Praise for Richard Herman

The Warbirds

'An imaginative action story told to perfection' – Clive
Cussler

'This is the sharp end, with vivid descriptions of air
combat, the smell of hot oil and fear' – *The Times*

Force of Eagles

'Truly edge of the seat exciting' – Dale Brown

Firebreak

'Richard Herman – himself a former pilot with 200
combat missions under his belt – spins a superb web
of tension' – *Oxford Times*

Dark Wing

'Could very well be tomorrow's headlines' – Clive
Cussler

Iron Gate

'Reading Herman is like gripping an electric cable and
having a charge of electricity sent through; you hang
on because you simply can't let go . . . Herman at his
breathtaking best' – *Oxford Times*

T*

'Realistic and suspen
provoking story' – *P*

Ag*

'"Thinking man's" thrillers that out-Clancy Clancy'
– *Kirkus*

Also by Richard Herman

The Warbirds
Force of Eagles
Firebreak
Mosquito Run
Dark Wing
Iron Gate
The Power Curve
Against All Enemies

About the author

Richard Herman is a former combat pilot who has flown over 200 missions himself. He was stationed in Vietnam, West Germany and Great Britain. He has flown the F-4 and the C-130 and received five medals, including the Bronze Star. He retired from the US Air Force in 1983 with the rank of Major after serving for twenty-one years. He has written eight previous highly acclaimed thrillers: *The Warbirds, Force of Eagles, Firebreak, Mosquito Run, Dark Wing, Iron Gate, The Power Curve* and *Against All Enemies*. He and his English-born wife now life in Gold River, California.

Edge of Honour

Richard Herman

CORONET BOOKS

Hodder & Stoughton

First published in Great Britain in 1999
by Hodder and Stoughton
First published in paperback in 1999
by Hodder and Stoughton
A division of Hodder Headline PLC

A Coronet paperback

10 9 8 7 6 5 4

ISBN 0 340 73826 X

Typeset by Palimpsest Book Production Limited,
Polmont, Stirlingshire
Printed and bound in Great Britain by
Omnia Books Limited, Glasgow

Hodder and Stoughton
A division of Hodder Headline PLC
338 Euston Road
London NW1 3BH

For all the cadets
who made the journey through the Sally Port
at New Mexico Military Institute.

Dwell on the past and you'll lose an eye;
forget the past and you'll lose both eyes.

Russian proverb

PROLOGUE

The archangel Michael loved heights.

Mikhail Vashin was sure of it as he stood at the big window on the top floor of his three-story penthouse apartment high above Moscow. Not that he was religious, far from it. But lately, he was feeling a special relationship with the celestial deity he was named after. Perhaps it was because of the weather. The mild winter had aided in the construction of his new skyscraper complex looming on the skyline three kilometers away. *Six more months,* he told himself, finding consolation in the speed of construction.

And it was perfect weather for the funeral. The sky was bright and clear for early April and the temperature cold enough to keep the snow from turning to slush. But not too chilly for the orchestra, or the girls, to perform outside.

Mikhail Vashin looked to the south, still gazing at the Towers, as he went over the funeral arrangements in his mind, checking off each item in the complex scenario. The heavy bulletproof glass in the window distorted his short, chunky frame and made him look even heavier. His four-thousand dollar Savile Row suit – Vashin detested the current Italian style popular with his contemporaries – draped perfectly over his barrel chest and thickening waistline. He rubbed his chin and sighed. His barber had given him a close shave two hours earlier but his five o'clock shadow was already showing.

A loud crack echoed across the big room and the three

men sitting on the luxurious brocaded couches fell to the floor. Mikhail Vashin never flinched. Stoically, he had quit counting attempts on his life when the number reached his age. He laughed as the men picked themselves off the floor. 'There,' he said, pointing to the glass chip on the outside of the bulletproof window. The fresh half-moon indentation made by a bullet was aligned with his forehead. 'I want the shooter.'

'He'll be dead by tonight,' one of the men promised.

Vashin snorted. They didn't understand. 'Such accuracy. The range had to be at least six hundred meters. Hire him.'

The men nodded with murmurs of 'Da'. It was one more brick in the legend surrounding Russia's wealthiest man. At thirty-six, Mikhail Vashin controlled eight percent of his country's gross domestic product – his goal was fifteen percent – and he was one of the richest men in the world. When asked by a *Newsweek* reporter in a recent interview what he wanted, Vashin had declined to answer. Instead, an aide had answered for him. 'Mikhail Vashin wants more.'

The funeral of Boris Bakatina was a major step in that direction.

The tall and stunning blonde who served as Vashin's personal assistant appeared at the door. She was holding a leather folder with a stopwatch and chronometer clipped to the cover. 'It's time, Mikhail,' she said in English. Geraldine Blake's accent was decidedly British upper-class. Even though his English was very limited, he nodded. Geraldine spoke into her personal telecommunicator, this time in Russian, and punched the stopwatch, setting events in motion.

Tom Johnson, who had been trained by the United States Secret Service and had stood post for a United States president before seeking more gainful employment with Vashin, spoke into the whisper mike under the cuff of his shirtsleeve. The elaborate security mechanism that surrounded Vashin sprang into action as he descended in the elevator from his lofty perch.

Mikhail Vashin was pleased and allowed himself a rare smile. He had found Geraldine and Johnson on the Internet and hired them on the spur of the moment. Yet both had worked out beyond his wildest expectations. Not only was Geraldine super-efficient as his personal assistant, she gave his organization a touch of class, which it desperately needed. And Johnson had rebuilt the security system that protected him. The bulletproof glass window in his penthouse and the security zone that floated around him were proof of that. Together, Geraldine and Johnson insulated him from the *vor*, the Honorable Thieves of Russia.

The irony of it amused Vashin. He was the most powerful of the godfathers of the *vor*, and that made him a target. Yet two foreigners, bought and paid for with hard currency and dependent on him for their own survival in Russia, were his most loyal supporters. He loved the Western ethic that made money, honestly earned, the arbiter of fidelity and morality.

Geraldine Blake reviewed her notes in the elevator. Her lips drew into a thoughtful pout. 'Mikhail, I know it's distasteful, but you must be among the first to kiss the body. Otherwise—' She deliberately did not finish the sentence. For Vashin not to kiss the forehead of Boris Bakatina would be an admission of guilt. Although the *patsani*, the young and unruly street thugs who made up the bulk of Russian criminals, collectively called the Mafiya, knew that Vashin had ordered the assassination of his partner.

'You English are too sensitive,' Vashin told her. 'The embalmers are the best. Bakatina is cold wax.'

'And nothing but wax,' an aide added. 'They couldn't find his head.'

Mikhail Vashin's face was impassive. That, too, was part of the arrangements.

The seven-car convoy, with Vashin's silver Bentley sandwiched in the middle, arrived at the cemetery on schedule. The other automobiles drove past the entrance while Vashin's car drove through the ornate iron gates. The black limousine bearing Viktor Kraiko, the President of the Russian Federation, was right behind him. The order of arrival was a message being sent to the CIA agents recording the funeral with their long-lens cameras over a kilometer away. Geraldine twisted in the seat beside Vashin to look at Kraiko's limo. She glanced at the chronometer on her clipboard. 'At least the filthy sod is on time,' she groused. 'The girls know he's coming. It cost us extra. They wanted sables.'

'It's nothing,' Vashin said. 'Besides, the furs will keep them warm.' He found the topic distasteful and changed the subject. 'Where did you place the orchestra?'

'Next to the trees behind the grave,' she answered.

'And they know when to begin the 1812?'

'On my signal,' she answered.

'Good,' Vashin replied. 'All must go smoothly. I don't want to upset Natalya. Losing Boris has been an ordeal for her and the children.'

'Natalya' – the dropping of the widow's married name another signal – 'is most appreciative of the funeral and sends her thanks.' Geraldine gracefully uncrossed her legs and prepared to make a smooth exit from the car. In public, style and grace were everything to Vashin.

Vashin waved a hand, his blunt fingers flashing an impeccable manicure. 'It is the least I could do for my sister.'

Tom Johnson was riding in the front seat and frowned as the Bentley coasted to a stop. An obscenely long Mercedes-Benz limousine was pulling away in front of them. He spoke into the intercom. 'The Cossack is here.'

Color drained from Geraldine's face. 'I was assured Gromov had agreed to the arrangements,' she said nervously. Yegor Gromov was the chairman of the Federal Counter-Intelligence Service, the old KGB in democratic sheep's clothing. When the Soviet Union had collapsed, Gromov had given the KGB a facelift and masterminded the organization's rape and pillage of the Russian economy. In the process, he had become Russia's new Caesar.

A flick of Vashin's hand. 'It's nothing.' Geraldine breathed more easily as an aide opened the rear door and Vashin stepped out. A line of toadies lined the walk leading into the cemetery. Vashin's eyes narrowed when he saw Oleg Gora, the contract killer who would, with Vashin's help, someday rule the second largest family of the Russian *vor*. Gora bowed his head in respect.

Vashin proceeded slowly up the path to the grave site. At one point, he stopped and waved to the large crowd hanging on the wrought-iron fence surrounding the cemetery. 'Give them money in Boris Bakatina's name,' he ordered. 'One-hundred-dollar bills, US.' Behind him, Viktor Kraiko, the President of the Russian Federation, also waved at the crowd. He was booed for his efforts. Behind Kraiko, the lesser lights of the Russian government and *vor* were arriving to pay their last respects. They were a seamless mix of comrades who understood each other perfectly and, for the most part, worked together with little friction. Especially now.

Most of the mourners had been standing in the snow since early morning, claiming a ringside vantage point for what had to be the funeral of the decade, an extravagance even by *vor* and Mafiya standards. They watched in silence as Vashin approached the open gold-and-crystal coffin resting on top of the freshly dug grave. What happened next would determine so much. Those nearest saw the tears flow down Vashin's cheeks as he bent over and kissed the recently deceased on the forehead. A long and sustained murmur of relief swept over the collected heads of the *vor* as they repeated Vashin's gesture before lining up at the lavish buffet tables. The quantity of food, vodka, caviar, and champagne spread out before them had not been seen at a public banquet since the days of the last Czar.

More than a few of the knowledgeable breathed in relief when Vashin embraced the father of Boris Bakatina. A bloody civil war among the Honorable Thieves would not rage in the streets of Moscow.

Vashin spoke quietly to his sister before strolling past the banquet tables. His progress was slow as everyone wanted to speak to him and gain his patronage. He worked the crowd for an hour, and finally broke free when the Moscow State Orchestra returned from a break and took their seats. He asked where Viktor Kraiko was, knowing the answer. The President was back in the trees with the girls, the expensive prostitutes who worked Moscow's most famous nightclub, Le Coq d'Or. The girls had agreed they would wear only leather boots and the sable fur coats as they reaffirmed, with any guest privileged to be invited to the funeral and who was so inclined, the act glorifying the life-force.

'Tell Viktor Kraiko it's time,' Vashin said to Geraldine.

A worried look spread across her smooth and perfect features and she made a helpless gesture. 'Perhaps it's too early.' She didn't want to be part of the parade of women servicing the randy satyr who had captured the Russian presidency after Boris Yeltsin. Kraiko might have been loony as a fox and a fascist, but he appealed to a large percentage of the Russian populace, who harbored a nostalgia for the security and glory of the Soviet Union.

'It's time,' Vashin repeated. This time Geraldine did not hesitate and she spoke to the orchestra before walking up the path leading into the trees. It was an occupational hazard that went with the business. Vashin spoke to an aide. 'Please tell Yegor Gromov that I would like to meet.' The aide was stunned. For Vashin to ask for a meeting with the old KGB general was an admission of subordination. Vashin turned and walked into the trees, heading for the meeting place while the orchestra played the low opening refrain of Tchaikovsky's 1812 Overture. The seven most powerful godfathers of the *vor* who made up the Circle of Brothers followed him.

A few minutes later, Yegor Gromov marched into the small clearing with twenty-six bodyguards. The absolute power that went with being the KGB's master for twenty years had become part of his nature, and age had not diminished his military bearing or sense of command. He stared at Vashin and the godfathers.

'Thank you for joining us,' Vashin said deferentially.

Gromov jerked his head in acknowledgment and said nothing as seven of the eight men who made up the government's Security Council were escorted into the clearing by their bodyguards. Only Vitaly Rodonov, the Minister of Defense and Gromov's principal ally, was absent. Gromov calculated the order of battle. His bodyguards outnumbered all the others combined. It puzzled him that Vashin should have so few of his own. Gromov jutted his chin at the politicians. 'Why are they here?'

'Merely as a courtesy,' Vashin said, his voice oily smooth. Kraiko came out of the trees with Geraldine. A flick of Vashin's hand and all the bodyguards withdrew out of earshot and formed a security cordon at the edge of the trees. Geraldine joined the cordon as she rearranged her hair and dusted snow off her clothes. She wished she could hear what was being said.

Vashin turned immediately to business. 'Yegor Sergeyevich,' he began. Gromov stiffened. Only his friends and allies dared use his patronymic. He turned to leave but Vashin reached out and grabbed his arm. 'It is best to listen.'

'Is this why you begged for a meeting?' Gromov replied. 'To assault me?' He brushed Vashin's hand aside. Without looking, he knew his bodyguards were flying across the clearing. Vashin was already a dead man.

'It's time to retire,' Vashin said.

Gromov snorted. Vashin didn't deserve a reply. Where were his bodyguards? He looked around. Only the torpedo Oleg Gora was walking across the snow. Gromov's bodyguards had switched allegiance and were merely witnesses to the proceedings. Gromov turned and faced Vashin, the politicians, and the Circle of Brothers. Now it all made sense. Vashin and the godfathers were standing side by side with Kraiko and the Security Council. The *vor* and the political establishment had openly merged. He was the last major obstacle on Vashin's path to absolute power and only Minister of Defense Rodonov remained in his way.

'So this is more,' Gromov said. He heard the crunch of Gora's footsteps in the snow. The orchestra reached the finale of the 1812 as its crashing cannons and pealing bells swept over the clearing. Gora flipped a wire garrote over Gromov's head, pulled it tight, and twisted. Gromov kicked twice before he passed out. But he was still alive when Gora dropped him into the snow. The torpedo flicked open a large knife and cut into Gromov's neck, cleanly separating his head above the thoracic vertebra.

Vashin evaluated Gora's skill with professional interest: the businessman demanding performance for his investment. 'Send Gromov's and Bakatina's heads to the Poles,' he ordered.

Kraiko bent over and was sick in the snow. 'Why?' he gagged, his face spattered with vomit.

'I want to send them a message.'

As Vashin expected, Kraiko did not understand. But the Security Council and the Circle of Brothers did.

Part One

Part One

CHAPTER ONE

Warrensburg, Missouri

The phone call came just after four in the morning. At first, Matt Pontowski ignored it and buried his head deeper in the pillow. Most likely, it was for Sam and she would answer it. But Samantha Darnell wasn't there. The phone rang a fourth time and he rolled over, reaching for the offending instrument. 'Pontowski,' he muttered. He never used his rank, brigadier general, when answering the phone.

'General Pontowski, would you please hold for the super-intendent of NMMI.' It was a male voice he did not recognize, and suddenly he was fully awake. The empty feeling left in Sam's wake was engulfed by a rogue wave of panic.

He clenched the telephone as he waited, and the grisly images that haunt parents when their children are away from home came out of the shadowy recesses of his subconscious. *Little Matt is just sick,* he told himself. But would the super-intendent of New Mexico Military Institute personally call for that? Probably not. It had to be bad news, very bad. *Get a grip!* he raged to himself. *You're obsessing.*

The male voice was back. 'I apologize for the delay, but the General is still on the other line. He'll be with you in a moment.'

Pontowski grunted an answer. Years of flying and com-manding the 442nd Fighter Wing, an Air Force Reserve outfit of A-10 Warthogs, had conditioned him to be calm and in control at all times, regardless of the circumstances. He fought the urge to shout, 'Is my son okay?' Instead, he waited. Why did he ever let his only son, his living link to Shoshana, go off to the military academy known simply as The Hill?

'General Pontowski,' the superintendent finally said, his voice carefully modulated and carrying weight, 'John McMasters here. Sorry to keep you waiting, but I was talking to the White House. Your son was in a fight with Brian Turner. No one was really hurt.' The superintendent paused to let his words sink in. Like every parent with a son or daughter at NMMI, Pontowski knew that Brian Turner, the son of the 44th President of the United States, had enrolled in NMMI in the same ninth-grade class as Little Matt.

Pontowski shook his head in disbelief. Then it hit him. Brian Turner was a strapping fourteen-year-old with at least six inches and forty pounds on Little Matt. It was with good reason his son carried his nickname, and rumor had it that Brian Turner was a spoiled bully.

'Little Matt in a fight?' Pontowski finally replied. 'That's hard to believe. How badly was he hurt?' A vision of Little Matt with a bloody nose and his face streaked with tears flashed in front of him. The poor kid was probably terrified.

McMasters didn't answer for a moment and Pontowski's fears started to rise, only to be submerged by a deep anger. Had Brian Turner mauled his son? Or had the Secret Service gotten involved and done something stupid? 'For the record,' McMasters said, 'Mr Pontowski beat the living hell out of Mr Turner, who is now in the infirmary.'

The White House

Maura O'Keith entered her daughter's bedroom just after seven o'clock in the morning. Madeline O'Keith Turner was sitting at the small table, drinking coffee and reading a newspaper, still wrapped in an oversized white terry-cloth robe, her brown eyes bright and clear. 'You're up early,' Maddy Turner said, a gentle smile on her face. Maura was not at her best in the morning, while it was Maddy's favorite part of the day.

Automatically, Maura pulled a hairbrush from her ever-present handbag and stood behind her daughter. She started to stroke Maddy's dark brown hair, evaluating the stylist's work from the day before. Maura had been a hairdresser most of her adult life, and liked the way the stylist was highlighting her daughter's hair with an auburn tint and covering up the gray that was beginning to streak back from her forehead. 'The superintendent at NMMI telephoned early this morning. I took the call. It was nothing serious so I didn't wake you.'

'What's Brian been up to now?' Maddy asked, recalling her meeting with General McMasters. 'I was hoping he'd stay out of trouble a little longer.' NMMI did not tolerate problem students.

'He was in a fight with another cadet. He got roughed up a bit and he's in the infirmary. The doctor says he's fine.'

'What the hell was the Secret Service doing? It's their job to protect him. Was it hazing? General McMasters assured me there is no hazing at NMMI.'

Maura recognized the signs. Like most mothers, Maddy was overprotective of her son. She brushed her daughter's hair harder. 'There was no hazing and Brian started the fight.'

'With who? Was some upper classman harassing him because he's my son?'

Maura brushed a little harder, trying to get Maddy's attention. 'It was another freshman like him.'

'Some hulking Cro-Magnon recruited to play football?'

'No. The other cadet was much smaller. They call him Little Matt.' She could tell from the way Maddy's shoulders slumped that she would listen now. The older woman dropped into the chair beside her daughter. She eyed the flaky croissants on the table. 'I've got to go on a diet,' she moaned.

Maddy laughed at the way her mother changed subjects, putting her at ease. 'If you can't be happy with your weight at sixty-nine, when can you?'

'It's easy for you to say. You haven't gained a pound in ten years.'

It was true – Maddy Turner still had a trim figure. But in private moments in front of her bathroom mirror, she hated the middle-age sag that was assaulting parts of her body. Madeline O'Keith Turner sighed and faced the truth. 'Brian's a bully, isn't he?' No answer from Maura. 'Should we leave him at NMMI?'

'If we can.'

Maddy shook her head. 'I can't break away every time he gets into trouble.' She looked at her mother. 'Can you fly to New Mexico and sort it out?'

Maura nodded. 'I'll take Sarah with me.' Sarah was Maddy's eleven-year-old daughter, a happy, uncomplicated little girl who hadn't discovered boys – yet.

'You knew I'd ask, didn't you?'

Again, Maura nodded. 'I asked Richard to arrange it.' Richard Parrish was Maddy's efficient chief of staff. 'We're leaving this morning.'

Maddy stood up. Her day had started. 'Thanks, Mother.'

At exactly eight o'clock, Turner left the second-floor residence of the White House and made her way down the hall, heading for the West Wing. Because it was summer, she was wearing an off-white linen business suit with a simple light blue blouse. As always, her hemline ended six inches above the floor. Turner had made it the accepted style and certain fashion mavens had predicted that if she ever raised her hemline, the world would turn upside down at the sight of presidential legs. Her makeup was undetectable and perfect, highlighting her high cheekbones. She wore little jewelry, only small earrings and the delicate and intricate gold chain that had become her trademark necklace. Her husband had bought it for her on their honeymoon in Greece and she was never seen without it.

Her daily commute to work was a well-rehearsed drill as Richard Parrish and her personal assistant, a quiet, handsome young man named Dennis, flanked her. Dennis slouched along, never taking notes or consulting a calendar. He had a photographic, computer-like mind that never failed him. But each evening, after escorting Turner back to the residence, he would update the computer on his desk – just in case. Besides his qualities of discretion and total dedication to Turner, hidden underneath his bland surface was the personality of a pit bull.

Parrish was talking. 'The Attorney General is very worried and wants to act now.'

'Frank is always worried,' Turner replied. 'He sees a crisis around every corner and a conspirator behind every tree.'

'Sometimes he's right,' Parrish told her. 'I asked Mazie to join us.' Mazana Kamigami Hazelton was Turner's National Security Advisor. Better known as Mazie to her friends, the petite and beautiful Japanese-Hawaiian was commonly referred to as 'the Dragon Lady' in the halls and offices of Congress.

'Mazie will keep him honest,' Turner said.

'Keep the Attorney General honest,' Dennis intoned, entering it in his mental computer.

'Delete that,' Turner ordered. Dennis did. He opened the door to the Oval Office and Madeline Turner entered the arena.

Until she retreated to the residence in fourteen hours, she would seldom be alone. Every minute was scheduled. Before lunch, she would hold a policy review meeting, a staff meeting, and a cabinet meeting. In between, a succession of two groups and three individuals would troop through the Oval Office for a brief introduction to the President. The morning would climax with a press conference, which always took longer than scheduled. After lunching with three federal judges and six members of Congress, she would spend thirty minutes in the Rose Garden for photo opportunities with various visiting dignitaries, swim forty laps in the pool, meet with her national security advisory group, meet eight more people in the Oval Office, and spend time with her chief of staff and his assistants, planning future trips and events. Then she would change into formal attire to speak at a 'Save the Children' banquet. She would finally return to the White House at 10 p.m. But her day was not finished. She always read for another two hours before retiring. And some time in between, she would have to call Maura and her son.

All told, an easy day.

The three men who made up Turner's Policy Review Committee and Mazie Hazelton were waiting for her. Since the Attorney General had asked for the meeting, he sat on the end of the couch closest to Turner's rocking chair. He nervously fingered his notes as she sat down. Madeline Turner was famous, or infamous, depending on the point of view, for galloping through meetings.

The Attorney General cleared his throat and began. 'Special Services claims Yaponets is a bigger problem in prison than on the outside,' he said. Special Services was the Department of Justice's spy system inside the federal prison system, and Yaponets, Russian for Japanese, was a senior godfather from eastern Russia and the leading member of the Russian Mafiya currently in an American jail. He was a burly, sixty-four-year-old man and anything but Japanese.

'What's the problem?' Turner asked.

'He's organizing crime on the outside from the inside,' the Attorney General answered. 'He's using our prisons as a command center, a recruiting ground, and as a graduate school for criminals.'

'Isolate him,' Turner said. 'Take his telephone away. Throw him in solitary.'

'We would if we could,' the Attorney General said. 'But the ACLU and prisoner rights organizations would be on our case in a flash. Not to mention some of the highest-priced legal assassins in the country.' Silence. A fact of life in the United States was that ROC, or Russian organized crime, had bought access into every aspect of American life through large charitable donations, political campaign contributions, and astronomical retainer fees paid to some of the craftiest lawyers in the United States.

'What happened to deportation?' the President asked.

'That's what I was going to recommend,' the Attorney General replied.

Now it was Richard Parrish's turn. As Turner's chief of staff and primary political advisor, he was always looking for hazards. 'That's political suicide. Senator Leland will beat us silly claiming we're soft on crime and that we caved into ROC.'

'So by being tough on crime and throwing the bastards in jail,' the Attorney General added, 'we actually help ROC achieve its ends.'

'It makes you long for the Cosa Nostra, doesn't it?' Sam Kennett, the Vice-President, said. 'At least the "men of honor" were American.'

'And not too bright,' the Attorney General said.

'Don't sell them short,' Mazie Kamigami Hazelton said. She sat motionless in her chair, an Asian doll whose dainty feet didn't quite reach the floor. Her words were so soft and low that it was hard to hear her. But they all fell silent when she spoke. 'I agree with DOJ.' The Attorney General beamed. Too often, the National Security Advisor was on the other side of the fence from the Department of Justice, and time had a perverse way of proving her right. 'We need to export our problems, not warehouse them. Exchange him.'

'For who?' This from the Attorney General.

'Not for a who,' Mazie said. 'For a what.'

'What do you have in mind?' Turner asked.

'Exchange him for a nuke,' Mazie answered.

The Hill

The immaculately restored blue-and-white T-34 Mentor approached from the north. It was flying at exactly 500 feet above the ground and 140 knots indicated air speed as it crossed the green fairways of New Mexico Military Institute's golf course. Pontowski rocked the wings of the old Air Force trainer he and Little Matt had lovingly rebuilt as he pulled up and headed for the airport to the south of town. The few golfers, all alumni and their guests, looked up. 'Jet jockeys,' one of the golfers muttered, ignoring the fact the T-34 had a propeller.

In his office on the second floor of Lusk Hall, Lieutenant-General (retired) John McMasters sat at his desk and shook his head. 'That will be Matt Pontowski,' he told the commandant, who stood at the big windows overlooking the NMMI's campus. 'He likes to make an entrance.'

'Nice airplane,' the commandant replied. 'But he looked kind of low. Do you want to report him for buzzing?'

'Matt Pontowski knows the limits,' McMasters replied. 'He was at the minimums.'

'Still,' the commandant persisted, 'it might be setting a bad example for the cadets. And what will the Secret Service say?' With Brian Turner on campus, the concerns of the Secret Service were a fact of life.

McMasters sat back in his chair. He needed to make a point to both the cadets and the Secret Service. 'Get the word out that Pontowski did it by the rules and was at the legal minimum altitude. If the minimums weren't good enough, they wouldn't be the minimums.' The commandant nodded and headed for the door. McMasters waited until he had left before calling his residence. His wife answered on the second ring. 'That was Matt's plane,' he told her. 'I told the driver picking him up to drop him off at the quarters. He'll probably want to change and you can soften him up before sending him over.'

Lenora McMasters knew exactly what to do.

Forty minutes later, a female cadet saluted Pontowski when he emerged from the car depositing him at the superintendent's quarters. 'Mrs McMasters is waiting for you,' the cadet said as Pontowski returned the salute. Pontowski was impressed with the girl's presence and appearance. She was neatly turned out in a Class E BDU, battledress uniform, with rolled-up sleeves and brightly shined boots. She was five feet six inches tall, on the husky side, and her blonde hair was pulled into a tight French braid. 'She's baking cookies for the Rats,' the cadet said, a pretty smile playing with the corners of her mouth.

Pontowski glanced at her name tag. 'Thank you, Miss Trogger.' She held the door for him and pointed him toward the kitchen. 'Now that smells good,' he said. The cadet led the way, moving with the coordination of a well-trained athlete.

Sarah Turner saw him first. 'I hope you know how to bake cookies,' she said, taking the newcomer in. She examined him with a wisdom far beyond the average eleven-year-old, and knew the single star on each shoulder meant he was a general. She put his age at about the same as her mother's, forty-six. He was tall, a little over six feet, and his gray-green flight suit hung on his lanky frame. His hair was brown, the cowlick at the back barely controllable, and his blue eyes were set close together. She didn't like his prominent, hawlike nose and didn't know it was a Pontowski trademark his grandfather had made famous.

'Sarah,' Maura O'Keith said, 'be polite.' She held up her hands in resignation. They were covered in cookie dough. 'Maura O'Keith. Glad to meet you.'

Pontowski gave a low laugh and, rather than attempt to shake hands, gave her a light kiss on the cheek. 'I never baked a cookie in my life, but I'm willing to learn.'

Lenora McMasters came across the kitchen, wiping her hands on a towel. They embraced. 'Welcome back to NMMI, Matt.'

'Doing the cookie lady routine?' he said, holding her at arm's length.

She laughed. 'I have no secrets from you, do I?'

Pontowski smiled but said nothing. Lenora McMasters was a beautiful fifty-eight-year-old who was equal parts empress dowager and mother hen. Today she was being the latter, softening the shock of military life for the new sixth class. But she was not a lady to trifle with and she and her husband made a perfect team.

'I'm Sarah Turner,' the little girl announced.

Pontowski turned to her and they shook hands formally. 'Matt Pontowski,' he replied. 'I'm pleased to meet you.'

'Is your son a big bully?' Sarah asked.

'Sarah!' Maura said.

'Actually,' Pontowski said, 'he's about your size. I don't think he's a bully.'

Lenora McMasters took charge. 'Matt, you probably want to shower and change. Why don't you do that while we finish up here. Then Zeth' – she shot a look at the cadet – 'can take you all over to John's office.'

'Thanks,' Pontowski replied. 'Save a cookie for me.'

'The guest suite is up the stairs and straight ahead,' Lenora said. They all watched as he disappeared out the door. 'We first knew Matt when he was a lieutenant,' Lenora explained.

'What was he like then?' Maura asked.

'A typical fighter pilot. All macho and full of himself. He cut quite a swath among the young ladies. Then he got married, thank goodness.'

'Why thank goodness?' Sarah asked.

'Well,' Lenora explained, shooting another glance at the cadet, Zeth Trogger, 'sometimes young women act very foolish when they get around handsome young men. Especially fighter pilots.' The McMasters were always teaching.

'Isn't he the grandson of President Pontowski?' Sarah asked.

Lenora confirmed it. 'Yes, he is.' Her eyes grew thoughtful. 'I can remember the day President Pontowski died in 1995 as clearly as yesterday.'

'I remember my mother crying,' Zeth said. 'We were watching the funeral on TV and General Pontowski was giving the eulogy at the National Cathedral. But that was before he was a brigadier general. His wife was there in the front row. She was beautiful.'

'Yes, she was,' Lenora said. 'Matt was devastated when she was killed.'

'What happened?' Sarah asked, her interest now totally aroused. Lenora hesitated, not sure what to tell the young girl.

'You might as well tell her,' Maura said. 'She won't quit pestering people until she finds out.'

'Well,' Lenora said, 'Shoshana was murdered by assassins at Tokyo's Narita airport. But she was very brave and killed four of them before they shot her.' She felt an explanation was in order. 'Matt met Shoshana in Spain. He was there on leave. She was a Mossad agent – that's the Israeli CIA – and on an assignment. Later, she and Matt met again in Israel. Unfortunately, war broke out between the Arabs and the Israelis again. It was touch and go for the Israelis for a while. Shoshana served as a medic in the war and was wounded. She suffered some severe burns. But she recovered nicely. They married a year later.'

Zeth Trogger's eyes opened wide in amazement and respect. 'When was she killed?'

Lenora thought for a moment. 'Matt was in southern China

with the American Volunteer Group at the time, so it would be six years ago, 1996.'

'They call my mom a widow,' Sarah said. 'What's a man called?'

'A man is called a widower,' Lenora replied.

'He is very attractive,' Maura added, her voice soft and thoughtful.

The White House

About the time Matt Pontowski stepped out of the shower at NMMI, Madeline Turner sat down with her security advisory group. Unlike her famous kitchen cabinet, the friends she gathered around her for political advice, the four members of this group were chosen solely for their analytical minds and keen insights into international threats to the security of the United States. As Turner's National Security Advisor, Mazie Hazelton was the group's nominal leader. But the three men, Sam Kennett, the Vice-President, Stephan Serick, the Secretary of State, and the DCI, or Director of Central Intelligence, all carried equal weight. However, in the end, it was Madeline Turner who dictated the security policy of the United States.

'Madame President,' Mazie began, 'we're getting some strange signals out of eastern Europe. I'm certain we're seeing a major shift in Russia's foreign policy.'

'We have seen no shift in policy,' Stephan Serick, the irritable Secretary of State, announced in obvious disagreement. 'Only the usual fumbling. Viktor Kraiko is lucky he's still President and is holding on by his fingertips. He hasn't had a new thought rise above his belt buckle in two years. Maybe after the Russians replace him something different will emerge. But not now.' Serick's Latvian accent always became stronger when he talked about his old enemy, Russia. For him it made no difference the Soviet Union had fallen apart. The hatred was still there.

Mazie let the cranky Serick spew a little more venom before answering. 'Russia's economy is stabilizing,' she said.

'So?' Serick snapped. 'And Russia's military continues to

shrink and the old KGB is in shambles since Gromov, that old bastard, died last April.'

'We now believe,' the Director of Central Intelligence said, 'that Gromov was executed.'

'Utter nonsense,' Serick grumbled. He stood up and limped around the room, his basset-hound jowls quivering as he spoke. 'My God! The man was seventy-eight years old. He died of old age.'

The DCI glanced at his notes. 'Then why did his head show up in Poland along with Boris Bakatina's?'

'Boris Bakatina?' Turner asked.

'The chief godfather of the Russian *vor*,' the DCI answered. 'The *vor* are the old-guard criminals, Honorable Thieves. They're different from the Mafiya who are the new kids on the block. Mix them all together and you've got ROC, Russian organized crime.'

'We think they lost their heads in a power struggle,' Mazie added.

'That's an awful pun,' Turner said. 'This is bizarre. So why are we spending time here?'

It was a question for Mazie to answer, and given the way Turner worked, she didn't have long to do so. 'We're getting reports of increasing interaction between high-ranking Russian politicians and ROC. We're not exactly sure of the contours of this new relationship, but Poland seems to be a frequent subject of discussion. Then we received three separate reports that these two heads were sent to the Polish Mafia in mid-April.'

'Old news,' Serick scoffed. 'Over four months old. Criminals sending each other presents does not constitute a change in foreign policy. We're wasting our time.'

'We think it was a message,' Mazie said. 'Their mouths were stuffed with gold coins, mostly Krugerrands.'

'So what was the message?' Turner asked.

Mazie spoke slowly, choosing her words carefully. This discussion wasn't going to last much longer. 'Gromov and Bakatina were the highest-ranking survivors of the old guard, one political and one criminal. They were dinosaurs left over from the Soviet system that raped both Russia and Poland. The message was very clear. The heads were a peace offering. The gold indicates there is money to be made from the death of the old system. It was an invitation from Russian organized crime to do business.'

'Rubbish,' Serick grumbled. 'This is all too bizarre. I'm more worried about what's going on in Germany.'

For the first time the Vice-President spoke. 'Bizarre, yes. But it makes a kind of weird sense. The Poles, including the Polish Mafia, carry a lot of hatred for the Russians. It would take a powerful gesture on the part of the Russians for the Poles to trust them.'

'Do we have anything concrete,' Turner asked, 'that suggests such an alliance is taking place?'

The DCI answered. 'We have monitored a huge increase in telephone calls and personal contacts between some very strange parties.'

'Such as?' Turner asked.

The DCI consulted his notes. 'Viktor Kraiko engaged in long conversations with Mikhail Vashin.' Vashin was a new name for Turner and she said so. 'Vashin,' the DCI explained, 'is a shadowy figure. After the removal of Boris Bakatina, he appears to be the new leader of Russian organized crime. He's even got the Circle of Brothers, that's the senior godfathers of the *vor*, under his thumb.'

Turner's fingers beat a tattoo on her desk in a well-known signal. They were about finished with the subject. 'If I understand what you're telling me, we're seeing some new mix of the political and criminal leaders of Russia. What exactly is the threat stemming from all this? Are there any domestic implications for us?'

'I'm not exactly sure,' Mazie replied.

'At best,' Serick said, 'it means a legitimization of criminal activity.' He snorted. 'Nothing changes in Russia.'

Turner recalled that morning's discussion about Russian organized crime and Yaponets. 'Mazie, keep on top of this and talk to the Attorney General.' She paused. Mazie was one of her most trusted advisors and was obviously concerned about the situation. As President, did she need to do more? She turned to the Vice-President. 'Sam, next week—' Her voice trailed off.

Sam Kennett laughed. 'I'll add Poland to my European vacation.'

'No one,' Serick grumbled, 'goes to Poland for a vacation.'

The Hill

Zeth Trogger led Maura, Pontowski, and Sarah from Quarters One to Lusk Hall, the administration building. She set a slow pace for Maura O'Keith and patiently answered Sarah Turner's endless questions about NMMI. Zeth's answers were right out of the Parents' Handbook, and Pontowski smiled. 'What class are you in?' he asked.

'Third class, sir,' Zeth answered. She was a senior in high school.

'Why did you pick NMMI?' Sarah asked.

'My dad's an alumni and I always wanted to come here.' She gave the little girl a serious look. 'It's a tough school. My Rat year was the hardest thing I've ever done.'

Pontowski studied the cadet. Zeth Trogger had beautiful green eyes that flashed with intelligence and spirit. An eighteen-year-old on the cusp of womanhood, she was definitely feminine and curvy. But she wore no makeup and her only concession to femininity was her long hair which was held up in a tight braid. She walked with the confidence of an athlete. 'Sports?' he asked.

'I'm on the soccer team,' Zeth answered.

'I didn't know you had a woman's soccer team at NMMI.'

'We don't,' she answered. She led them to the superintendent's office on the second floor. She held the door for them to enter and then waited outside.

General McMasters ushered Maura to a seat at the large conference table while Pontowski held a chair for Sarah. The little girl beamed at him, reveling in the courtesy. Nelson Day, the commandant of cadets and a retired army colonel, joined them and sat next to Maura. 'Well,' McMasters began, 'we do have a problem here.' He turned the meeting over to Colonel Day, who was responsible for cadet discipline.

Day quickly reviewed the basics. The two Rats in question were in the same squad and had taken an instant dislike to each other, mostly because Mr Pontowski was not as well coordinated and as strong as the others and slowed the squad down. Animosity had flared and the two boys finally decided to settle their differences in a more direct fashion. The other cadets had cooperated and helped them sneak out of their rooms in Hagerman Barracks late at night. Somehow, they had gotten into the tunnels of NMMI, which were really little more than a series of interconnected basements between the barracks and adjoining buildings.

'How did they get past the Secret Service?' Maura asked.

McMasters shifted into a bureaucratic mode. It was the way he covered his impulse to smile at what the cadets had done when he had to be the disciplinarian. 'Well, the Secret Service is embarrassed.' He described the security arrangements in detail. 'They were geared for intruders, not for cadets going into the tunnels from the inside. We've already fixed that.'

Maura kept shifting her gaze to Pontowski. 'General McMasters,' she said, reading the discussion right, 'I know you're worried about losing your most famous student, but this sounds to me like a minor ruckus between two boys who don't know how to settle their differences peacefully. I only have one question. Can you fix it?'

'I think we can,' McMasters answered.

'They're going to walk off at least ten demerits,' Day said. 'That's ten tours in the Box.' The Box was the quadrangle in the center of Hagerman Barracks, and a tour was fifty minutes of marching back and forth.

'Shouldn't we hear their side of the story?' Sarah asked. She gave Maura a questioning look. 'That's only fair, isn't it?'

Maura and Pontowski nodded in agreement and the two miscreants were brought in. Brian Turner was a tall, strapping, good-looking boy who, physically, was going on eighteen. Little Matt was a frail, skinny kid who looked all of eleven. Yet both were within six months in age. Brian had a bruised eye and swollen lip. Little Matt only had a Band-aid over his right knuckles. The commandant asked each for his side of the story, and Brian went into some detail justifying his actions and why he had lost the fight. He had slipped on the wet concrete floor and Little Matt had unfairly hit him in the face four or five times before he could regain his balance. Little Matt only said that he did it and that the facts were correct.

'How did you get into the tunnels?' Day asked.

'I don't know, sir,' Little Matt answered. 'The door was open.'

They had a problem. Picking a lock was a serious offense but finding the guilty party would be very hard, and did they really want to pursue it and kick some cadet out of NMMI? 'General McMasters,' Pontowski said. 'May I suggest you give the cadets some wiggle room on this so they can learn from their mistakes? Issue a blanket warning on how serious it is to pick a lock and fix the door.'

'I agree,' Maura said.

'It appears we're in agreement,' McMasters said. 'Colonel Day, it's in your court.'

Day fixed the two cadets with a hard look and called in Zeth Trogger. 'Mr Turner, Mr Pontowski, meet your new squad leader. As of now, you are roommates and are welded hip and thigh. You will do everything as a pair and you will learn to get along. Any questions?'

'Please, sir,' Brian begged, 'not a girl.'

'Why?' Day asked.

Brian stammered an answer. 'Ah . . . ah . . . girls can't hack it.'

Colonel Day grew very serious and put weight in his voice. 'How long have you been at NMMI, Mr Turner?'

'Almost three weeks,' came the answer.

'Then you have a lot to learn,' Day said. 'They're all yours, Miss Trogger.'

'Outside,' Zeth ordered. Pontowski smiled. There was iron in her order. The two Rats double-timed out the door with Zeth right behind them.

McMasters stood and walked to the big windows overlooking the campus. 'I think you need to see this,' he said. They all joined him at the windows. Below them, the two cadets were standing at attention while Zeth leaned into them, her face a mask as she spoke. 'I imagine,' McMasters said, 'that she is explaining a few facts of life to them.'

Zeth's face was exactly thirty inches away from Brian's nose. 'We seem to have a basic difference of opinion here,' she told them, her voice low-pitched yet hard as nails. 'If you're right and girls can't hack it, then—'

Brian interrupted her. 'Get out of my face, Trogger. You got to stay thirty inches away.' Then, not so sure of himself, 'That's what the regulations say.'

Her laugh was not reassuring to either of the boys. She knew she was at the exact distance allowed by the Blue Book. She leaned in another inch, challenging him. 'That's twenty-nine inches.' She pulled back. 'This is thirty, dirtbag. If you got a tape measure, use it. Otherwise, stifle yourself or you'll be walkin' tours.'

'You think I'm gonna march any freakin' tours?' Brian retorted. 'Look, I'm gettin' out of here and there's nothing you can do to me.' He motioned to the two men standing in the doorway to Lusk Hall. 'See them? They're Secret Service. You touch me and they'll be all over you like stink on shit.'

Zeth cast a look at the two men. They were standing rock still, faces impassive, well within earshot. For a moment, she was confused, off balance. Then she recovered. 'You mean like when Pontowski reached out and touched you?'

Brian blinked, worry now written on his face. She pressed her advantage. 'I don't have to touch you, dirtbag. I'll heap so much shame and ridicule on you that you'll be on the World Wide Web under WWW dot Buttjoke dot com.' She motioned at the agents. 'And they won't do a thing about it. Mr Pontowski, a knowledge question. What do you get when you cross Brian Turner with an ape?'

'I do not know, ma'am.'

'A retarded ape.' She leaned into Brian. 'Hey, dirtbag, I did that one without trying. Wait until I go high speed on the Internet. You'll love it. Check your good buddies who are supposed to guard your worthless butt. Are they laughing?'

Brian chanced a glance. One of the agents was smiling, and he heard Little Matt laugh.

Zeth was on a roll. 'Stifle yourself, Pontowski. Only one thing is gonna save your two worthless butts.'

'What's that?' Brian asked, defiance still in his voice. But it was all false bravado and Zeth knew it.

'You two becoming the best Rat buddies who ever marched a tour in the Box. You two will be showdogs for the Corps or the butt of every joke for a year. Your choice. Drop and give me fifty.'

Brian sneered. 'Right after you, *Miss* Trogger.' The challenge was obvious.

Zeth dropped to the ground and rapped out fifty fast push-ups, the maximum allowable as punishment. She bounced to her feet. 'Now drop,' she commanded. The two boys fell to the ground and struggled to repeat her performance.

'How many?' Brian asked through gritted teeth.

'Until I get tired,' she shot back. She intended to let them go the full fifty but both were running out of steam. 'Save me from wussies,' she moaned.

CHAPTER TWO

Moscow

'Natasha, I'm Geraldine Blake, Mr Vashin's secretary,' the Englishwoman said in perfect Russian as she extended her hand in a businesslike manner. The girl, still in her teens, gently shook the outstretched hand and nodded, her blonde hair flowing gracefully around her face. Everything about her shouted youth, grace, education and breeding, exactly what Vashin wanted. Geraldine Blake spoke to the guard at the elevator door and he, in turn, spoke into his palm radio. A voice answered and the guard jerked his head. The elevator was descending from the penthouse. They waited in silence until the doors opened, revealing two more guards. Geraldine motioned the beautiful prostitute to enter first. The doors closed behind them.

'Please do exactly what you are told, Natasha,' Geraldine said, 'and everything will be fine. Whatever you do, don't lie.' The girl gave a little nod, her eyes filled with fear. 'Take off your wrap,' Geraldine said. The girl handed her the expensive silk cloak draped around her arms. She wore a simple, low-cut, flimsy black dress that revealed her lovely shoulders. The dress barely reached the girl's thighs and was a gossamer cloud designed to showcase her beauty. It had cost over a thousand dollars in Milan.

One of the guards frisked her, his hands moving roughly

over the delicate fabric of the dress. Then he reached under her short hemline and groped inside her panties. He ran his fingers from front to back, poking and prodding for a hidden weapon. The girl's face was impassive as she endured the search. 'How old are you, Natasha?' Geraldine asked.

'Seventeen,' came the answer. Her voice was soft and sweet.

'You are a very foolish girl,' Geraldine said. 'But I'm sure Mr Vashin will understand because of your age.' The girl was trembling. The doors slid open and the Englishwoman led the way into the penthouse. Mikhail Vashin was standing in front of the architectural model of his skyscraper complex, Vashin Towers. It had become his favorite spot, and he never seemed to tire of it, especially late at night. A man sat on one of the heavily brocaded couches across from Viktor Kraiko, the President of the Russian Federation. Two guards stood in front of the elevator doors.

'Is this the girl?' Vashin said, his voice dull and flat. Geraldine recognized the tone and nodded. She wanted to leave but knew that was impossible. 'Well,' Vashin said, turning to the girl, 'are you the one they call Little Dove?' The girl's voice was barely audible when she answered. 'You have nothing to fear from me,' Vashin said. He held out a closed hand and opened his fingers. Resting on his palm were a pair of beautiful amber cufflinks mounted in silver. The amber droplets glowed with a golden warmth and richness. Encased in each gem was an identical insect, both with extended wings as if they were ready to fly. But they were of a species not seen on earth in over ten million years.

'The silver mountings are nothing,' Vashin explained, 'a convenience. But the amber is priceless and has been part of Poland's history for six hundred years. They were stolen by the Nazis in 1942 and later confiscated by the Soviets. I decided it was time to return them to their rightful owners' – he gestured at the man sitting opposite Viktor Kraiko – 'as a token of Russian goodwill. You were to make Mr Gabrowski comfortable, be his companion, and warm his bed. Surely, you are well paid for your charms. So why did you steal the cufflinks?'

The girl's eyes filled with tears. 'Because they are so beautiful and . . . and I wanted a special gift for my boyfriend's name day.' Her head hung low and she whispered, repeating herself. 'They are so beautiful.' It was a plea for understanding.

'Indeed they are,' Vashin said. He reached out and lifted her chin. A strand of errant hair fell around her left cheek, making her even more vulnerable. 'Undress,' Vashin said. The girl threw Geraldine a quick glance and reached for the straps of her dress. With a quick motion, the dress fell to the floor. She wore only black panties and shoes. Without hesitating, she hooked her thumbs into the panties and stepped out of them. She stood there, tall and radiant in her youth. Vashin handed her the cufflinks. 'Please return these to Mr Gabrowski.'

Natasha did as commanded and walked over to the man sitting on the couch. 'Put them on his cuffs,' Vashin told her. She knelt in front of Gabrowski as she fastened the cufflinks on to his shirt cuffs. Her long fingernails made the task difficult. Finally, she was finished and stood. Gabrowski ran his hand down her stomach, lingering for a moment. 'Come here,' Vashin ordered. Obediently, Natasha returned to him, all eyes rooted on her. She stood in front of Vashin, her hands dangling at her side. He reached out and fondled her breasts. 'So young and firm,' he said. 'So beautiful.' He squeezed hard, released, and squeezed harder. Her eyes filled with tears but she didn't move. 'You do not steal from my guests,' he said. 'Because of your foolishness, your boyfriend is dead.' He squeezed again, his blunt fingers digging into her flesh. She cried out.

'So young,' Vashin sighed, releasing her. 'You may leave.' She knelt to gather up her clothes on the floor but he stepped on them. She looked up and he shook his head. He jerked his chin toward the elevator. She stood. 'Leave your shoes,' Vashin ordered. She stepped out of her black pumps and walked quickly across the room, totally naked. As she reached the two guards, one inserted a key into the elevator lock and twisted it fully counter-clockwise. She stood at the closed doors. They silently opened but there was no elevator. The girl gasped as the other guard placed a hand between her shoulder blades and gave a hard shove. She tumbled into the black pit and her scream echoed for what seemed an eternity as she fell thirty stories. It halted abruptly. The guard twisted the key and the doors closed.

Kraiko sweated heavily and his face was deathly pale. For a moment, Vashin was certain he would be sick, like he was at the cemetery. 'Politicians,' Vashin said to Gabrowski, 'do not have a stomach for obedience. But Viktor is learning.' He shook his head in pity. 'I give you my word,' Vashin said, 'that we are honorable men and can be trusted.' He made a slight motion toward Kraiko. 'Not like politicians.'

Kraiko wanted to escape. 'It's late,' he croaked, fighting the bile rising in his throat. 'Can we finish this tomorrow?'

'Of course.' Vashin looked at his guest. 'Is there anything else we can do for you tonight?'

Gabrowski studied Geraldine and smiled. 'I have always found Englishwomen very appealing,' he said.

'Of course,' Vashin replied. He nodded at Geraldine and she walked toward the stairs descending to the guest bedroom. 'We will finish our business tomorrow morning.'

The Hill

Brian Turner stood in the middle of the dorm room in Hagerman Barracks and checked the time. Just after 8 p.m. Friday night and less than two hours to Taps. He and Little Matt had been preparing for Saturday morning's room inspection since returning from supper, and he was bored with the entire drill. 'Stupid,' he muttered, 'fuckin' stupid. I gotta get out of this place.'

Little Matt finished arranging the drawer in his locker and pushed it closed. 'Your locker is gross. We ain't gonna make it.' Saturday's inspection was always a killer. He fell silent when he heard footsteps on the stoop, the cement walkway outside the room, come to a halt.

'Who gives a shit,' Brian muttered, oblivious to the person standing in the open door. Little Matt jumped to his feet and came to attention.

'Mr Turner,' Zeth Trogger said, 'read what the Blue

Book has to say about profanity. Page one dash twenty-nine, I believe.'

'Little Miss Blue Book,' Brian mumbled under his breath, an obvious reference to the deputy commandant, nicknamed Colonel Blue Book, who took reports and administered punishments for infractions of the rules listed in the book of cadet regulations.

Zeth ignored the remark and looked around the room. 'Gross, absolutely gross. You'll never pass. Haven't you wussies learned anything?' She walked around the room and ripped the bunks apart before trashing Brian's locker and desk. Then she inspected Little Matt's locker, leaving it undisturbed. 'Marginal, but it will get by.' She groaned loudly at the sight of Brian's desk and destroyed it.

Brian's face filled with anger. 'You can't do that. You're history, Trogger.'

'Really?' she answered, surveying her handiwork. 'What for? Hazing? Fagging? Get a clue.' She stood on a short ladder to work on Brian's bunk, which was above his desk. 'Got a dollar, wuss?' Brian handed her a dollar bill. 'Watch, wussie, and check the time.' She used the dollar bill as a measure to fold the blanket and sheet into a white collar. Next, she folded the corners at a perfect forty-five-degree angle. Then she remade Little Matt's bed before arranging Brian's locker and desk. She finished by putting Little Matt's desk in inspection order. She stepped back and raised her hands when she was finished. 'That's how it's done. How long?'

'Thirty-eight minutes,' Little Matt answered.

'Yeah!' Brian said. 'About time someone cut us some slack here.'

'Really?' she replied. The two boys stared in horror as she dismantled the bunks. 'I'll show you how it's done, but you have to do it.' She spun around and walked out the door. 'Have a nice evening, wussies. See you in the morning.'

'Bitch,' Brian muttered.

'I didn't hear that,' Zeth called from the stoop.

'Look,' Little Matt said, pointing in excitement. Zeth

Trogger had left the lockers and desks in inspection order.

'She's still a bitch,' Brian muttered.

Williams Gateway, Arizona

The blue-and-white T-34 Mentor descended to 4,000 feet as Pontowski followed the published arrival procedures for landing at the air show. He peered into the morning haze and tried to find the distinctive landmarks that pointed to Williams, the old Air Force pilot training base that had been closed and turned over for civilian use. A tinge of nostalgia tugged at him, for, in many ways, this was a homecoming. He wished Little Matt were with him in the back seat of the T-34, but Saturday on Labor Day was just another duty weekend and Monday a normal class day at NMMI.

Pontowski had been born at Williams AFB when his father was a second lieutenant in pilot training. Twenty-two years later, after Pontowski had graduated from the Air Force Academy, he had returned to Williams also as a second lieutenant for pilot training. Now the old memories flooded back as he approached the airport. *I must be getting sentimental in my old age*, he thought. He shook his head. *Pay attention to business and fly the airplane.*

He overflew the published checkpoint and made the required radio call. 'Willie Tower, Mentor Three-Four-One-Five ten miles southeast for landing.' Ahead of him he could see a double string of airplanes lined up for landing. But the airport was still lost in the haze.

'Mentor One-Five,' the tower replied, 'you're number four for runway three zero right following a Cessna. Report field in sight. Maintain spacing.'

As the arrival procedures dictated, he did not acknowledge the instructions. There were too many aircraft arriving at the same time and the frequency was jammed with radio calls. Ahead of him, he could see the Cessna he was to follow, and he slowed to 100 knots, the published approach speed. The Cessna pilot was a professional and was at the same airspeed. Now the triple parallel runways emerged from the haze and he could see the built-up area and parking ramp on the southwest side of the field. Suddenly, a bright red Marchetti 260 zoomed up in front of him and shot through his altitude. The pilot rolled ninety-degrees as he bled off his excessive airspeed and pulled down into the landing flow of traffic, less than 200 feet in front of Pontowski. But he had lost too much airspeed in the maneuver and was twenty knots slower.

Pontowski's reaction was automatic, honed by years of flying. He rolled to the right, pulled the Mentor's nose up, and firewalled the throttle. He cleared the Marchetti's tail by less than fifty feet. It was a classic near miss in the landing pattern caused by a jerk who thought he was too good a pilot for the rules to apply to him. 'Willie Tower,' Pontowski radioed, 'Mentor One-Five breaking out of traffic to the north. Will reenter.' The heavy radio transmissions prevented him from explaining why. He was too seasoned a pilot to get angry in the air and would sort it out on the ground.

Fortunately, there was a professional in the control tower. 'Aircraft cutting off the Mentor, say intentions.'

A cool voice came over the radio. 'Marchetti Whiskey Romeo Two' – the next two numbers were garbled – 'landing Williams for the air show. Ah, I do need to get on the ground.'

'Are you declaring an emergency?' the tower asked.

'Not at this time,' the Marchetti pilot replied. He had told the tower that he had a problem that needed taking care of but not severe enough to declare an emergency.

'You're cleared to land runway three zero right following the Cessna. Call tower on a land line when you're on the ground.' The controller wasn't done with the incident.

This time the pilot's response was not so cool. 'Rog on the phone call.' Then, 'Sorry 'bout that, Mentor.'

Pontowski snorted in disgust. If the Marchetti had a real problem the pilot should have been talking to approach control and been well clear of the heavy traffic landing for the air show. He downgraded his opinion of the pilot to flaming asshole and didn't bother to respond. But another voice did. 'The butthead needs to take a leak.'

Pontowski couldn't help himself. 'Rog on the leaking rectum.'

The air show was well organized and Pontowski was quickly marshaled into a parking spot beside six other T-34s after he landed. The old Air Force trainers were in the row next to the military displays that were a featured part of the weekend, much like the air shows at Paris or Farnborough. He shut down as the other T-34 pilots wandered over to greet him. They had all met before. He climbed over the canopy rail and stood on the wing as he slid the canopy closed. Two rows down, in the midst of the military hardware, he could see four bright red Marchettis. Even on the ground, the little Italian trainer looked like a hot rod. *One of the aerial demonstration teams,* he decided. His eyes narrowed. He hoped the show's air boss was having severe doubts about one of their pilots.

'Hey, Matt,' one of the Mentor pilots called, 'what the hell happened out there? That sonofabitch almost nailed you.'

'He came damn close,' Pontowski answered. 'Claimed he had an emergency.'

'His only emergency,' another pilot said, 'was taking a piss. Never saw anyone get out of a plane so fast after landing. He relieved himself right on the ramp.'

Pontowski nodded. 'Suspicions confirmed.' They shook hands all around, old friends bound by a common interest in T-34s.

'Are you going to file a near miss?' the first pilot asked.

Pontowski thought about it for a moment. 'The tower's on top of it. But I do need to talk to him.' He walked across the ramp, slowed by the large crowd of spectators already at the air show before the heat grew too intense. He made a mental note to cover the Plexiglas of the Mentor's tandem cockpit before it got too hot.

A pudgy, fair-haired man in his early thirties was talking to a mixed crowd of civilians and foreign military officers about the Marchettis. He was wearing a tight red Nomex flying suit festooned with patches on the shoulders and chest. A gold name tag identified the wearer as Sammy Beason. Pontowski wouldn't have been caught dead wearing it.

'Quite an outfit,' a voice said behind him. Pontowski turned to the speaker, a tall, slender man with white hair. 'Bob Bender,' the man said, a broad smile on his face and his hand outstretched. 'Aren't you Matt Pontowski?'

Pontowski immediately recognized the four-star general. 'Guilty, sir.' Even in civilian clothes, Robert Bender was all military hard lines and unbending attitude. The general was a legend in the Air Force: a former Thunderbird solo pilot, a fighter jock who had flown every high-performance jet in the inventory and shot down two Iraqi MiGs in the Gulf War. Recently, he had commanded Air Combat Command, and was now the vice-chief of staff of the Air Force, rumored to be in line for chairman of the Joint Chiefs of Staff. But there was more. He was a commander men and women trusted and would follow willingly into combat, even at the risk of death.

They shook hands. 'What brings you here?' Pontowski asked.

Bender shook his head. 'That gentleman.' He was looking directly at the Marchetti pilot.

'I need to explain a few things to him,' Pontowski said.

'I'd rather you didn't,' the general said. Pontowski waited for an explanation. 'He claims he had an intermittent electrical malfunction,' Bender added.

'That can't be duplicated on the ground. Who is he anyway?'

'Sammy Beason controls an airline, a basketball team, and who knows what else. He got them when his father retired. Unfortunately, he's also the CEO of World Security Systems.'

Pontowski was beginning to get a clue. World Security Systems, or WSS, was the world's leading private arms merchant. But WSS had taken it to a much higher level. Besides supplying weapons to the highest bidder, the company also provided military expertise, support services, and training programs. WSS could deliver, on demand, export licenses for some of the United States' most technologically advanced weapon systems. Further, for the right price, they could provide a turnkey, combat-ready military force. They could do all this because Sammy Beason, through his father, had access to some of the most important politicians in the country. 'So what is he doing here?' Pontowski asked.

'Peddling an all-up tactical fighter force under the cover of a pilot training program. WSS provides the instructors, the planes, weapons, maintenance, and training. The client provides the airbase and the student pilots. While the students are being trained, the so-called instructors function as combat-ready pilots. *Voilà*, instant air force. As you can see, there is some interest.'

Pontowski's eyes narrowed. 'I'd like to undermine the interest in that program.'

Bender smiled. 'I might be able to arrange that. Can you hang around for a few days?'

Washington, D.C.

It was a congenial group that gathered at Secretary of State Serick's Georgetown townhouse for a garden party celebrating American labor. But the only people who had ever turned an honest day's labor were the waitresses, waiters, and caterers. Most of the women were wearing bright summer dresses, although two pairs of designer jeans were to be seen. But those were worn by the young and thin trophy wives. The men all wore light summer sports coats with open-necked shirts. If a society reporter had been present, she would have noted all the dignitaries and overlooked Herbert von Lubeck, the first secretary to the German deputy minister for economic research.

But a political commentator or reporter would have looked at the group differently. Why were so many high-rollers still in the city on the last summer holiday and at a party for such a minor foreign functionary? The answer was in the second-floor den where Stephan Serick was examining the excellent Havana cigar Herbert von Lubeck had given him.

'A gift from Cuba's new President,' von Lubeck said in German.

Serick breathed deeply and savored the cigar's aroma before lighting it. 'Excellent,' he replied, also in German. 'Unfortunately, we won't be importing any of these for some time.'

'A very short-sighted policy, my friend. But one that my government encourages. Our trade with Cuba benefits greatly by your absence.'

Serick rolled the cigar in his fingers, apparently more interested in the cigar than in von Lubeck's unusual candor. On the surface, von Lubeck had a minor post in an obscure office of the German government. In reality, he was a plenipotentiary with far-reaching powers and was in the United States for a definite purpose. Serick doubted that his visit had anything to do with Cuban cigars. 'Like a good cigar,' Serick said, 'foreign policy is not made in a day.'

'The key is good soil and land,' von Lubeck said. 'Without them, nothing can grow to its proper size.'

The Secretary of State chose his next words carefully. Since the country had united in 1990, Germany's agriculture sector had been the weak spot in its economy and was holding it back. 'Ah, yes, your agricultural base.'

'We are pursuing certain initiatives to correct that deficiency,' von Lubeck told him.

Serick put on his 'how interesting' expression to mask what he really thought. The State Department had been flooded with disturbing reports about renewed German interest in its pre-World War II territories in Poland. On the face, it seemed fair enough: the German government was helping its citizens who had lost land in Poland after the communist takeover in 1945 to reclaim their holdings or seek compensation. But what was going on below the surface was far more worrisome. The Germans were using this policy as a cover for buying large tracts of Polish land.

'The Poles,' von Lubeck said, rolling his own cigar in his fingers, 'are asking for our help in modernizing their agricultural sector. We believe that would be beneficial to both countries.'

'Beneficial?' Serick asked, packing a ton of meaning into that single word. Von Lubeck only smiled in response, and Serick decided it was time to flash a little of his famous irritability. 'We feel a German expansion in that direction could destabilize eastern Europe,' he said, still speaking in German. It was easy to sound cranky in that language.

Again, von Lubeck smiled. 'Exactly the reason for this conversation, my friend. Germany has no intention of reclaiming its lost lands. We are content with the current Polish border along the Oder and Neisse rivers. This is simply an economic endeavor. German agriculture is much more efficient and this, I must emphasize, this will prove beneficial for both countries.'

'Then why don't you invest in Polish agrobusiness instead of outright purchase of land?' Serick replied, pulling off the diplomatic gloves.

Von Lubeck showed no sign of surprise at Serick's revelation that the United States knew what was going on. He waved a hand in dismissal. 'There is a certain, ah, shall we say inherent instability in Polish affairs. We merely want to ensure a sound base for our investments.'

Serick humphed. He knew how Germans interpreted stability. 'The United States will not allow a change in Poland's borders.'

Von Lubeck guillotined the end of his cigar with a silver cutter. He wanted to say that what the United States wanted was becoming less and less important. Instead he offered, 'That certainly is not our intention.'

Serick knew how quickly intentions could change. He gave a diplomatic sigh of resignation to encourage von Lubeck. 'We understand,' the German said, falling for it, 'the problems you are having with the lack of resolve and consistency in your current administration.' He lit his cigar and puffed it to life. 'Your poor Mrs Turner is in over her head.'

Didn't the world learn anything from the Okinawa blockade? Serick thought. Within weeks after assuming the presidency upon the death of President Roberts, Madeline Turner had to resolve a major crisis in the Far East. China had blockaded

Okinawa in an attempt to drive a wedge between the United States and Japan. The world had moved perilously close to nuclear war when fighting broke out. Turner had contained the crisis and brought the Chinese to the negotiating table. But it had been a near thing.

Von Lubeck came to the heart of the matter. He was amazingly candid. 'Our goal in eastern Europe is economic and political stability, which only Germany can provide.'

Because you don't think Maddy Turner can, Serick mentally added.

Williams Gateway, Arizona

The real business of the air show was conducted on Tuesday after the crowds and most of the civilian aircraft had departed. Only a few corporate jets, the military displays, and a lone blue-and-white T-34 Mentor remained on the ramp. The potential buyers had all been wined and dined by the contractors and builders, the right call-girl or toy boy provided, and any other required service taken care of. Now the hard sell could begin.

Bender was still in civilian clothes when he met Pontowski outside the old operations building. 'I remember this place well,' Pontowski said, recalling his days as a student pilot.

Bender nodded. 'I went through training here too.' He paced slowly back and forth. 'My sources tell me WSS has two very interested clients in their all-up pilot training program.' He named two countries, one in eastern Europe, the other in North Africa. 'Iran and Libya are financing the projects under the table. We can live with the North African venture, but the eastern European deal is in entirely the wrong place at the wrong time.'

Pontowski frowned. He understood the factors that could destabilize a region only too well. 'Not good,' he allowed. 'Do we have any counters on the table?'

'We might be able to get something going in eastern Europe – if we can discourage them from going with WSS.'

'Any ideas how?' Pontowski asked. Bender shook his head.

'Well,' Pontowski continued, 'let's go listen to WSS's pitch. You gotta know the opposition.' They entered the building and found seats at the back of the room where WSS was presenting its program.

Sammy Beason was on the stage, still wearing his flashy red flying suit. He started the program by welcoming them all to 'the finest and most versatile pilot training program in the world', and turned it over to his experts. Pontowski was impressed with the Madison Avenue presentation. Finally, it was question-and-answer time, and Beason was back on the stage. 'In the final analysis,' he concluded, 'our program is the best in the world because of our pilots.' He introduced four men in the front row, who stood up as he called their names. They were the same four pilots who had flown the Marchettis in an aerial display on Saturday, Sunday, and Monday. The crowd had roared its approval, especially at the inverted bomb burst that climaxed the show. The last pilot to stand was an Iraqi, Johar Adwan.

'I'll be damned,' Pontowski muttered under his breath. He listened as Beason claimed the pilots were typical of WSS's staff. He allowed himself a tight smile when Beason added that they were acknowledged as the world's 'four top guns'.

'Hey, Joe,' Pontowski called to the Iraqi. 'I heard you gave it up after I shot you down.'

Every head in the room turned to Pontowski. Johar Adwan went rigid, then a big smile spread across his face. 'Matt Pontowski,' he said. 'Always the big mouth. You got lucky that day.'

'Yeah,' Pontowski conceded, 'you're right. It wasn't a fair fight, two vee one.' He paused. 'Say, what happened to your wingman after I stuffed him?' Every pilot in the room caught on. It had been Pontowski against Johar and his wingman and Pontowski had won.

'The planes were unequal,' Johar allowed, still smiling. 'If we were evenly matched—'

Bender interrupted. 'Mr Beason, you can settle this argument. Maybe a little ACT? Johar against Matt in your Marchettis.' ACT was air combat training, basic dogfighting where two of the same type aircraft went one on one.

Beason jumped in front of Johar for damage control. He had heard of Pontowski and didn't want to take any chances. If there was going to be a demonstration with potential buyers looking on, he wanted the results carefully orchestrated in advance. 'Unfortunately, we don't have the airspace.' He shrugged his shoulders in resignation. 'The FAA.' The Federal Aviation Agency controlled the use of airspace in the United States and was dedicated to flying safety.

Bender stifled a smile. 'The box is still activated,' he said. The box was a small piece of the sky over Williams's triple runways that the FAA had designated for acrobatics and aerial demonstrations at the air show. The show's air boss in the tower controlled the box, and the pilots and owners of performing aircraft assumed all the risk.

'I don't see how,' Beason stammered.

'According to your brochure, your Marchettis are configured with HUDs' – head-up displays – 'that have airborne video recorders to tape this type of training. We can all watch it from the ground and then review the tapes afterwards in the debrief.' Bender smiled at Johar. 'I assume we're dealing with professionals here.'

'Sounds good to me,' Pontowski said. 'I don't mind taking an observer along in the left seat.' The Marchetti was a two-place, side-by-side trainer where the passenger or instructor sat in the left seat. Half the men in the room were on their feet, eager to volunteer. Afraid that someone important would want to fly with Johar in the Marchetti, Beason said he would fly with the Iraqi. His face paled when he saw the cold look in Pontowski's eyes.

Two hours later, Beason was on the edge of panic as Johar taxied his red Marchetti to the active runway. 'Do not worry, Mr Beason,' the Iraqi said. 'Pontowski may be good but I seriously doubt if he is proficient in the Marchetti. I am.' Beason felt an overpowering need to urinate when Pontowski moved into position off the left wing, his side of the aircraft, for the taxi out.

43

The tower cleared them on to the runway. 'You are cleared into the air-show box, ground to five thousand feet. Maneuver parallel to and over the runways. Reposition over the open area northeast of the box.' It was a reminder to stay over open areas and keep the nose of the aircraft pointed away from any buildings or people. It was a constraint Pontowski could live with.

'Now we get to go fly and fight,' Pontowski told his passenger, a Polish Air Force officer named Emil with an unpronounceable last name. As briefed, he taxied into position on the right of the Marchetti. Johar Adwan would lead the takeoff, which was exactly what Pontowski wanted. Johar was sitting in the right-hand seat of his Marchetti and glanced at Beason in his left seat. He then made a circular motion with his forefinger to run the engines up. Pontowski shoved his throttle full forward and rode the brakes. Johar tilted his head back and then dropped his chin, the signal to release brakes. The two aircraft moved in unison down the runway, rapidly gaining speed.

They lifted off together. Pontowski snapped the gear handle up and mentally counted to ten, the time it took for the gear to retract. Johar was a fraction of a second slower. Pontowski felt his gear lock at the count of nine. He immediately jerked his aircraft forty-five degrees to the right, pulling four Gs. He leveled off less than fifty feet above the ground and turned back to the original heading to keep Johar in sight. 'Fight's on,' he radioed. The maneuver had given him nose-tail separation from Johar. His reflexes were still rattlesnake quick and he turned back into Johar, crossing behind and accelerating. They were at midfield. As Pontowski expected, Johar lost sight of him and pulled up. Pontowski rolled out at Johar's six o'clock and followed him in the climb. He was in the saddle, a perfect position from which to employ an aircraft's cannon. 'Guns, guns, guns,' he radioed, pulling the trigger on the stick. But there was no gunfire, only a laser beam illuminating the spot on Johar's aircraft where the bullets would have hit. The fight was over and it was all recorded on the videotape. Pontowski hit the radio transmit button. 'Splash one Marchetti.'

'*Fantastique!*' Emil shouted.

But Johar had other ideas. He leveled off at 1,000 feet and accelerated straight ahead, gaining speed to separate and reengage. But Pontowski nosed over and dived under him, using gravity to help him accelerate. He rapidly closed on the Iraqi, who was now directly above him. Johar snap-rolled to the right and saw Pontowski still beneath him. The Iraqi pulled on the stick and started a loop.

'An Immelmann ain't gonna save your ass,' Pontowski grunted, fighting the Gs as he followed the Iraqi. He slipped his aircraft to the left, falling into Johar's eight o'clock, the side of the aircraft Beason was sitting on and in Johar's blind spot. 'Betcha can't do a belly check in a loop.' Again, Johar had lost sight of him. 'He knows we're here,' Pontowski explained to Emil, 'but he can't resist a peek to be sure. Watch.'

As expected, Johar flew a half-loop and rolled upright the moment he reached the top. Again, he snap-rolled. Pontowski rolled with him, still camped at his eight o'clock.

'Where is he?' Johar shouted over the intercom. Beason's head twisted to the left and his panic turned into pure fear when he saw Pontowski in tight formation, rolling with them. Beason had flown acrobatics, but never anything like this. A cooler head would have said, 'Bandit camped at our eight o'clock.' But words totally failed him.

'*Merde!*' Johar shouted. He partially snap-rolled his Marchetti to the left, doing a belly check to that side. But Pontowski had anticipated that maneuver and rolled with him, holding his position, still in Johar's blind spot. Beason was vaguely aware of the warm feeling in his crotch as he lost control of his bladder. But the fight was far from over. The engines on both aircraft screamed in protest as the pilots kept them at full boost and dived for the ground.

'Sucker!' Pontowski shouted as he followed Johar. Much to his delight, he discovered he had even more overtake than before. He set up for a high-to-low attack followed by a high-speed overshoot. At 300 feet above the ground, he deliberately overshot Johar and nudged his nose over. He was hoping Johar would see it and do the opposite. He did. The

Iraqi pulled up to reduce his speed and to add to Pontowski's overshoot problem. But Pontowski was already pulling on the stick and rolling into Johar, countering the overshoot. He had to get rid of the speed generated by the dive and the bellowing engine. Johar instinctively turned into Pontowski as they entered a series of climbing, crisscrossing nose-to-nose turns and overshoots. 'We're in a scissors,' Pontowski explained to Emil. He was thoroughly enjoying himself. 'Now we got to see who can fly the slowest and get behind the other guy.' Emil laughed.

But all was not equal light and joy in Johar's cockpit. 'Knock it off!' Beason screamed. Johar ignored him as he again turned into Pontowski. His stall warning horn was blaring as their airspeed decayed. But Beason's screaming drowned it out. Suddenly, at 2,000 feet above the ground, Johar's Marchetti departed controlled flight and snapped inverted, entering an upside-down spin.

Pontowski zoomed clear and radioed, 'Knock it off and recover.'

Getting out of an inverted spin is tricky and requires a series of actions best described as unnatural acts. Fortunately, Johar was an accomplished pilot, knew what to do, and had enough altitude to recover. But Beason decided to vote and cast his ballot by doing what appeared normal. He stepped on the rudder pedal opposite the rotation and pushed the stick forward in the sequence required to recover from an upright spin. The result was to raise the Marchetti's nose and put them into a fully developed inverted spin.

By the second full turn, Pontowski knew the Marchetti was in trouble and yelled the recovery procedure over the radio. 'Step on the pedal that has resistance! Back pressure on the stick!' He watched the Marchetti enter the third turn and tasted bile in the back of his mouth. His instincts told him what his mind rejected: Adwan and Beason were dead.

The Marchetti smashed into the ground upside down at the 2,000-foot-remaining mark on runway 12 Left, well inside the aerial demonstration box.

Pontowski banged his fist against the canopy rail. 'God damn it to hell!'

Emil touched his arm, trying to calm him. 'It was combat, my friend.'

'This is peacetime,' was all Pontowski could think of.

'We are never at peace,' the Pole answered.

CHAPTER THREE

The White House

Dennis, Madeline Turner's personal assistant, stood in front of her desk in the Oval Office, his hands clasped in front of him as they went over her daily schedule in detail. Richard Parrish, her chief of staff, sat on a couch making notes. 'Dennis,' Turner said, 'for God's sake, at least look like you're taking notes. It makes me more comfortable.'

'Yes, ma'am,' Dennis replied. He turned to business, not the least chastened. 'Mr Serick and Mrs Hazelton are first on the agenda and waiting outside.'

'Richard, do you have anything before we get started?' Turner asked. Parrish stood and handed her a memo on Serick's meeting with von Lubeck while Dennis ushered in the Secretary of State and Mazie. Dennis closed the door behind them and left. Turner could read over 1,200 words a minute with close to 100 percent comprehension and, by the time they had sat down, she had read and digested the memo. 'I hope you had a nice holiday,' she said, welcoming them back from the Labor Day break.

'We were at Kennebunkport with Went's mother,' Mazie replied. Mazie's husband, Wentworth Hazelton, was the scion of the Hazelton family, who moved in rarefied social and political climates. But more important, his mother was Elizabeth

Martha Hazelton, better known as E.M. to her friends and as the Bitch Queen of Capitol Hill to her enemies.

'How is the Queen these days?' Parrish asked.

'She had an interesting guest Saturday and Sunday,' Mazie said, 'a Herbert von Lubeck.' Serick's head almost twisted off as he turned to look at her. 'They spent a great deal of time together in private conversations,' Mazie added. 'I don't know what they were talking about.'

Serick looked as if he were on the verge of a stroke. 'The bastard,' he finally sputtered. 'I talked to him Monday and he didn't mention meeting with Hazelton. He's playing games with us. I don't trust him.'

Turner tapped Serick's memo as she considered the implications. Without a word, she handed it to Mazie to read. 'I think we're dealing with an expansionist Germany.'

'I'm not so sure,' Mazie said. 'I've dealt with Germany before and they might just be testing the waters. I found them opportunistic, not imperialistic. There is a difference.'

'Ah, yes,' Serick said. 'You're referring to the UN peacekeeping mission to South Africa. A fiasco.'

'It did result in a certain stability there,' Parrish said.

'Temporary at best. Soon it will go the way of the rest of Africa below the Sahara.'

'I'm not familiar with that operation,' Turner said. 'Or the current situation in South Africa. Put together a briefing book on it.' Parrish made a note to create another blue binder. Turner's staff had learned the hard way not to procrastinate and it would be ready that afternoon. 'The important question,' she said, 'is whether there's any domestic fallout or other linkage here.' Turner was still concerned with von Lubeck and Germany.

'There may be a linkage with what's going on in Russia,' Mazie said. 'The CIA reported that Viktor Kraiko was at a series of meetings with Mikhail Vashin and a Pole, a man named Gabrowski, over the weekend. We don't have anything on him and think he was using an alias.'

Serick's voice was a low rumble. 'What we are seeing inside Russia is nothing more than criminals capturing the legitimate government. The Germans may be opportunistic or imperialistic, depending on your point of view, but they are not criminal. So what is the linkage?'

'Poland is undergoing an economic renaissance since being admitted to the European Union,' Mazie answered. 'Maybe the Russians want a piece of the action. The Germans might see that as a threat. Historically, Poland has always been the shatter zone when Russian and German interests collide.'

Turner was ready to move on to another subject. 'Enough about shatter zones. I don't want to be blindsided on some domestic issue because of what we missed in Germany, Eastern Europe, or Russia.' She tapped her right forefinger for emphasis, a gesture which they all caught. Her orders came fast. 'Mazie, stay on top of the situation. Richard, I want the FBI and the CIA looking for any attempt by the Germans or Russians to buy political influence here, specifically through campaign contributions and lobbying efforts. Stephan, I want State to keep Mazie fully informed on what you're seeing in that part of the world.' She paused. 'I'd like to get rid of Rudenkowski.' Lloyd Rudenkowski was the United States ambassador to Poland, a political appointee she had inherited from President Roberts when he died in office.

Parrish coughed for attention. 'Because of the Polish renaissance, Warsaw has become a political plum. Rudenkowski's appointment made mega-points with the Polish-American community.'

'Not to mention mega-contributions to the party,' Serick muttered. 'Thankfully, we have an excellent Deputy Charge of Mission in Warsaw and he can cover for any appointee with an open checkbook and a large bank account.'

'Get me a short list,' Turner said.

'It will be on your desk by this afternoon, Madame President,' Serick replied. He would warn her in a private memo that Rudenkowski had political clout and how his removal could cause problems. They quickly reviewed the three other security issues on the agenda and five minutes later were finished. It was exactly 8.23 a.m. The day had barely started, and Madeline Turner was seven minutes ahead of schedule. Parrish buzzed for Dennis to usher in the next group.

'Oh,' Turner said, 'I want to speak to General Bender.' Parrish and Dennis exchanged glances.

Williams Gateway, Arizona

The inspector from the FAA's Flight Standards Office in Phoenix was temporarily in charge of the accident investigation. Until the investigators from the National Transportation and Safety Board, or NTSB, arrived, it was his job to secure the scene of the accident and gather evidence. Because there had been two major aircraft accidents over the holiday weekend, the NTSB was slow in arriving and the FAA inspector had progressed to interviewing Pontowski. Bender joined them for the interview, acutely aware of the anguish weighing on Pontowski. They were all airmen and accepted the hazards that went with flying. But Pontowski had to live with what had happened and always ask, 'What if?'

After taking an oral statement, the inspector reviewed the four videotapes from the accident. The first one had been taken from the control tower where the air boss had videotaped the entire flight from takeoff to the final, cataclysmic crash. The audio portion recorded all radio transmissions heard or made by the tower. The second video was shot by a WSS cameraman from a platform on the opposite side of the field. And while the audio recorded the reactions of the spectators, the sound was of little use. The last two tapes were from the HUDs of the Marchettis and recorded the flight as Pontowski and Johar Adwan had seen it.

But without doubt, the audio portion of Johar's video was the most important because it recorded Johar's shout of 'Let go the stick!'

After the video had been rewound, the FAA inspector glanced at his notes and then at Pontowski. 'This is the best-documented accident I've ever seen. But did this qualify as an aerial demonstration?'

'It was a demonstration of air combat training,' Pontowski

explained. 'ACT is not choreographed like a normal aerial demonstration. But it does have rules.' He handed the inspector a cassette tape. 'I tape-recorded the prebrief. I flew the mission as briefed and we were inside the box.'

They all listened to the tape. 'I think it's pretty obvious what happened,' Bender said.

The FAA inspector nodded in agreement. 'That was no time to have someone else voting on the stick.' Again, he looked at Pontowski. 'But damn, you were pressing the envelope.' He held up his hand to shut off discussion. 'I know, I know. You had clearance to perform a multi-ship aerial demonstration in the box. But this was not what we had in mind. You had a lot of confidence in Adwan's abilities. Perhaps your confidence was misplaced.'

The 'what ifs' were back, pounding at Pontowski, demanding their price. Slowly, he shook his head, still trying to quiet his demon of responsibility. 'Johar Adwan was a good pilot. I flew against him in combat and was damn lucky to have survived.' He read the disbelief on the inspector's face. 'He never lost situational awareness yesterday.'

'How can you be sure of that?' the inspector asked.

'Because there was no fire. I looked inside the wreckage when I retrieved the videotape from his HUD. Johar had turned the ignition and fuel selector valve off before impacting the ground. He knew he was going to crash and never gave up.'

The inspector closed his notebook and gathered up the tapes. 'Well, we have a lot of work to do.' He paused. 'General Pontowski, I'm going to have to ask you for your log book.'

Pontowski shook his head. 'I'll send you a certified copy.'

'Please, don't play games with me.'

The two men looked at each other, neither wanting to get into an argument. But they were staking out the boundaries of the investigation. Pontowski almost said the FAA was not the Gestapo but was saved when the door opened and a man and a woman carrying briefcases marched in. Both were dressed in dark business suits. The man snapped out a business card and handed it to Bender because he looked like he was in charge.

'Jonathan Slater from Fine, Schlossmaker, and Traube.' The woman sat down and clicked open her slim briefcase. Bender read the card, frowned, and handed it to the FAA inspector. Fine, Schlossmaker, and Traube was a high-powered law firm with offices in every major city in the United States. Just to get them to answer the telephone required a yearly retainer fee of $50,000. 'We represent Mr Beason's family,' Slater announced as if he spoke for an ecclesiastical power.

The woman handed the FAA inspector a subpoena. 'We're filing a wrongful death action against all parties for the death of Samuel Beason and subpoenaing all relevant documents.' She reached for the tapes.

The FAA inspector slapped her hand. 'Don't get grabby,' he told her. He unfolded the subpoena and started to read.

A cellphone buzzed and all five reached for their handsets. It was for Bender. He flipped his set open. 'Bender here.' Even in that simple greeting, there was authority. He listened to the summons from the White House. No emotion crossed his face. He broke the connection and waited for the inspector to finish reading the subpoena.

'You had better get a federal judge involved,' the inspector told the lawyers.

'This is a court order,' the man said. 'Are you defying it?'

The inspector shook his head in disgust at the legal gimmicks lawyers would try, even very high-priced ones, when they were out of ideas. 'Wrong court.' A little smile crossed his face. 'We'll provide you with copies at the proper time.'

The two lawyers exchanged glances. 'We're sorry you've chosen not to cooperate,' the woman said. The smile never left the inspector's face as the two lawyers retreated, slamming the door behind them.

'Eat shit,' he muttered. 'They want to bury the tapes.'

Pontowski decided he liked the man. 'You'll have my log book as soon as I can find a Xerox and make a copy for myself.'

'Thank you.'

'I have to get back to Washington ASAP,' Bender told the

two men. 'There's a plane waiting for me at Sky Harbor.' Sky Harbor was Phoenix's international airport twenty-six miles away. But to get there through traffic and into the terminal could take over an hour.

'I can fly you there in the Mentor,' Pontowski offered. It was quickly arranged.

'I hope you're coming back,' the inspector said.

'Are you making me an offer I can't refuse?' Pontowski asked.

'Well, we still got three Marchettis that are good to go and since Fine, Schlossmaker, and Trouble want to gather evidence, maybe we can model the accident for them.' Pontowski didn't reply, but the idea of reflying the accident appealed to him. 'Perhaps,' the inspector continued, his face solemn but his eyes giving him away, 'we could take those two legal beagles along.' He paused. 'Since they're gathering evidence, of course.'

'Most assuredly,' Bender allowed.

'Now that's an offer I can't refuse,' Pontowski replied.

The White House

Dennis escorted the four local politicians from Maddy Turner's hometown in California into the Oval Office and checked his watch. It was late afternoon and they were thirty-five minutes ahead of schedule. He beat a hasty retreat to ensure the photographers were ready to record the meeting. Then he made a panic phone call to Maura O'Keith. They had a problem.

Photographers loved Turner. She was naturally photogenic and captured the camera. Unfortunately, the same could not be said for one of her guests. One woman, who happened to be the mayor and one of Turner's most avid supporters, had a sense of fashion caught somewhere between bag lady and troll. Dennis shuddered at the thought of a photo of the two together. Such pictures had a life of their own and always came back to haunt the White House. Five minutes later, Maura was in the secretary's office as Dennis explained the problem. The intercom buzzed. They were ready for the photographers and Dennis wished that Turner was a little less efficient in shortening her schedule.

Maura spoke to a secretary, appropriated her scarf, and followed the photographers into the Oval Office, tying the scarf around her shoulders. She made a pretense of examining her daughter's hair, pronounced it fit for photographing, and generally acted like a mother, which thoroughly charmed the visitors. Then she did the same for them. She lingered over the mayor and smiled. 'I know just the thing. It's the light in here, you know.' She produced a hairbrush from her ever present handbag, brushed the woman's hair back on one side and curled it down and around the other cheek. She stepped back, surveyed her handiwork, and then draped the secretary's scarf around the woman's shoulders and tied it with a loose knot. The improvement was dramatic and the photographers went to work. Maura spoke to the woman when Dennis ushered them out. 'The scarf looks so much better on you. Why don't you keep it as a souvenir of your visit?' The woman beamed at her.

As usual, Parrish stayed behind to go over the next day's schedule. 'That's about it, Madame President. Nothing's brewing so you should have a quiet evening.'

She leaned back in her chair. 'Did Stephan send over a list of names to replace Rudenkowski?'

Parrish nodded and extracted the list from his folder. 'And this,' he said, handing her a private memo.

Turner looked through the list and the brief biographies before reading the memo. 'So Stephan is certain that replacing Rudenkowski will have adverse fallout.'

'Well,' Parrish said, 'he has made major campaign contributions to Senator Leland and does have influence. Stephan probably figures he paid for the ambassadorship and deserves to keep it.'

'Richard, my instincts tell me Poland is going to be a problem. Exactly how, I'm not sure. I want a professional over there as head of mission. But if I read Stephan's memo correctly, Rudenkowski will cause problems if I request his resignation.'

'Big problems, Madame President.'

She stared at the painting over the fireplace, considering her options. 'Check and see if there's something else we can offer him.' She thought for a moment. 'And have the FBI and Treasury take another look into his background. Poke around a bit but keep State out of the loop for now. I want to be sure there is nothing that could prove embarrassing if it became public knowledge.' Parrish understood perfectly. It was the old carrot-and-stick approach. 'Like Patrick used to say,' she said, thinking of Patrick Flannery Shaw, her former chief of staff, 'kiss them on the cheek before you kick 'em in the charlies.'

'I never realized Shaw was that subtle.'

'Patrick had his moments,' Turner replied, thinking of all she had learned from him.

'Will there be anything else, Madame President?'

'I was hoping to speak to General Bender today.' It was a gentle reprimand to the effect that her staff had not done their job.

'We found him in Arizona,' Parrish said. She arched an eyebrow. Parrish rushed to add, 'He will be available tomorrow. When would you like to see him?'

'Whenever it's convenient.' That was her code for, It had better happen tomorrow.

It was a quiet evening at home. Sarah was sitting on the floor wearing a headset and listening to music while she did her homework. Maura was sitting in a recliner reading one of her fashion magazines with her knitting in her lap. Occasionally, she drifted off to sleep, only to give a little honk and wake herself up. In the background, the TV was tuned to CNN. Madeline Turner was curled up in the corner of her favorite couch wearing a baggy track suit and woolly socks. She was reading the blue binder on the UN South African peacekeeping mission she had requested that morning. The room was a scene of domestic tranquility paparazzi would have killed for to photograph. But

Maddy's fierce protection of her family's privacy made that impossible.

Maura gave another little honk and woke up. 'Mother,' Maddy asked, closing the three-ring binder, 'you met Matthew Pontowski at NMMI. What was your impression?'

'Little Matt?' Maura asked, still drowsy.

'No, his father.'

Now the older woman was fully awake. It had been a long time since her daughter had asked her opinion about a single man. 'He's very attractive,' she replied. 'A widower, you know. Lenora McMasters told me all about him. He was very wild in his younger days when he was a fighter pilot.'

Maddy shook her head in disapproval. She had met too many Pontowskis in her time; good-looking men who reeled women in with far too much success and ease. 'The top-gun image,' she said. 'I never knew if they were talking about their penis or their airplanes. Why do women fall for it?'

'Fall for what?' Sarah asked, pulling off her headset.

Both women sighed in resignation. Once Sarah joined in a conversation, she pursued a topic with bulldog-like determination. 'The things men do to attract women,' Maddy answered.

'Oh,' Sarah replied, apparently satisfied with that answer. Then, 'Mom, who are the Moody Blues?'

'An old rock and roll group from the early 1970s,' Maddy answered. 'I don't think they're still recording.'

'I never liked them,' Maura said.

'Your father and I loved them,' Maddy said. 'We used to sit and hold hands listening to them.' She caught Maura's amused look and, for a moment, was back with Brian Kelly Turner. Indeed, they had listened to the Moody Blues, but they weren't exactly holding hands. They were usually in bed making love. The sex had been wonderful. But there had been a rough spot when she discovered she was pregnant and not sure if she wanted to marry him. However, Brian Kelly Turner had pursued her so doggedly that she finally gave in. Then she had a miscarriage.

But it was an excellent marriage that had grown stronger

over the years. His death from a heart attack while playing tennis at forty-eight had devastated her. It had happened in the middle of the election when she was running for vice-president on the Quinton Roberts ticket. Patrick Flannery Shaw had used her husband's death as the springboard to victory. He turned around the losing campaign by casting her as a devoted mother of two young children gamely soldiering on. It had worked because it was true. It also covered up her thin political record and captured eighty-eight percent of the woman's vote.

'Maddy,' Maura said, drawing her back to the moment and Matt Pontowski. 'People do change, you know. Why did you ask?'

'I'm reading about a peacekeeping mission he was on in South Africa. Apparently, he was involved with a woman down there, Elena Martine, the head of the UN Observer Mission.'

'Didn't we meet her at a reception?'

'How could I forget?' Maddy replied. Elena Martine had been introduced by the French ambassador and had been the star of the evening, upstaging every woman there. More than one tongue had been seen wagging or drooling, depending on the sex of the owner. As a result, Elena had gone on every Washington hostess's blacklist. No wife in her right mind wanted a temptation like Elena floating around the cocktail and dinner party circuit.

'What's wrong with Little Matt's dad being involved with someone if he's single?' Sarah asked.

'It all depends on the circumstances,' Maura answered. 'He *was* in Africa to do a job for his government. I remember something on the news. How did it turn out?'

'Actually, not bad,' Maddy answered. 'There was some fighting but the current situation seems fairly stable – for Africa.'

Sarah climbed on to the couch and cuddled up to her mother. 'Mom, are you ever going to get involved with another man again?'

Maddy knew it was futile to avoid the subject. 'Not while I'm President, Chubs.' She playfully poked the eleven-year-old's ribs. Sarah was skinny as a rail and had never been chubby. But her brother Brian had often called her Chubs to irritate her.

'Mother!' the girl protested. 'I'm being serious.'

'So am I, darlin'.' Maddy hesitated, searching for the right words. 'If I became romantic with a man while I'm President, it would become a political issue. Unfortunately, truth is the first casualty in politics. Too many people would twist the truth and use a relationship to keep me from doing my job. It wouldn't be fair to the country or the man. Or you.'

'Why do they want to keep you from doing your job?'

'Because some people see the world differently than I do.' She changed the subject. 'Bedtime.'

Maura snorted, demanding their attention. 'Tell her the rest.'

Sarah looked confused and Maddy gave a mental sigh. *Why do children have to grow up so fast these days?* she thought. 'What your grams is talking about is power. Many people are in politics because they want the power to make other people do what they say. They'll lie, cheat, and steal to get power and keep it. They want to be important. They want everyone to know who they are and treat them special, even when they don't deserve it.'

'Oh,' Sarah said. 'You mean they're on an ego trip. My teacher is on one all the time.' She scooted off the couch and gathered up her books. 'Personally, I think being truthful is more important than anything else, and if you like someone, you shouldn't be afraid of getting involved.' She kissed Maura on the cheek before giving her mother a peck and flouncing out of the room.

'Out of the mouths of babes,' Maura said, her words barely audible.

'Whatever are you talking about?' Maddy said, returning to her reading.

CHAPTER FOUR

Moscow

Mikhail Vashin hated everything about General Colonel Peter Prudnokov: the classic good looks, the perfect fit of the Air Force uniform on his tall, athletic body, and the aura of command that drew people to him, including Geraldine Blake. And she knew better. 'Please, Peter Davydovich,' Vashin said, using the three-star general's patronymic, 'sit down. This is an honor and I am pleased that you should think of me.'

Prudnokov looked uncomfortable. He knew the price of the meeting would be high, maybe too high for him to pay. 'It's a small problem,' he said, 'that I cannot solve. Yet it is one that deeply upsets my family.'

'And the problem?' Vashin knew, but he wanted to hear the general beg for help.

'It's my daughter. She is missing and we cannot find her.'

Vashin's hatred ratcheted up a notch at Prudnokov's self-control. 'And you would like my help?' A simple nod answered him. 'We are not the police,' Vashin said. Again, the general nodded in acknowledgment of the obvious. Vashin fixed him with a cold look, wanting to humiliate and crush the man. He was everything Vashin was not: from a prominent family, protected and pampered as a youth, educated, and then given the inside track to career and promotion. Prudnokov was a child of the *nomenklatura*, the élite of the Communist

Party who had ruled the Soviet Union for their own benefit. But times had changed and the *nomenklatura* were a relic of the past, like the Bolsheviks and czars.

Now it was Vashin's turn. The grinding poverty of his childhood, the endless deprivations in the name of Soviet socialism, the early death of his mother from overwork and abuse, the refuge his father found in vodka, were all behind him. But there was no satisfaction for Vashin, there was no redemption, there was no cure. The brutal system that had degraded and scorned humanity had left a darkness in his soul, a vague quest for 'more' that was rooted in hate, paranoia, and the desire for revenge. It was the stuff that gave birth to a Hitler or a Stalin.

'Peter Davydovich,' Vashin said, opening negotiations, 'I understand you have recently been given a new command.'

Again, the irritating nod. 'Your information is correct. I am now the commander of Transport Aviation.'

'Is Transport Aviation still flying paid cargoes?'

A snort from the general. 'It is how we pay for fuel, maintenance, and pilot proficiency. A commercial venture.'

'But you do have landing rights in other countries not available to normal civilian aircraft?'

Prudnokov fully understood what they were negotiating. 'We have many residual rights left over from our Warsaw Pact and peacekeeping commitments.' He decided it was time to sweeten the negotiations. 'Because of our treaties, Transport Aviation aircraft are not subject to customs inspections or import duties. Of course, we are willing to allow, shall we say, special friends to use our services.'

'I have interests that will pay extra to use these services,' Vashin said.

'We are more than glad to accommodate our friends, provided they help us and pay on time.'

'Of course,' Vashin replied. He needed the security only Transport Aviation could provide, and the general wanted his daughter back. It was a done deal. 'Perhaps some of my people can help in the search for your daughter. Do you have a picture?' The general handed him a photo and Vashin studied it, his features as bland and noncommittal as the general's. 'A beautiful girl. I can understand why you are so worried. She could be a movie star.' He forced a sigh. 'Children. They have no respect these days.'

'She's a good girl,' the general said. 'But her head is filled with trash about love and romance from watching LTV and the movies.'

Vashin buzzed for his secretary. She was standing in front of him within seconds. 'Geraldine, I want to help Peter Davydovich find his daughter.' He handed her the photo.

'A very pretty girl,' Geraldine said. She thought for a moment. 'Perhaps Tom would be the best one to handle this.' She stabbed at her personal telecommunicator and within seconds the former Secret Service agent came through the door. Tom Johnson was a big man who could have played defensive guard on a pro football team. His hair was cut short Marine-style, and he had a classic Prussian bulge on the back of his neck. Vashin explained what he wanted and Geraldine handed him the photograph. Johnson asked a few questions in a deep guttural Russian.

'Peter Davydovich,' Vashin said, bringing the meeting to a close, 'we will be glad to help. But perhaps you can do another small service for us. A service we'll be glad to pay for.'

'Certainly,' Prudnokov replied. 'Anything that is reasonable.'

'I don't know the right words, but you have fake devices you use for special weapons training. I understand the smaller, suitcase-sized ones are very realistic.'

At first, the general was confused, not sure what Vashin wanted. Then he understood. 'A simulated weapon? That's all you want?'

Vashin smiled. 'That's all.'

Prudnokov stood to leave. 'I'll see what I can do.' Geraldine escorted him out.

Johnson stared at the photograph for a few moments. The image of Little Dove smiled back at him. 'Who can resurrect a dead girl?'

Vashin shrugged his heavy shoulders. 'There are no miracles.'

The White House

Bender was processed through the southwest appointment gate and walked north on West Executive Avenue. Images of an earlier time when he was the acting National Security Advisor tickled his memory. A White House intern met him at the entrance to the West Wing. 'Good morning, General Bender. The President is expecting you.' He walked through the west entrance and the memories were in full flood.

'Quite a few things have changed since you were last here,' the intern said as they walked down the hall. It was an obvious statement. The heavy presence of the Secret Service was muted and, while Bender knew they were present, they weren't as visible as before. Other than the Marine guard at the entrance, he hadn't seen a single military uniform. He suppressed the urge to ask if the chairman of the Joint Chiefs had to wear civilian clothes when he came to the White House.

When they neared the Oval Office, Bender caught a glimpse of a shaggy bear of a man shambling down the quiet corridor. 'I see Mr Shaw is still here,' he ventured. There was no answer. *Why does she keep that bastard around?* Bender raged to himself. *Politics. Nothing really changes. Especially politics.* He mentally chastised himself for being so cynical about politicians. *She is your commander-in-chief.* He was honest with himself and admitted Madeline Turner was turning into a good president. But like so many other presidents before her, she had to grow into the job.

She had been openly hostile to the military at first. But during the crisis over Okinawa, when Congress and most of her own administration had deserted her, Bender had convinced her that she could rely on the Joint Chiefs of Staff. It was a crash course in the bare-knuckle use of power for Turner, and the steel that lay hidden behind an attractive face and pleasant manner finally emerged. Thanks to Bender, she learned how to use the military as an effective instrument of national power.

Only Bender appreciated the irony of the situation. While he honored his oath, respected the office of the President, and would always be loyal to his commander-in-chief, he simply didn't like Madeline Turner.

The intern turned Bender over to Dennis, who led him into the Oval Office. 'Robert,' Turner said, standing to greet him, 'thank you for coming.' She extended her right hand, genuinely glad to see him. He gently took her hand in his. 'I think you know everyone here,' she said, looking at the four members of her National Security Advisory Group.

Mazie Hazelton rose gracefully from her seat and walked quickly into his arms. 'I've missed you,' she said, her voice a whisper. Bender was obviously embarrassed by Mazie's uncharacteristic display of emotion and hesitated before folding his arms around her. The top of her head barely came to his chest. Then she was gone and back in her seat.

A gentle smile played across the President's face as she sat down. She motioned to a spot on the couch beside her rocking chair. 'Did I see a blush there?'

He forced a little smile but managed only to look guilty.

She reached out and touched his arm. 'Still the same.' Her words carried a soft warmth. 'My unbending general.' It was the old play on his name, the unbending Bender, and, for a moment, they were friends. But then it was all back in place. She was the commander-in-chief and he was her subordinate. She felt his defenses stiffen as the walls rose into place. 'Robert, are you abreast of the situation in Poland?' she asked, turning to business.

'Only vaguely. Economy doing well, standard of living on the rise since becoming a member of the EU, some problems with joining NATO.'

'The reason I ask is because Lloyd Rudenkowski is resigning as ambassador. I want to appoint you in his place.' Bender looked at her in shock. She knew he wanted to be appointed chairman of the Joint Chiefs of Staff when the current chairman retired the following year. But she needed him now. 'Because of the situation in Poland, I want a competent person heading the mission to Warsaw. I was going to offer Rudenkowski a cabinet position to induce him to resign. But when Treasury did an expanded background investigation, he came up dirty. Very dirty.'

Bender nodded, not offended in the least by her political maneuvering. 'Isn't Rudenkowski one of Senator Leland's boys?' Senator John Leland was the chairman of the Senate Foreign Relations Committee and ruled like a feudal warlord. But there was more. Leland had led the attempt to force Turner to resign during the Okinawan blockade. His hatred of Turner and her administration was deep, personal, and irrational.

Serick grumped. 'Leland is North Carolina's permanent revenge on the United States for losing the Civil War.'

Turner laughed. It started easy and low and ended like a crystal bell. Her face came alive and her eyes danced with humor. 'Stephan has testified before the good senator too many times.'

'Leland sponsored Rudenkowski and pushed his nomination through the Senate,' Vice-President Kennett explained.

'Leland's push was more like a ramrod,' Serick added.

'Getting my name past Leland's committee will be a problem,' Bender said, hoping his shot for the chairman of the Joint Chiefs was still alive. 'He'll want to even some scores. Especially after Okinawa.' He was reminding them of a political reality. His advice and support of Turner had been critical in fending off Leland's attack on her presidency during the blockade.

'I don't think so,' Kennett said. 'Leland will be more than glad to forward your nomination to the Senate with a favorable recommendation after I explain things to him.' He handed Bender a folder summarizing the recent investigation into Rudenkowski's background.

Inside the folder was a photograph of the ambassador being presented the Navy Cross. The accompanying citation and newspaper article described how Lieutenant (j.g.) Rudenkowski had been in command of a riverine patrol boat in Vietnam. During a two-boat river sweep, he had gone to the aid of the lead patrol boat that had been caught in an ambush by the Viet Cong. He had attempted to rescue the first boat, but each time was driven off by heavy machinegun fire from the shore. Only after the lead boat had exploded and all hands had been lost, and after sustaining heavy casualties on his own boat, did Rudenkowski withdraw. Only he and a badly wounded bosun's mate survived.

A second photograph in the folder showed a much older Rudenkowski, wearing his Navy Cross, locked arm in arm with Senator Leland at an election rally. Underneath that was a financial statement revealing that Rudenkowski had contributed over a million dollars to an election campaign fund controlled by Leland and his cronies. The final document was a sworn statement by the bosun's mate on the riverine patrol boat to the effect that Rudenkowski had never tried to rescue the first boat and had immediately retreated, leaving the crew to its fate. Two miles downstream, Rudenkowski had taken a wrong turn and stumbled into another ambush. Thinking the bosun's mate and the rest of the crew were dead, Rudenkowski had returned to base. Because of his wounds, it was six weeks before the bosun's mate remembered all that had happened. Before he could report the truth, Rudenkowski had reached out and bribed him to confirm his version of the ambush. At first, the bosun's mate had been rewarded with money and women. The drugs and threats came later.

'Why did the mate finally come clean after all these years?' Bender asked.

'He's dying of leukemia and wants to go with a clean slate,' Kennett replied. 'Leland's standing too close to Rudenkowski so he'll go for a quid pro quo: our silence about Rudenkowski for his support on your nomination.'

The DCI listened to the discussion and said nothing. He longed for the good old days when the option of wet operations easily solved a problem like Rudenkowski. But times had changed.

Bender felt an empty void; he wanted to be the chairman of the Joint Chiefs. But now the ambassadorship to Poland was all he was going to get. Then another thought came to him. His wife, Nancy, would love it. 'I would like to talk it over with my wife and think about it,' he said.

'Certainly,' Turner said. 'I'd like to forward a nomination to the Senate next week. When can we expect your answer?'

'You'll have it tomorrow morning.'

'What's the matter?' Maura asked. They were sitting in the family room off Maddy's bedroom after dinner. As usual, Sarah was doing her homework on the floor while wearing headphones, listening to music.

'I offered Robert Bender the Warsaw embassy today.'

'He'll make an excellent ambassador. Besides, I like him. And his wife. She's lovely.' Maura picked up her knitting and her clicking needles beat a fast rhythm. 'Why is that bothering you?'

Maddy sighed. Her mother could be as stubborn as Sarah once she got her teeth into a subject. 'It's how we're doing it. There are times I hate politics. We should be exposing a man for what he is. Instead, he's going to get away scot-free so I can send a decent ambassador to Poland.'

For all her seeming naïveté, Maura was an astute observer of the political scene. She made the connection. 'I never did like Rudenkowski. Too smooth and oily.' The needles clicked. 'Senator Leland is a problem, isn't he?'

Maddy nodded. 'He's a real bastard.'

Sarah pulled off her headset. 'Who's a bastard?'

'Young ladies don't use profanity, Little Miss Snoopy,' Maura said.

Maddy frowned. 'You were eavesdropping, weren't you?'

'I was an innocent bystander,' Sarah argued, making her case. She gathered up her books. 'I'll study in my room.' She knew when to make a tactical retreat.

'No phone calls until you're finished,' Maddy called.

'Yes, Mother.'

The two women waited until the door was closed. 'I'll never understand what motivates men like Leland,' Maura said.

'Patrick does,' Maddy replied, referring to her first White House chief of staff. There were times she missed his shrewd advice and hardball approach to politics.

Maura dropped her knitting into her lap. 'That's because he's one of them. Maddy, I've watched these people and listened to them. Oh, I know there are some good men and women here who deeply care about our country. But far too many came to Washington for all the wrong reasons. They're not here to help people, only themselves. And they don't care who they hurt in the process. You should change the constitution and make every elected politician swear an oath that "First, I will do no harm".'

'Like a doctor.'

Maura picked up her knitting, her lecturing done. 'And I'd kick Patrick Flannery Shaw all the way back to California.'

Maddy smiled. Maura O'Keith was her moral gyroscope, always upright and true. 'Yes, Mother.'

The Hill

Brian Turner rubbed his close-cropped hair and tried to make sense out of the biology book in front of him. It wasn't going to happen. 'Hey, Maggot,' he whispered to Little Matt, 'do you really understand this shit?'

Little Matt looked nervously around the library. The rules of the Toles Learning Center were strictly enforced and he didn't want any more demerits. They had just finished walking ten punishment tours for the fight. 'Yeah. It's a snap.' Another quick look around. 'I'll help you when we go back to the room.'

Temporarily satisfied, Brian pushed back his chair and wandered into the book stacks. They still had ten minutes to go on the first half of night study hall and, at 8.15, they would have five minutes to return to their room for another seventy minutes of enforced study. He hated it and promised himself for perhaps the five hundredth time he would escape NMMI at the first opportunity. He started a mental countdown to Family Weekend at the end of September. He rounded a book stack in a back corner and stopped when he heard a rustle of clothes in the next aisle. He chanced a peek. It was Zeth Trogger and a first classman locked in a passionate embrace. He beat a quick retreat back to the table. 'Hey, Maggot,' he muttered. 'Check that out.' He nodded in the direction of the book stacks. Rick Pelton, the Regimental Executive Officer and second highest ranking cadet at NMMI, was walking out of the book stacks. A few moments later, Zeth emerged from another aisle.

'So?' Little Matt replied.

'They were sucking tongues big time.'

'Pelton making it with the Trog? No way. He can have anyone he wants. PDA gets you what? Eight Ds?' PDA was public display of affection and worth eight demerits. 'Who's gonna risk eight tours for kissing the Trog? Besides, his buddies will dump on him big time.'

'I'm telling you he was doing it with the Trog.' It was time to go, and they gathered up their books to make the quick march back to Hagerman Barracks. An ever-present Secret Service agent trailed along, out of sight and unobtrusive. 'Hey,' Brian said, 'maybe he likes her.'

'Sure he does,' Little Matt said, mustering up a fourteen-year-old's worldly cynicism.

'They're screwin',' Brian announced.

'Gimme a break.'

'Everyone fucks, Maggot. Even your parents.'

'Obviously. We're here, aren't we? Read your biology book.'

'Not my mom, not any more.'

Little Matt conceded the point. 'Being President is different. My dad had a girlfriend, Sam Darnell, who lived with us. I really liked her and kinda hoped they'd get married.'

'Was she good-looking?'

'She's beautiful.' For a moment Little Matt was on the edge of tears.

'Do you remember your mom?'

'Kinda. I was only seven when it happened.'

'I'd just turned twelve,' Brian told him. He paused, trying to remember his father. But the image was out of focus and gray. 'But it's getting hard to remember.' Another pause. 'Do you think your dad will ever get married again?' Little Matt shrugged an answer. 'Is your dad really a fighter pilot?' A nod. 'Did he ever shoot down another airplane?'

'Yeah, four of 'em. But he doesn't talk about it.'

'No shit? That's really neat.' Brian recalled the time he had met Little Matt's father in McMasters's office. The image was sharp and clear. Little Matt's father looked like a fighter pilot, lean and cool. They climbed the steps together and walked along the stoop to their room.

Rick Pelton was waiting for them. 'Inside,' he ordered. The two Rats hurried inside and came to attention beside their bunks. Pelton stalked around the room, giving it a quick inspection. He stood in front of Brian, their noses almost touching, exhaling loudly. 'Do I have bad breath, Dirtbag?' No answer. 'Smart. Keep your mouth shut and you'll stay out of trouble.'

Brian wasn't having any of it. 'Don't even think about it. I got real muscle down in the TLA's office.'

Pelton's eyes drew into narrow slits. The Secret Service monitored Brian from the Tactical Leadership Advisor's office. 'Fuckin' Secret Service. You start talking and I'll dog your Rat buddy over there night and day. He'll love chairing. All because you can't keep your fuckin' mouth shut. Got it?'

'I got it' – a long pause – 'sir.'

Pelton gave Brian a hard look, spun around, and marched out of the room. 'Oh, shit,' Little Matt moaned. 'They saw you. What's chairing?'

'Beats me,' Brian replied. 'But I think you got problems.'

Williams Gateway, Arizona

The lawyer seemed out of breath from the short walk to the Marchetti. 'I've never flown in a little airplane,' she said, her breath coming in short pants. Pontowski fitted the parachute to her, careful not to touch her in any way that might offend. He showed her how to tighten the leg straps. 'Can you tuck them in?' she asked. Pontowski did as she asked, all too aware of her bare midriff, abbreviated T-shirt, and tight jeans. He had to admit that Kate Winston was much more human when away from Jonathan Slater, the senior partner at Fine, Schlossmaker, and Traube.

Pontowski waited until the FAA inspector had finished fitting Slater's chute and was helping the lawyer into the cockpit of their Marchetti before motioning Kate on to the wing. He helped her climb over the rail into the seat. Her breasts brushed lightly against his shoulder as he helped her fit and tighten her safety harness. 'I'm really looking forward to this,' she murmured. He walked around to the other side and climbed in. The cockpit of the Marchetti was a tight fit for two people, and he was having second thoughts about the two lawyers coming along when they reenacted the accident. Her perfume tantalized him with a soft citrus scent.

As briefed, they started engines together and taxied to the runway. From the control tower, the little red planes looked like ants as they moved into takeoff position. 'This is gonna happen real fast,' Pontowski warned her. 'Whatever you do, don't touch the controls.' She nodded, her eyes wide. The FAA inspector gave the signal and they were rolling, exactly as Pontowski had done at the air show. The moment his gear was up, he made the tactical split, again pulling four Gs. Immediately, he said, 'Fight's on,' and turned back into the lead ship. The FAA inspector pulled up exactly as Johar had and Pontowski fell into the saddle for the shot. 'Gun, guns, guns,' he radioed.

'Knock it off,' the inspector replied. Then, 'My boy isn't doing too well.'

'What's the matter?' Kate asked, disappointed that the flight might be over.

'Slater's probably sick and about ready to toss his cookies,' Pontowski answered.

'From that? That was fun. Do we have to land?'

Pontowski keyed his radio. 'Jim, let's go out to the training area and do the rest at altitude. We can set five thou as the floor.' The FAA inspector agreed and they climbed out in tight formation, switching lead and wingman twice. 'He's good,' Pontowski said, taking the measure of the inspector.

'We'll use five thousand feet as the floor for maneuvering and never go below it,' he explained.

'Does that mean five thousand feet represents the ground?' Kate asked.

'You got it,' he replied, impressed with her quick understanding.

She wiggled in the seat, distracting him. 'Wouldn't it be more realistic if we did it lower, closer to the ground like you did in the air show?'

'I'm not so sure your buddy could take it. Besides, it's safer this way.'

She seemed disappointed and sat in silence as they flew out to the training area over the desert. The FAA inspector checked them in with Phoenix Approach and quickly set up the next maneuver with Pontowski chasing him in a climb. Twice they went through the Immelmann followed by Pontowski's overshoot. Satisfied with the results, they entered the scissors in an exact recreation of the air show. Then, at 7,000 feet, the inspector's Marchetti departed controlled flight and flipped into an inverted spin. 'Knock it off and recover,' Pontowski radioed, the same as before.

But this time, the inspector went through the recovery procedures and safely recovered the Marchetti. 'I was wings level with five hundred and sixty feet to spare,' he transmitted. They went through the maneuver again. But this time, the inspector entered a fully developed inverted stall, just as Johar had experienced. The aircraft was still inverted when it fell through 5,000 feet, where the ground would have been if they had been at the same altitude as the air show. 'Shit-oh-dear,' the inspector radioed. 'You have to hold it with wrong stick and rudder to make it happen. The bird wants to fly out of it naturally.'

'What does that mean?' Kate asked.

'Jim just confirmed what we saw and heard on Johar's videotape. Beason was on the controls.'

'Do you want to try it?' the inspector radioed.

Pontowski looked at the lawyer. 'Oh, yes,' she said.

Again, they repeated the scissors maneuver, only this time

Pontowski did the spin. But his Marchetti would not flip inverted and they entered a normal spin. They only lost 600 feet before recovering. 'Can we do that again?' Kate asked.

'We can try.' He keyed the radio. 'Miss Winston wants to do it again. She wants to see the world from upside down.'

'Ah,' the inspector answered, 'maybe we should RTB. My guy looks kinda green. Oops, he's puking his guts out.' The lawyer's stomach had caught up with him once they were flying straight and level.

The two planes joined up in a loose formation for the leg back to Williams. 'I love it,' Kate said. 'That was the most exciting thing I've ever done.'

Before Pontowski could answer, an annunciator light on the control panel blinked at them. He scanned the engine instruments. The oil pressure gauge was reading zero. 'Jim, I've lost my oil pressure,' he radioed. 'I'm gonna have to shut the engine down.'

'There's a fairly straight part of a dirt road at nine o'clock, two miles,' the inspector replied. 'Shut 'er down while I check it out.' He nosed his Marchetti over and stroked the throttle, racing for the ground while he radioed Phoenix Approach about the emergency. Pontowski went through the engine shut-down procedures and set up his glide airspeed while the inspector overflew the dirt road. 'It's looks kinda rough, Matt. Plus there's a series of high-tension power lines crossing the road. You might want to look somewhere else.'

'It's pretty rocky out here,' Pontowski radioed. 'Unless I see something more promising, I'll go for the road.' The inspector answered with two short clicks on the radio button. When all was said and done, it was Pontowski's decision. 'The road is the smoothest piece of real estate around here,' Pontowski told Kate, an obvious understatement.

Kate sucked in her breath when she saw three sets of power lines that made big droops as they crossed the dirt road in front of them. 'Can we make it?' she asked.

'No problem,' Pontowski answered.

Her breath was coming in short bursts. 'We don't have enough altitude!'

'Check the road,' he ordered. 'Look for potholes.' He concentrated on the power lines as he descended.

'I see some holes,' Kate shouted. They cleared the first power line by fifty feet. Ahead of them, she could see the next high-tension wire. 'We're not high enough to fly over it!' she screamed.

'Who said anything about flying over,' Pontowski replied, his voice calm and measured. He dropped a notch of flaps and hit the gear handle, lowering the landing gear. The sudden drag caused the Marchetti to drop like a rock without changing its attitude. They dropped beneath the second power line and flew under, touching down on a smooth section of road. 'Nice, baby, real nice.' He was talking to the Marchetti as they rode out a series of rough bumps. They rolled to a stop and he radioed that they were down safely.

He slid the canopy back as the other Marchetti flew by and did a wing wag before heading for Williams. 'Cheated death again,' Pontowski told her, pulling off his helmet.

Kate turned to him, her eyes wide and unblinking as she removed her helmet. Then her hands pulled at the quick release on her safety harness and it fell away. She reached for Pontowski's face and pulled him to her as she twisted in the seat. Her mouth was on his as her tongue explored his mouth. 'Please, please,' she whispered.

Her fingers pulled at the leg clips on her parachute and the straps fell away. He released her chest strap and she shrugged off the parachute harness. She came out of the seat in a fluid motion. He crawled out of the cockpit as she ran around the tail of the airplane and threw herself into his arms. Her mouth captured his tongue and she sucked. At the same time, she pulled at his shirt. 'I've got to go to the bathroom,' she said. She pulled free and ran for the bushes, unbuttoning her jeans.

Pontowski looked around and saw a cloud of dust coming down the road toward them. 'A car's coming,' he said. Kate's head bobbed up from behind a bush.

A sheriff's patrol car pulled up and stopped. 'Everything okay here?' the deputy asked, a big smile on his face. He was looking at the bushes where Kate had disappeared.

A scream answered him and Kate ran out of the bushes, pulling up her pants. 'A scorpion bit me!' she shouted.

'Where?' Pontowski asked.

She turned and pulled down one side of her jeans and panties, revealing a red mark on a well-shaped buttock. 'Oh dear,' the deputy said. 'One of us will just have to suck it out.'

CHAPTER FIVE

The White House

Maddy Turner stood in the shower and let the hot water course over her head. *Forty-seven*, she thought. The water felt good and she turned up the pressure. Her skin tingled and came alive and, for a moment, she was young again. She turned off the water, wrapped a big towel around herself, and stepped out of the shower. Automatically, she checked the clock. Just after 5 a.m. *Who's the master here? You or me?* She knew the answer. She was a slave to the clock.

She toweled her hair, feeling rested and fresh after a good night's sleep. Then the number was back. Forty-seven. How many good years do I have left? She reached for the hairdryer and her towel fell away. She glanced at herself in the mirror. *Would a man still find me attractive?* As quickly as it came, the thought was gone and she pulled on a white terry-cloth robe to finish drying her hair. She heard a knock at the door.

It was Mary, one of the interns who rotated the night duty in the residence. 'Madame President, I'm sorry to disturb you but since I saw your light on—' She didn't finish the sentence. The light in question was the motion detector system that tracked the President's movements in the White House.

'It's okay,' Maddy said. 'I was awake. What's the problem?'

'The watch officer just received a message from the CIA and thought you should see it. It's a category three.'

Maddy's heart stopped racing. A category three message only required the President's attention.

'The watch officer said it's about the exchange of a nuclear weapon and you would want to know about it.'

'Please call my maid,' Maddy said, still drying her hair. She reached out and traced '47' on the foggy mirror.

Maura and Sarah were finishing their breakfast when Maddy joined them. 'I'm famished,' she said, sitting down. Two small gifts and an array of cards were in front of her.

'Happy birthday, Mom,' Sarah sang. She bounced out of her chair, handed Maddy another card, and kissed her on the cheek. Maddy opened Sarah's card first. It was a hand-painted sketch of flowers blended with real rose petals. 'I made it in art class,' Sarah announced. The inscription inside wished her a happy forty-seventh birthday, and more flowers twisted around the numbers.

'It's beautiful, darling. Thank you.' She opened the other cards. One was from Maura, the other from Brian. But it was Brian's gift that caught their attention. It was a beautiful set of turquoise-and-silver earrings. She tried them on. 'I love them.'

'They go very well with your suit,' Maura said. 'Very Southwest.'

'Humph,' Sarah muttered. 'Someone must have reminded him it was your birthday. I bet Mrs McMasters picked them out for him.'

'Be nice,' Maura said. She cast a critical eye over her daughter. 'Have you been up long?'

'Since five. Something came up.'

Maura looked worried. She was not a sophisticated woman, but every instinct warned her that Maddy had to be protected from being swamped with minor problems or details. 'Couldn't someone else have handled it?'

'Probably. But I was already awake so I got dressed.' A steward set a plate in front of her. 'Thank you, Felipe,' she said. She set to work devouring the light breakfast.

Maura laughed. 'Well, there's nothing wrong with your appetite.' She changed the subject. 'Have you thought about the Family Weekend at NMMI? It's less than two weeks away.'

Maddy dabbed the corners of her mouth with a napkin and took a sip of coffee. 'I'm not going to be able to make it. Why don't you go?'

'Brian will be disappointed,' Maura said.

'I know.'

'Can I go?' Sarah asked, suddenly very animated.

At exactly eight o'clock, Turner's chief of staff and personal assistant escorted her to the West Wing. 'I'm sorry, Madame President,' Parrish said, 'there was no need to wake you. He should have called me first. It could have waited.'

Turner did not reply for a few moments. It was a problem common to every major organization. The night duty watch officer who worked for Parrish had overreacted, partly out of zeal, partly to shine in front of the boss. But in this case, the boss was the President of the United States. The message that had started it all was going to require her personal attention anyway, and no real harm had been done as she was already awake. But did she need to send a wake-up call to her staff and do some fine-tuning? Then she thought about the message. That was another problem that needed fixing. She considered her options. 'Dennis,' she said to her personal assistant, 'we need privacy.' The young man walked on ahead to wait for them by the elevator.

'Richard, there was no damage done this time. I was already awake. But *you* should have made the decision to disturb me or Maura. That's the way I want it.'

'My apologies, Madame President. The watch officer knows that.'

'Then fire him. But do it right. Ask for his resignation first and offer him another job. But not in the White House. This is a minor thing, in-house only, and I don't want any bad publicity out of this.'

'Yes, ma'am.' He waited for her to start walking. But

from her stance, there was more coming. He braced himself.

'Have you had a chance to read the message?' she asked.

He nodded in answer. 'Talk about a screw-up.'

'That's what I thought. It couldn't have come at a worse time. Richard, I've got to rely on our people to do things right. Otherwise, we're dead in the water and a sitting target. Am I making myself clear?'

'Yes, ma'am.'

Good, she thought. 'When I go in there, I'm going to shake things up. I want people to get the message: No more screw-ups.'

'Madame President, what may seem like a gentle shake to you will register on the Richter scale.'

'Good. I want some shaking going on.'

'How upset are you?'

'Minor damage only. Four point five on the Richter scale.'

Parrish got the message. Everything Madeline Turner did was tightly calculated, even when she was angry. He followed her the rest of the way to the Oval Office. The three members of her Policy Review Committee and Mazie Hazelton waited for her. For a moment, Turner considered making Mazie a permanent member of the committee. She quickly discarded the idea: better to keep functions compartmentalized and bring Mazie in as needed. She motioned them all to be seated. Dennis shut the door and retreated to his desk, glad that he had not been invited to stay and face her wrath.

Turner did not sit down. Instead, she leaned against the front of her desk and folded her arms. She stared at them. 'What went wrong?'

Silence. Then Mazie started to speak, her voice calm and flat. 'As you know, we had arranged to exchange Yaponets for a tactical nuclear weapon, specifically a five-kiloton satchel weapon that had been stolen by the Russian Mafiya from the Ukrainians.' Turner gave a little nod, telling everyone that she was up to scratch on the details about the Russian godfather imprisoned in the US. 'The exchange went as planned,' Mazie continued. 'DOJ flew Yaponets to Syria and once the weapon had been delivered to the CIA in Estonia, we turned him over to the Russian embassy in Damascus.'

'So what went wrong?' Turner asked.

Now it was the Attorney General's turn in the barrel. 'The CIA examined the weapon before cabling to release Yaponets. It checked out. Correct weight, correct radiation signature. It was only when we got it back to our labs and disassembled it that we discovered it was a training device.'

'So we were taken,' Turner said. 'They got Yaponets for nothing and we got mud kicked in our faces. Lovely.' She shook her head. 'How difficult is it to verify that a nuclear weapon is a nuclear weapon?' There was no answer. 'Don't we have people at Sandia or Livermore labs who do this sort of thing?' Again, no answer. 'Were they even brought in?' She didn't wait for a response. 'Do you have any idea what Senator Leland will do with this?' She paced the floor. 'The Senate Foreign Relations Committee is scheduled to start hearings tomorrow on General Bender's appointment as ambassador to Poland.' She gave Vice-President Kennett an approving look. 'Thanks to Sam, we've worked out a deal with Leland. We let Rudenkowski off the hook and he forwards Bender's name to the Senate floor with a favorable recommendation.'

'Madame President,' the Attorney General said, 'these are two separate issues. There is no linkage here.'

'Tell Leland that,' Turner snapped.

'Why should he even know about it?' This from Parrish.

Phoenix, Arizona

The offices of Fine, Schlossmaker, and Traube were decorated in a mix of Southwest chic, bad art, and legal pomposity. At first, Pontowski wasn't sure if he was in a tourist trap or a decorator's showroom. A secretary held the door to the conference room for him, the FAA inspector, and two members of the NTSB accident investigation team. They sat at the huge table. 'May I get you a drink,' the secretary offered. 'Coffee, tea, juice?'

'Coffee would be fine,' Pontowski replied. She disappeared.

'Nice table,' the FAA inspector said, running his hand over the highly polished surface.

'All part of the game,' Pontowski told him. 'It's meant to intimidate.'

Kate Winston entered and sat down gingerly on the opposite side of the table. The lawyer's business suit was in total contrast to the tight jeans and scanty T-shirt she had worn for the flight. 'Good morning, gentlemen, General Pontowski.'

'Good morning, Miss Winston,' Pontowski answered in the same tone. 'I hope you're recovered from the flight.'

'Oh, yes.' A little smile flickered at the corners of her mouth. 'It was an experience.'

'For both of us.'

'Mr Slater will be here in a moment,' she told them. 'Mr Beason, Sammy's father, will also be here.' From the look on her face, Pontowski knew she was against the senior Beason attending the meeting because they would be discussing the accident in detail. And all the evidence pointed to his son as the cause.

Jonathan Slater, the senior partner in charge of the Phoenix office, held the door open for Daniel Beason. Beason was in his late sixties, six feet tall, with a full head of gray hair. His face was red and splotchy. At one time he had been handsome, but heavy drinking, smoking, and womanizing had ruined his health. Now he was grossly overweight and his breath came in short pants. 'May I introduce Mr Daniel Beason?' Slater said. They all stood to shake hands. But when Pontowski extended his hand, Beason turned away and sat down at the head of the table. 'Shall we get started?' Slater said.

The head of the NTSB team passed out folders and led them through the preliminary investigation report. He finished by outlining the results of the flight when Pontowski and the FAA inspector had recreated the accident profile. He looked sadly at the elder Beason and spoke in bureaucratic tones, trying to soften the reality of what he had to say. 'The second flight modeling the mishap fully supports the documentation—'

Beason interrupted him. 'I don't give a damn about your documentation.'

'The documentation in question is the videotape from the mishap aircraft,' the team chief said. He took the mental equivalent of a deep breath. No government official willingly incurred the wrath of Daniel Beason. He plunged ahead. 'The accident occurred when the mishap pilot, Johar Adwan, did not have full control of the aircraft. The audio portion of the cockpit videotape indicates the pilot and copilot were fighting over control of the aircraft.'

Beason shot to his feet and leaned across the table, his right hand outstretched, forefinger pointed at Pontowski. He was shaking in his rage. 'That bastard killed my son and you're telling me he's going to walk!'

'Please, Mr Beason,' Slater said soothingly. 'These are not criminal proceedings.'

Beason's finger was still wavering at Pontowski. 'You're not getting away with this!' His face was bright red.

Kate Winston came out of her seat and rushed over to Beason. She leaned against him and took his hand, guiding him back into his seat. 'Please, Mr Beason. We understand. We truly do.' It seemed to work and the old man slowly gained control. She gave them all a cautionary look. 'Perhaps another day?' she ventured.

'I want to hear what *he* has to say,' Beason rasped, obviously meaning Pontowski.

'Mr Beason,' Pontowski said, the pain in his voice obvious. 'I am very sorry and I would give all I have for this not to have happened. But it was not my idea for your son to go along as a passenger. Nor did I cause the accident. I was simply there, a helpless bystander when the Marchetti went out of control and entered an inverted spin.'

'You're not walking away from this.' Beason stood up. 'I'll see you in court.'

Pontowski wanted to be gentle. 'And your son's actions will be held up to public scrutiny. Is that what you want?' For a moment, silence ruled.

'Confusion in the cockpit of the mishap aircraft was the

primary cause of the accident,' the NTSB team chief said. Beason spun around and marched out of the conference room. The FAA inspector folded his hands and fixed Slater with a hard look. 'There is absolutely no doubt what happened. Your client's son panicked and took control of the aircraft at a critical moment. He caused the accident. I don't think you have a case that will stand up in court.'

'So you're also an expert on courts?' Slater asked.

'No,' the team chief replied. 'But I was involved with the TWA Flight 800 court case. Believe me, I know what the legal defenses are.'

'I suppose you're also a lawyer,' Slater snapped.

'As a matter of fact,' the team chief said, 'I am. Don't embarrass your client with a case you can't win.' He paused for effect. 'Daniel Beason has quite a track record. If you lose this one, which you surely will, he'll turn on you.' He snapped his briefcase shut. 'Think about it.'

The room rapidly emptied, leaving Pontowski alone with Kate Winston. She walked around the table and stood next to him. 'Mr Beason has been terribly hurt by the death of his son.'

'I know. I'd be devastated if my son was killed. But Sammy Beason was a poor pilot. Even worse, he didn't know it. Bringing that out in court, which I will, is only going to hurt him more.'

Kate looked at her hands, wanting to tell him he was right. There was something drawing her to Pontowski that had nothing to do with his good looks. And that made him even more attractive. She raised her head, her eyes bright. She reached out and touched his cheek. Her hand was warm and gentle. 'Matt, we need to talk.' Her voice trailed off.

'Your reaction after we landed? That was normal. Also the need to relieve yourself or a sudden thirst is very common.'

'And you'd have taken advantage.' Anger laced her words.

He shook his head. 'No. But it was a chance for you to understand a little of what's involved.'

She stared at the floor. 'It did get Jonathan's attention. He finally proposed.'

'Slater?'

She nodded. 'And I accepted. I wanted to warn you about Beason.'

'He is your client. Don't say anything you'll regret later.'

'Matt, he's furious that we didn't confiscate the videotape from Sammy's airplane and destroy it.'

'Isn't that tampering with evidence?'

She nodded. 'He's out of control and we're trying to withdraw from the case.'

'Should you be telling me this?'

Conflicting emotions tore at her. 'No. But he's playing dirty and wants to get you personally. Be careful.'

Pontowski gave a little humph. 'I've been there before.'

'He's playing the political card and has bought himself a senator.'

'They come cheap these days.'

'Please, be serious.'

'I am.'

Washington, D.C.

Bender took his seat at the witness table in the committee hearing room and waited for the senators to settle in behind the long table that barricaded them at one end of the room. Aides hovered behind each senator, ready to be of instant service. Two senators quickly left the dais when they saw the first TV camera, only to return a few minutes later in makeup. An air of anticipation hung over the packed audience as TV crews set up more cameras. They had all come to witness the best show in town. Senator John Leland was going to live up to his reputation as Madeline Turner's most ardent opponent and crucify yet another one of her nominees.

Leland was the last to enter and sit down. He rapped the committee to order and made his opening remarks. He used the customs and courtesies of the United States Senate to rule like a feudal monarch, and only the constant attention of the TV cameras held him in check. He smiled at Bender. 'First, let me thank you for coming on such short notice, General Bender. This won't take too long.'

Knowing smiles broke out among the aides. Leland was at his best when shredding ambassadorial nominees not on his personal short list of campaign contributors. Bender was lucky even to be sitting in front of the committee, and would be dispatched in short order.

He only sounds friendly, Bender thought, recalling the last time they had met face to face. It had been in the Cabinet Room in the White House the night Leland and his cronies had tried to force Madeline Turner to resign as President. Bender's words were engraved in his memory. 'The President,' he had said, 'is engaged in a national emergency. You are no longer welcome in her house, and she wants you to leave. May I suggest you do so immediately.' Those were not the words a man like Leland ever forgot – or forgave.

'I notice you're not wearing your uniform,' Leland said.

Bender moved the microphone closer and adjusted it so that he would not have to lean forward to speak. *Keep it short and sweet*, he cautioned himself. 'Sir, I hope my record while serving our country speaks for itself. But today, I am here as a civilian, not a member of the armed forces.' His answer seemed to go down well with the committee, and the TV cameras lingered on him.

Leland pontificated for a few moments about the committee's responsibilities until the cameras were back on him. An aide handed him a note. Daniel Beason was on the phone and wanted to talk to him. It was a summons not even Leland could ignore. 'What's this about?' he grumbled to the aide.

'He didn't say,' came the answer. 'But I think he may not like Bender.'

Leland dismissed the aide and opened the folder on talking points his staff had prepared. He flipped to the page of hostile questions. 'General Bender,' he began, 'what do you know about Poland? For example, can you tell us about their national anthem?'

Bender suppressed a smile. 'Of course, I've heard it and could try humming a few bars. But believe me, with my musical abilities, that might cause an international incident.' Laughter echoed behind him and a few of the senators smiled. 'It's based on the song General Jan Dabrowski adopted for the army of Polish exiles he raised in Italy in' – he paused, searching for the date – '1797, as I recall.'

The senator from Illinois beamed with approval. 'The date is correct,' she said. 'I first heard it when I was a child. It is very stirring.' Then she hastened to add, 'My family is Polish-American.'

Leland humphed and went on to the next question. He looked over his reading glasses and frowned. The TV cameras were spending far too much time on Bender. He needed to change that. 'I'm told the Poles are very aware of their history, General. How does that affect their current policies?'

'The Poles remember their history because, as a nation, they are always in trouble. They are a small country caught between two major powers, Germany and Russia, which have a habit of dividing their country up and erasing it from the map.' Scattered applause rippled through the audience.

Leland hid his anger by smiling. He glanced at his notes. It was his turn to appear knowledgeable. 'Ah, yes. You are, of course, referring to the Three Partitions in 1772, 1793, and 1795. All over two hundred years ago.' The implication that the partitions were too old to be relevant hung in the air.

'Yes, sir, I am. But if you speak to the Poles, they will tell you of the fourth partition in 1939 when Germany and Russia invaded their country and again divided it between them.' Bender leaned forward to make his point. 'They have learned from their history and don't want it to happen again.' The applause was widespread and prolonged, led by the senator from Illinois.

Leland smiled graciously and passed on the questioning. He drummed his fingers on the table. He wanted to dispatch Bender on the spot and send him back to the White House in a box. But the conversation with Vice-President Kennett in the sauna of the Senate gym was too fresh in his memory. Rudenkowski was a problem and Kennett had offered an easy solution. In the end, the TV cameras made the decision for him.

By the time the third senator had finished his questioning, only Bender was getting any camera attention. It was time to get the general out of the country and defuse the Rudenkowski bombshell before it exploded.

He also made a note to return Beason's phone call.

Madeline Turner was as alone in the pool as a president can be. Two female Secret Service agents, both trained as lifeguards and paramedics, sat at opposite ends, their feet in the water, as she churned out lap after lap. A tall African-American woman, also in a swimsuit and wearing an open robe that flapped behind her, revealing a lithe and athletic figure, paced the side of the pool beside Maddy, a stopwatch in her hand. 'Come on, girl,' Noreen Coker called, 'you can do better than that. One more lap. Go, go, go.'

Maddy put on a burst of speed and stroked hard, finishing the last lap. She held on to the edge of the pool, breathing deeply. 'You've been impossible since you lost weight. I liked you better when you were fat.'

'Can't help it,' Noreen replied. 'Not since I got sanitized, sanforized, and Oprah-ized. Talking to that woman changed my whole attitude about exercise and being skin-ee.' She struck a pose, causing her robe to fall away. 'Great butt.'

'You're getting worse,' Maddy said, pulling herself out of the pool. She was wearing a dark blue tank suit and white bathing cap.

Coker undertook a critical survey of her friend. 'You look fantastic. Poor thing. You got it but you can't flaunt it.' Their laughter joined as Noreen helped her into a terry-cloth robe.

Noreen Coker was a congresswoman from Los Angeles and one of Maddy's best friends. They had met in the California State Legislature when they were freshmen, Maddy a senator, Noreen an assemblywoman. At the time, Coker weighed over 250 pounds and was given to flashy clothes, wild hairdos, and outrageous statements. But Maddy saw through the façade. Underneath was an extremely intelligent and shrewd politician who knew what it took to get elected and how to get things done. Later, Coker had gone on to the House of Representatives, and when Maddy arrived in Washington as the Vice-President, the old friendship was rekindled.

Within a month of her arrival, Maddy had gathered Noreen and a small coterie of friends around her as personal advisors and a support group. After she had become President, the group became known as the kitchen cabinet, and were often called the ultimate insiders. To a person, they were discreet, totally honest, and completely loyal. But Noreen was more. She was a she-bear protecting her young when it came to her friend.

Inside the dressing room, Noreen automatically flicked on the TV. It was set to C-Span, and a commentator was standing in front of the Capitol, microphone in hand. 'Only Senator Leland voted against General Robert Bender's appointment as ambassador to Poland. Inside sources were surprised that Leland even let the committee consider Bender's appointment, much less come to a quick vote. Could this signal the end of the senator's long hostility to the Turner administration?'

'Don't bet on it, child,' Noreen said to the TV. She listened to the soundbites from the committee hearing. 'Oh, you did good, Bobby Bender.' She turned to Maddy, who was almost dressed. 'Our boy got a slam dunk this time. But Leland is hard on rebounds. He'll be back.'

Maddy pulled on her shoes. 'I knew the committee would like him.' She didn't mention the deal Kennett had struck with Leland.

Gostomel Air Base, Ukraine

The women walked across the parking apron of the semi-deserted airbase fifteen miles north of Kiev. They were all young and pretty and carried their own luggage. Most walked in silence, but a few of the sixteen-year-olds, happy to be out in the night air after being cooped up in the shabby barracks for over a week, chattered about their new jobs in the West. They formed a single line, waiting to board the Ilyushin Il-76. The Il-76, the workhorse of Russia's Military Transport Aviation, was not what they had expected. The high-wing, T-tailed, four-engine cargo plane bore a striking resemblance to the United States' old C-141 StarLifter that had been retired from active service.

Only one woman showed any hesitancy about giving up her passport to the man checking off their names. But a sharp command from one of the guards escorting them ended that. Like the others, she handed over her passport and walked up the ramp and into the lighted cargo deck. No seats had been rigged and she sat on her suitcase. The man collecting the passports did a quick count. 'Forty-seven fresh cunts,' he said, speaking Russian. He handed over a small aluminum suitcase to the men guarding the women. They huddled around and quickly counted the money. 'Yes?' the first man asked. 'All is correct?'

The man holding the suitcase replied in Russian. 'As agreed, two thousand dollars each, ninety-four thousand dollars US.' He spoke to the others in Ukrainian and they trooped off the aircraft, leaving the women to their new masters. The Il-76 started engines and taxied for the runway. Within minutes, it was airborne and turned to the northwest, heading for Minsk in Belarus. The creaky aircraft never climbed above 12,000 feet for the thirty-minute flight, and made only one radio call, when it crossed the border into Belarus.

The radar antenna on top of the 345-foot tower outside Bialystok, Poland, swept the horizon every five seconds. The twin parabolic reflectors were stacked one above the other and rotated in unison, feeding information through a cable net to a bunker two miles away. A sign over the bunker's blast doors announced it was the home of Crown East, the easternmost of three radar early-warning and ground-controlled intercept sites that formed a chain across central Poland. Inside the bunker, the radar operator on duty noted the track of the Il-76 in his log and marked it down as routine traffic. He did not bother to track it to Machulishche, an old Soviet airbase outside Minsk, Belorusskaya, nor to wake the tactical threat officer.

*　　*　　*

A follow-me truck was waiting for the Il-76 when it cleared the runway at Machulishche. The big plane lumbered after the truck, following it to a remote parking apron where heavily armed guards surrounded two low cargo carrier trucks loaded with pallets. The Il-76 shut down its engines as the first cargo carrier backed up to the aircraft's loading ramp. The first three pallets were quickly pushed on board and the truck pulled away. The women had to move to make room for the cargo, and most stood beside the stacks of white plastic-wrapped bricks, holding on to the cargo netting. The high-grade cocaine was worth more than them.

The second cargo carrier pulled up and three more pallets were rolled on board. As with the cocaine, there was no attempt to disguise the half-kilo bricks of tarry hashish. A third truck rolled up and a line of men formed a chain to pass cardboard boxes on board. The boxes were broken open and the bricks of high-potency marijuana, sensimilia to be exact, were stowed around the pallets, filling the cargo deck. Finally, the women were left sitting on top of the drugs.

Less than an hour after landing, the Il-76's pilots started engines and made one radio call. On the other side of the airfield, two pilots walked leisurely out of an underground bunker. The cargo plane taxied for the active runway and, without waiting for clearance, took off into the clear night. But this time, the Il-76 leveled off at 5,000 feet as it headed directly for the Polish border, 160 miles away.

The two pilots walking across the apron climbed into their waiting Sukhoi Su-35 fighters and strapped in. The Su-35s were single-place, twin-tailed, twin-engined fighters about the same size as the US F-15 Eagle. An observer, unable to see the foreplanes mounted above the intakes, might confuse the two. But unlike the Eagle, which went out of production in the early 1990s, the Su-35s were brand new and, with their advanced avionics, a serious threat to the United States' newest fighter, the F-22 Raptor. The pilots finished cocking their jets for a scramble. Now they had to wait.

*　　*　　*

The radar operator sitting in the darkened bunker at Crown East swore silently in Polish. The P-50 radar, known to NATO as Barlock, was going out of calibration – again. The Polish Air Force had inherited the system from the Warsaw Pact and it was showing its age. The operator cursed the radar's Soviet makers and manually tuned it. A blip caught his eye. Then it was gone. He retuned the radar and caught it again. He noted the azimuth and distance: 075 degrees at 150 nautical miles. He called out the target and the plotter stirred to life, angry at having her sleep disturbed. She plotted the target on the Plexiglas situation board at the back of the room.

'An airliner taking off out of Minsk,' the young woman muttered.

'It's tracking toward us. I don't have a flight plan and there is no radar transponder. It should be squawking a code.'

The girl shrugged. 'Russian maintenance.' They had heard all the rumors about the deplorable state of Russian aircraft.

The operator studied the scope. 'It's definitely heading toward us. Still no squawk. Wake the tac officer.' The tactical threat officer stumbled out of his cubicle and zipped up his pants. He rubbed his eyes as he looked over the radar operator's shoulder. 'I have an unknown, sir. No flight plan or IFF squawk.' Again, the operator called out the azimuth and distance for plotting as he activated the computer's automatic tracking system. Much to his surprise it worked, and a readout appeared on the scope. 'The target is still heading directly for us.' He changed the antenna into sector sweep for confirmation. 'Maybe it's an airliner headed for Warsaw with a malfunctioning transponder. You know the Russians.'

'They act like they still own the world,' the tac officer muttered. He bit his lip. It was still a bogie, an unknown target, that would penetrate Polish airspace in eighteen minutes. 'Notify sector command,' he ordered, sending the problem upstairs. The radar operator made the radio call without bothering to activate the encryption circuits.

The controller at sector command answered immediately, his voice loud and clear over the clear radio channel. 'A single target at that speed and altitude is no threat. It's probably a Vnukova flight.'

'Damn,' the radar operator said. Vnukova was the call sign for Russian diplomatic aircraft with special overflight rights left over from the days of the Warsaw Pact. The name came from the airport twenty miles southwest of Moscow where the flights supposedly originated. 'They're still required to file a flight plan and be transmitting the proper IFF code for identification.'

'Their whole system is screwed up,' sector control answered. In six words, he had explained the lack of a flight plan and IFF squawk.

'Why not a Bravo?' the radar operator ventured. A Bravo was a practice scramble of fighters setting air defense alert. 'We can use the practice.'

Sector control considered it. Fuel and flying time were very costly and he'd have to justify the scramble. But the pilots did need the practice. He hit the Klaxon button. The two fighter pilots in the alert facility next to sector command were jolted out of a sound sleep and raced for their waiting aircraft, two F-16s recently purchased from the United States.

The intelligence listening post at Brest in Belarus had monitored Polish communications for years and was still manned. The technician on duty intercepted the radio call between Crown East and sector command scrambling the F-16s, and passed it on as a routine matter. Normally, it would have died in the bowels of the military command structure. But on this particular night, the system worked as designed and a green light from the Minsk control tower flashed at the Su-35s sitting alert on the ramp. Immediately, the Su-35s' big Saturn AL-35 turbofan engines spun to life and the fighters fast-taxied for the runway. The pilots made a formation takeoff in afterburner, not because they required the extra thrust, but for the fun of it. Besides, the air force wasn't paying for the fuel.

They needed less than 4,000 feet of runway to become airborne. They climbed to 400 feet and did a tactical split at the end of the runway, falling into an easy route formation 200 feet abreast. Both pilots slaved their autopilots to the terrain following/avoidance radar and dropped to 150 feet above the ground. Satisfied the system was working, they accelerated to .96 Mach, 630 nautical miles per hour. They would catch the Il-76 in thirteen minutes, just before it penetrated Polish airspace.

The two F-16s the Polish pilots were flying were not new aircraft. However, they had been completely refurbished by General Dynamics and equipped with zero-time engines before being sold to the Polish Air Force. Ultimately, the program would lead to the Poles manufacturing F-16s under a licensing agreement. But so far, the program was stalled because of the American refusal to include more highly advanced avionics, or black boxes, that upgraded the F-16's capability. Still, the Polish pilots loved the hot performance and reliability of the jet. They only wished they had more of them and could log more flying time.

Considering they had started cold from a sound sleep, the scramble went smoothly enough. The F-16s were at the end of the runway, ready for takeoff, in nine minutes. But sector command delayed their takeoff while they tried to establish radio contact with the approaching Il-76. Lacking success, the controller finally launched the two F-16s when the Il-76 was thirty miles from the border.

The handoff to Crown East was routine and the radar operator directed the F-16s to enter a racetrack pattern fifty miles back from the border with one leg oriented toward the incoming bogie. Now three different agencies — sector command, Crown East, and civilian air traffic control — were trying to establish radio contact with the oncoming Il-76. There was still no response, and the tac officer in the bunker passed control over to his weapons officer, the radar controller in charge of directing the actual intercept. Like many officers in the Polish Air Force, she was young and new at her job. And this was her first live intercept. The Il-76 penetrated Polish airspace.

Her voice shook as she broke the two F-16s out of orbit. 'Archer One and Two, you have a bogie at zero-seven-zero degrees, forty-five nautical miles. Fly vector zero-seven-zero. Visually ID and report only. Weapons safe.'

'Weapons safe,' Archer One replied, making sure his master arm switch was in the off position. He broke out of orbit and set his airspeed at .85 Mach, 510 nautical miles per hour.

'I have contact, on the nose, at forty miles,' Archer Two called over the radio. His pulse-Doppler radar had easily found the Il-76 and he locked it up. Almost immediately, the APG-68 radar broke lock. 'Negative lock,' he radioed. He tried again with the same results. Then he remembered to check his radar warning receiver to see if he was being jammed. There was no symbol on the warning display, only a chirping tone in his headset. He disregarded it.

Archer One also had the Il-76 on his radar and was experiencing the same problem. Then it hit him. Their radars were interfering with each other. 'Turn your radar to standby,' he ordered, keeping his own radar in 120-degree, four-bar scan. Now he tried to lock up the target. Nothing. The weapons officer at Crown East continued to direct them into the intercept, giving them headings to set up a stern conversion.

The two Su-35s were still on the deck, directly underneath and at co-speed with the Il-76. Their radars detected the two oncoming F-16s and their wingtip jammer pods successfully jammed the F-16s' radar, hiding their presence and denying the F-16s a radar lock-on. Automatically, the fire control system in the lead Su-35 sorted the threat and assigned targets to the R-77 missiles carried on the fuselage underneath the intakes. The R-77 was the most advanced air-to-air missile in the Russian inventory and nicknamed the 'AMRAAMSKI' as it was comparable to the United States' highly advanced AMRAAM, or Advanced Medium-Range Air-to-Air Missile. When the data had been downlinked, an in-range marker flashed on the aircraft's wide-angle HUD. The pilot hit the pickle button on his stick and two missiles leaped off the rails. Now they waited.

Archer One, the lead F-16 pilot, kept scanning the night sky outside. 'Do you have a visual?' he radioed.

'No visual,' came the answer.

'The bogie is at your two o'clock, ten miles, slightly high,' the weapons controller at Crown East radioed. 'Fly zero-three-zero.' She was directing them away from the Il-76 to give them turning room to convert to the bogie's stern. The two F-16s turned to the new heading, still searching the sky for a visual contact.

'We should see his lights,' Archer Two radioed.

'Looking,' Archer One replied.

But they had never been taught how to do a proper visual scan, especially at night, and they never saw the two rockets arcing up at them from their deep four o'clock position.

'Archer One, right turn to two-five-zero,' the weapons controller radioed, turning the interceptors back into the bogie. 'Target will be coming from your three o'clock to your nose, two miles, slightly high.' No answer. 'Archer One, how copy?'

'What happened?' the tactical officer demanded.

'I don't know,' the weapons controller replied. 'I've lost all contact.' She went through the lost communications procedures while the radar operator retuned the radar. Nothing.

'You stupid woman!' the tac officer shouted. 'Two aircraft don't just disappear.'

The radar operator's voice came through their headsets. 'The bogie is squawking now and we are in radio contact. He's using a Vnukova call sign; a diplomatic flight. He's calling for landing at Modlin.' Modlin was an airbase twenty miles northwest of Warsaw where the Russians had landing rights.

'Has the Vnukova flight seen the F-16s?'

'He claims not,' came the answer.

'What happened?' the tac officer asked. There was no response.

CHAPTER SIX

Moscow

The motorcade of two black Mercedes-Benz sandwiching the Bentley hurtled down the center of Granovsky Street. It was a throwback to the 1970s, the heyday of Soviet rule, and policemen waved off traffic and pedestrians, clearing the way to the Kremlin's Borovitsky Gate. The barrier at the gate was raised and one of the three guards managed to wave them through, not bothering to salute. The motorcade drew to a halt in front of the Red Steps and Mikhail Vashin climbed out of the Bentley. He stood in the cool morning air, savoring the moment. Deep in his soul, his peasant heritage told him that fall was in the air and to prepare for winter. But his days in the cold were over. The spring of Mikhail Vashin was about to begin.

He climbed the steps and entered the building. Viktor Kraiko, the President of Russia, and Yaponets were waiting to escort him. 'The guards at the gate,' Vashin said to Kraiko. 'Sloppy. Fix it.'

'He can't,' Yaponets said. 'But I can.'

Vashin grunted. Yaponets got things done, often with a mere word or look of disapproval. He was a man with authority, a trait Russians understood instinctively. Vashin handed his overcoat to Kraiko, who passed it on to an aide. 'Tell me, Viktor Ivanovich, who controls the Security Council today?'

'I do,' Kraiko answered, trying to sound confident. Russian politics were a shifting quagmire of quicksand that changed with each tide.

'The meeting will go smoothly?'

'Rodonov will be difficult. He has questions about last night.'

Vashin snorted again. Vitaly Rodonov was the Minister of Defense and the last stumbling block in his way. So far, Kraiko's advice to avoid a direct confrontation with Rodonov had been sound. But that time had ended.

Two guards opened the doors to the ornate conference room where the Soviet Politburo had once met. The men waiting inside were silent as Kraiko took his seat at the head of the table. The meeting was supposedly Kraiko's idea. But they all knew the truth of it. Kraiko played his role to the hilt and motioned Vashin to the podium at the bottom of the table. Arranged on Vashin's right were the most powerful leaders of Russian organized crime. On his left were the same men from the Security Council who had attended Boris Bakatina's funeral. But this time, the Minister of Defense was present, completing their number.

'Mikhail Andreyevich,' Kraiko began, 'let me welcome you and your compatriots.' As titular head of the Russian government, Kraiko could still be counted on to perform with some dignity.

'Give the President a drink,' Rodonov said. 'It will help his backbone.' Every eye was on him. 'We know why we are here.'

'Ah,' Kraiko said, trying to regain control. 'The incident in Poland last night.'

'It was an ambush,' Rodonov said, 'arranged behind our backs. It was the senseless act of criminals to protect a cargo of drugs and whores.'

Kraiko tried to put the best face on it. 'Our military transport aircraft are guaranteed the right of transit by treaty, much like the Allies enjoyed with the Berlin corridor during the Cold War. The Poles tried to deny us that right last night. What happened was—'

Rodonov interrupted him. 'Murder. Unfortunately, we are involved.'

'You are involved,' Vashin said, 'in the rebirth of our country. Soon, Russia will reclaim its rightful place in the world.' Loud applause, mostly from the Mafiya side of the table, echoed over his head.

'Why Poland?' Rodonov demanded.

'Poland is our gateway to western Europe.'

'For what?' Rodonov demanded. 'Your drugs?'

Kraiko was sweating. 'Poland has access to the West we lack. We must be able to move through Poland into Europe without interference.'

'And you do this by antagonizing the Poles?' Rodonov replied.

'We spoke to them in a way they understand,' Vashin replied.

'I repeat, why Poland?'

Vashin stared at Rodonov. Few people dared to question him like this. 'Because Poland is part of Russia. It is our natural buffer against the West.'

Rodonov interrupted him. 'This is the twenty-first century, not the nineteenth.'

Vashin spoke with a calm he didn't feel. 'An independent Poland is an insult to Russia. Stalin knew how to deal with that abortion.'

'Ni pizdí,' Rodonov muttered. It was a fine Russian phrase that roughly translated into 'Don't bullshit me'. He slapped his hands on the table. 'Why Poland?'

The men sitting on Rodonov's side of the table had the same question. They were masters of reality, or at least what was real in Russia, and it was time for Vashin to take off the gloves. He did. 'I want to make Poland the central distribution point for the world's narcotic industry. That requires total freedom to move our products without interference or monitoring of any kind.' The men listened in silence as Vashin outlined his plan. It was criminal activity on an industrial scale that required a union of legitimate government and organized crime. If it worked as Vashin promised, it would bring a river of money and wealth flooding into Russia, changing the balance of economic power in Europe and Asia.

'And if the Poles object, what then?' Rodonov asked.

'Our brothers in the Polish Mafia will prevent that. They are presenting Adam Lezno and the Polish government with other problems to occupy their time. Soon the Poles will turn to us, more than willing to exchange their lust for freedom for security.' Heads nodded in agreement around the table. Poland would become a tool for rebuilding the Russian empire.

'Poland is only the first step,' Vashin promised. 'Follow me and the future is ours.' Only Rodonov did not join the heavy applause that echoed over the room.

The meeting was over and Yaponets escorted Vashin to his waiting car. 'Rodonov is a problem,' Yaponets said.

'Sew him up,' Vashin muttered.

'And Kraiko?'

'Not yet. He can still be of some use.'

The Hill

Brian threw down his pencil in disgust. He hated writing book reports. He glanced at his watch – 9.33. Where was Little Matt? Night study hall was over and he should be back from the library. He wandered out on to the stoop and joined two other Rats, who were looking over the rail. There was a commotion in one corner of the quadrangle below them. 'What's going on?' he asked.

'They got Little Matt,' one of the Rats answered. 'Someone said they're going to chair him.'

'Oh, shit,' Brian muttered, wishing he hadn't bragged during a bullshit session on the stoop about seeing Zeth and Rick Pelton, the Regimental Executive Officer, sucking tongues in the library. He turned and ran for the stairs.

But two upper classmen were waiting for him. 'Go back to your room,' one of them ordered.

'I'm going to the TLA,' Brian said.

'You ain't got a problem for the TLA. Your Rat buddy does.' They backed him slowly along the stoop and into his room. 'Next time, keep your fuckin' mouth shut.' They glared at him menacingly. 'This involves Pontowski, not you, so keep the fuckin' Secret Service out of this. Got it?'

'I got it,' Brian promised. He slammed the door behind him and flopped down on his bunk. 'Fuckin' bastards,' he muttered. He renewed his promise to leave NMMI as soon as possible. He would do it over Family Weekend during the last weekend of September when he saw his mother. *Nine days*, he thought, starting a countdown calender. He came to his feet. 'Ah, shit,' he moaned. He might be leaving but Little Matt liked NMMI and wanted to stay. Now Little Matt was in trouble because he had shot his mouth off. *Tough shit*, he told himself. *It's a free country and I can say what I want*. 'Ah, no,' he said to himself. He had to do something, anything. But he didn't want Little Matt to get into more trouble. The cadets outside might keep him from reporting to the TLA what was happening, but they couldn't keep him off the phone. He dialed Zeth's number, hoping the telephones had been turned back on after night study hall. They had.

Zeth answered on the first ring. 'Some upper classmen grabbed Maggot,' he said, using his nickname for Little Matt. 'Someone said they're going to chair him. I didn't see which way they took him.'

'They used to do it in the Box,' Zeth said. The Box was the quadrangle in the center of Hagerman. 'But that's too risky now. It will get them dismissed big time. They're probably in the tunnels where you duked it out.'

'What are they going to do to him?' Brian asked.

'Put a bag over his head,' Zeth answered, 'strip him naked, tie him to a chair and spray him with shaving cream.'

'Can they get away with that?'

'Not if I can help it,' Zeth answered. She broke the connection, grabbed her flashlight, and ran for the back of the museum next door to Hagerman Barracks. She skidded down the steps and banged on the door to the tunnels. 'Open up, you freakin' assholes!' she yelled. Nothing. She shone her flashlight on the door. The recently installed lock and bolt system, thanks to the Secret Service, would defy a safe-cracker. *Where did they take him?* she wondered. Then it came to her. She raced for the parade field. She had to hurry. Time was short before the bugle sounded Call to Quarters. Ahead of her, on the far side of the parade field, she saw a cluster of dark figures lugging something up to the reviewing stand.

A cadet stepped out of the shadows and stopped her. 'Leave it alone,' he warned her.

'No way,' she growled.

'Forget it, Zeth,' the cadet said. 'Pontowski has the smallest pecker I've ever seen on a Rat.'

'You an expert on Rat penises now?' She barged past and ran across the field. Ahead, the shadowy backs of cadets formed a wall. She put on a burst of speed. 'Hey!' she yelled. One of the upper classmen turned in time to take the full blow of her running block. He fell over as she crashed into the circle, fully expecting to see Little Matt strapped naked to a chair. She had arrived in time and Little Matt was okay. But she was furious. 'You sons of bitches!' she screamed.

'Hey, Zeth,' one of the cadets said, trying to soothe her, 'we're not going to hurt him.'

'Damn right you're not,' she shouted. The cadet put a hand on her shoulder and tried to pull her out of the circle. It was a mistake. She rounded on him and threw a punch directly into his chest. Zeth was a conditioned athlete, big for a woman her age, and not afraid of any man at NMMI. Her fist was doubled into a hard knot and she punched like a man, straight from the shoulder, putting her weight behind the blow. She hit him in the sternum and knocked the wind out of him. He went down, gasping for a breath that wouldn't come.

'Who's going to give him mouth-to-mouth?' she challenged. She advanced on the closest cadet. 'How about you? You going to put a liplock on him? Save your buddy?' The other cadets stared at her, their eyes wide as she challenged them. 'Afraid to kiss a guy?' she shouted. She snorted and bent over the prostrate cadet. She grabbed his jaw and jerked his mouth open before blowing a big puff of air into his lungs. It worked and he gasped for air.

She stood up. 'Which one of you dumbshits thought this one up?'

'This is none of your business,' the ringleader said. 'Drop it. Quit playing mother hen.'

'I'm taking care of my troops, asshole!' She advanced on the speaker, her right hand knotted into a fist.

'She's crazy,' another cadet said. 'Let's get the hell out of here.' They all took it as good advice and ran toward Hagerman.

'Do it again,' she yelled, 'and I'll cut your balls off!' She turned to Little Matt. 'You okay?'

'Yeah,' he muttered. 'Who do I tell?'

'The TLA,' she answered. 'But if I were you, I wouldn't. Not if you want to stay here. This is serious and the commandant will kick the assholes out. But you'll be blamed for it. Find another way to even the score.'

The two undercover Secret Service agents posing as track coaches and living in the top-floor apartment of the north tower of Hagerman Barracks had recorded the entire incident through a night vision scope. 'Should we tell the superintendent?' one asked.

'Nah,' the other replied. 'Brian wasn't involved and she stopped it before they got started.' He thought for a moment. 'I wish Brian would grow up and think about his buddies for a change.'

The other agent agreed. 'He's a spoiled bastard.'

The White House

Madeline Turner relaxed into her chair and sipped the freshly brewed tea she loved. The cup in her hand was from a beautiful and delicate creation that was being called the 'Turner Collection'. *Is that what I'll be remembered for?* she wondered. It was a quiet moment in her day and she savored the serenity of her private study. Unlike the Oval Office next door, this retreat had become her place.

She glanced at the grandmother clock in the corner. It was time to end her day. She leaned forward and set her cup down before resting her elbows on her desk. She clasped her hands together and considered what she was going to do. The silence around her was punctuated by an occasional sound, little more than a murmur in the background of the real world outside. She lived in a confined world where every word she uttered, every move she made, every hand she reached out for, was considered the people's business. Yet in the end, it always came down to this: she was alone.

The intercom buzzed. 'The Senate just approved Bender,' Parrish said. 'They're on their way back.'

'Please show them right in,' she replied, breaking the connection. She had a few more moments to herself. She focused her thinking on the problem at hand, determined to move it to a back burner so she could move on to other issues. Her decision made, she thought about Brian's phone call. *I'm not going to let him quit*, she thought. *Not yet.*

A polite knock on the door rechanneled her attention as Richard Parrish held the door for Sam Kennett to enter. Mazie and Bender followed him in. As usual, Parrish settled into a corner chair, at the meeting but not part of it. What he had to say would come later when he was alone with the President. 'Well done,' Turner said. 'That was the fastest confirmation vote we've had.'

A rueful look spread across the Vice-President's face. 'We paid a price for it. Leland's on a slow boil and the pressure is building.'

'Is he going to be a problem?' Bender asked.

'Not for you,' Kennett answered. 'For us. Leland considers the appointment of ambassadors his personal bailiwick, regardless of what the Constitution says.'

'The good senator,' Turner said, 'doesn't have to live with the consequences of what he does. We do. Robert, I'm worried that Poland is destabilizing and Russia is a major player.'

'And has delusions of empire,' Mazie added.

'When we were in Poland on vacation,' Kennett said, 'I got the impression of a country on the edge. Everyone was worried about crime and the Russians. Unfortunately, the Secretary of State has a different interpretation.'

'That's why Stephan is not here,' Turner replied.

'In Serick's defense,' Mazie said, 'the exact contours of the problem are still emerging. We simply don't know who is doing what to whom. He's also worried about the Germans and, to be perfectly honest, so am I.'

Turner nodded. Mazie was one of her most valued counselors because she was not afraid to disagree. Turner steepled her fingers and studied them. 'I will not see Poland partitioned a fifth time, not in my presidency.'

'Madame President,' Kennett said, 'I don't think we have to worry about that. This is the twenty-first century.'

'I hope you're right. Robert, find out what is going on over there. I want to know where we can help and what we can offer them to stabilize the situation. I want to put some counters on the table.'

Bender was stunned. These were explicit marching orders and his spirits soared. He was done with the endless meetings, the talking, the political give-and-take that marked life in Washington. He was returning to the danger zone where the action was. He was back on the wire! Then reality came crashing down. He was still an ambassador reporting to the Secretary of State. Everything he said or did would be filtered through the bureaucracy of the State Department. Hard experience had taught him that bureaucracies were immovable objects with a life of their own, resistant to change. 'One of the best fighter pilots who ever strapped on a jet always said that when things go wrong, get aggressive. I don't think the State Department is quite ready for that approach to foreign policy.'

'There will be resistance,' Mazie said, thinking about her husband, who was a comer at State. 'We need to set up a separate reporting channel so we know what you are telling State.'

'That's easily arranged,' Parrish said. 'But Serick will be furious if he learns about it.'

Turner drummed her fingers on her desk. The meeting was

about over. 'I want results. We are not going to be caught with our options down. Mazie, open up a back channel to Robert and stay on top of the situation.' She looked around the room. 'Anything else?' Head shakes answered her and the meeting was over.

As usual, Parrish stayed behind to confirm the next day's schedule. 'I think Robert understands what I want,' she said.

'He does,' Parrish assured her. 'Did you see how he came alive? He's an old war-horse. Sound the bugle and he charges. But I'm worried that he might overstep his bounds. That could cause problems with Leland.'

'Not to worry,' Turner said. 'Robert has a wonderful sense of presence.' Her personal assistant came through the door. 'Ah, Dennis. We're about finished here.' It was a gentle reprimand to the effect that he was late.

'My apologies, ma'am,' Dennis said. 'I was talking to the Secret Service. They're wondering if Brian is coming home.'

Turner sank into her chair. 'No. I want him to stay at least until the end of the semester unless there are other problems.'

'His roommate is having some problems with a first classman.'

'Why?' Turner asked.

'The lead agent isn't sure. But apparently it's resolved now.'

'Did the Secret Service tell General McMasters?'

'No. Per your instructions they only go to the superintendent if it concerns Brian. Otherwise, they go with the flow and don't interfere. The agent has good words about the place and is going to enroll his daughter.'

'That's quite a recommendation,' Turner said, feeling better about her decision to keep Brian at NMMI. 'See if he can find out exactly what the problem was.' She thought for a moment. 'What's the schedule for Maura and Sarah?' Dennis rattled off times and arrangements from memory. 'I wish I could go,' Turner said. 'I wanted to pin on his cadet boards.'

CHAPTER SEVEN

Detroit

The motorcade moved with majestic dignity through the heart of the city. Inside the President's limousine, Turner's advisor on domestic affairs kept up a running commentary on what she was seeing. It was urban renewal on a scale not attempted in fifty years, and the rusting city had undergone a turnaround, coming alive with promise and hope. The advisor assured her it was only the beginning and much remained to be done. But by attending the dedication ceremony that launched the second, and most critical, phase of the program, the President was ensuring the support the city needed.

'And it melds perfectly with your address in Chicago to the National Association of Investment Bankers,' her chief of staff, Richard Parrish, added.

Turner suppressed a twinge of regret. She would have preferred to have been at NMMI with her family. She focused on a large block of dilapidated buildings. A cyclone fence with razor wire on top surrounded the burnt-out, rat-infested complex. It was an eyesore of monumental proportions. 'Who does that belong to?' she asked.

The domestic affairs advisor checked his notes. 'Here it is. At one time, the Army. But now, HUD. HUD was the Department of Housing and Urban Development, one of the more bureaucratic-laden agencies in the government.

'So it's ours,' she replied. She pointed at a group of young men clustered around an opening in the fence. 'Are those drug dealers?'

'We wouldn't be driving by if they were,' the advisor answered. 'Drug dealing is high tech now, call and deliver, strictly out of sight. They're most likely gang members who can't handle the technology and are unemployable, even as criminals. At best, they might be part-time runners.'

Turner said firmly, 'Richard, I want something done about this.'

'I'll check into it, Madame President.' No one in the limousine made a note or seemed overly concerned.

Turner spoke in a low voice, her words even and without emotion. 'I want action on this. Fortunately, I know how bureaucracies work. They nod their heads in agreement, put it to the bottom of the pile, and hope I'll forget about it. That's not going to happen here. I want a memo on my desk by close of business Tuesday outlining what we are going to do, when we are going to do it, and who is in charge. If that memo is not on my desk, or if it's bureaucratic hooey, I want the two highest-ranking GS-17s who are responsible for those buildings in my office Wednesday morning. And I assure you, it will not be a pleasant meeting.'

She picked up the phone next to her and spoke to Dennis in the front seat. In a few crisp sentences, she summarized what she had said. Dennis would not carry out her directions, but he would ensure they were not forgotten. The domestic affairs advisor keyed the phone on his side of the car. He chuckled to himself. A lot of bureaucrats were going to wish Madeline Turner had gone to New Mexico instead of to Detroit.

The Hill

Matt Pontowski walked around Little Matt's room and smiled. The bunks were inspection tight, the lockers in perfect order, and the floor spotless for Family Weekend. 'Just like when I was at the Academy,' he said. He examined his son's desk. A framed photo of him and Little Matt in front of their T-34 stood between the telephone and computer monitor. 'You really like it here?'

'Yeah, I guess so.' Little Matt shifted uneasily from foot to foot. He looked good in his uniform and was proud of his new shoulder boards that Pontowski had pinned on after the parade, but something was bothering him. 'Dad, I want to go to the Zoo like you did.' The Zoo was the Air Force Academy at Colorado Springs. 'I want to fly fighters.'

'Just like your great-grandfather and grandfather,' Pontowski said. Conflicting emotions tied his stomach in a tight knot. Pontowski's father, Matthew Zachary Pontowski II, had been killed in Vietnam flying F-4 Phantoms. Did he want his son to be the fourth in the long line of Pontowskis whose destiny was tied to the profession of arms as practiced by men who fought and died in fighter aircraft? Little Matt was a sweet kid, small for his age, and uncoordinated, not the stuff of fighter pilots. Yet he wanted to hug his son for wanting to carry on the family tradition. 'Well, son. You've got lots of time to think about it.'

'Think about what?' Brian asked from the doorway. Like Little Matt, he was wearing his new shoulder boards that had been awarded after that morning's parade. His sister Sarah and Maura O'Keith were standing behind him.

'Nothin',' Little Matt muttered.

Sarah bounced into the room and climbed the ladder on to Little Matt's bunk above his desk. 'Hey, Chubs,' Brian said, 'stay off Maggot's bunk. He'll get stuck with two demerits. That's two hours' walking tours.'

'It's okay,' Little Matt said. Sarah smiled at him.

Maura and Pontowski exchanged greetings and the customary pleasantries about the activities flowing around Family Weekend. There had been a major change in the afternoon's activities because the visiting football team from Hobbs had had to cancel at the last moment. Sarah sat on the edge of Little Matt's bunk, her feet swinging back and forth as she watched Brian shift his weight from one foot to the other. He was obviously uncomfortable and bored with the weekend. 'Well,' Maura said, 'what's next on the agenda?'

'There's an intramural soccer game instead of football,' Little Matt said. 'It starts in ten minutes. Zeth, she's our squad leader, is playing. She's really something, the only girl on the regular team.' Sarah climbed down off the bunk and Little Matt quickly brought it back to inspection standard. 'It doesn't take long to do this,' he told her. 'Zeth taught us how.'

With the room in inspection order, they headed for Stapp Parade Field, where temporary goals had been set up for the game. Pontowski was surprised when Sarah slipped her hand inside his as they walked. 'Did you fly down in your airplane like last time?' she asked. He nodded. 'Can I go for a ride?'

'That's up to your grandmother,' he told her.

Brian came alive. 'You got your airplane here? That's cool. Can I go too?'

'Brian wants to go to the Air Force Academy and fly fighters like General Bender did,' Sarah announced. 'We used to talk to him all the time when he worked in the White House.'

'Shut up, Chubs,' Brian grumbled.

Pontowski arched an eyebrow at Maura, an unspoken question. 'Well,' she said, 'I suppose it's okay.'

'Great,' Brian said. 'Let's go.'

'How about after the soccer game?' Pontowski ventured. Brian sulked and followed them into the bleachers behind the reviewing stand where Little Matt had almost been chaired. The teams were already on the field as the team captains flipped a coin for the kickoff. 'Is that Zeth, center midfield?' Pontowski asked. Little Matt confirmed his guess. Zeth's team won the toss and two forwards stepped into the circle for the opening play. The referee blew his whistle and one of the forwards faked a pass to the side, stepped over the ball and back-kicked it to Zeth. She moved the ball downfield with speed and finesse. 'She's good,' Pontowski said admiringly. 'Watch how she can drop the ball to her feet, keep it there, and pass off accurately.' The tempo picked up and it became obvious that Zeth was controlling the center, causing constant disruption when the opposing team tried to bring the ball downfield. 'She's fierce,' he said. 'I wouldn't want to play opposite her.'

'Do you play soccer?' Brian asked.

'I used to,' Pontowski answered.

'He played on the Academy's team,' Little Matt said. 'He was an All American.' Brian focused on Zeth, seeing her in a different light.

The forward playing opposite Zeth was the ringleader of the cadets who had tried to haze Little Matt. The other cadets had ragged him unmercifully because Zeth had stopped him and now he had a chance to even the score. 'Stay out of the way, Trog,' he threatened. 'I'll run right the fuck over you.'

'Like last time?' She faked a move and scooted past him. But he threw out an arm and hit her in the breasts, hard. She ignored it and scrambled after the ball, hoping the referee saw the foul. But there was no whistle as she bumped shoulders with the midfielder bringing the ball downfield. She crashed into him again and took the ball away. She broke down the sidelines, charging the defending fullback between her and the goal. Her feet flashed and she passed the ball across the field in front of the goal. Her team's forward was there and he drilled the ball into the net. Zeth trotted back up the field while the spectators cheered.

The forward was waiting for her. 'Sorry 'bout the tit slap.' There was no apology in his voice.

The other side had the ball and again she bottled up the center. But this time she held back, always keeping the forward between her and the ball. 'Go for the ball, Zeth!' her coach yelled from the sidelines. But she concentrated on the cadet in front of her.

The forward grinned. 'Tits hurting?'

'A little,' she said.

'Can't stand the pain, don't play the game.'

The opposing goalie kicked the ball upfield after a missed goal. Zeth put on a sudden burst of speed and charged the ball, bringing the forward with her. But she easily outran him. She almost smiled when the angles were right. Her right leg swung in a full kick, her momentum and body weight behind it. The ball was an artillery shell with a flat trajectory as it bounced off the forward's face. He fell to the ground and she trotted over to him. The ball's seams were imprinted on his cheek. 'Sorry 'bout the head slap,' she said.

'Yes!' Little Matt shouted, coming to his feet. 'She nailed him.' Brian was right beside him, shouting and pounding on Little Matt's head. Little Matt jumped on Brian's back and they danced around as two trainers helped the dazed forward off the field.

'Grams,' Sarah asked, 'what happened?' Maura explained how the forward had fouled Zeth and gotten away with it. The kick decking him had simply been a form of rough justice delayed. She didn't realize how rough and how delayed. 'When did you learn about soccer?' Sarah asked.

'I was one of the first soccer moms when your mother was growing up,' Maura said.

'Mom played soccer?' This from Brian.

Maura laughed. 'Only for one season. That was before soccer was popular. She wasn't very good and it was to impress some boy.' She led the way out of the stands. 'Well, Matt Pontowski, how about that airplane ride? I just might want to go up myself.'

'Ah, come on, Grams,' Brian moaned.

'May I come in?' Zeth asked from the doorway. It was Sunday evening and Brian and Little Matt were studying, the iron routine of NMMI back in place after Family Weekend. She stepped inside and sat on the floor, her back against Brian's locker. 'I thought you were bailing out?'

'I'll finish the year then bail. That was a great kick. You really nailed that asshole.'

'Is that why you changed your mind?' she asked.

'A little bit. But it was everything. My grams was so proud when she pinned on my boards. And Sarah kept taking pictures. And I went up for a ride in General Pontowski's airplane. I've never done acrobatics and he taught me how to do an aileron roll. It was great.'

Zeth was persistent. 'So why are you staying?'

'I'm not sure.' He thought for a moment. 'Maggot's dad said that flying fighters was the most fun thing he's ever done in his life. He also said it was the hardest thing he's ever done. You have to really work to get it and nobody cuts you any slack. I guess that means I gotta work for it if I wanna do it.' Brian pulled into himself, thinking. 'Maggot's lucky. He's got a great dad.'

'Why do you call him Maggot?' Zeth asked.

'It seems to fit,' Brian replied. Then another thought came to him. He looked at Little Matt. 'You okay with that?'

Little Matt shrugged. 'It's okay. And you got a cool mom.'

'So why don't you two introduce them?' Zeth asked. She got up to leave. 'Think about it.' She walked out of the room.

Little Matt shook his head. 'Stupid. Can you see your mom in bed with my dad doing it?'

'No way,' Brian answered. 'They're way too old.'

Over western Poland

Nancy Bender sat in the seat next to her husband, enjoying the attention Delta Airlines bestowed on its first-class passengers. She was a small, dark woman, in total contrast to her tall and fair husband. He was intellectual and analytical while Nancy was intuitive and spontaneous in her thinking, making wild leaps and quick judgments. Where he was prudent and reserved, she was lively and outgoing. Nothing seemed to match. Yet it was a good marriage and they complemented each other in ways that grew stronger over the years. Their marriage had endured rough passages, especially when their only child, Laurie, was killed in the crash of an F-15E. But they had made it.

She glanced at her husband. Bender was still working his way through the mass of material the State Department had given him during what he called the Foggy Bottom Charm

School. At first, the charm school had been little more than briefings on social protocols, and every hard question he raised was answered by 'Your Deputy Charge of Mission will brief you on that aspect'. Then he became cold and hard, the way only a general can. The bureaucrats responded by dumping a pile of documents on him, fully intending to bury him under an avalanche of information. Little did they know he would sort through it all, finding what he needed.

Nancy twisted in her seat, ignoring the queasiness in her stomach which she attributed to middle age and the onset of menopause. 'A girl could get used to this,' she said, looking out the window. Bender agreed with her. The perks and privileges that went with being the President's representative far exceeded anything they had enjoyed in the Air Force. 'Robert, what wing has the letters SP on the tail of its fighters?' Years of being the wife of an Air Force officer had taught her about tail markings, but she couldn't remember what they all stood for.

'The 52nd Fighter Wing out of Spangdahlem, Germany. Why?'

'Well, there're two F-16s out there with SP on the tail.'

Bender leaned across and looked out her window. Two F-16s painted air-superiority gray were camped in a loose formation 2,000 feet abeam of the airliner. He watched them for a few moments as one pulled up and away, leaving the other alone. His eyes narrowed. 'Miss,' he called to the flight attendant. 'Have we crossed into Poland yet?' She told him she would check and walked forward to buzz the pilots. She was back in a few moments confirming his guess.

'I only see one now,' Nancy said, looking out the window again. 'Where did the other one go?'

'I imagine he's on the perch, above and behind us.'

Nancy looked at him, recognizing the tone in his voice. They would discuss it later, when they were alone. The F-16 on their wing collapsed on to the airliner, now only 500 feet away, close enough for Bender to make out details. The Fighting Falcon had two wing tanks for long-range cruise and a full set of air-to-air missiles. An AIM-9 infrared missile hung on each wingtip with a mix of AMRAAM radar-guided missiles and AIM-9s on the wing pylons. But they were not painted blue, signifying they were for training. These were the real thing. They had an escort.

Why hadn't he been told about it? This was the type of surprise he didn't like. He made a mental note to shake a few trees when he landed. Another thought came to him. What had the President said about putting counters on the table? He considered the possibilities. 'Just one of the perks that comes with the job,' he told his wife, making light of it.

'Why are you smiling?'

'I'm not.'

'Oh yes you are, Robert Bender. I saw those steely blues flash. I know when you're smiling.'

He changed the subject. 'You know, I just might like this job.'

'I knew you were smiling,' she said, giving his hand a little squeeze.

The VIP lounge at Okecie, Warsaw's international airport, was filled with dignitaries waiting for the arrival of the Delta flight bringing the new ambassador. The room buzzed with gossip as Winslow James tried to quiet the rumors surrounding Robert Bender and his wife. James was a fussy, potbellied man, pushing fifty. He was always neatly dressed and careful with his words. He was also a hard-working professional diplomat who had worked his way up through a series of posts and was now the Deputy Charge of Mission. Neither he nor his superiors were happy about Bender's appointment as ambassador, and the back-channel lines had been humming about how to handle the latest incumbent, who was neither a political appointee nor a professional diplomat.

'Winslow,' a voice said behind him, 'what a nice reception.'

James turned and suppressed a groan. It was Jerzy Fedor from the Council of Ministers. Fedor was in his late thirties, and had a lean, ravaged look about him that was in total contrast to his buoyant good humor. James was not sure exactly what

Fedor did in the cabinet, but he did seem to survive every change in government and moved in the highest circles. 'Is it true?' Fedor asked.

Winslow James forced a smile. 'Is what true?'

'Your new ambassador is a jet jockey, a cowboy top gun.'

'I wouldn't describe General Bender in those terms,' James replied, putting on his best diplomatic face. 'At one time, he flew fighters. But he's retired. As you are probably aware, he has the full confidence of President Turner.'

'So I've heard,' Jerzy Fedor said, ambling off into the crowd.

James's wife joined him. She was holding a large bouquet of flowers for the new ambassador's wife. 'What did he want?' she asked in a tone reserved for vermin and snakes.

'Who knows? He's probably more interested in the hors d'oeuvres and the wine than Bender.' He looked around. 'Well, I see everyone is here and the airplane has arrived.' They walked together to the head of the jetway where Bender and Nancy would be deplaning. They would be the first off so James and his wife could hustle them through the doors into the VIP lounge, where they would be separated from the other passengers. The welcome inside would be neatly choreographed to make Bender feel like a VIP and to insulate him from the real Poland as quickly as possible.

As planned, James greeted Bender and Nancy when they stepped off the jetway. The two men shook hands while James's wife presented Nancy with the bouquet and welcomed her to Poland. They walked together into the VIP lounge for the welcoming ritual with the Polish Minister of Foreign Affairs. As protocol required, Bender said a few words about how happy he and Nancy were to be in Poland. Then it all fell apart. Before James could hurry them to the waiting limousine, Bender and Nancy walked around the room, introducing themselves and shaking hands. 'Robert Bender,' he said, extending his hand to a man standing near the back.

'Jerzy Fedor,' came the answer.

'Of the Polska Partia Przyjaciol Piwa,' Bender replied,

butchering the pronunciation of the Polish Beer-Lovers' Party.

Fedor laughed. 'You have done your homework, General. But we have gone respectable. Our party is now part of the Little Coalition.' He leaned forward and stretched out his hand. 'But I must tell you it was more fun when we were the PPPP.' They shook hands.

'What lovely cufflinks,' Nancy said, instantly regretting the breach of protocol.

'Ah,' Fedor replied, 'a family heirloom. For me, amber is like Poland, very old but warm and alive to the touch.' He fixed her with an intense gaze. 'We Poles are incurable romantics. Where else could you find a political party like the PPPP with the goal of having lively political discussions in pubs serving good beer?'

James interrupted them, trying to get the reception back on track. 'General Bender, your car is waiting.'

Bender introduced himself to a few more people before allowing James to escort him and Nancy outside. 'Please join us,' he said. James closed his door and hustled around to the other side, motioning to his wife to follow them. Inside, Bender turned to business. 'I want a staff meeting in one hour,' he said.

James started to protest but the look on Bender's face warned him it would be fruitless. 'Of course, sir.' He made a mental note to call his superior at the Eastern Europe Desk in Washington right after the meeting.

The number of people waiting for Bender in his office on the second floor of the embassy was much smaller than he had expected. 'Please get the defense attaché,' he said, 'and the CIA station chief.' The staff exchanged nervous glances as James made the phone calls. Within moments, the two men were in the room and James introduced them. 'Please bear with me during these first few weeks,' Bender began, 'while I learn exactly what you all do and how you do it. You need to know three things about the way I do business. First, if I ask you about something that is not in your area, I expect you to refer me to the right person and stay involved. Second, it's okay to disagree with me. But have your act together when you do. Third, I don't like surprises and I got one on the flight into Warsaw. We were escorted by two F-16s out of Spangdahlem Air Base in Germany. I was not told about it in advance.'

'Sir,' the attaché said, 'the escort was my idea. As you are probably aware, two Polish F-16s on an air defense mission were shot down four weeks ago. It was a routine intercept of a cargo plane. We suspect the Russians did it, but we don't know why or how.'

'I am aware of the shootdown,' Bender replied. 'But that was not the way to tell me that the Poles cannot guarantee the security of their own airspace.'

'Sir—'

Bender held up a hand, cutting him off. 'I know. It was not your fault that I was not given advance warning. But that is exactly the breakdown in communication that I want stopped. Keep the players informed. Also, on the drive in from Okecie, I counted eight patrol cars along Aleje Ujazadowskie in the vicinity of the embassy. And I must admit, the embassy's security arrangements are impressive. This place is a sealed fortress. Am I wrong in the assumption that security is a major concern?'

Everyone in the room was fully alert. Bender had been in Poland less than three hours and was already comfortable with the local geography and had focused on a major problem. He was not going to be a political appointee adroitly corseted by the professionals on his staff. 'That's a true statement,' the CIA chief of station said.

'The situation is extremely complex,' the political officer added.

Bender gave her an encouraging nod. 'And we're going to make sense out of it.' He glanced at the calendar on his desk. 'This is Thursday. I want a detailed assessment of the security situation on my desk by Monday morning. Include a list of programs we can make available to the Poles so they can help themselves. Please tell your staffs I'll be touring the embassy tomorrow morning to meet them.' The session was over and his staff set a new record in retreating to the safety of their offices.

The political officer was a very worried woman, and outside she cornered the protocol officer, the other high-ranking woman on the staff. 'What do you think?'

The protocol officer gave her a sympathetic look. 'It's going to be very interesting.' The two women were silent as Winslow James rushed past, muttering something about cowboys and jet jockeys.

'He is very attractive,' the political officer said.

'That won't be a problem,' the protocol officer added.

CHAPTER EIGHT

Moscow

Geraldine Blake answered the phone and jotted down the message. *This will be trouble*, she thought. She dialed another number and spoke in Russian for the benefit of the technicians monitoring the line. 'Tom, I may need you in a few minutes. Are you available?' The technician on duty automatically annotated the time of the call to Thomas Johnson, Mikhail Vashin's chief of security whom everyone called the American. Johnson said he would be at his desk. 'It might be better if you were in the penthouse,' Geraldine said, this time in English.

She broke the connection, thought for a few moments, and called Le Coq d'Or, Vashin's nightclub. *Best be prepared*, she told herself. 'Please send Naina and Liya to my office.' She listened for a moment. 'I don't care what time it is. Do it now.' She put the phone down and looked at her watch. It would take at least thirty minutes for the girls to arrive. She could delay the inevitable that long. She took a deep breath. Part of her job as Vashin's personal assistant was to anticipate trouble.

At exactly 2.07 p.m. the two girls walked into her office. Both were young, beautiful, and elegantly dressed. But more importantly, the two prostitutes were well trained. Geraldine gathered up her folder and personal telecommunicator and marched into the penthouse. She handed Vashin the note from the phone call. 'This came in from Minsk a few minutes ago.'

She waited patiently as he read, the cool business professional ready to serve her employer. As expected, the eruption built slowly. 'Vitaly Rodonov has overstepped his bounds,' Vashin said. Strain played at the edge of his voice. 'He may be the Minister of Defense, *but he does not confiscate my cargo.*' His voice shifted pitch, growing more shrill. 'No one does that! Do you know the dollar value of what he stole from me?'

Geraldine opened her folder and read the manifest. 'Eight cargo pallets of high-grade cocaine, weighing five hundred kilos each, is a delivered value of forty-eight million dollars; two pallets of hashish, same quality, weighing seven hundred kilos each, is a delivered value of approximately ten million dollars; fifty-four girls, delivered value approximately half a million dollars. Total amount lost, exactly 58,340,000 dollars.'

'Delivered value!' Vashin screamed, his face mottled with fury. 'Street value returned to us is four or five times that! I lost a *quarter-billion dollars* because Rodonov confiscated one cargo!' He banged his fists on his desk as a stream of invective spewed over the room, and started to shake. 'The bastard! I wanted him in the ground four weeks ago! Where is Yaponets?'

Geraldine did not hesitate. She punched at her telecommunicator and summoned the godfather. Then she called for Johnson. In less than thirty seconds, Johnson was in the room. 'Why isn't Rodonov dead!' Vashin shouted, barely understandable.

'I'll check it out,' Johnson said, his voice calm and matter-of-fact. Hit contracts weren't his job but, increasingly, he was branching into other areas. 'I imagine it's because he's guarded by professionals. Sooner or later, they'll make a mistake and our men will be waiting.'

For a moment, Vashin seemed rational. 'Where is Yaponets?'

'He's on his way,' Geraldine said soothingly.

Then the dam burst, Vashin's rage in full flood. He lunged at Johnson, who was closest to him, screaming a torrent of obscenities in Russian that were all but incomprehensible. Johnson took the blow in his face. He was a wall and didn't move. Vashin spun around and kicked at Geraldine. But he missed and hit the leg of a table. He fell to the floor and rolled as his body shook. He swallowed his tongue and started to choke. Johnson and Geraldine bent over his flailing body and held him down. The American forced Vashin's mouth open while Geraldine fished out his tongue. She stroked his face, trying to calm him.

'I can give him a sedative,' Johnson said.

'No drugs or needles,' Geraldine replied. She shouted at one of the guards. 'Get Naina and Liya! They're in my office.' The guard ran from the room while Johnson pinned the bucking man to the floor. The two girls ran up and stepped out of their shoes. They fell down beside Vashin, one on each side, and scooted under Johnson to help sandwich Vashin with their bodies. Vashin wrenched his right arm free and smashed his fist into Naina's face. She cried out in pain but only hugged him more tightly, stroking his cheek and whispering softly, cooing to him like a mother to an infant. Liya hummed a lullaby as she stroked his crotch. Slowly, Vashin quit shaking and Johnson got up. His nose was bloodied and he had a vicious bite on the edge of his left hand. He wrapped it with a handkerchief and said nothing.

Vashin pulled at Naina's dress while Liya undid his belt. She pulled his pants off, taking his shorts with them. Naina guided him into her as he rocked rhythmically back and forth, licking the growing bruise on her face. He climaxed and rolled off. Liya cuddled against his back, still humming the lullaby while he sucked on one of her fingers. She rocked him to sleep.

Johnson let out his breath. 'That was bad.'

'I've seen worse,' Geraldine told him.

Vashin sat on one of the heavily brocaded couches with Naina and Liya still beside him. His clothes were neatly arranged and only his flushed face betrayed the fury that had swept over him. Geraldine handed him a cup of tea drawn from the ornate silver samovar that had once been in the Hermitage in St Petersburg. He looked at Naina, almost adoringly. 'Thank you,' he murmured. Geraldine read the signs correctly and motioned for the girls to leave. Vashin's hand lingered for a moment on Naina's arm before she departed.

When the door was closed behind them, Vashin walked to the heavy plate-glass window overlooking Moscow. Mist swirled in front of him, blocking the view. He touched the inside of the bullet chip. The glass was smooth to his touch and, for a moment, he thought of the chip as the icon of his life, dented and scarred on the outside, but polished and whole on the inside. 'The problem of Rodonov is still with us.'

'Rodonov is beneath you,' Geraldine said. 'He's not worth your time.' Vashin stared out the window, his face a blank mask. She knew he was listening. 'But he is very popular with the people. Perhaps it would be better if he were disgraced first. Perhaps a honey trap? Who knows? That might solve the problem.'

Vashin became animated and turned to Johnson. 'In your movie *The Godfather* a troublesome senator is caught with a brutally murdered prostitute in a whorehouse. What will the people think of their hero Rodonov if that happens to him?'

'He will be disgraced,' Johnson said, 'and the problem solved.'

'Arrange it,' Vashin ordered. Geraldine and Johnson exchanged glances, not sure who he wanted to do it. But it was not a question either dared ask.

'This is all new to me,' Johnson said. 'I'll need to talk to the right people.'

Geraldine was more practical. 'A honey trap will need the right bait.'

'Naina and Liya,' Vashin said.

Geraldine made a note to train two new girls.

A knock at the door claimed their attention and Yaponets entered. 'Leave us,' Vashin ordered. Geraldine and Johnson quickly left as Vashin returned to the big window.

'Another fit?' Yaponets asked.

Vashin didn't answer immediately. Eventually he said, 'I had a dream last night. I was floating over Moscow drifting in clouds.' He gestured out the window. 'It was like now. I couldn't see a thing, but I knew Moscow was down there.'

Like many Russians, both men were deeply superstitious. 'Perhaps it's a sign,' Yaponets said. 'You must wait.'

Vashin accepted the wisdom of the older man. 'Geraldine says Rodonov is beneath my concern.'

'She may be right,' Yaponets allowed. 'No one can stand in your way. Not now.'

'There is one,' Vashin said. 'The President of the United States.'

'She's only a woman.'

'She's more than that,' Vashin said. He paced back and forth, fixated on the image he had conjured. 'I want to know everything about her. What are her weaknesses, her strengths? Where does she live in her heart?'

Yaponets shrugged. 'Where do all women live?'

'This one is different.'

'What do I tell Geraldine and the American?'

'Nothing. This is beyond them.'

Warsaw

The black limousine flying the American flag turned right out of the US embassy and drove down Aleje Ujazadowskie. It motored silently down the elegant avenue, past Chopin's monument in Łazienki Park, and turned left into the Belvedere, the official residence of the President of the Republic of Poland. The distance was exactly one kilometer, sixth-tenths of a mile. 'We should have walked,' Bender said, taking in the beautiful day.

Winslow James suppressed a very undiplomatic sigh. No matter how gorgeous the day or short the distance, ambassadors did not walk when they presented their credentials to the President. 'Security is always a problem,' he said. The limousine pulled to a stop and the waiting honor guard came to attention. The Minister of Foreign Affairs greeted Bender when he emerged from the back seat. They walked slowly up the steps, chatting amiably, with James in close tow.

The palace sparkled, fresh from a recent renovation. 'Very beautiful,' Bender said, making the required small talk.

'Indeed,' the minister replied. They reached the double doors leading into the reception chamber. 'As you know, the President is recovering from a heart attack. So he will be in a wheelchair and the meeting will be short.' They entered the room. Waiting at the far end was Adam Lezno, the old lion who had struggled for Poland's freedom since 1956. He had been beaten by the secret police, imprisoned, and forced into exile. But he had always returned to the fray, fighting for an independent and democratic Poland. Now he was an old man, but the fire still burned within.

The Minister of Foreign Affairs made the introductions while James handed over the leather folder holding President Turner's formal letter presenting Bender as her official emissary to Poland. Lezno waved it to an aide. 'Come,' he said to Bender. 'It is too nice a day to be inside.' Another aide pushed his wheelchair into the garden while Bender walked beside them. Outside, Lezno was more relaxed. 'I hate formality. I suppose it's necessary, but it takes too much time, of which I have very little left. General Bender, my country is in trouble.'

'President Turner is aware of your problems and very concerned,' Bender replied. He decided to pull the gloves off. 'That's why I'm here.'

Lezno chuckled. 'You are a man of my heart, direct and to the point. I was in the hospital during your confirmation hearings and watched you on CNN. I was impressed when you knew of our national anthem. Do you know the words?' He started to sing in English, 'Poland had not yet been destroyed—' He stopped. 'It sounds better in Polish. The song is our history. We are a small country caught between Russia and Germany. Apparently, they have not changed and once again want to erase us from the map.'

'Times are different now.'

Lezno snorted. 'The means are different. The Germans talk of the frontiers of 1937 and buy land in western Poland. We are living with eighty-five million Germans on our border.

Their birthrate is increasing after years of decline. Soon they will again look to the east for *lebensraum*. The quest for living space is deeply rooted in the German psyche. But the Germans are not fools. The first step is to repudiate the Warsaw Treaty of 1970 which recognizes the Oder and Neisse rivers as our common border.'

'World opinion, Mr President, will not allow that.'

Again, the snort. 'Last Monday, Berlin filed a brief with the International Court of Justice in The Hague claiming Willy Brandt and his government did not represent all of Germany when he signed the treaty. Therefore, it is invalid and must be renegotiated.'

Bender stiffened. Why hadn't he been told? It should have been in the read file that was on his desk every morning. 'I will advise my President of your concern,' he said.

'My country needs more than your sympathy,' Lezno said. 'Look at what the Russians are doing. They are turning my country into a cesspool of crime and drugs.'

'Mr President, we can help you with that particular problem. I should receive specific instructions in the near future.'

They turned back toward the palace. As they approached, another man joined them. It was Jerzy Fedor from the reception at the airport. 'I believe you have already met,' Lezno said. 'Jerzy is my expert on internal security. Perhaps you two could discuss those specific instructions you mentioned. In private.'

'Most assuredly,' Bender answered. Another thought came to him. *He knows about the security aide package we cabled to Washington yesterday.*

'General Bender,' Lezno said, 'do not underestimate Poland. Yes, we have problems that we must solve and we do need help. But we are much stronger than you realize.'

Winslow James was waiting for Bender by the entrance, ready to lead him through the departure ritual. In a few moments, they were back in the limousine and headed north on Aleje Ujazadowskie. Bender raised the privacy window to the front seat. 'I must apologize for not making myself clear last week, Winslow. I really do hate surprises and I received two of them during my conversation with President

Lezno. We need to discuss my read file and communications security.'

The ride back to the embassy turned into the longest journey of Winslow James's life.

The White House

Madeline Turner studied the President's Daily Brief, or PDB for short. It was a slickly printed, highly professional document produced by a committee at CIA headquarters in Langley, Virginia. It was never more than twelve pages long and contained the best intelligence the CIA could produce. Only seven people were on its distribution list and all copies were carefully analyzed after being read. The paper contained a trace element that emerged under a special light if the PDB had been through a copy machine or a scanner. Turner reread the item on Mikhail Vashin and laid the report on her desk. *We've got an agent on the inside*, she thought. *The information is less than three days old and too detailed.* 'Richard, did you read the item on Vashin?' He nodded. 'What do you think?'

'Very unstable and very dangerous. Personally, I'd like to hear what Mazie and the DCI think' – he glanced at the PDB – 'without a few bureaucratic layers filtering the information.'

'Get them on the schedule for this afternoon.'

Parrish made a note, picked up the PDB, and buzzed for the next meeting. The door to the Oval Office opened and the key staffers responsible for the day-to-day running of the White House trooped in. Parrish signed the PDB over to the security officer, who turned and left, closing the door behind him.

Like most of her working groups, this one was small and numbered only six people, including her mother, Maura O'Keith. Madeline Turner's greatest strength was her ability to choose outstanding subordinates she could trust to act independently, never compromising themselves or the White House. The administration group was a well-rehearsed team and the meeting went smoothly.

The social secretary went over the list of coming events, always careful to check that Dennis was in full agreement with the schedule. As usual, the secretary ended with requests they had to turn down. Turner's chin came up when she heard the name Amadis Escalante.

For a moment, she was back in the past, an awkward and gangling teenager in an art gallery in New Mexico. The portrait of a Mexican-American woman, worn down by poverty, privation, and childbirth, had captured her heart. A woman spoke softly behind her. 'How old do you think she is?'

'Eighty, eighty-five,' Turner answered, turning around.

The voice belonged to a huge woman, well over six feet tall and very heavy. 'She's forty-seven,' the woman said. She smiled gently at the stunned look of disbelief on the teenager's face. 'I know, I painted her. I'm Amadis Escalante. What's your name, child?'

'Maddy Turner.'

'Are you an artist?' She studied the teenager and answered her own question. 'No. You are meant for more important things.'

All of Maddy Turner's self-doubts and teenage insecurities crashed down on her. She gazed at the portrait. 'I can't do anything.'

'Yes, you can. If you listen to your heart. Like now.'

Turner came back to the present. Her staff was silent, waiting for her. 'I'm forty-seven,' she murmured. Her eyes glistened with memory. 'I met Amadis when I was fifteen.'

The social secretary responded instinctively and related how the New Mexico Council for the Arts had invited the President to dedicate the Amadis Escalante Museum of the Arts. 'The museum is in Ruidoso and you can stay at the family compound on the Escalante Ranch. It's rustic but very beautiful.'

'Please accept the invitation,' Turner said.

Mazie Hazelton sat on the couch in the President's private study, her eyes on Turner. Mazie had never seen the President so angry. Her gaze was fixed on the carpet, her arms folded as she walked back and forth. She stopped and pointed at the

DCI, who was sitting across from Mazie. Her voice was flat and hard. 'Let me see if I understand this right. The CIA has an agent next to the Russian madman who may be Russia's next dictator. The madman has ordered our agent to assassinate the Minister of Defense, Vitaly Rodonov, who happens to be a good guy and is helping to stop the drug trade going through Poland.'

'I wouldn't describe Rodonov as "a good guy",' the DCI answered. 'At this point, he's an unknown quantity. We need to know more about him.'

'But Rodonov,' Turner continued, 'could be a possible successor to Viktor Kraiko, the current President of Russia who happens to be Vashin's toady.' Again, the DCI confirmed her understanding of the situation. 'However, this is a way for our agent to make his bones with Vashin, and that would give us a pipeline right into the heart of his operation. So you want to preserve our agent at any cost.'

'I didn't say that, Madame President,' the DCI protested.

'Damn.' Maddy resumed her pacing, working the problem. She stopped and whirled toward the DCI. 'The only options I've heard are either to let our agent do it or pull him out.' She sat down behind her desk. Like any government bureaucracy, the CIA dealt the cards and forced the card they wanted played. 'Well, I don't buy it,' she announced. 'Mazie, there must be something else we can do.'

Mazie half closed her eyes. 'Tell the agent to delay while we have NATO request an immediate conference with Rodonov. The goal is to get him out of Russia and out of harm's way. Once he's in Brussels, we tell him about the plot on his life.'

'What would be important enough,' the DCI asked, 'to get Rodonov to a meeting with NATO?'

'We create a situation,' Mazie replied, 'no Russian Minister of Defense can ignore. As part of General Bender's proposed security aide package to Poland, NATO wants Russian landing and overflight rights in Poland revoked. Rodonov comes to NATO to discuss the issue and gets some of their rights back. That way, he returns to Russia a hero and has been of some use to Vashin. It might be enough to save him.'

The DCI shook his head. 'I've read Bender's security proposal. Serick and the State Department won't buy it. It's dead in the water.'

'It is not dead until I say it is,' Turner said. 'Call Robert back for consultations.'

The Hill

Brian and Little Matt slammed into their room after lunch and threw their hats into their lockers. Because it was Saturday and there was no formation at the noon meal, they were in good spirits, looking forward to a weekend free of marching tours and little homework. Brian saw the flashing light on the telephone and hit the message button. It was from Dennis at the White House. 'Brian, your mother is going to be in New Mexico next weekend to dedicate the Amadis Escalante Museum. She'd like you to join her for the weekend. Please give me or your grandmother a call.'

'All right!' Brian said. 'I'm gone.'

'You'll need a special furlough,' Little Matt said. 'We got that biology test Tuesday. You flunk it and you're restricted.' He thought for a moment. 'Talk to the Trog.' Brian agreed and Little Matt called Zeth's room.

Zeth met them in the cadet lounge in the John Ross Thomas building. 'It's gonna take some doing to get out of here on a Friday,' she said. 'You'll need a chaperon.'

'The Secret Service?' Little Matt ventured.

'I got a better idea,' Brian said. 'I ask Maggot to come and his dad chaperons us.' They looked at one another, thinking the same thing. The idea of Brian's mom and Little Matt's father meeting was in the back of their minds, growing and taking shape. Zeth approached it like a matchmaker while the boys were more like neophyte wheeler-dealers, ready to test their conspiratorial wings. Brian smiled. 'And that way—'

'They meet!' the three chorused together. Brian and Little Matt did a high-five, slapping their hands together. They walked back to the boys' room, where Brian called the White House. He was put through immediately to Maura and jotted down the details. Then Little Matt called Pontowski, barely able to contain his excitement. Zeth sat at Little Matt's computer and composed a request letter as the two boys peered over her shoulder.

'Do you think we can do it?' Little Matt wondered.

'What about biology?' Brian asked.

'Hit the books,' Zeth told him, pulling the letter out of the printer. 'It's high speed next week. Don't get stuck with a D.' A 'D' was a demerit that could get them walking a tour over the weekend and restricted to post. 'Don't blow this one,' she cautioned, wishing she could go with them.

CHAPTER NINE

Near Ruidoso, New Mexico

Pontowski let the scenery wash over him as he drove west out of Roswell Friday afternoon. Like all aviators, he checked the sky and found the far horizon. It was a gorgeous fall day in the high desert, perfect for flying. For once, he was content to be earthbound. Behind him, Little Matt and Brian joked and exchanged good-natured insults, happy to escape NMMI for the weekend. Zeth Trogger sat in the front seat beside him, looking wistfully out the window, not joining in the banter.

The desert scrub gave way to low trees and more grass as they entered the Hondo Valley. Now the landscape conjured up an image from an earlier time. *So much like Israel*, he thought, *yet so different*. Suddenly, two F-16 Vipers flying low level crossed the road in front of them at 1,000 feet above the ground. Once clear of the road, the pilots slammed the jets back down to 300 feet and disappeared over a low hill. Now the memories were back, bursting through the floodgates of time.

He was back in the cockpit of an F-15E, flying low over the desert terrain of the Golan Heights. Then he was challenging Iraqi SAMs and two Su-27 Flankers. Ambler Furry was in his back seat, his voice a cool fountain in the heat of combat. Pontowski laughed to himself as Furry's words echoed in his memory. 'Shit-oh-dear. We ain't got no right wing.'

Somehow, Pontowski recovered the F-15 Eagle from the midair collision with Johar Adwan and made aviation history. Then he was on the beach near Haifa with Shoshana as they made their peace.

But like the land around him, it was different now. Time had tamed the raging torrent of loss and regret. All that remained was a gentle current of remembrance. The pain of Shoshana's death was gone.

'Dad,' Little Matt said, breaking his reverie, 'were those F-16s?'

'That's right. Did you see the CC on the tails? They were out of Cannon Air Force Base, the 27th Fighter Wing.'

'You could tell all that?' Brian asked. The boys started talking again, full of themselves and the day.

Pontowski glanced in the rearview mirror. Because of the unusually warm weather, the boys were still wearing their class A summer uniforms with short-sleeve white shirts and dress blue trousers. His son's voice was familiar, but resonated with a new-found confidence he had never heard before. *Matt's growing up fast*, Pontowski thought, unconsciously dropping the 'Little'. A twinge of sadness poked at him: his son was changing and he was missing it. Still, he liked what he was hearing, the give-and-take of boys growing to manhood. He glanced at Zeth Trogger. 'Are they always like this?' he asked.

'Unfortunately,' she replied. She gave him an encouraging smile. 'They'll grow out of it.'

'Grow out of what?' Brian asked.

'Sounding off like an idiot,' Zeth shot back. Brian grumbled an answer under his breath and the boys shut up. 'That's better,' Zeth said. 'General Pontowski, I want to thank you for inviting me to come.'

'Mrs McMasters suggested it,' Pontowski said. 'It sounded like a good idea to me.' He smiled. When Lenora McMasters decided on something she was a bulldog. Why send two cadets when three would give NMMI more of a presence in the national media?

Zeth looked out the window at the river. 'That's the Rio Hondo. You'll see a sign on your left in about five miles.' She paused. 'I know a back way to the ranch. It's cool.'

'Are you from around here?' Pontowski asked.

'I grew up here. My folks own the ranch next to the Escalantes. They live in Santa Fe now. They don't come here much any more but I love it.'

'Did you know Amadis Escalante?'

'Yes, sir.' She pointed to a dirt road on the left. 'Turn here.'

Pontowski slowed and turned on his blinker to warn the black sport utility vehicle behind them that he was turning. The personal radio the Secret Service had given him buzzed. As expected, the agent following them wanted to know about the change in route. He handed the radio to Zeth. 'You tell them where we're going.' She took the phone and talked to the agent. Pontowski listened and followed the route she described. They crossed the river on a low wooden bridge and followed a dirt road that led to an unused polo field. A tractor was mowing the weeds as the President's arrival party prepared a landing pad for her helicopter. They came to a dilapidated corral and stables where a horse pranced along the fence, greeting them. A roadblock was next, and Pontowski rolled to a stop.

A tall, heavily built man with dark hair approached the car. 'General Pontowski, I'm Special Agent Sanford with the Secret Service.'

Brian leaned forward, a rare smile on his face. 'Do you remember me, Mr Sanford?'

Sanford returned Brian's smile. At the White House, Brian had always called him by his first name, Chuck. He stuck a massive hand through the window and they shook hands. 'How could I forget? It's good to see you. How's it going?'

'All right, I guess. Any chance we can shoot some hoops?'

'You got it.'

Sanford turned to Pontowski. 'General, the compound is already sealed. You need to give us a heads-up call before anyone leaves. Otherwise, we'll stay out of your way.' He smiled at Zeth. 'Miss Trogger?' She nodded in answer. 'We need a photograph so everyone will know who you are. Security.' He held up a Polaroid camera. 'It would be better if you were standing.'

She frowned. 'I look terrible in pictures.'

'That's why they call her the Trog,' Brian said.

Zeth looked uncomfortable as she got out of the car. Away from the comforting routine of NMMI, she was very unsure of herself. Like the boys, she was wearing a summer class A uniform with pants. As usual her hair was pulled back into a tight braid and she looked quite severe. Sanford snapped a photo, then quickly took a second, and she got back into the car.

'When does my mom get here?' Brian asked.

'Later this evening,' Sanford answered. 'So you got plenty of time to settle in and look around.'

'Can we go for a horseback ride?' Zeth asked. 'We can go over to my folks' ranch. The ride is really cool.' Brian and Little Matt chimed in with enthusiasm.

'Sure,' Sanford said. 'I'll tell the stables to expect you.' He stood back and waved them through. 'Park on this side of the compound. We want to keep the cars out of sight.'

The Escalante ranchstead was controlled chaos as they parked and walked into the family compound. Secret Service and communications specialists were everywhere, preparing for Turner's arrival. Pontowski estimated there were at least forty people scurrying around. The compound itself was a cluster of adobe buildings with tile roofs arranged in a U shape. It was not the product of an architect or some master plan. Instead, the Escalante family had added buildings and rooms as needed over the years. At the back, buildings either touched or were connected by an adobe wall, presenting a fortress-like effect to the outside. But inside, the rooms and buildings all opened on to a well-tended flower garden and expanse of grass. A lanai-covered brick walkway tied everything together.

A very pretty woman Pontowski estimated to be in her late twenties showed them to their rooms. The boys were bunking together and Zeth was rooming with Sarah, the President's daughter, in the family quarters. The woman then led Pontowski through the garden to his room at the far end of the compound. It was not large, maybe twelve feet on a side. An easy chair faced a fireplace and a bed was tucked into the corner. He looked around. 'Very nice,' he said. An oil painting of an old woman hung over the fireplace and caught his attention. 'Is that by Amadis Escalante?'

The woman smiled at him. 'Oh, yes. Most everything here is.' He dumped his bag on the bed. 'Oh dear,' she said, 'the bed is too small for you. I'll switch you with someone else.'

'Not to worry,' Pontowski said. 'I like the room. I'll just sleep at an angle.'

She touched his arm and gave him a grateful look. 'Well, if you need anything else—' Her voice trailed off.

He gave her a smile and shook his head. She gave her hair a pretty toss and repeated her offer, making it much more obvious. *Very pretty*, he thought, watching her leave. *But what is she thinking of? The Secret Service probably has the place wired for sound.* He changed into jeans and cowboy boots before wandering outside and into the garden.

The boys charged out of their room and ran across the grass. 'There's a problem,' Little Matt called. 'They only have five horses.'

'Right,' Pontowski said. 'Brian can only go if two agents go along and Zeth knows the way. So that only leaves one extra horse. Why don't you go and I'll sack out for a while.'

'Thanks,' Brian and Little Matt said, echoing each other.

Pontowski watched them march off together. They were a far cry from the boys their age he saw in Kansas City and Warrensburg. 'Great kids,' Chuck Sanford said from behind him.

'I thought you were going with them.'

'Nope,' Sanford replied. 'I can't ride. In fact, last time I got near a horse, it bit me.'

'Brian obviously likes you.'

'I used to shoot some basketball with him and General Bender in the White House gym.'

'You know the general?'

'Oh, yeah. I was with him when the Vice-President was shot.'

'Wasn't an agent killed?'

'My partner, Wayne Adams.' Sanford pulled into himself, recalling President Turner's first six months in office. 'It was a crazy time and everything was coming apart. Bender was like a rock.' He looked at Pontowski, coming to the reason for the conversation. 'Sir, Maura O'Keith asked me to talk to you. I think you know why Brian is at NMMI. But do you know about the heat your son is taking because of him?' Pontowski shook his head. 'Apparently, Brian shot off his mouth about some upper classman. So the upper classman's buddies did a little hazing on your son in retaliation.'

'What did the Secret Service do?' Pontowski asked.

Sanford shook his head. 'Nothing. We're under orders only to intervene if it involves Brian's safety. Otherwise, we just go with the flow and let the place run itself. In this particular case, Brian called Zeth and she stopped the hazing before it really got off the ground.'

Pontowski remembered the boys' reaction at the soccer game when Zeth had drilled the other cadet with a well-placed shot. 'Does this have anything to do with her tuning that cadet in the soccer game?'

'He was the ringleader,' Sanford answered. 'She's a pretty gutsy girl.'

'Indeed she is.' Pontowski thought for a moment. 'Is my son in any real danger because he's Brian's roommate?'

'We don't think so,' Sanford answered.

'Then why am I worried?' Pontowski said.

'Maybe you should talk to the President about it.' Pontowski gave a little nod and said he would do that. *That will be an interesting conversation,* Sanford thought.

Maura O'Keith made the introductions and studied her daughter's face as she shook hands with Pontowski. She listened as they made small talk about the boys, who were still out riding with Zeth. 'Sarah,' Maura said, 'scat. We need to have a private conversation.'

'You're going to talk about Brian,' Sarah said. 'Why can't I stay and defend him?'

Maddy laughed. 'Beat it, little Miss Jurisprudence.' Sarah flounced out of the room in a huff. 'Maura tells me you're worried about Brian and your son being roommates,' Maddy said.

'Somewhat,' Pontowski replied. They fell into a relaxed discussion about the hazing incident, and he was surprised how easy it was to talk to her. She seemed more like a mother than the President of the United States. He had always thought of her as being bigger. Then it hit him. Hard. Up close and personal, Maddy Turner was a captivating woman, far exceeding her public image. And he liked the way she turned her head to look at him.

'I can have the Secret Service take a more active role. It won't happen again.'

'I don't think that's necessary. Zeth nipped it in the bud before it got started. If we pursue it, General McMasters will have to dismiss the ringleaders. The cadets will see that as punishment for something that didn't really happen and that will create a backlash in the Corps. I'm not so sure we want that. Little Matt hasn't mentioned it and he's on top of the world right now. So no harm, no foul. Besides, Zeth may have solved the problem and that's what leadership is all about.' He gave Maddy his best lopsided grin. 'You should have seen her deck the ringleader in the soccer game.'

They talked for a few more minutes then Maddy had to end it, pleading the press of other business. Pontowski stood and again they shook hands. Maura concentrated on her daughter's face as he left. 'Well?' she asked.

'I'm going to make Agent Sanford the lead agent at NMMI and tell him to keep an eye on Pontowski's son.'

'Not that,' Maura said. 'Him.'

'Whatever are you talking about, Mother?'

★　★　★

The boys trailed along with the presidential party as they toured the Amadis Escalante Museum for the Arts prior to the dedication ceremony on Saturday morning. 'Hey, Maggot,' Brian muttered, 'we gotta get out of here.'

'With the Trog on duty?' Little Matt replied. 'Give it up.' The mention of Zeth was enough to kill any thought of escaping, and they hurried to catch up. Thankfully, the dedication ceremony was well organized and lasted only forty minutes. The discipline of NMMI paid off and the boys had no trouble playing their assigned roles in front of the TV cameras covering the event. Afterwards, they marked time at the reception and plotted what they would do at the ranch.

'Where's the Trog?' Brian wondered.

They roamed the room until they found her with Pontowski. When Little Matt saw the woman with them, he started to hurry. Then he stopped and straightened his uniform. 'How do I look?' he asked.

'Locked up,' Brian told him. 'What's the big deal?'

Little Matt didn't answer as he marched purposefully toward his father and Samantha Darnell. 'Hello, Sam,' he said. Then he was in her arms, no longer the well-turned-out cadet but a fourteen-year-old boy, safe with a woman who loved him.

Sam held him at arm's length and took him in. 'You've changed,' she announced. 'You're not Little Matt any more.' Matthew Pontowski IV drew himself up and returned her smile. It was true, he was no longer Little Matt.

'I call him Maggot,' Brian said, eager to join the conversation.

Sam laughed. 'What a terrible nickname.'

'I don't mind,' Matt said. 'It seems to fit.'

Sam extended her hand to Brian. 'I've heard all about you. I'm Sam Darnell.'

Brian fell back on his training as a cadet and shook hands with her. 'Pleased to meet you, ma'am.' He wanted to say something witty, but words escaped him.

Across the room, Maddy spoke to Maura and Dennis. 'Who's the woman with Brian and General Pontowski?'

'She *is* stunning,' Maura said.

'That would be Samantha Darnell,' Dennis said. 'She's a director with CNC-TV and is here covering the dedication. At one time she was, you might say, the significant other in General Pontowski's life. But they've been separated for some time now.'

'Oh, I see.' Maddy turned to meet more local dignitaries.

Sarah tugged at her grandmother's hand. 'What's the matter with Mom?'

'Nothing, Little Miss Nosy.'

'Why am I always Little Miss this or that?'

'Because you're growing up too fast.'

Maura O'Keith was coming out of the ladies' room when she saw Zeth watching TV in the museum's visitors' lounge. The sound of a reporter's voice describing the dedication ceremony carried across the small room. TV coverage was so much a part of Maura's life that, normally, she paid no attention. But judging by Zeth's reaction, something was wrong. She sat down beside the girl and watched the news clip. It was good coverage and Maddy was at her best. But Zeth was clearly upset. 'Did I miss something?' Maura asked.

Zeth shook her head, on the verge of tears. 'I saw myself on TV. I *am* a trog.'

Maura examined the girl's face and turned her chin from side to side, examining her hair. She loosened Zeth's French braid and let her hair fall. 'Is a trog some new word or just how you feel about yourself?' Zeth didn't answer. 'Stand up. Let me look at you.' Zeth did as she ordered. 'Yes,' Maura murmured, examining her uniform and lack of makeup. Then she asked, 'Would you like to go shopping with me this afternoon?'

'I don't have any money,' Zeth answered.

'Not to worry,' Maura answered. 'Do you mind if Sarah comes along?'

Brian and Matt were wearing blue blazers and dark gray trousers for the dinner that culminated Saturday's activities. Since it was a political fundraiser where the guests paid 500 dollars a plate for the privilege of eating with the President, they were not in uniform. 'Hey, Maggot, where's the Trog?' Brian asked, 'I haven't seen her since lunch.'

'I think she went shopping with your grandmother and Sarah,' Matt replied. They wandered outside to wait for everyone to gather for the trip to Ruidoso Downs Jockey Club where the dinner would be held.

Pontowski joined them, also wearing a blue blazer and gray slacks. 'It looks like we all have the same uniform,' he said. 'Wow,' he muttered, looking over their heads. The boys turned and were speechless. Zeth stood in the doorway. Her hair tumbled to her shoulders and shimmered in the soft light. Maura had applied a light makeup so skillfully that it blended perfectly with her smooth complexion and gave her a radiant glow. She was wearing a simple dress with spaghetti straps and a full skirt that ended just above her knees. A white shawl was draped over her bare shoulders.

'Trog?' Brian and Matt said in unison, not believing what they were seeing.

'If you snooze, you lose,' Pontowski murmured. He stepped around the boys and extended an arm. 'May I?' She took his arm and he escorted her down the walk to the waiting cars.

The boys were still in a confused state when they returned from dinner at the Jockey Club. They had been pushed aside as every young man, and a few not so young, clustered around Zeth at the reception. One young man, a tall cadet from the Air Force Academy, had talked to the boys and quizzed them about her. Then, using his inside knowledge, he moved in. Within a very short time, he had totally captured her attention. She was still glowing from it all when she joined them. 'Okay, wussies,' she said, deciding to let them back into her good graces. 'It's poker time. I'll find some cards and chips. Meet me in the kitchen.'

'I don't know how to play poker,' Matt protested.

'It's about time you learned,' Pontowski said.

'Great,' Brian moaned. 'Now she's a card shark.'

'Can I play too?' Sarah asked.

'Until your bedtime,' Maura replied, checking her watch. She stood up. 'I'll keep things under control.' She walked after the kids, leaving Pontowski and Maddy alone.

Pontowski settled into a leather easy chair near the fire. 'Is it like this every day?' he asked. Maddy gave a little laugh, low and musical, and sank into the chair next to him. She kicked off her shoes and stretched her legs to the fire.

'This was an easy one,' she replied. 'Probably because it was something I wanted to do.' She turned to look at him and, as before, the way she did it captivated him. 'I was fifteen when I met Amadis,' she explained. She looked into the fire and remembered. 'She had painted a portrait of an old woman. I thought the model had to be at least eighty years old. Amadis said she was only forty-seven. Can you believe that? I'm forty-seven now. That painting really touched me.'

'I think,' Pontowski said very slowly, 'that it's hanging in my room.'

'It can't be.'

'It's an easy thing to check.'

Without a word, Maddy stood and, without bothering to put on her shoes, followed him into the cool night air.

A Secret Service agent standing post in the garden spoke into the whisper microphone under the cuff of his black windbreaker. 'Magic is moving.' Inside the temporary command post, a light flashed on a control panel, tracing Turner's path as she moved down the garden. Once she and Pontowski were out of earshot, the agent filled in the details. 'Magic is with Pontowski and heading in the direction of his room. She's not wearing shoes.'

One of the agents on duty in the command post studied the control panel. 'Is our commander-in-chief fraternizing with one of the troops?' he asked, deadpan.

'Don't go there,' Chuck Sanford ordered.

*   *   *

'I love desert nights,' Maddy said as they approached his room. He held the door open and turned on the light. A fire had been built in the fireplace and the room was too warm. He left the door open. She stood in front of the mantel and gazed at the portrait. 'That's it,' she said. 'But I don't remember it being so small.'

'When you're young,' Pontowski said, 'emotions make things bigger.' He stood beside her; they were almost touching. On impulse he stepped up to the fireplace and took the painting down, bringing it back to her. 'It is small,' he said.

She held the painting and stroked the canvas. 'Her brush strokes were so delicate.' She handed it back to him.

'There's something taped to the back,' Pontowski said. He turned the painting around for her to see. 'I think this is for you,' he said, peeling off an envelope. Bold lettering was scrawled across the face.

For Maddy Turner

Turner carefully broke the seal and pulled out a card. On one side was a bill of sale made out to her. She turned it over.

Always listen with your heart
Amadis Escalante

'The date,' Maddy said. 'It's when I was fifteen.' She looked at Pontowski. 'She knew. Even then, she knew.'

Pontowski examined the card and the envelope. 'Look at the date on the envelope. It's the day before you were sworn in as Vice-President.'

'Why did she backdate the bill of sale?'

'I think,' Pontowski said slowly, 'she's telling you she remembers and she wants you to have the painting. By backdating the bill of sale to before you were Vice-President, she arranged it so you don't have to turn it over to the Smithsonian or the Treasury Department.'

'I can't keep it.' Then his words struck home. 'You said "she's telling you she remembers" like she's still alive.'

Pontowski handed her the painting. 'She is. In this.' Their hands touched and, for a reason he did not comprehend, he leaned forward and kissed her. It was a light kiss, little more than a brushing of lips. But for a moment they lingered. 'Oh,' she whispered. Then she kissed him back, this time for much longer. 'I need to get back and tuck Sarah in,' she said finally, drawing away and smiling at him. He had seen her smile many times on TV but this was different. She glowed with a radiance no camera could capture and it was meant for him alone. It captivated him and yet he was lost.

Pontowski followed her out of the room, turning off the light but leaving the door open. Another Secret Service agent dutifully reported her movements to the command post.

Sunday's breakfast was a family affair. Sarah was bright and cheery while the boys and Zeth were still half asleep from their late-night poker session. Maura was on her second cup of coffee and finally coming alert. Maddy sat at one corner of the table, elbows resting on a dinner mat while her hands cupped a steaming mug of coffee. Pontowski was sitting at the far corner, and occasionally he would glance at her. Their eyes met twice and a little smile played at the corner of her lips. 'Well,' she said finally, 'I'm going for a ride. Who's coming?'

Matt groaned loudly, claiming he wanted to sack out, and Brian said he was going to 'shoot some hoops'. Sarah glanced around the table. 'I've got homework. Zeth and General Pontowski can go.' She gave Zeth a meaningful look.

Zeth understood. 'I've got homework too,' she said. 'We can do it together, if you want.' That decided it, and Pontowski stood up, waiting for Maddy. He followed her outside.

'We need to talk,' Maura said before the boys could escape. She walked to the door leading into the kitchen and called. 'Dennis, we need you.'

Maddy's personal assistant joined them and sat down. He folded his hands in front of him on the table and spoke in a smooth and quiet voice. 'As you know, everything President Turner does is news and she may be photographed riding with General Pontowski. The media will try to blow it up into some big romance because they were seen alone.'

'Big deal,' Brian snorted. 'They're not alone. What about the Secret Service? They'll be with them.'

'I assure you,' Dennis insisted, 'the Secret Service won't be in the photo. The reason I'm bringing this up is to warn you that you might be asked questions by reporters or people who will sell what you say to the press.'

'So what should we say?' This from Matt.

'The truth,' Dennis said. 'But don't embellish it, don't make anything out of it. General Pontowski was here as your chaperon and they went for a horseback ride. That's all there is.'

'That's the truth,' Matt said.

'Yeah,' Brian added. 'They're hardly talking and I don't think they even like each other.'

Part Two

CHAPTER TEN

St Petersburg, Russia

Vashin was pleased. The banquet room in the Hermitage shimmered with the elegance and grandeur of Czarist Russia. The champagne and caviar were the best the world could produce, and even an acknowledged wine connoisseur representing a consortium of French banks raved over the vintage wine flowing freely. The chefs flown in for the event had outdone themselves. The dinner was a triumph. Not that he was surprised, not after the dream.

It was still crystal clear. He was floating in clouds and suddenly there was a break in the weather. Below him was St Petersburg and the Hermitage. When he mentioned the dream to Geraldine, she became very serious and told him not to ignore it. It had to mean something. Men like Vashin had dreams for a reason. He believed her and moved the dinner to the Hermitage.

But without doubt, Geraldine was the star of the evening. Vashin had never seen this side of her, confident and regal, the perfect hostess to charm the fourteen bankers who had accepted his invitation to come to Russia. Half of them wanted to sleep with her and the American from Chicago wanted to marry her. For a moment, Vashin considered that possibility for himself. But just as quickly, he rejected it. Better to keep his wife and maintain the image of a responsible husband and father of four children.

Geraldine herded the bankers into the Czar's study for cigars and cognac. It was the final act. Vashin had studied the dossiers and ranked them in terms of resistance. The Swiss banker would be the hardest to convince, the Chinese the easiest. But if Geraldine was right, every one of these men could be bought. It was simply a matter of approaching them in the right way. He followed her into the smaller and much more intimate study and stood by the fireplace. He waited for the men to become comfortable. If all other inducements failed, there were the gifts.

He started to speak in Russian as Geraldine translated into English, a language the bankers understood. He was certain the message behind his words was equally clear. 'Again, thank you for coming.' Each had been flown in separately on a private jet. 'I hope you have enjoyed your visit.' Geraldine had been meticulous in pandering to their individual interests and needs. 'But all good things must come to an end.' It was time to talk business.

The carrot came first. 'As you know, my country is reaching out to the world in new endeavors.' The Russian Mafiya was dominating the drugs trade. 'Fortunately, we are achieving some success.' The money was flowing in in obscene amounts. 'Now we must direct the fruits of our labor into new investments.' We need to launder the money. 'But this is beyond our field of expertise.' We want you to do it for us. 'What we need are men of your stature and business acumen to guide us through the intricacies of investment opportunities in your countries.' Can you bribe the politicians? 'Together, we can all benefit in this combined endeavor and we are most generous in rewarding our friends and allies.' You're in for a hefty percentage if you come on board.

The Swiss banker swirled his cognac before taking a sip. 'Herr Vashin, your proposal is most interesting, certainly worthy of my colleagues' consideration. But we have heard many stories about the dangers of doing business in your new Russia.'

Vashin smiled, trying to be reassuring. 'It is true that, in a manner of speaking, a few Russians have lost their heads'

– a nervous titter worked its way around the room – 'in ill-timed ventures. But they were not businessmen and that was in the past. We are now dealing with a higher level of sophistication.'

The American banker from Chicago guffawed. 'Talk about happy horseshit—' A warning look from Geraldine cut him off.

Instead of translating the remark verbatim, she said, 'They're a little skeptical.'

The stick came next. 'Please,' Vashin said, 'I know you must all think about it and confer with your principals. We do understand your reluctance to join in a new endeavor with an untried partner. If you choose not to participate, there will be no hard feelings, only the hope that we can do business in the future. For now, it is more important that we gain your goodwill. As a remembrance of your visit with us, may I offer some gifts for you and your families?'

On cue, Geraldine threw open the double doors and a string of waiters entered. Some were pushing carts laden with gifts, others carrying paintings or priceless icons. Each banker was first presented with a Fabergé egg for his wife or, as the case required, his mistress. The gifts kept coming, each one carrying an inscribed gold tag with the name of the man's children and closest living relatives.

A deathly silence ruled the room. The gifts announced that Vashin knew where, and how, they lived.

The Swiss banker was the first to recover. 'These are most flattering and I cannot thank you enough. We will be talking in the very near future.' The others rapidly agreed and the evening was over. They had much to think about.

The German banker was the last to leave. He joined Vashin by the fire and spoke in Russian. 'Chancellor Gunder sends his regards and asks if you would consider meeting with his representative to discuss matters of mutual interest.'

'I would be honored,' Vashin replied.

The White House

Madeline Turner glanced at the carriage clock on the mantel. It was 7.20 a.m. and she was alone in her office in the residence on the second floor. She tried to concentrate on the Quadrennial Defense Review in her lap but the combination of bureaucratic and military jargon defeated her. *I need an interpreter for this*, she thought. Felipe, her favorite steward, poured her another cup of coffee. She took a sip, enjoying the aroma, as she waited for her kitchen cabinet to arrive for breakfast.

Noreen will be first. Noreen Coker was the most direct of the four friends who were her personal advisors and support group. She read another page of the Quadrennial Defense Review and dropped it in a briefcase in frustration. *I'm missing something here.* A knock at the door, a tactful pause, and Noreen entered. Turner smiled. 'I'm glad you're early. We need to talk.'

The tall African-American congresswoman from Los Angeles collapsed into an overstuffed chair. 'For God's sake, coffee. No normal human being gets up at this hour.' Felipe handed her a steaming cup.

'Thank you, Felipe. That will be all.' The steward withdrew, leaving them alone. Turner studied her friend. 'Are you putting on weight?'

An unhappy nod from Noreen. 'Is it obvious?'

'A man?'

Another nod. 'He's no good but he does stir my bones.'

'I hope that's all he's stirring.' Turner wanted to say more but Noreen knew the rules in Washington. Women politicians had to be masters of the double standard. What a male politician could get away with was a career-breaker for a woman. 'I'm glad you're early. There's something we need to discuss. I'm thinking of running for reelection.'

Somewhere deep in Noreen a switch turned and the consummate political professional emerged. She was no longer the flashy congresswoman who represented a poverty-stricken district but the shrewd Washington insider. 'I'm not surprised. You've got the political base to capture the nomination. But most incumbents do, unless they're total idiots. Most of the press loves you but a few of the bastards run with Leland and his pack. We can handle them. It's too early to announce and you need to play coy for a while, at least until after the congressional elections next month, perhaps until after the first of the year. We've got to keep the opposition guessing for as long as possible. Otherwise, they'll get organized and start raising money. Finances will be a problem for us. We'll need someone with muscle.'

'I know. I was thinking of bringing Patrick in.' Patrick Flannery Shaw was Turner's former mentor and chief of staff who had fallen from grace and had been banished to the basement of the White House.

'Don't stand too close to that man.'

Turner didn't answer. But she knew the truth of it. The ugly fact of life in national politics was the amount of money needed to mount a successful presidential campaign. Raising it was not the problem. Keeping it at arm's length was. Shaw would do the dirty work and be the lightning rod drawing the anger of her opponents. And the more successful her campaign, the stronger the attack. After the election he would have to disappear into the background or she would dump him. Turner glanced at the clock. 'The others should be here.' She rose and led the way into the dining room where her kitchen cabinet gathered for breakfast.

'Maura will be against it,' Noreen cautioned. 'She hates this place.' The switch moved and the façade was back in place. 'Girl, you'd think I'd know better than to mess with a man at my age.'

Joe Litton, the press secretary, stood aside as Madeline Turner took the podium in the press briefing room. Everyone was standing and applauding, and even Sam Donaldson had exchanged his sharklike grin for a warm smile. As the senior correspondent, Donaldson was the dean of the press corps and sat front and center. 'Madame President,' he said, 'the pictures of you horseback riding with Brigadier General Matthew Pontowski have received wide coverage. Is there some romantic interest here?'

For a moment, the room was absolutely silent. Donaldson was not one of Turner's tame reporters on whom she could rely to spin her side of the story. She gave him a little smile. 'Not that I'm aware of, Sam.'

'So should we assume you're horse fanciers?'

'Well, you could assume that, but we're not. Brian and General Pontowski's son are roommates at NMMI. We have a common interest as concerned parents. Sam, you graduated from there. You know how difficult the freshman year is.'

Donaldson looked down as if caught up in his own memories. Elizabeth Gordon from CNC-TV was next. She was one of Turner's tame reporters. 'Madame President, is it true that Amadis Escalante willed you one of her paintings?'

'Not exactly willed,' Turner replied. 'There is some confusion about whether it's a gift or not. I was quite moved by the thought and the painting. For the time being, it's hanging in my bedroom. But after I leave the White House, it will be sent to the Smithsonian as part of the national collection.'

Her answer satisfied the reporters and they turned to the hard questions about the economy, defense, and public education. The press secretary leaned against the side wall and relaxed. It was going to be a good day.

The black limousine took the long way from Foggy Bottom to the White House. Normally, the drive from the State Department lasted only a few minutes. But Stephan Serick, the Secretary of State, needed the time to abuse his two deputies. His hands twisted in a vain attempt to strangle his cane. 'The President knew about Bender's security aide package before I did. Why?'

'We're still staffing it,' the head of the European desk said. 'It arrived on my desk less than two weeks ago.'

Serick scowled, but the man was right. Two weeks was not even time for the head of a desk to clear his throat, much less digest and forward a cable from an ambassador. Two months was more reasonable. 'Unfortunately,' Serick grumbled, 'you do not have to discuss it with the President. I do.'

'Bender has overstepped his bounds,' the under-secretary said. 'Ambassadors do not initiate major policy proposals.'

Serick almost shouted. 'This one has.' His heavy jowls quivered and his Latvian accent grew thick. 'How did she learn about it?' From his glare, the two professional diplomats knew they were in trouble.

'Not from State,' the under-secretary said. 'Turner recalled him for discussions and the National Security Advisor talked to him when he arrived.' Mazie Kamigami Hazelton was a much-hated person in the State Department, referred to only by her title, never her name.

'And what is our position on this so-called security aide package?' Serick asked.

Two heads shook as one. State didn't have a clue.

The limousine went through the southwest appointment gate and deposited Serick at the west entrance to the West Wing. A Marine guard opened the door and Serick stumped into the White House, his right hand clenching his cane, still trying to strangle it. Dennis was waiting for him and led him into the Oval Office.

'Good afternoon, Madame President,' Serick said. He nodded at the other members of the President's National Security Advisory Group and sat down next to Sam Kennett, the Vice-President. He nodded at Bender and Mazie. As usual, the DCI did not even look up to acknowledge his presence. Richard Parrish, Turner's chief of staff, was sitting against the back wall.

Turner gave Bender a little half-smile. 'Well, Robert, I believe your security aide proposal has ruffled some feathers.'

'I must apologize,' Serick said. 'I haven't had a chance to review it.' He muttered something about 'the press of other business'.

Turner enjoyed watching Serick squirm. 'Robert, can you summarize the high points?'

'Basically, it's a two-part package. We provide the Poles with the ability to create an FBI-type organization. Second, through the Defense Security Assistance Agency and the NATO connection, we upgrade the Polish Air Force.'

Serick grumped. 'And the desired results?'

'The goal,' Bender explained, 'is to give the Poles the capability to combat organized crime and to control their own airspace.'

'The first I understand,' Serick said. 'But why the concern over the control of airspace?'

'Because the Russian Mafiya leapfrogs at will around and through Poland using air transport. It's a fast, efficient way to move drugs and people, and it avoids ground interdiction. You can't arrest them unless you get your hands on them.'

Serick stood up and stomped around the room. 'This is too simple and ill conceived. Besides, I am more concerned with what the Germans are doing.'

'I haven't seen any recent intelligence in the President's Daily Brief about that,' Turner said.

The DCI coughed for attention. 'We received a report this morning about a high-level meeting in St Petersburg between Mikhail Vashin and a group of foreign bankers. The Germans invited Vashin to a follow-up meeting with Chancellor Gunder. My analysts think they're reconciling areas of conflict.'

Mazie was worried. 'Are we seeing a new alliance?'

Turner rocked gently in her chair as the discussion went around the room. As always, Serick was at his best when playing balance-of-power diplomacy, but this time something felt wrong, out of kilter. She interrupted them. 'What do we need to implement Robert's proposal?' It was her way of telling them she had made a decision.

'We already have the funding,' Kennett said.

Serick muttered, 'By what stretch of the imagination?'

'Discretionary funding in the Omnibus Crime bill and under Foreign Military Sales to NATO,' Kennett replied.

'I'll need two project officers to manage the programs,' Bender added. 'Someone from DOJ and someone from Defense.'

Serick's face turned three shades of mottled red. He was losing control. 'Madame President, I must protest. An embassy is an extension of your diplomatic arm, not an action agency.'

'Does the CIA concur with that statement?' Mazie asked

sweetly, looking directly at the DCI. He tried to become invisible and not answer the question. As it did in many countries, the CIA maintained a formidable presence in Warsaw – the entire third floor of the United States embassy was occupied by the Agency.

Turner stood and walked to the front of her desk. The meeting was almost over. 'Robert, work with Richard. He'll get whoever you need from DOJ and Defense. Stephan, please keep Mazie informed from now on so we can react in a timely manner. Any questions?' There weren't any and they all stood to leave. 'Robert, please stay a moment.'

Serick led the way out, stamping his cane in frustration. A major policy decision had been shoved down his throat.

'There goes one angry man,' Richard Parrish said.

'He'll get over it,' Turner replied. 'Robert, are you familiar with the latest Quadrennial Defense Review?'

'I helped write it.'

'Please tell me exactly what it means.'

Bender took a deep breath. 'Essentially it's a question of readiness. Contrary to the official line, combat readiness is going down at an alarming rate. Our current state of readiness is at the lowest it's been since before the Korean War in 1950.'

'But the Secretary of Defense tells me we are at an all-time high. I haven't heard a single general speak out in disagreement. Least of all you.'

'The Secretary of Defense is telling you what he thinks you want to hear. I was the vice-chief of staff of the Air Force and owed my loyalty to the chief of staff who, in turn, owed his loyalty to the chairman of the JCS. We've had some frank, even brutal, discussions about readiness. But when all is said and the decision made, we speak as one voice. As a subordinate officer, I could not contradict the JCS.'

'But you are now.'

'I'm no longer in that chain of command and you asked me a direct question.'

'If I had appointed you chairman of the JCS, would you have gone against the Secretary of Defense?'

'Absolutely. Or I would have resigned if he didn't let me

tell you the—' He stopped in mid-sentence. He had almost said 'tell you the truth'.

Clearly upset, Turner paced back and forth. 'Our poor state of readiness, is it a question of money?'

'Partially, but not totally.'

'What are the most critical issues I need to know?'

'Speaking just for the Air Force, three come to mind. First, strategic airlift is broken. We need to double the size of the C-17 fleet and supplement it with an equal number of tactical cargo planes similar to the C-130. Then we need to take a hard look at long-range aviation.' He paused, searching for the right words.

'And the third issue?'

He bit the bullet. 'Madame President, women are in the military to stay but—' His voice trailed off.

'Go on.'

'We need to reevaluate their role in combat before it's too late.'

Bender and Parrish braced themselves for her explosion. But it didn't come. Instead she issued a very quiet 'Why?'

'We've got problems integrating women into combat specialities. Because of the political climate, a commander will be crucified if he, or she, even suggests there might be something wrong. How can we solve a problem we can't talk about?'

Turner steepled her fingers and looked at the painting of Thomas Jefferson over the fireplace. Her silence was actually very brief but seemed to last a lifetime. 'Well, I did ask the question.' Again, silence. Then she said, 'Robert, we're having a dinner party next week. Can you and Nancy make it?'

'We'd be delighted, Madame President.'

'Always so formal. Will it ever be Maddy?'

'Please forgive me, Madame President. It's just my nature.'

Turner smiled. 'Then until next week.' She settled into her chair and watched him leave. 'My unbending Bender,' she murmured.

Dennis came through the door for the day's wrap-up. 'Senator Leland is stirring the pot again.'

'I wish that man would go away,' Turner muttered. 'What's he up to now?'

'He's filed a congressional enquiry with the Pentagon and the FAA on behalf of Mr Daniel Beason. It involves the death of his son in an air-show accident.'

'Leland and Beason in the same bed is bad news,' Parrish said.

Turner frowned. 'Any fallout for us?'

'There shouldn't be,' Parrish answered. 'But I'll check into it.'

'Don't. Let the system handle it. Leland will see any interest on our part as interference.' She spun around in her chair and gazed out the window. The sun was setting and the President's Park was encased in long shadows. 'Dennis, I've invited Robert and his wife to the party next week. Please take care of it.' She turned around. 'And I want to invite General Matthew Pontowski to sit at my table.'

'Ah, Madame President,' Parrish stammered. 'After the press conference today, would that be wise?'

'It's time to give poor Clarence a break,' she answered. Justice Clarence Wood was a widowed Supreme Court justice who served as Turner's companion for functions that required an escort.

Parrish and Dennis exchanged worried glances.

The Hill

'The Trog just walked in,' Brian said. He and Matt were standing in the new cadet side of the Post Exchange in John Ross Thomas Hall sipping Cokes. Until they were yearlings, they had to stand at the high tables in the section reserved for new cadets. But at least they were safe from upper classmen. Zeth looked at them but said nothing and walked down the short flight of stairs to the lounge.

'Something's buggin' her,' Matt said.

A rare look of concern crossed Brian's face. 'Yeah.' Then he reverted to his norm. 'So who gives a shit?'

'I guess I do.' Matt sucked at his straw and drained his Coke. He picked up his backpack and followed her.

'Wait a minute,' Brian said. 'I'll go with you.' He dumped his Coke in the trash can and trotted down the stairs after Matt. They found Zeth at a small desk against a wall. She stared at a test paper. From four steps away they could see the big red F emblazoned on the front page. 'You blow a big one?' Brian asked.

Zeth nodded. 'It doesn't make sense. I spend more time studying chemistry than all my other classes together and I still blow it.'

Brian sat down opposite her and looked at the test. He didn't understand a word of it and handed it to Matt. 'Hey, Maggot,' he said, enjoying the chance to rag her, 'this looks like a piece of cake to me.'

Matt read the questions. 'Carbon compounds is tough.'

'Tell me,' Zeth said. 'This is my second shot at chemistry. If I don't make it this time—' She stopped. There was no grade inflation at NMMI and approximately twenty cadets a year flunked out for grades.

'Take biology or geology,' Brian said. 'They're easier.' Then he relented. 'That's what I'm doing.'

'I'm not a total wuss,' she said.

Something in her voice reached Brian. 'Then you gotta go for it. Look, why don't you let Maggot tutor you? He's getting me through biology. He knows all about this—' He almost said 'shit'.

Zeth looked at Matt. 'You do?'

Embarrassed, Matt shifted his weight from foot to foot. 'Yeah, I guess so. It just sorta comes naturally.'

Brian got up and shoved Matt into his chair. 'It won't hurt to give it a try.' He picked up his backpack and headed out the door. He was always a little uncomfortable in the formal lounge. Then he reconsidered and went back inside. He dragged a chair up beside Zeth and sat down, joining in the study session.

'The simplest organic compounds are called *hydrocarbons*,' Matt began, listing a sequence of formulas. 'Now watch how they're related.'

Chuck Sanford, the Secret Service agent on duty, sat behind the desk with NMMI's hostess, the trim and proper lady responsible for supervising the lounge and teaching cadets the social graces. 'Well, I'll be,' he muttered, watching the three cadets.

'Mr Turner is turning into a gentleman,' the hostess pronounced. 'I've seen it happen before.'

CHAPTER ELEVEN

The White House

The blue Air Force staff car joined the line of vehicles pulling up to the White House. The driver was nervous, and she kept glancing in the rearview mirror to check on her passenger. Pontowski sympathized with what the young airman was going through. 'Your first time?'

'At night, yes, sir.' The car jerked to a stop. A Marine guard opened the door and Pontowski got out. Automatically, he gave the short jacket of his dark blue formal uniform a tug. 'Your hat, sir,' the driver said, handing him his wheel hat.

'Thank you,' Pontowski replied, tucking the hat under his arm for the short walk inside. 'I always feel like a penguin in this outfit.'

'You look great, sir,' the driver said, confirming the truth of it. The mess dress uniform fitted him perfectly, and he looked as if he had stepped out of an Air Force recruiting poster.

Dennis was waiting for him. 'General Pontowski, this way, please.' Instead of going up the steps with the other guests, Dennis led the way to the second-floor residence. 'You'll escort the President down the main staircase,' he said. 'At the bottom landing, stand aside and the President will proceed with the honor guard. An aide will take you to the State Dining Room where she will join you at the head table.'

Pontowski gave a low laugh. 'Been there, done that.'

Dennis recovered nicely. 'Ah, yes. When your grandfather was President. I doubt that much has changed.' He held open the door and Pontowski entered the family quarters. The old memories came rushing back, and for a moment he was a young second lieutenant and his grandfather was the President of the United States. He smiled when he saw his grandmother's favorite chair by the fireplace. The elegant and kind woman called Tosh had really raised him after the death of his parents. Then he saw it. His grandfather's portrait hung over the fireplace.

'The likeness is startling,' Maura said from behind him. 'He was a handsome man.' Pontowski turned around. 'No hugs,' she declared. 'You'll ruin the get-up.' Then she hugged him anyway. 'Ouch. Those medals are sharp. What are they for?'

He pointed to the Distinguished Flying Cross. 'Well, this one is because my group had forty percent fewer cavities and—'

She touched another medal, interrupting him. 'That's a Purple Heart, isn't it?'

'I had a bad day.'

'Please, be serious.'

'Must I?'

'Yes, Matt, you must. Maddy likes you, more than she's willing to admit. Sarah adores you and Brian . . . well, let's just say you're the good example he needs in his life.'

'But this is Washington,' Pontowski pointed out, 'and there are no rules for the first woman president. Especially a widow.' His grandfather had taught him well.

'She can be hurt,' Maura murmured, not thinking at all of Washington and its immortal politicians and bureaucrats who treated presidents as temporary interlopers on their terrain.

The door opened and Maddy walked in with a beaming Sarah. 'Wow,' Pontowski managed. It was a classic understatement.

'You look lovely, darlin',' Maura said. Maddy was wearing a slim floor-length dark blue evening dress with narrow straps that gave full play to her bare shoulders and intriguing hints of a trim figure. Her trademark gold chain was gone and, in its place, she wore a thin diamond necklace. The small pendant earrings matched perfectly. 'I love your hair,' Maura said, passing her most critical judgment. Maddy's hair was pulled back off her face and held in a simple arrangement that fell to her shoulders. But it was her gown that demanded a second look and would spur the fashion pundits to create new superlatives for understated elegance and glamour.

'We seem to be a matching pair,' Maddy said, joining Pontowski by the fireplace. She reached out and adjusted his bow tie. 'Oh. It's a real one. I didn't know men still knew how to tie them.'

'My grandmother taught me.'

'Wasn't she English?' Maura asked.

'The Lady Wilhelmina Crafton. Everyone called her Tosh.'

'Tosh,' Maddy mused. 'What an unusual name.'

'I don't know where it came from. I asked them about it once but they only smiled at each other. I think it goes back to when they met. My grandfather was flying with the Royal Air Force in World War Two and was wounded, actually pretty badly. My grandmother never used her title after they were married. She became an American citizen in 1952.'

'She was an elegant First Lady,' Maura added.

Dennis knocked and entered with Justice Wood, Maura's escort for the evening. 'Madame President, it's time.'

'Thank you, Dennis.' She turned and took Pontowski's arm, leading the way into the hall.

'Your daughter,' Justice Wood murmured to Maura, 'is going to set the fashion industry on its ear, not to mention a few tongues wagging.'

The dinner party was, by White House standards, a semi-official event in honor of the new president of the Académie française, that convocation of France's intellectual élite dedicated to preserving all things French. The elderly gentleman was touring the United States with his new wife, the former Elena Martine, who was thirty years younger. As the guests of honor, they sat at the head table with the presidential party. Elena had intended to be the star of the evening in a shimmering gold and dark red gown that had been created by a Parisian fashion house for the occasion. But Maddy upstaged everyone. Elena tried to recover by charming them with her French accent while Justice Wood trotted out his rusty French. Then Pontowski joined in, his French near perfect. Elena's husband was impressed that an American could carry on a conversation in the language, and said so.

Bender and Nancy were seated at a nearby table with Senator John Leland and his wife. 'Robert,' Nancy said, 'isn't she the woman Matt was involved with during the South African peacekeeping mission?'

'I believe,' Bender said, 'she was head of the UN Observer Mission at the time. He had to interact with her.'

'I mean romantic involvement.'

'She's very attractive,' Leland's wife said, joining the conversation.

'She's too flashy,' Leland said grumpily. 'And far too young for that old fool.'

'They *are* French,' Leland's wife said. 'Look how she keeps touching Pontowski. Maddy must be furious.'

'The President is absolutely gorgeous tonight,' Nancy said, leading them away from speculation on the President's frame of mind.

Leland humphed. 'She shouldn't dress like that.'

'You might say she's upholding the national honor,' Bender said, deadpan.

Nancy reached out and touched her husband's hand. '*Robert*. I believe you just made a funny.'

Leland's eyes narrowed as he considered the possibilities. In the low-pressure atmosphere of Washington ethics, a boyfriend was fair game.

In a show of gallantry, the guest of honor asked Maddy to dance when the music started. She rose gracefully and they walked on to the dance-floor. 'Matt,' Elena said, 'shouldn't we join them?' Reluctantly, Pontowski stood and offered her his arm. 'Do you remember when we first danced at the state dinner in Capetown? You were wearing the same uniform and ever so dashing.'

He allowed the memories out of their carefully walled

niches, where he would return them as soon as possible. 'And you were wearing dark pink.'

'You do remember,' she cooed in French. 'Do you remember afterwards?'

He didn't answer, but the memory of her standing nude by the big window overlooking Bantry Bay as golden firelight played on her skin was vivid and fresh as yesterday. He made a mental resolution to keep it all in the past where it belonged. Elena moved into his arms and they started to dance. Other couples joined them, and soon the dance-floor was full. When the music ended, Maddy and Elena's husband joined them. Maddy touched Matt's arm, establishing her rights for the next dance, and when the orchestra started to play a waltz, most couples left the floor. Maddy arched an eyebrow as if to ask if he knew how to waltz. 'Tosh taught me,' he answered. 'She loved to dance.'

Maddy stepped into his arms and they picked up the beat, moving in perfect step. The waltz is a formal, stylized dance meant to showcase the couple's skill and the woman's gown. But when it is done right, the couple blend into one and move with a sensuous grace. Unlike the tango, in which the dance is a graphic reenactment of seduction and sexual conquest, the waltz can be a public, but very proper, display of courtship and hidden affection. The other couples on the dance-floor moved aside and watched as they spun around. Finally, the music ended and the audience applauded. Maddy's face glowed with emotion. 'Oh,' she finally managed, breaking contact, 'that was nice.'

Elena watched them return to the table, determined to have her time in the spotlight – and with Pontowski. 'Be careful, my pet,' her husband cautioned in French. 'We're here to build bridges.'

The evening turned into a rare success, partly because of Maddy's new image and partly because of the vivacious Elena, who knew how to work an audience. But mostly because everyone knew who Matt Pontowski was and wanted to discover if he was more than just the President's escort for the evening. For all appearances, Maddy was the perfect hostess, but inwardly she knew that Elena was encroaching on her territory. She fumed with anger.

Late in the evening, Maura leaned her head next to her daughter's. 'Don't let her upset you,' she murmured. 'She'll be gone in a few days. Besides, he's not interested in her.'

'Whatever are you talking about?' Maddy replied, a little testy. She glanced at Pontowski, not knowing how to read him. Was Maura right or was he infatuated with an old flame who was almost offering herself to him? A commotion in the far corner caught her attention. Someone had collapsed on the dance-floor. Maddy stood and saw Bender hovering over his wife. 'Get Dr Smithson,' she ordered. Within moments, the White House doctor was with Nancy Bender, and she was sitting in a chair. Then Bender and Smithson helped her into another room.

'Let's call it a night,' Maddy said. She motioned to an aide to start the farewell protocols. Twenty minutes later, she was in the residence with Maura and Dennis as Pontowski said goodnight and left. 'Dennis, please check on Mrs Bender.' He hurried out to do as ordered. Now Maddy could give full play to what was bothering her. She paced back and forth in long strides, her legs whipping at the gown's skirt. 'That woman will never step inside my house again. Can you believe it? The obvious way she fawned over Matt? And he liked it! You would've thought they were lovers and her husband a blind dolt.'

'Cuckold, dear,' Maura said. She had to suppress her laughter. 'There's nothing between them.'

But Maddy wouldn't let it go. 'There may not be – now.'

Maura touched her daughter's arm. 'Everyone has a past. She was long before you.'

'Mother! I know what men think with.'

Dennis knocked and entered with Dr Smithson. 'Mrs Bender is fine,' the doctor said. 'We'll run some tests tomorrow. I imagine we'll find she needs vitamins and perhaps iron.'

'That's a relief,' Maddy said. Then she added, 'Iron? Is she anemic?'

'Most likely. She may be expecting.'

'She's pregnant? At her age?'

Maura chuckled. 'It does happen.'

Maddy glared at her mother. 'What is it with these Air Force men? Do they run around with permanent erections?'

'It's the women that make them that way, dear.' Maura collapsed on a couch and sighed. 'What a wonderful evening!'

Georgetown, Washington, D.C.

Nancy Bender leaned across the breakfast table in the elegant guest house the State Department maintained for VIPs. She touched her husband's hand. 'Quit playing the great stoneface and say something.'

'Are you sure?'

'They say home tests are very accurate.'

'But—' It was one of the few times in his life that Bender was at a loss for words. He covered his frustration by pouring another cup of coffee.

'It does happen. Menopause does things to your, ah, timing.'

'But—'

'I'm forty-eight and that's what you get for marrying a child bride. Besides, I haven't taken precautions in years. I didn't think it could happen after all that time of wanting another child. Maybe I didn't care.'

'But—'

'Stop sounding like a stuck record. It's because of those cold Polish nights with nothing to do. That's why there'll always be a Poland.'

A wide smile spread across Bender's face as he shook his head in wonder. He reached for her hand. 'I do love you.'

'You had better. I feel fine, so what's on the agenda for today?' Then another thought came to her. 'I can hardly wait to see the look on Winslow's face when we tell him.'

'I may have to explain the mechanics to him,' Bender said with a straight face.

★　　★　　★

Pontowski was driven to the Georgetown guest house that same morning. Bender was waiting for him. 'Thanks for coming,' he said, showing him into the sitting room. 'Matt, I'd like you to meet Peter Duncan.'

Duncan stood and the two men shook hands. He was short, a fraction over five feet five inches tall, and built like a tree stump. His jet-black hair, unbelievably fair skin, and pale blue eyes declared he was black Irish. His South Boston accent confirmed it. 'The pleasure is all mine, General Pontowski.'

'Don't let Pete fool you with his Irish cop routine,' Bender warned. 'He's been a cop, FBI special agent, lawyer, and DOJ prosecutor.'

'And now you have me sounding like I can't hold a job,' Duncan protested. He settled back in his chair. 'At heart, I'm still a cop.'

'Which is why he's here,' Bender added. 'Pete, this laid-back, devil-may-care jet jockey is here because he's like you. He's done many things. But in his heart, he's always been just one thing: a fighter pilot.'

The two men looked at Bender, wondering why they were in the same room. Matt gave him his lopsided grin. 'Why do I get the impression I'm about to be hosed out of the saddle. Cut to the chase, General.'

'Gentlemen, I want you to help stabilize the situation in Poland.'

'The man's mad,' Duncan muttered. 'That means taking on the Russian Mafiya. Tell your insurance company and they'll cancel your life assurance.'

'It can't be that bad,' Pontowski said.

'It is,' Bender replied. He sat back in an overstuffed chair and studied them. He had set the challenge and knew his men. It was one of the reasons he was a general.

Duncan's voice became soft. 'What do you want us to do, General?' Underneath his calm exterior, his heart was beating rapidly.

'Pete, I want you to help the Poles create a viable anti-crime task force similar to our FBI but with more muscle. Matt, the

Poles need a tactical air force that can control their own airspace. We're selling them F-16s through NATO, but they need training. That's where you come in.'

'Are these related in some way?' Pontowski asked.

Duncan tried to look bored, but he had read the reports coming in from every major law enforcement agency in America and western Europe. 'Is St Patrick Irish?'

Pontowski laughed. 'As a matter of fact, no.'

'Poland's airspace is effectively uncontrolled,' Bender explained. 'Russian organized crime is using it as a shipment tube for drugs.'

'I'm not current in the F-16.'

'Five weeks at Luke Air Force Base can fix that,' Bender said.

'So what's my cover in Poland?'

'You'll head up my Office of Defense Cooperation responsible for selling the Poles training packages. But your real job is to give them a full-up tactical air force.'

'Like the package World Security Systems was selling at the Williams air show?'

'Very similar.'

'That will really piss Beason off,' Pontowski said, recalling the last time he had met the senior Beason. Then another thought came to him. 'I've never been to Poland.'

'It's always nice to visit the old sod,' Duncan allowed, reminding Pontowski of his heritage. 'Count me in.'

'But it's the wrong sod for you,' Pontowski said.

'True,' Duncan replied. 'But the Irish love lost causes.'

The White House

Sam Kennett and the three women who composed the kitchen cabinet clustered around Turner in a protective huddle in her private study next to the Oval Office. Opposite them sat Patrick Flannery Shaw, the consummate political bandmaster. He was a shaggy bear of a man in a rumpled dark brown plaid suit. His tie and collar button were loose and his shoes needed a shine. Shaw was a man who could destroy the political opposition, intimidate the media, and raise campaign money by the truckload. He cared little for legal niceties and less for ethical principles. But they all knew why he was there. He won elections.

'Well, Mizz President,' Shaw drawled, his old confidence back in place. 'It's nice to be among friends.'

Secretary of Health Gwen Anderson's hackles were up. 'It's Mrs President or Madame President.' She looked at Turner. 'Do we really need him?' Her tone of voice proclaimed she would gladly perform a brain transplant on Shaw without benefit of anesthesia.

Shaw regrouped. 'Madame President, I suspect I'm here because you're going to run for reelection. You can manage a campaign without me, but I can do it better than anyone else.'

Gwen Anderson glared at him. The memory of how he had taken her out of consideration for the vice-presidency was still sharp and painful. She looked at Kennett. 'Sam, you're a wonderful vice-president and my friend. But I can never forgive that man for what he did to me.' She focused all her wrath on Shaw. 'If you're so damn good, convince me.'

Shaw's whole life revolved around politics, and he stayed awake at night plotting the destruction of his political enemies, whom he simply called *the bastards*. At one time, he had mistakenly lumped Anderson with them. 'The bastards are hurtin' for a candidate. If they get on the stick, they might be able to groom someone to run against Sam here in six years. But for 2004 they're hurting.'

'Tell us something we don't know,' Anderson muttered. 'The only way they can win is by attacking the President. It's going to be a dirty campaign.'

'They've got the money and backing to do it,' Kennett added.

Shaw's big head slumped, his chin on his chest. 'Madame President, you're going to win because I'm gonna make you the greatest president who ever sat in the Oval Office.'

Anderson was skeptical. 'And how do you propose to do that?'

Shaw came to his feet, remarkably agile for his weight. He paced the office, alive and animated. 'We stake out the moral high ground and never budge. We run on one issue – a vision for the future. We have one message – only the President has the moral integrity and courage to lead the nation forward. Our focus is the middle class and our finances are above reproach.'

Anderson's voice was full of disbelief. 'Do you really think that Ronnie Reagan's "morning in America" feel-good policy is going to work when the attack ads start?'

'They won't,' Kennett replied.

'Right,' Anderson scoffed.

Kennett gestured at Shaw. 'They won't because of him. Everyone knows he wrote the book on dirty tricks and below-the-belt tactics. He's the master and no one can match him. We keep him in the background, always waiting, ready to leap on the first fool who crosses the line. He's our hold card no one wants played.'

'Are they that afraid of you?' Maura asked Shaw.

Shaw chose his words carefully. More than anyone in the room, Maura was the one he had to win over. And she hated his guts more than Gwen Anderson. 'I'd like to think they are.' Shaw tried to sound humble, but it ran counter to his nature. 'You can never be certain, but last week Dan Beason offered me a consulting job at two point five million per year with a five-year contract.' They all knew who Daniel Beason was. 'Duties to be negotiated after signing the contract.'

'They really want to sideline you,' Kennett said, amazed at the amount of money.

'That's why it will work,' Shaw replied.

'I'm intrigued,' Turner said. 'Lay it out.' She knew the way Shaw worked, and she listened as he took center stage and orchestrated the opening movement for her reelection. When she had heard enough, she raised a hand, cutting him off in mid-flow. 'We'll talk next week.' The meeting was over.

Maura was the last to leave. For a moment, they were alone. 'Are you sure? Do you really want this?' she asked.

Turner gave a little nod. 'More than you'll ever know.'

There were tears in Maura's eyes. 'He's telling you what you want to hear.'

'I know.'

CHAPTER TWELVE

Bonn, Germany

The motorcade drove in stately grandeur up the twisting drive to the palace overlooking the former capital of West Germany. Vashin gazed out the window as they approached the magnificent structure. 'The dream came back last night,' he confided to Geraldine.

'Was it the same or different?'

'Much the same. I was drifting in clouds. Suddenly the mist parted and I could see a golden ray of sunlight shining on the Kremlin. It was the most beautiful thing I've ever seen.'

'Were you still in the clouds?'

'Yes. It was like I was ready to descend to earth.'

The Mercedes-Benz limousine turned into the driveway and coasted to a stop in front of the main entrance. Von Lubeck came down the steps between the flags and honor guard. 'The man meeting you is Herbert von Lubeck,' Geraldine said. 'His official title is first secretary to the Deputy Minister for Economic Research—'

Vashin waved a hand, cutting her off. 'He's nothing. This is an insult. I'm wasting my time here.'

Geraldine shot a worried look at Tom Johnson, the former Secret Service agent. She had to smooth over Vashin's ruffled feelings. 'I've heard that von Lubeck speaks directly to the Chancellor.'

Johnson saved it in the nick of time. 'In Washington, he was treated with kid gloves and had direct access to the Oval Office. He's the man who gets things done with the Germans.'

Vashin finally nodded as the door was opened. He stepped out and greeted von Lubeck like a long-lost friend, and they walked into the palace. Geraldine gave Johnson a look of relief. 'Thanks, Tom. As you Yanks like to say, I owe you one.'

Johnson grinned. 'How about tonight? And bring a friend.'

'Male or female?'

'Female. Young, pretty, and blonde.'

'And if she has a German accent?'

'Then we'll have our own international piece conference.'

Geraldine caught the pun and arched an eyebrow.

Von Lubeck stood in front of the fireplace as he lit his cigar. For a moment, he savored the warmth that held the cold November night at bay. He rolled the cigar and puffed it to life. It was late and they had been dancing around the subject most of Saturday afternoon and well into the evening. It was time to start negotiations. 'It has been a delightful evening, my friend,' he said, speaking Russian. It was one of the five languages he spoke fluently. He poured himself another brandy and freshened Vashin's vodka. 'Unfortunately, there are complications.'

'There are always problems. In Russia they are short-lived.'

'Yes, I see.' And von Lubeck did. It confirmed the German estimation of Vashin as a vicious, illiterate peasant. But a very dangerous one. 'Then you are aware of the latest difficulty?' No response from Vashin. 'Your Minister of Defense is traveling in secret to Brussels to meet with NATO.'

Vashin's head snapped up at the mention of Vitaly Rodonov. 'When?' His stomach churned in anger.

'Four days from now, on Wednesday.'

'Why?' Vashin spat the word out.

'The United States wants NATO to restrict your diplomatic landing rights in Europe, starting with Poland.'

Vashin forced his anger back into its cage. 'I can't allow the' – he almost said the bitch – 'United States to do that.'

Von Lubeck studied his guest, wondering if he would throw one of the fits German intelligence had reported. The extensive dossier had thoroughly bisected Vashin and described him as a clever sociopath suffering from epileptic fits. But close up and in the flesh, von Lubeck saw only an illiterate Russian peasant. His instincts told him it was time to speak in terms a peasant understood. 'The Americans have a phrase: a dog never shits in its own back yard.'

'In Russia, a dog shits where he wants.'

'German dogs shit where their masters want and most Germans see Poland as their back yard.'

Vashin's head jerked toward von Lubeck. Geraldine had told him the Germans were interested in 'respective areas of interest in Poland.' But he hadn't believed her. Only recognized heads of state dealt with such matters. He was surprised to see a pleasant smile on the German's face.

'You see, my friend?' von Lubeck ventured. 'We have a problem.' He waited for Vashin's reply, but as expected the cagey peasant wanted to hear more. 'As long as the Russian dog only shits in eastern Poland and none of the shit flows into Germany, we can reach an accommodation.'

'Sometimes shit flows in directions which the Russian dog did not intend.'

Von Lubeck nodded in understanding. Vashin was telling him he could not keep drugs out of Germany once they hit the streets. 'That is not a problem if the Russian dog doesn't care how we clean it up.'

'We need a map of Poland,' Vashin said.

The Hill

Zeth barely nodded when she hurried past Brian and Matt in the dining hall. Her lips were compressed into a narrow line. 'What's eating her?' Brian asked. Matt shrugged. They finished supper, stacked their trays, and left to take advantage of the thirty minutes before night study hall began. They wandered into the cadet lounge in John Ross Thomas Hall where Zeth was sitting in a corner looking despondent.

'Is everything okay?' Matt asked.

Zeth pulled a letter out of her pocket and unfolded it. She reread it, still in a state of disbelief. 'Do you remember when we went to dinner at the Ruidoso Jockey Club? I met a Zoomie there.'

The boys nodded, recalling the tall third-class cadet from the Air Force Academy they had met. 'Yeah,' Brian said. 'He was cool.'

'I invited him to the dance Saturday night and he accepted.' She folded the letter and put it back in her pocket.

'Cool,' Matt echoed.

She hung her head in despair. 'I can't go unless I get my GPA up to two point zero.' She stood up. 'I got to call him.'

'Is it chemistry?' Matt asked. A slight nod in answer. 'Don't you have another test tomorrow?'

Again, the little nod. They could tell she was on the edge of tears.

'I need to get at least a B. But I won't know the results until Friday, and then it'll be too late to stop him from coming down.'

'You won't bust it,' Matt assured her.

Brian came alive. 'Tell your teacher why you got to know the results. I bet he'll grade it right away.'

'Yeah,' Matt said. 'And we hit the books right now.'

Suddenly, Brian didn't look so happy. 'What about our math test tomorrow? I thought we were going to study for it tonight.' He needed Matt to help him as much as Zeth did.

'We can wing it,' Matt said.

Brian stomped off, unhappy to be studying on his own. 'Right. Wing it.'

The White House

It was a quiet dinner in the family dining room in the residence. The table had been shortened to make it more intimate, and Sarah sat opposite Pontowski while Maura and Maddy faced each other. 'Did you know,' Sarah said, 'that everybody's name here but mine starts with an M? Maura, Madeline, and Matthew.'

'And there's Matt,' Maura said, thinking of Pontowski's son.

'Let's see,' Pontowski said, making a show of it. 'The letter M is the thirteenth letter and shares the center of the alphabet with N.'

'Do you always think in terms of numbers?' Sarah asked.

'Sorta,' Pontowski conceded.

'Good,' the little girl announced. 'You can help me with my math homework.' She slipped off her chair and dragged him to the family room.

Maura shifted and came to her feet. 'I've got to lose some weight,' she moaned. She followed Maddy. 'I'm glad you invited him to dinner,' she murmured.

'Well, he is in town and I wanted to talk to him—'

'About the boys, no doubt.'

'Exactly,' Maddy replied.

'He's a hunk,' Maura murmured.

Maddy raised her eyebrows. 'Do you think so?'

Maddy was content to let Sarah dominate Pontowski's attention as he helped her with her homework. Maura's knitting needles clicked in the background as she watched TV and gave an old-fashioned patina to the evening. Finally, it was Sarah's bedtime, and Maddy hustled her daughter off. Maura stirred to follow her. 'I'll tuck her in,' Maddy said, leaving them alone. Sarah set a speed record getting into bed and gave her mother a goodnight kiss. 'Mom, I really like him.'

'So do I. But that's a secret between you and me.' She gave Sarah a playful tickle. 'So don't tell anyone, Chubs.' She kissed Sarah on top of her head and turned out the light. 'Sleep tight.'

Pontowski was talking quietly to Maura when she rejoined them in the family room. Maura faked a yawn and excused herself, claiming it had been a long day. Once alone, they made small talk, taking little steps of discovery on the path to a stronger relationship. An inner voice told her it was time to take a giant leap forward and see where they landed. Regardless of how they felt about each other, she was, above all, the President of the United States.

'Matt, I was talking to Robert, General Bender, the other day about the Quadrennial Defense Review and the subject of women in combat came up. He said there were problems we need to address now, before it's too late. Doesn't your fighter wing have women?'

'Yep, sure do.'

'Are you having problems?'

Pontowski sensed why she had brought the subject up. 'Maddy, I'm personally against women in combat. But the military is an extension of the government and we implement government policy. If my government wants women in combat, I'll put them in combat. But every decision has a price. Unfortunately, in the military, the bill comes due in combat when lives are at stake.'

She took his hand in hers and held it. 'You never answered my question.'

'We have problems. But my wing is a Reserve outfit, so what I'm experiencing may be unique. The real problem is that I'm not allowed to talk about it. My bosses tell me to integrate women. End of discussion. Problems and results are not part of that equation. So I stand tall in the grass, salute, and say "Yes, sir" and do the best I can.'

His tone of voice was matter-of-fact, his manner easy and relaxed. He was not challenging her or asking for a special understanding. Maddy's intuition shouted they were on the same wavelength. 'Can you be more specific?'

Again, his answer was straightforward. 'The attrition rate among women is too high, which means a decrease in readiness.' He felt her hand stiffen at the word that Bender had focused on. Misreading her reaction, he automatically started to massage her hands as he talked, concentrating more on them than on his words. 'On the flight line and in maintenance, women suffer more physical injuries, which means more medical care. That's not a problem in Missouri, but it will be in a forward operating location where there's limited medical care and I need every person I've got available for duty.'

'Ummm,' she murmured. 'That feels good. Matt, would you—?' She gave him a pleading look.

He laughed, enchanting her. 'You want your feet rubbed!'

She scooted back and brought her feet up, dropping them in his lap. 'How did you know?'

'You're dealing with a fighter jock here, madam. We know the way to a woman's heart.'

She stifled her reply. Instead she asked, 'When do you leave?'

'It's back to Knob Noster tomorrow—'

'Knob Noster?'

He laughed, again drawing her to him. 'That's the name of the town where my base is located. It'll take me a couple of days to clear my desk and turn the wing over to my replacement. Then it's on to Luke Air Force Base for a quick refresher in the F-16. I'll be there for five weeks, then off to Poland.'

'Will you be in the States for Christmas?'

'That's the plan. I finish training on December twentieth.'

She glanced at her watch. 'Matt—'

'I know, time to go.'

Maddy reached out and touched his cheek. 'It was a lovely evening.'

'It was. Thanks for inviting me.' They stood and she walked with him into the hall. Outside, an intern from the social office was waiting to escort him out. Again, they said goodnight and shook hands. But it was really more of a caress than a formal goodbye.

She closed the door and sat down by the phone. After thinking for a few moments, she picked it up and called Dennis.

'Is it set up?' She listened for a few moments and said, 'I'll be right down.' She walked to the window and looked out over the park as images of Pontowski kept demanding her attention. 'Only daydreams,' she murmured to herself. She walked back out into the hall.

Behind her, the Secret Service agent on duty spoke into his radio. 'Magic is moving.' In the command post directly below the Oval Office, the lighted panel traced her steps as she rode the elevator to the basement and headed for a small staff break room not far from the kitchen.

Dennis was waiting for her. 'He's on his way.' Turner nodded and stepped inside. On one table was a bottle of Jack Daniel's, a tumbler of water, a bowl of peanuts, some glasses, and a root beer. She sat down and poured herself a drink from the bottle of root beer.

'This will do fine,' she told Dennis. 'We used to meet late at night in party headquarters in Sacramento. I'd cry a lot, he'd drink, and we'd talk.' For a moment, she was back in California, a freshman state senator, in over her head, and very alone.

'Madame President,' Shaw said from the doorway. He smiled when he saw the bottle of Jack Daniel's. He knew what she was doing. 'Just like old times.' He sat down and poured himself a drink. Then he grabbed a handful of peanuts and munched a mouthful. He glanced over his shoulder at Dennis, who was sitting beside the closed door. His presence announced that the rules had changed. 'Patrick,' she began, her voice friendly and relaxed, 'I've been thinking about what you said last week. I like your approach.'

Instinctively, Shaw sensed it was truth-to-tell time or he would end up back in some California city running elections for a desperate mayor or wannabe assemblyman. 'Madame President, it was what you needed to hear.' All traces of his Southern accent were gone. 'To make it work, I'll need to set up a war room similar to Clinton's and make the appropriate noises. I'll put a stable of tame reporters together and leak stories about how you have to keep me in check. The bastards will be so busy looking over their shoulders at me that you can scamper home free.'

'What about finances?'

'I'll set up a committee to reelect the President and then disappear into the background. But I can still open doors, twist arms, and crack heads. All behind the scenes, naturally.'

'Naturally. And the money?'

'All of it goes through the committee. I'll have a screening process in place to make sure it's clean and then promptly reported. Clean as a hound's tooth.'

'My role in all this?'

'You never get involved with the filthy stuff.' He leaned forward, rolled the glass between his big hands, and stepped through a time warp. They were back in Sacramento and he was the master lecturing an eager student on the game. 'Some bastard or foreign country will make a run at you and try to buy influence with a gawdawful campaign contribution. I'll try to catch 'em but one might get through. That's when plausible denial is everything. You've got to keep it at arm's length so you can sacrifice the subordinate who got too eager, or careless, overstepped the bounds, and got caught. It's the same dealing with the CIA and intelligence.'

'Patrick, you do know what will happen after the election?' Her voice was soft and full of concern.

Shaw's face broke into a big smile. She was still the perfect student. 'In this business, usin' people is like eatin' a good T-bone steak: you gnaw the bone, suck the marrow out, and throw what's left to your dog.' He would have to make a very public exit from public life. Then after the proper amount of time had passed, he would be back, the privileged friend and advisor with direct access to the President. But this time he had it wrong.

Brussels

They were as mismatched a pair as ever walked the halls of NATO. Mazie was doll-like while the tall and rangy Bender towered over most of the bureaucrats who made a career working for the political arm of the North Atlantic Treaty Organization. Mazie recognized the symptoms immediately:

empty offices, too many casual conversations, and people wandering the halls. 'This place needs a swift kick in the ass,' she muttered to herself.

'My sentiments exactly,' Bender replied in a low voice. As outsiders, they saw what the bureaucrats refused to acknowledge: NATO was an alliance that had lost its mission. Yet it kept rolling along because of its own mass, a juggernaut without a compass. 'The real action is at SHAPE where the working troops are.' SHAPE, Supreme Headquarters Allied Powers Europe, was the military arm of NATO headquartered near Mons, thirty miles southwest of Brussels. 'This is where the pretty people do their thing.'

She looked at him and laughed, her voice a tinkling bell in the staid corridors of the formal and sterile building. 'Who would've ever thought – the Frump, here with the pretty people.' Bender arched an eyebrow, not understanding. 'When I worked for Bill Carroll, they called me the Frump.' William Gibbons Carroll was a former National Security Advisor who had died of ALS, Lou Gehrig's disease.

'You, frumpy?'

'I was a little butterball.'

'Sometimes people get hung up on images.'

'For a woman, it's everything. It's really stupid.'

An aide held the door open and they entered a private study. The two Russians waiting for them stood. One was a civilian, the other a three-star general. 'Robert,' the general colonel said, 'it has been a long time.' The two men shook hands. They had met when both were lieutenant-colonels observing each other's military exercises during the Cold War. 'Minister Rodonov, may I present Mrs Mazana Hazelton and General Robert Bender.'

Vitaly Rodonov extended his hand and held Mazie's longer than protocol required. 'So charming,' he murmured in English.

'She is not window dressing,' the general colonel warned in Russian. Russian military intelligence had a full file on her, most of it wrong.

'They call me the Dragon Lady in the White House,' Mazie replied in the same language.

Rodonov smiled and laughed. 'I like you already.'

'I didn't know you spoke Russian,' Bender said.

She gave him a sweet smile. 'A little.'

With the introductions over, they sat down. Mazie went right to the heart of the matter and talked about the drugs coming out of Russia and what was happening in Poland. 'The problem is that Mikhail Vashin is using diplomatic flights to transport drugs in huge quantities.'

Rodonov managed to look only mildly embarrassed. 'The situation is very complicated at the present time.'

Mazie understood perfectly. Rodonov could not control what was happening. 'Without the proper constraints,' she said, 'NATO may be forced to cancel your landing rights.'

Rodonov had not survived the upheavals in Russia by being slow or stupid, and he instinctively sensed when he had an ally. 'Such a development would embarrass my office.'

Mazie reached out and touched his hand, astounded by his candor. If NATO canceled Russia's landing rights, he would be blamed and removed from office, maybe even feet first. 'That is not our intention,' she said.

'Perhaps there is a middle ground,' Bender said. 'It is our interpretation that diplomatic protection only extends to the aircraft itself and the crew.'

Rodonov nodded. Whatever was on the aircraft was fair game once it was unloaded. 'We may have an understanding here.' He visibly relaxed. Now he could return to Moscow and claim a victory. Even Vashin should be pleased.

Now it was time for the Americans to reciprocate. 'We are fairly certain, as you are probably aware,' Mazie said, 'that Vashin has ordered your assassination.' She handed him a list of the men who were contracted to take him out. 'I hope this is helpful.'

'We would appreciate,' Bender said, 'knowing in advance what flights Vashin is using.'

'All of them?' the three-star general asked.

Bender was dumbfounded. The problem was much worse

than anyone suspected. 'It would be helpful if we knew when the flights were scheduled.'

Rodonov glanced at the general colonel. 'As you know, Peter Davydovich commands Transport Aviation.' He didn't add that this was why the general was at the meeting. 'I'm confident that certain protocols regarding notification can be established, which,' he went on, deadpan, 'do not violate our treaty rights. Why don't you work them out while Mrs Hazelton and I discuss other matters?'

Bender and the general withdrew to an inside office, leaving the other two alone. Again, Mazie came right to the heart of the matter. 'Are you aware that Vashin was in Bonn last Saturday and reached an understanding with Herbert von Lubeck?'

'I didn't know they had met,' Rodonov replied.

'Apparently, they agreed on "areas of interest" in Poland; Germany in the west, Russia in the east.'

Rodonov allowed the worry he felt to show. 'Please assure your President that neither I, nor, for that matter, anyone on the Security Council, wishes to change the status quo in Poland. But please remember our history. We cannot allow a remilitarized German presence on our borders.'

'I'll tell her,' Mazie promised.

'Tea?' Bender asked, remembering the time he and the general colonel had worked together.

'How can you drink that piss you Americans call tea?'

Bender laughed. 'You haven't changed a bit. How's your family? I remember your daughter. She was just an infant. What a beautiful baby. She must be . . . what? Seventeen now? Do you still call her Little Dove?'

CHAPTER THIRTEEN

Minsk, Belarus

The weather was unusually clear for mid-November when the Ilyushin Il-76 passed over Minsk. The city lights twinkled in the early dark as its citizens finished work and streamed into the streets, some to relax and enjoy the weekend, but most to work at their second job. Few looked up at the sound of the descending military transport aircraft. But a taxi driver duly noted its time of arrival and made a phone call. Within minutes, the information was passed to the third floor of the American embassy in Warsaw.

The Il-76 was cleared for a straight-in landing at Machulishche, the old Soviet airbase ten miles south of the city. A follow-me truck escorted it to the parking ramp that had once been occupied by an air regiment of MiG-23 Floggers. Now only the blackened scorch marks left by the exhaust plumes of jet engines remained, marching in rows of exclamation marks. A procession of three trucks and a bus packed with soldiers made its way out of the shadows and stopped behind the Il-76. A line of young women carrying luggage filed off the aircraft and were told to wait under the wing.

There was no delay in loading the aircraft and the men went about their duties in a well-rehearsed drill. No sooner was the cargo on board than the bus pulled up and let the soldiers off. They trooped on board the aircraft, lugging their weapons and equipment with them while the women climbed on the bus. The pilots started the engines and the big plane taxied for the runway. But this time the tower read a clearance for them to proceed as filed to Modlin Air Base in Poland. Four Sukhoi Su-35 fighters taxied out of nearby bunkers and awaited their turn to take the active. The tower cleared the Il-76 for takeoff and the four Su-35s rolled on to the runway. Three minutes later they took off at twenty-second intervals, chasing the big cargo plane.

The radar operator at Crown East, the Polish radar early-warning and ground-controlled intercept site outside Bialystok, Poland, started tracking the Il-76 the moment it climbed through 4,000 feet. He dutifully noted that its radar transponder was squawking the correct code for a diplomatic overflight. But it did not have a flight plan. He spoke to the tactical threat officer, who immediately called sector command.

'We have a target tracking inbound from Minsk,' the tac officer said. 'It's squawking the correct IFF code for a diplomatic flight but I don't have a flight plan.'

On cue, a voice with a heavy Russian accent came over the radio. 'Crown East, this is Vnukova inbound for Modlin Air Base.'

The radar controller's fingers flew over his controls, patching the radio frequency on to the communications net before he acknowledged the call. 'Vnukova aircraft calling Crown East, be advised we do not have a flight plan on your flight. Do not penetrate Polish airspace without clearance.'

'Crown East, be advised a flight plan is not required.' The pilot's tone mimicked the controllers. 'We are under treaty clearance.'

The tac officer spoke to sector command over a discreet land line. 'I don't like this, sir. It is similar to September eighteenth.' The Poles referred to the loss of their two F-16s by the date of the incident.

The silence from sector control was painful. Finally, the

voice said, 'Stand by. Keep monitoring their track while I contact headquarters.'

'Good luck,' the radar controller muttered to the tac officer. 'They've all gone home for the weekend.' He fine-tuned the old P-50 Barlock radar. Something was wrong. The return was far too strong for an Il-76 at that distance. He called the tac officer over. 'Sir, I think we're dealing with two aircraft flying in formation.'

'What game are the stupid Russkies playing now?' the young man said. He keyed his microphone and relayed the radar controller's suspicions to sector command.

'I have no response from headquarters,' sector answered.

'We need a decision,' the tac officer said.

Again, the silence was painful. 'I do not have enough information,' sector said. 'You are authorized to respond as the situation warrants.' Sector command had just bailed out.

The young tac officer did not hesitate. 'Scramble alert.'

'Scrambling now,' sector command said. He hit the Klaxon button, relieved that a subordinate unit had made the decision for him. In a nearby bunker, two pilots raced for their aircraft and clambered up the boarding ladders. The doors clanked open and each pilot settled into his seat and turned on his battery for radio and engine start. But only the lead aircraft cranked to life. The second aircraft had a dead battery. The pilot gave his lead a helpless look as a crew chief ran for the auxiliary power unit. But it was missing. In disgust, the lead pilot taxied alone and raced for the end of the runway. He was airborne two minutes later.

The climb-out and handoff to Crown East was routine, and within minutes the F-16 pilot was vectored on to the Il-76. He got his first radar paint at sixty nautical miles and locked on. Almost immediately, his radar broke lock and started to strobe. But for a fraction of a second, the F-16's anti-jam circuits burned through the strobing. Then the strobing was back. But in that brief quarter-second, the pilot saw five distinct radar returns clustered in a tight vee formation. What he didn't see were two of the radar returns peeling off and heading for him.

The loss of the two F-16s had been much discussed among the Polish pilots, and each had come to his own conclusions about what to do if they were caught in a similar situation. The Polish pilot immediately turned his radar to standby and let Crown East run the intercept. His eyes kept dancing back to his radar warning receiver. The chirping tone in his headset alerted him to a hostile attack radar, but there was no symbol on the scope. The pilot was not a coward, nor was he a fool. It was time to run for cover. He stroked the afterburner and did a split-S, an inverted half-loop, for the ground. The F-16 pulled six Gs at the bottom as the pilot pulled out. He kept the throttle in full afterburner as he raced for home.

The maneuver saved his life. The two Su-35s that had been converging on him broke off their attack run and rejoined on the Il-76, which was in a descent for landing at Modlin Air Base outside Warsaw. It called the tower for landing clearance.

'Vnukova aircraft calling Modlin,' the tower replied, 'be advised the runway is closed.'

'Modlin tower, be advised we are on a diplomatic clearance and will be landing in six minutes.'

'Do not attempt a landing. There is a vehicle on the runway.'

'Please clear the runway,' the Ilyushin pilot replied. Two of the Su-35s raced ahead in tight formation. They made no attempt to configure for landing and flew down the runway at 500 feet. At mid-field they pulled up and stroked their afterburners. They went through the Mach going straight up and the characteristic double-boom shock wave shook the tower and the small truck parked on the runway. The truck driver got the message and quickly drove on to the grass, clearing the runway. The vehicle became mired in the soft earth, but the driver was a very focused man. He bolted out of the cab and kept running, leaving the engine running.

The Il-76 pilot shaded his landing to the opposite side of the runway and his left wingtip missed the truck by thirty feet. The big cargo plane taxied to parking and shut down engines. The ramp at the back of the aircraft was lowered and soldiers streamed out. They ran into position, establishing a defensive cordon around the aircraft. They waited.

Almost immediately, a lone black Mercedes-Benz drove up and a lean and ravaged-looking figure emerged from the back seat. It was Jerzy Fedor from the Council of Ministers. He walked up to the soldiers as bolts slammed home, charging the weapons, and addressed the first man he approached. 'Let me speak to the officer in charge.'

The Russian colonel who stepped out of the shadows was relieved to see Fedor. Now they could play out their respective roles and follow the script. 'My government,' the colonel said, 'must protest at this crude attempt to deny our landing rights as established by treaty.'

'We,' Fedor said, speaking in Russian, 'are only following the treaty to the letter. Of course you have the right of landing and transit. However, we must insist on inspecting all cargo and passengers to ensure you are in compliance with the treaty agreements.'

'And who will perform this inspection?'

'That's why I'm here.'

'I can't allow it,' the colonel said.

Fedor gave an audible sigh and spoke into his telecommunicator in Polish. Immediately, the sound of diesel engines cranking to life and treads rumbling across concrete could be heard. The first tank emerged out of the shadows and stopped. It was followed by five others. The Il-76 was surrounded. 'This is not a good day to die, my friend. Come, we are reasonable men and can reach an understanding.'

The colonel nodded. The pro forma moves had been completed. He spoke to his aide and the captain ran back to the Ilyushin. Four men came out, each carrying two aluminum suitcases. They double-timed over to Fedor's car and piled the suitcases inside. 'The money is in negotiable US securities,' the colonel muttered.

Fedor handed him the completed inspection forms. 'You are cleared to proceed. However, anything you unload here does not have diplomatic protection once it leaves the airbase.' He climbed back into the Mercedes-Benz.

The colonel's eyes narrowed into thin slits of hatred as he watched the car disappear into the night. 'Polish whore.' Behind him, trucks unloaded the Ilyushin.

Camp David, Maryland

The mood was relaxed as the President's staff went about their Saturday morning duties. Only the Navy commander carrying the football, the black leather briefcase with the nuclear release codes, wore his normal uniform. Everyone else, like Turner, dressed casually. The weather was unusually mild. Maura and Sarah were on the main deck outside the presidential lodge. Inside, Turner was with Parrish and Noreen Coker.

The door opened and an aide entered carrying a briefcase of classified material. A woman's laughter echoed down the hall and was suddenly hushed. Turner shook her head and smiled and, on cue, a little squeak of laughter scurried in before the door closed. 'Your staff, what a happy bunch,' Noreen commented.

'They like to get away,' Turner replied. 'It's much more relaxed up here.'

'I'm envious,' Noreen replied. 'I wish my staff blended so well with my mood.'

'Whatever are you talking about?'

'Madame President,' Parrish said, handing her the PDB. 'I'm sorry it's late but apparently there was some late-breaking intelligence. It's on the last page.'

Turner opened the slickly printed President's Daily Brief and read the latest intelligence the CIA had to offer. Her face froze. 'Apparently our agreement with Rodonov is worthless.' She flung the PDB at Parrish. 'The Russians forced a cargo of drugs through Poland last night. A big cargo. They used soldiers. Apparently, Mazie and Bender's meeting with Rodonov accomplished nothing. It may have even been counterproductive.'

Parrish quickly read the offending article. 'It's too soon to tell. It may be linked to the meeting between Vashin and the Germans. We need to wait and see.'

Turner paced the floor. 'Why do I sense the Russians are driving events and not us? More importantly, why am I spending so much time on this?'

'Time to go,' Noreen said, standing up. 'This isn't for me. Besides, I got a heavy encounter of the most personal kind tonight.'

Normally, Turner would have taken a moment to share a personal confidence with her old friend. 'We'll talk next week,' she said, still pacing. Noreen waved goodbye and spoke to the two secretaries on her way out. Turner kept pacing. 'The Russians are sending us a message that I don't like. I want to hear from the DCI.'

'I'm not sure he's in town this weekend,' Parrish said.

'Someone at Langley must know what's going on.'

'I'll see who I can find.' Parrish left to speak to his assistant. Outside, he confirmed the rumor Noreen had started. The word spread and the lodge was hushed as Turner called for more members of her staff as she turned to other problems. The helicopters were placed on alert and the White House notified that the President might be returning early.

Her staff easily accepted the one overriding fact about Maddy Turner: she was a workaholic.

The Hill

The ballroom on the second floor of John Ross Thomas Hall was packed with cadets and their guests. The DiscStaff, a cadet social club, had brought in the most popular disk-jockey in El Paso for the Saturday night dance and the big room was rocking. General McMasters and his wife made a brief appearance and, as usual, Lenora came loaded with home-baked cookies for the refreshment table. Also as usual, the Rats rushed the table and the cookies vanished. She smiled as she looked over the dance-floor. 'I hardly recognize some of our young ladies. Look at Miss Trogger. With her hair down, she's a totally different person.'

McMasters sighed inwardly when he saw Zeth. She was wearing the dress Maura O'Keith had bought for her and wearing her hair and makeup in the same way. 'I believe,' he said in a low voice, 'that our Miss Trogger is the star of the evening.' It was true. More than a few of the cadets and guests from town were vying for her attention.

Lenora McMasters knew how her husband worked. 'This is not the time for second thoughts,' she murmured. 'Besides, dances like these are good for relations with the townies. They see the cadets as normal, everyday kids. Just like them.'

The superintendent had reservations about allowing a civvies dance. For some reason, the cadets put on civilian clothes and forgot they were still cadets. While the conditions for this dance dictated that the boys wear coats and ties and the girls modest dresses, the girls were pushing the standard to the limit. 'If the minimum wasn't good enough,' he muttered to himself, 'it wouldn't be the minimum.'

'John, this is the twenty-first century.'

'I know.'

'You can trust them.'

'They're still kids,' he muttered. He smiled for one of the chaperons who was taking photos of the dance. 'Time to go, before I see something I don't want to see.'

'Hey, Maggot,' Brian said, 'check out the Trog.'

'Yeah, I saw her.' They talked loudly to be heard over the music.

'The studlies are really hounding her.'

'She can handle it,' Matt replied.

'Handle what?' a voice said behind them. They turned around and were facing Rick Pelton, the Regimental Executive Officer.

'All the attention,' Brian answered.

Pelton agreed. 'She is something else.' His eyes narrowed into slits. 'Who's that tall townie she's talking to?'

'He's a third classman at the Air Force Academy,' Brian told him. 'We met him at a dinner with my mom.'

'He's cool,' Matt added. The three cadets watched as the couple moved on to the floor and started to dance. The combination of light, the flowing motion of Zeth's hair, and her dress created a lovely picture. 'Where did she learn to dance like that?' Matt wondered, giving voice to what they all were thinking.

'What the hell is he doing here?' Pelton wondered, now very interested in Zeth and taking the measure of the intruder on his territory. Pelton and the newcomer were both the same age and in the same class at college. However, the Air Force Academy was still the Air Force Academy, and that put Pelton at a disadvantage. But he was much better looking and more athletic.

Brian couldn't help himself and stirred the pot. 'I'd guess he's checking out the Trog.' The music slowed. The couple were clinched in a tight embrace. 'I think she's using him.'

'For what?' Pelton asked.

'To make you jealous.'

'Gimme a break.'

'You gonna let some zoomie bastard just move in?'

Pelton snorted and walked away, looking for some of his buddies. 'Why are you egging him on?' Matt asked.

'It's fun. You got a short-term memory problem? He's the bastard who chaired you to get back at me, remember?'

'He wasn't there and Zeth stopped it.'

'Yeah, but he was behind it.' They watched as Pelton joined the couple and talked to them. The two young men shook hands and Zeth even danced with Pelton for one number. Then she was back with the Air Force Academy cadet and Pelton joined a few of his classmates who were with their girlfriends.

Brian laughed. 'Aced out.'

One of the girl Rats came up and asked Matt to dance. He blushed brightly. 'I don't know how.'

'I'll teach you,' she said, her eyes sparkling with fun and something more than just friendship.

'See you later, studly,' Brian said. He wandered through the big double doors and down into the games room in the basement.

Pelton was shooting pool with a buddy. 'Askin' a freakin' zoomie to the dance,' the other cadet said. 'What a bitch.'

Pelton lined up his shot. 'You got that right.' He took the shot and sank the ball.

Warsaw

Bender arrived at the embassy on Monday morning at exactly 7.30. It was the time he always came to work, and he was a little concerned that his staff hadn't got the message that he liked to start early. But rather than ride roughshod over long-established traditions, he decided to give it some time and see if they figured it out for themselves. An embassy staff was a far different critter than a staff in the Air Force where young and eager officers only wanted a chance to show what they could do. With that group, he had to chase them out of the office or they would have worked horrendous hours. The Marine guard came to attention as Bender stepped into the elevator.

'Good morning, sir.'

'Good morning, Corporal Kincaid,' Bender replied. The Marine was shocked. Not only did Bender know his name, he recognized his rank. The previous ambassador could distinguish a Marine from a cow, but that was about it. Forget about knowing names.

Rather than hit the button to the second floor where his office was located, Bender descended to the basement and walked into the communications section. The clerk on duty was surprised to see him. 'Good morning, sir.'

'Good morning, Miss Clement.' Her mouth opened in surprise that he remembered her name. 'I'd like to see my read file, please.'

'The DCM's secretary hasn't collated it yet.'

'No problem. I'll do it.'

'Sir, I don't know—' Her voice trailed off. Then she showed him the stacks of folders holding the cables that had come in over the weekend. 'Most of these came in Friday night after the close of business in Washington.' The timing did not surprise him as bureaucrats liked to clear their desks for the weekend and sent most of their letters and cables out on Friday afternoon. But the amount of message traffic was staggering, far surpassing anything he had experienced in the Air Force.

'Is it always this much?' he asked.

'Oh, no, sir. This was an unusually light weekend.'

He quickly thumbed through the folders. Then he noticed the Daily Intelligence Summary, which he had never seen before. He extracted the cable and read it. He replaced the message and thanked the clerk. She beamed as he left, little suspecting the anger beneath his calm exterior.

The corridors on the second floor were deserted when he came out of the elevator. As he neared his office, he caught a whiff of coffee. 'Someone's awake,' he mumbled to himself. He turned into the Red Room, the large office and reception area that separated his office from that of Winslow James, his Deputy Charge of Mission. The smell of the brewing coffee drew him to a small side office occupied by one of the interpreters who worked for the Chief of Mission secretary.

A young woman he had never met stood up. 'Good morning, Mr Ambassador. May I get you some coffee?'

He was stunned and, for a moment, speechless. She was tall, perhaps five feet ten inches, and on the heavy side, classically Rubenesque. Her soft brown hair hung in waves past her shoulders and highlighted beautiful, doe-shaped hazel eyes and high cheekbones. She had the most perfect mouth and lips he had ever seen and a flawless complexion. 'Black,' he finally managed to croak. 'I'm sorry, I don't know your name.' She smiled at him, and for the first time in his life he understood why some men reconsidered their marriage vows. Thankfully, he was a happily married man.

'Ewa Pawlik.' She pronounced her first name *Eva*.

'Ewa Pawlik,' he repeated.

Again, she smiled. 'In Poland, Eva is spelled with a *w*.' She placed a carafe and cup and saucer on a tray. 'I'm an interpreter and work part-time,' she explained, answering his unasked question as to why they hadn't met. Her English was near perfect; he could detect only a trace of an accent. She followed him into his office and poured him a cup.

'Well, Ewa, what do you do the other part of the time?' He expected to hear that she was a university student.

She captivated him with a serious look and suddenly the legend of Helen of Troy made sense. 'I help at my mother's surgery in Praga. She's a physician, Dr Elzbieta Pawlik.' Looking at her, he sympathized with artists who tried to capture the magic of true beauty and in the end always failed. 'Well, I must get back to work. Mr James likes to have a translated summary of the newspapers.'

He watched her as she walked away, gave a little shudder and forced himself back to reality. She was too beautiful to be true. He made a note to have security run a background check on her. 'Who else is here?' he said to himself. He punched at his telephone. He hit pay-dirt on the fourth try when Peter Duncan answered. Three minutes later, the former cop, FBI agent, and DOJ prosecutor was in his office, also holding a cup of Ewa's coffee.

'Lovely girl,' Duncan said.

Bender came right to business. 'Have you heard about Friday night?'

'If you mean the so-called diplomatic flight into Modlin Air Base with its cargo of drugs, no.'

Duncan had unknowingly pushed one of Bender's buttons. 'Don't play smart. You're wasting my time.'

'Sorry, sir. I learned about it Saturday night through my contacts with the MO. That's the police.' He tried to pronounce *Milicja Obywatelska* but failed miserably. 'I came into the office Sunday to check it out, but no one was at work. I even tried the CIA. No luck there either.' His face grew hard. 'This place is a model of inefficiency.'

Bender was impressed. Duncan had been in Poland less than a week. 'You didn't waste any time getting involved.'

'As I recall, those were my marching orders.' He leaned forward and tried to explain it. 'General, you'd opened the door to the police with President Lezno and I was able to walk right in. The Poles accepted me because, like them, I'm a cop. It's what I am. They got problems. But last week, I discovered there's a lot of good cops here. You can see it in their eyes, in the way they talk, the way they do business. They only want to do their job.'

'How long would it take to set up a special task force, organized and trained to target drug shipments?'

'It already exists – Special Public Services.'

Bender was incredulous. 'Special Public Services? It sounds like they're in charge of sewers.'

Duncan couldn't help himself. 'They are, more or less.'

'I sold the President of the United States a security aide package for Poland and I never heard of them. This makes me look like a fool.'

'Now don't go indulging in self-flagellation, General. It's not the type of special unit the Poles would talk about, least of all to diplomats. Besides, they got problems.'

'Such as?'

'Confused leadership at the top, poor mid-level management, and rotten intelligence. Not to mention lousy pay which breeds corruption. But the poor bastards are trying, especially at the operational level.'

'How long before the SPS is fully operational?'

'With a little tweaking, not long.' Bender looked doubtful. Duncan thought for a moment. 'I can arrange a tour so you can see for yourself.'

'Set it up for this week.'

Bender fixed Winslow James with an icy stare. He was doing a double burn over his discovery of the Daily Intelligence Summary and Duncan's revelation about the existence of Special Public Services. Had his staff deliberately omitted it from the security aide package to send him a message? Or was the omission the product of poor staff work? He didn't like either answer. He might have been ambassador for only six weeks but it was time to start sending some very direct messages to his people. He tapped his read file with a finger. 'Winslow, I noticed you included the Daily Intelligence Summary in my read file. Obviously, you talked to Miss Clement in Communications. That's good, because

I want my staff talking to each other. My question is, Why haven't I seen it before?'

James stammered something about what the former ambassador preferred. Bender tapped the file. 'When did you learn about the incident of Friday night at Modlin Air Base?'

'Is it important?'

'I'd say a drug shipment valued at approximately half a billion dollars that was forced through Poland at the point of a gun with an armed fighter escort is important.'

'Sir, we don't interfere in internal matters.'

'You didn't answer my question.'

James swallowed. 'This is the first I've heard of it.'

'Winslow, you're letting important things fall through the cracks. Starting tomorrow, you will receive an in-country situation brief every day you are on station. Further, I want a summary of that briefing in my read file. Speaking of which, it will be waiting for me on my desk when I arrive at seven-thirty.'

James spluttered. What Bender was ordering meant he would have to be in his office by six at the latest and his secretary even earlier. That wasn't why they had joined the foreign service. Then he saw a way out. 'Who will prepare the briefing?'

Bender glanced at the ceiling. 'As I recall, the CIA occupies the entire third floor of this building.'

'True, but they won't do it.'

'Would you care to bet your career on it?' Silence from James. 'Next, Peter Duncan is setting up a tour at a special police unit this week. Be sure it happens, and I want you to come along.' James started to protest but Bender held up his hand. 'Finally, please find a good obstetrician for my wife.' He allowed himself a little smile at the look on James's face. 'She's expecting.'

James recovered nicely. 'Congratulations, sir.' The meeting was over and he wandered back to his office in a state of mild shock. Pregnant secretaries, wives of younger officers and junior staff members were quite common. But not the ambassador's wife. It was unheard of. He stopped by his secretary's desk. 'Please have Ewa find an obstetrician for Mrs Bender.'

CHAPTER FOURTEEN

Moscow

Geraldine Blake and Tom Johnson flanked Vashin when he walked into Vashin Towers, the newest skyscraper complex in Moscow. 'I've had a team of independent security experts in here for a week,' Johnson explained. 'They've gone over every square millimeter and Vashin Towers is, without doubt, the most secure structure they've ever seen.'

'Not to mention,' Geraldine added, 'the most elegant.'

'Better than Trump Tower in Manhattan?' Vashin asked.

'Trump Tower is not even a distant second,' Geraldine replied. She guided him up the escalator to the mezzanine where he could view the entrance mall with its collection of expensive boutiques and restaurants. 'This is a master-piece,' she said. 'You have created the symbol of the new Russia.'

Vashin stood at the rail and took it in. Below him, people streamed in. The boutiques were busy, the restaurants booked weeks in advance, and every office space rented. Vashin Towers was an instantant success.

He turned and smiled. 'I'm pleased.' A wave of relief swept over the entourage surrounding him.

Geraldine stepped back. 'This way, please.' She led him to the marble-lined alcove and the executive elevator. The doors were open. They stepped inside and Geraldine said,

'The Center, please.' The doors closed. They were barely aware of movement.

A computer-generated woman's voice said, 'Good morning, Mr Vashin. I have scanned the building and it is secure.'

'The computer system,' Johnson told him, 'was designed and installed by Century Communications International. They are the best in the world.' Vashin grunted an answer. The name Century Communications meant nothing to him.

The elevator doors opened and they stepped into the Center, the new hub of Vashin's web that was six stories below street level. It was a modern and efficient office complex worthy of any international corporation. 'Your decision to build underground was inspired,' Johnson said, stroking Vashin's ego. 'It increased construction costs but paid off in increased security.' He sensed Vashin's impatience. 'Would you like to see the Action Room first?' Vashin nodded hungrily. They marched down the center hall and through what looked like a vault door, stepping on to a balcony overlooking an operations center. Rows of consoles faced huge computer-driven displays on the walls, and people scurried purposefully around on business. Half of the Action Room could have been a military command post. The other half was a finance center with links to every stock exchange in the world.

'Very good,' Vashin said. He barged ahead and into his new office complex. His desk was in the largest chamber and set against a huge picture window overlooking the Action Room.

'My God,' Geraldine whispered to Johnson. 'This is right out of a James Bond movie.'

'Where do you think we got the idea?'

Geraldine found her desk and looked into her computer monitor. An embedded security camera scanned her retina and the screen came to life. She signed on and was ready to go to work. She picked up a leather folder, which now integrated her telecommunicator and personal organizer and linked her into the computer system. She walked into Vashin's office. He was standing by the window, hands clasped behind his back and a rigid, triumphal scowl on his face. A warning bell tinkled in the back of her mind and, for a brief moment, she was looking down a dark corridor into the past. Then it was gone. 'Mikhail, whenever you're ready. The bankers are in the penthouse.'

She followed Vashin into the express elevator that connected his office to the penthouse. They shot 105 stories skyward. The doors opened and they stepped out. Vashin stopped and turned to the guard. 'Is it the same?'

The guard answered with a smile. He inserted a pass key and turned it counter-clockwise. There was a slight pause as the elevator moved up to clear the door. The doors opened silently and revealed the dark shaft. A blast of cold air hit them and Vashin smiled. The guard twisted the key, the doors closed, and the elevator descended back into place.

Thirteen of the fourteen bankers who had been in St Petersburg a month before were waiting for him in the conference room. Only the banker from England was absent. Vashin stood at the head of the table and motioned Geraldine to the podium at the other end. He spoke in Russian and thanked them for coming as Geraldine translated. He liked the way her voice was an echo of his. Then, as planned, he sat down and let her continue.

'Mr Vashin,' she said, speaking in English, 'is very pleased that you have decided to join him in this new venture. As you know, it is Mr Vashin's intention to establish Moscow as one of the world's leading financial centers.' She moved gracefully to the computer-generated displays on the back wall and used a sequence of charts and diagrams to outline Vashin's plans. Vashin concentrated on the bankers' reaction, trusting his instincts more than logic to interpret for him. It was Geraldine who was convincing them, not his grand plan.

She came to the heart of the meeting. 'Critical to Mr Vashin's goal is a strong banking system in Russia that has links to the world's international trade centers. By being essential components of such a system, your banks will—'

The banker from Chicago interrupted her. 'We know why we're here. We need to know how Mr Vashin intends to prime the system. Banks don't exist on promises or hot air.

We need cash reserves, under our control, to underwrite our business.'

'Sufficient funds will be deposited in your Moscow branch to create the reserves you require.'

Now it was the Swiss banker's turn. 'Our governments require us to identify the source of large deposits.' Vashin was up against the basic problem faced by all criminal organizations – how to legitimize illegally obtained money. The reserves and money priming the system had to be clean or the banks would lose their charters.

'Not to worry,' Geraldine replied. 'The funds will come to you by electronic transfer from recognized and long-established Russian banks.'

'And these banks will certify the money is legitimate?'

'Of course,' Geraldine replied.

'We can accept those transfers,' the Swiss banker said, 'if the funds were originally sourced in a bank recognized by the European Union or the US Federal Reserve system. However, if the funds are sourced in Russia, my charter requires the actual transfer of cash, securities, or gold to our control.' The other bankers confirmed that they had to live with the same constraints.

Geraldine's voice was matter-of-fact as she explained the problem to Vashin in Russian. 'We've got to put up the actual money before they will sign on.'

'How much?' Vashin asked.

Geraldine asked the question of the bankers and added up their responses. Her face paled at the total figure. Afraid to tell Vashin, she started to bargain, and finally got the initial funding down to two billion dollars each. She relayed the number to Vashin and he jerked his head in agreement.

'When can we expect it?' the Japanese banker asked in Russian.

Vashin thought for a few moments. He had the funds, in one form or another. But most of it was scattered around the world and had to be physically transferred into the Russian banks he controlled to start the laundering process. 'Soon,' he told the bankers. 'Before Christmas.'

The meeting over, Geraldine led the men into the dining room for a sumptuous luncheon. Vashin was struck by how easily she switched roles from an accomplished negotiator to a regal hostess. She was a consort worthy of an emperor.

The White House

Turner huddled with her speech writers and Richard Parrish in her study. The two men and one woman who wrote her speeches were, without doubt, the most eclectic group on the presidential staff and could rise to any occasion, swamping her with a torrent of appropriate remarks for the audience. They had to be since Turner made about three hundred speeches a year, ranging from casual remarks on the White House lawn to ceremonial addresses to the nation. But not only did they play with the power of the spoken word, they carefully crafted how and where she delivered it.

'Madame President,' the woman said, 'we may be wasting the issue on the National Guard Association. They're so glad you're speaking, it doesn't matter what you say.'

'We're floating a trial balloon,' Parrish said. 'Their response will be critical.'

'Avoid any mention of women in the military and it'll play like apple pie and motherhood in Iowa,' one of the men said.

'Okay,' Parrish said, 'we're agreed. Let's look at what's on the schedule for next week.' They quickly went over the upcoming events and which writer was responsible for what speech.

Dennis stuck his head through the door. 'It's time, Madame President.'

'Thank you, Dennis.' She rose and the speech writers vacated the room as another assistant brought in her coat and gloves.

Because her speech to the National Guard Association was an announced public visit, fourteen cars were waiting for her on West Executive Avenue. Her limousine was sandwiched between seven security vehicles for the short drive to the

Watergate complex, less than a mile away. The other six cars held her traveling staff. It bothered Turner that the elaborate security conditions placed her in a state of almost total isolation. She had never forgotten Maura's initial reaction and her simple comment, 'This turns people off.'

She had raised the problem once with the head of the Secret Service. He replied they had only received four threats against her life that week, an all-time low. She didn't ask what the all-time high was and that ended the matter.

As usual, a bank of TV cameras and reporters waited for her arrival. Again, the Secret Service scanned the crowd with hard looks, always hyper-vigilant. Patrick Flannery Shaw waited with the reception committee, a worried look on his face. The TV cameras recorded him speaking to her, although no one could hear his actual words. Turner paused and looked at him. He said something else and she gave him a little, but very obvious, push, pointing him down the hall. She sighed and shook her head with the look a mother has for her errant children. Her worried hosts ushered her into the reception area.

The small auditorium was still ringing with applause when Turner left the stage and said goodbye to her hosts. Parrish followed her. 'Your remarks about establishing an independent commission to evaluate combat readiness touched a nerve. I've briefed Joe on how to respond to questions.' Parrish led her down a side hall and to a back elevator. Free of the press, they entered a back door into the offices of Stammerville and Holt, media consultants. Patrick Shaw grinned when he saw her come in.

'Well, Mrs President,' he drawled, 'we sprinkled some dust on the waters.' He introduced her to the two men who would mastermind her campaign. For the next forty minutes, they outlined the realities of what it would take to elect her and a strategy to capture key states. An assistant came in with a videotape recorded from the CNN, Fox, and CNC-TV news channels. It was the first reaction to her speech. But the coverage centered mainly on the incident in the hall and not what she had said.

Shaw roared with approval when Liz Gordon from CNC-TV ended her coverage with 'We don't know what the President said to her old friend and advisor, Patrick Shaw. But it does appear he is in the presidential dog house. A knowledgeable insider told this reporter that she is rejecting his advice to run for the presidency in her own right.'

'Who's the knowledgeable insider?' Parrish asked.

'Me,' Shaw replied. 'Ms Gordon is in our stable.'

'What's the point?' Parrish asked.

Stammerville answered. 'The point, Mr Parrish, is to keep our opponents guessing as long as possible, not only about the President's intentions, but about Mr Shaw's role in the campaign.'

'Patrick's a liability,' Turner said. 'But he's critical to my campaign.' She stood and paced the room. 'This rift was staged to focus attention on Patrick, not the issue I raised with the National Guard. I'm deeply concerned about combat readiness in our armed forces. I wanted to air the idea of an independent commission on it without stirring up a partisan controversy. Identifying problems and finding right solutions may take years.'

Shaw frowned. 'You might not like the answers, Mizz President.' He wanted to tell her that independent commissions had the bad habit of revealing the truth, a definite liability in his world. 'If you're serious about winning, postpone the commission until after the election.'

Holt caught the slight tilt of Turner's head and the set of her mouth. His political instincts warned him this was not an issue they should raise during a campaign, and he had to change her mind. His words came slowly. 'By appointing an independent commission to evaluate combat readiness you may be opening yourself to criticism on a vulnerable issue. Better to wait and let the other side raise it. Then appoint the commission and claim it's far too serious a question for partisan politics.'

'And take it off the table,' Shaw added. He studied the President, hoping it was now a dead issue. But his instincts warned him otherwise.

'Madame President,' Holt continued, 'we need to finalize

two items. First, will it be Madeline Turner or Maddy Turner?'

The question was critical, for the answer would set the campaign's tone. Would it be presidential or would it be personal? An image of her imperial motorcade driving down an empty street flashed in her mind's eye. 'It's Maddy Turner.'

'Second, the timing of your announcement is critical. We recommend delaying it until after the first weeks of the year. Perhaps in February.'

Turner pulled into herself and reran all the old arguments. So much of it was gamesmanship, and logic said that Holt was right. But her instincts were sending a different message. She made her decision. 'Before Christmas.'

Shaw bit off his reply. She had gotten that one wrong.

Kutno, Poland

Winslow James sat in the back seat of the black staff car with Bender and Peter Duncan for the ride to the country manor house where the Pole's SPS, Special Public Services, was headquartered. It was a long ride into the countryside west of Warsaw, and the narrow two-lane road was congested with heavy truck traffic. 'This road,' James said, 'is the major artery connecting Warsaw to western Poland. As you can see, Poland needs a modern highway system.'

Bender listened while James listed Poland's transportation problems. He grudgingly gave his DCM high marks for understanding the country's economic infrastructure. But he wished James would sound more human. By all normal standards, he was a pompous, overbearing snob impressed with his position and himself. *He needs a shot of reality*, Bender told himself. Peter Duncan, on the other hand, was all Irish charm hiding a sharp mind and aggressive disposition. 'Pete,' he said, cutting James off, 'what's the agenda for today?'

Duncan handed him a schedule. 'Pretty much your normal dog and pony show in the morning with a luncheon at one o'clock. I've scheduled an hour for a private conversation with the commander afterwards, and they want to end the day with a tactical exercise.'

'Mr Ambassador,' James huffed, 'I do have to return to the embassy; the press of official business. I've arranged for a staff car to pick me up at noon.'

Bender nodded, his opinion of James slowly solidifying into stone.

The commander of Special Public Services was a big man, all hard lines and rigid attitude. His black combat fatigues were devoid of any sign of rank. The only distinguishing mark was a red shoulder patch shaped like a shield with a white SPS logo: two lightning-bolt *S*s flanking a *P* that turned into a double fishhook at the bottom. The commander towered over the much smaller Duncan, yet Bender sensed they were both cast from the same mold. Duncan's words about being a cop carried a fresh meaning. Bender listened, hearing pride and dedication when the commander spoke about his unit. 'Five years ago, law enforcement was in a shambles. We started to make real progress when our first graduates from your FBI's National Academy returned.'

James coughed for attention. 'Mr Ambassador, my car is here.' Without waiting for Bender's reply, he thanked the commander and almost ran to the waiting staff car in his rush to escape. Bender suppressed what he wanted to say. Until James was able to look beyond the façade of diplomatic bureaucracy and protocol and cope with reality, he would never be an effective diplomat.

The commander watched James leave. 'We have hundreds like him in our government. How did you get him out of his office?'

'With a crowbar,' Duncan replied.

The commander laughed. 'It is good he left. I told my exercise team to lay on a hostage exercise for this afternoon. It would have frightened him.'

Duncan perked up. 'Is it a live-fire exercise?'

'Of course not.'

'Where will it take place?'

'Finding where the terrorists have taken the hostage is part of the problem. I have given my intelligence section two hours to locate the hostage. If they fail, an informant will reveal the location to speed things along. Then you can see how a tactical squad responds and negotiations are started.'

Duncan said, 'So it will be near here.'

'Of course.'

A wicked smile crossed Duncan's face that made Bender think of a malevolent leprechaun. An unspoken understanding passed between the American and the Pole. 'I agree,' the commander said. He spoke into his telecommunicator, issuing orders in Polish. 'The exercise has commenced as of now.'

'What are you two up to?' Bender asked.

'Mr Ambassador,' Duncan answered, mimicking James, 'the interrogatory should only be used when the acknowledgment is acceptable.'

'Which means?'

'Don't ask the question if you can't stand the answer.'

'Will you please join my staff for luncheon?' the commander asked.

Following the meal, Bender and Duncan talked with the commander in his spartan office. 'My main problem is intelligence,' the Pole admitted. 'Our national intelligence service is worthless and our informant system is hopelessly compromised by the Russian Mafiya. It is so bad that we assume nothing is reliable.'

'We can make some of our national sources available to you,' Bender said. 'But if your system is so bad, how do we keep the information we give you from going directly to the Mafiya?'

This was Duncan's area of expertise. 'Limited distribution, through me to the commander.' He sketched a flow diagram as he talked. 'Ultimately, the SPS will have to create its own intelligence base. That means you'll have to find and develop your own sources. We can train your people on how to find and approach potential informants. We have some mighty fine arm-twisting techniques to ensure cooperation. You'll have to create a secure system, safe from compromise, to verify and use the information. Again, we can show you how. But you have to do it.'

The commander was not happy. 'For fifty years, informants kept the communists in power. It was the curse of our lives. Who could we trust? No one.' He hunched over and clasped his hands. 'After Poland was free, I waited for two years to make sure the old regime would not return. Then I killed my neighbor. That's how bad it was. Now you are telling me I must do the same thing. Will my neighbor kill me?'

'You don't have a choice,' Duncan said.

The commander looked at his watch. 'They should have located the hostage by now.' The tone of his voice announced that his intelligence section had failed. He picked up the phone and told his operations center where the terrorists had taken the hostage. 'I think you'll enjoy this.'

The commander was right and Bender had to work to maintain a poker face, the dispassionate observer merely recording events. The small, two-room farmhouse where the mock-terrorists had taken the hostage for the exercise was painted bright blue and typical of the ancient farmhouses in the area. But the owners had prospered in recent years and it had been deserted in favor of a newer home. Still, it served as a reminder of the not so distant past.

Duncan kept up a running commentary as the exercise unfolded. 'Rule number one, General, isolate and clear the area. Look how they sweep the vicinity of booby traps or ambushes before the terrorists are aware they are even here. I've seen cops rush up to a situation and get hosed down in crossfire. That's not going to happen with these guys. They're good.'

'And rule number two?' Bender asked.

'Establish communications and bug the place.'

'Then what happens?'

Duncan was enjoying himself and wanted to get involved. But that wasn't going to happen. 'Time, talk and tear gas.'

'I'm afraid I don't have time for that.' Then Bender remembered a similar exercise from years before. 'How long will they hold James?'

Duncan laughed. 'Well, sir, he is the hostage.'

Bender took the mental equivalent of a deep breath. He hoped the exercise was not out of control.

The commander drove up in a US-built Humvee bristling with antennas and packed with radios. 'General Bender, we're going to assume negotiations have reached the stage where we are giving the terrorists a getaway vehicle.' He pointed to a dark gray van and handed Bender a headset. 'A team has placed sensitive monitors on the outside walls and we can hear everything inside.'

Bender listened. He could hear a man whimpering, begging for mercy. A husky woman's voice kept reassuring him it was just an exercise. Then she added, 'You'll get your clothes back in a few minutes.'

Bender's mental deep breath became a gulp. 'Was it necessary to strip him?'

'Well, sir,' Duncan replied, 'that's what happens in real life. He's probably still got his shoes on and a bag over his head.'

The commander spoke into his radio. On cue, two men moved silently toward the back wall of the farmhouse. 'Always find the blind spot,' Duncan said. The men were against the wall and using hand signals to communicate. They attached a ribbon charge of C4 plastic explosive to the wall, outlining the opening they intended to create. 'That's the diversion,' Duncan explained. 'James is in the other room, so he's safe.'

'I hope so.'

When the charge was in place and the detonator armed, one of the men against the wall raised his hand, his fingers crossed. The charge was armed. The dark gray van drew up to the front of the farmhouse. The driver got out and opened all the doors to the van, showing that it was empty. The driver retreated to safety, leaving the engine running.

The back wall of the home exploded in a flash and one

of the men threw a stun grenade into the opening. Even in broad daylight the flash was blinding and the roar deafening. At the same time, six men burst out of the empty van and charged into the farmhouse. 'Where did they come from?' Bender gasped.

'A holographic image of the van's empty interior is projected in front of a paper curtain inside the cargo compartment.' Gunfire echoed from the farmhouse. Duncan never missed a beat. 'The assault team is hidden behind the curtain and just rips through the paper.' A naked James was hustled out of the farmhouse as more gunfire punctuated the scene. 'At this point,' Duncan said, 'the terrorists should all be dead or acting very friendly.'

The commander drove back up. 'The area is secure.' Duncan and Bender followed him over to the waiting van, where James was sitting, a blanket now around his shoulders. 'Mr James,' the commander said, 'thank you for volunteering to be the hostage. I hope it was a valuable learning experience for all of us.'

James glared at him. 'This was a gross violation of diplomatic immunity. For your information, I am the Deputy Charge of Mission representing the President of the United States.'

The commander gave him a sympathetic look. 'The first time is always the hardest. Unfortunately, if this were a real situation, you'd be dead. The assault team repeatedly shouted, "James, drop! Get down!" You stood up directly into the line of fire. Luckily, we were only firing blanks.'

'We will lodge an official protest with the Ministry of—' The sound of an arriving helicopter drowned James out.

They waited as the helicopter's engine spun down and the rotor blades slowed. 'We'll talk about it later,' Bender said, ending the discussion.

A lanky figure got out of the helicopter. The commander visibly stiffened as Jerzy Fedor walked up to them. 'Well, Mr Ambassador, what do you think of my SPS unit?'

CHAPTER FIFTEEN

Air Force One, over Illinois

Maddy Turner sat with her advisors as Air Force One descended into Chicago's O'Hare airport. Shaw leaned forward in his seat, explaining how Illinois fitted into her whirlwind tour of the six states critical to winning a presidential election. 'Illinois unlocks the Midwest. The bastards know it, the reporters trailing along sniffin' up our tail know it, and we know it. So don't worry about what they're thinking. Let 'em speculate, percolate, and scramb-a-late while we find out if you've got the political base to run in your own right. Think of Chicago as the key to Illinois. But Chicago is a tough objective. We're talking old-fashioned party politics: rigid organization, precinct captains, organizing the troops, getting out the vote.'

'You make it sound like a military organization.'

'In a sense it is. Chicago has a political machine with a rigid hierarchy and a command structure. The trick is to make the generals want to do what you want them to do.'

'And how do I do that?'

'Now we're talking leadership. You convince the generals you're the candidate who can win and Illinois is yours. Show 'em you've got the popularity to win and then challenge 'em to deliver the vote.' The FASTEN SEAT BELTS lights went on and they strapped in for landing. The 747 touched down and taxied to the commercial side of the field, well away from the passenger terminals and the interminable lines of airliners waiting for takeoff. Shaw looked out his window. 'We weren't expecting anything like this.'

Turner followed his gaze and caught her breath. A huge crowd strained at the barriers and waved crude, hand-lettered signs in the wind. There was a hint of rain and they were bundled up against the cold. Yet there was a spontaneity and warmth about them that echoed across the parking ramp. Conflicting emotions tore at her. Ego and vanity blended with pride and satisfaction while purpose and resolution drew her out of her seat and to her feet. And there was awe. But the echo of Maura's voice reminded her that she was still mortal and fallible.

Joe Litton, her press secretary, came forward before the aircraft had stopped. 'Madame President, the Secret Service says this is the biggest crowd they've ever seen at an airport. The reporters are hounding me for a quote. You might want to say a few words to them first.'

Shaw was still looking out the window. 'Go talk to them. Be humble, be awed.'

'I am,' Turner replied.

Shaw hunched in front of the window, trying to gauge the size of the crowd. He was brisk: 'You've got the popularity, Mizz President. Now challenge the generals to deliver the goods.'

Warsaw

Winston James was about to do the bravest thing in his life. He was going to resign as Bender's DCM. He carefully adjusted his tie, buttoned his coat, and marched resolutely across the Red Room and into the ambassador's office. 'Thank you for seeing me,' he began. Bender waved him to a seat. 'I'd prefer to remain standing. Mr Ambassador, I'm afraid we are at total cross-purposes here.'

'How so?'

'Apparently, sir, you are operating under several misconceptions. An embassy is *not* an action agency like the military.'

'And what would you call the entire third floor?'

'The CIA functions entirely within the scope of a legation as an intelligence-gathering body. We are, if you will, legal spies.'

'I assure you, Winslow, that what the CIA is doing is not legal.'

James refused to be swayed. 'Further, you appear to be under the illusion that, as ambassador, you are utterly free to conceive and act in policy formation. Nothing could be further from the truth. We are here to represent the President of the United States and implement her foreign policy, not make it.'

'And what if the President's foreign policy is for us to conceive and implement in certain areas?'

'Then you must do so. But not at the expense of the dignity and integrity of your staff.'

'You're still angry about the hostage incident.'

'I was abused,' James replied, his voice huffy and strained.

'I understand Ewa Pawlik was the interpreter in the staff car. What did she tell you when you were stopped?'

'She said it was a police exercise and to follow their instructions.'

'Have you ever planned or participated in a hostage exercise?' James shook his head. 'Then,' Bender continued, 'perhaps you learned something and will be better prepared if the real thing should occur. I understand there's an embassy operating instruction on terrorist and hostage situations.' Another nod from James. 'You're in a unique position because of your experience and I can't think of anyone who can speak with more authority than you on this subject. Perhaps this would be the ideal time to update the operating instruction and brief the staff. Perhaps even an exercise—' He stopped at the look on James's face.

'I might be able to do something in that regard,' James allowed, hedging his commitment.

'Why don't you think about it and get back to me.'

'Thank you, sir. I will.' James spun around and left. Halfway back to his office, he stopped and remembered his original purpose. For the first time in months, he was excited and felt good. He wanted to update the anti-terrorist/hostage operating instruction and test it. Perhaps it could even be a model for other embassies. His resignation could wait.

Air Force One, over California

Shaw was on a roll.

'We got momentum here, Mizz President. I've never seen anything like it. After the turnout at the airport, those Chicago fat cats rolled over and begged you to stroke their bellies.' He laughed. 'And you did. I never heard 'em purr like that. My Gawd, it was almost obscene, they were so contented. Now let's see if we can repeat it in the land of la-la.' An aide handed him the latest news clips taken off the Internet. He hunched over and studied them. 'It's a slow news day. We're on page one because nothin' else is hot.' He paced the President's cabin, waving the pages in the air like a fly swatter. 'Hollywood is the heart of the beast.'

'Hollywood doesn't have a heart,' Richard Parrish muttered.

Shaw shook his head. 'Americans crave theater. Entertain me, entertain me. But they also want someone to look up to and admire. Since we ain't got a king or queen to stand up and be deified, the public picks whoever is available. More often than not, the whoever comes from Hollywood. If you don't believe me, just schedule yourself opposite the Academy Awards and find out who comes in suckin' hind tit.'

'What's your point?' Turner asked.

Shaw sat down. 'This is gonna take a different approach. Substance doesn't count here, style does. In Chicago, you had to challenge 'em. Here you got to *wow 'em.*'

'How do you propose I do that?'

'Well, Mizz President, give 'em what they want and they'll come out every time.'

Turner felt equal parts annoyance and amusement. 'Patrick, I've heard that line before. Get to the point.'

'I had a fashion designer work up a new wardrobe for

this trip,' Shaw said. Turner arched an eyebrow in disapproval and he grew very serious. 'Trust me on this one, Madame President.' He gave a friendly shrug. 'Couldn't hurt to look.'

The chartered aircraft carrying the press on the presidential tour landed at Burbank airport thirty minutes before Air Force One arrived. The size of the crowd the Secret Service was predicting would have totally disrupted Los Angeles International and the airport authorities asked the White House to find another arrival location. Although the change was announced twenty-four hours in advance, there was still confusion, and many of the reporters could not find their TV crews.

Liz Gordon from CNC-TV scrambled to find her cameraman and was running toward the arrival area when Air Force One taxied in. Shaw had warned her to find a location that would give her a good shot of the President getting off the plane. Liz pushed her way through the crowd and bullied past lesser luminaries in the reporting world. Her cameraman was still setting up when the stairs were pushed against the forward entrance of the 747 and the door opened. Liz gave her hair a shake and did a sound balance. Then she was live, looking into the camera with Air Force One in the background.

'This is the fourth stop on President Turner's whirlwind tour. While it is becoming increasingly obvious that—'

'Go to the President,' a voice in her earphone said.

Gordon never missed a beat as she turned toward the aircraft. '—the President is personally testing the depth of her support in key states . . .' She stopped, at a loss for words, not sure if she was seeing the President or not. A woman stood in the doorway wearing a stylish hip-length leather jacket and very chic but impeccably tailored pants. A tie belt snared her narrow waist and the collar to her jacket was open enough to reveal a man's-style white silk shirt. Then it hit. It was Maddy Turner.

'Talk,' the voice in Gordon's earphone commanded.

'This is the first time,' Gordon managed to say, 'that the President has appeared in public wearing trousers. Judging by the reaction around me, she has caused a sensation. I hope the camera can capture the full effect she is having on this crowd. By simply changing her style of dress, she has reached out to them and said, "I am one of you".'

On board Air Force One, Shaw charted her progress from a TV monitor in the communications section. He grunted in satisfaction as he channel-surfed. The reaction was unanimously favorable. 'That got their attention,' he muttered to himself.

Warsaw

Peter Duncan collapsed on the couch in Bender's office. He was freshly showered and shaved but fatigue was etched on his face. He looked as if he hadn't slept in two days. Automatically, Bender buzzed the outer office for coffee. 'It's too early,' he grumbled. His staff still hadn't gotten the word he liked to start work early. Ewa Pawlik answered on the fourth ring and promised to bring a tray in.

'Problems,' Duncan muttered. 'I've been on a field exercise with Special Public Services for the last thirty-six hours. They're peaked and ready to go. I don't envy their commander. It's like having two hundred hungry Doberman pinschers in your back yard with their balls all tied to the same tree.'

'So what's the problem?'

'Intelligence.' He fell silent when Ewa knocked and entered with a tea cart.

'Your secretary is here,' she said, 'and Mr James has just arrived with your read file.' The two men watched her as she poured them coffee. Then she was gone.

Duncan sighed. 'Lovely girl. Some lucky devil.'

'I asked security to run an expanded background check on her,' Bender said. 'She came up clean.'

Duncan nodded. 'There are times when beauty is suspect in itself.' He took a sip of the strong brew and savored it for a moment. 'SPS is ready to go but we're not providing the intelligence they need.'

'Why?'

'I can't crack the system. Everyone in the embassy is

charming and friendly. They appear helpful and promptly pass the buck. No one's willing to make a decision.'

Bender's secretary buzzed. Winslow James was ready with the daily intelligence summary. Bender had him sent in. James marched into the office and handed him the thick read file and a summation of the local situation. He stood while Bender scanned the two-page document. It was accurate, brief and well written. 'I'm impressed,' Bender said. 'Make sure key members of the staff are on the distribution list.'

James frowned. 'The CIA will only participate if the intelligence summary is for your eyes only.'

'You got farther with them than I did,' Duncan groused.

Bender stood up. 'I think we need to speak to the gentlemen upstairs.' He led the way into the main corridor and to the elevator. 'How do we get it to stop at the third floor?'

James punched the button for the third floor and spoke into the speaker. 'The ambassador for Mr Riley.' The elevator rose slowly and passed the third floor. It stopped at the fourth. 'They don't like unannounced visits,' James muttered.

Bender hit the button for the third floor and spoke. 'Tell Mr Riley to meet me in the bubble room. Now.' He hit the button for the basement and the elevator rapidly descended. The doors opened and Bender again hit the button for the third floor. 'I expect Mr Riley in two minutes.' He marched out of the elevator and into the hallway. A Marine was sitting behind a desk, guarding a door. He stood and came to attention. 'Good morning, Corporal Kincaid,' said Bender. 'We need to use the bubble room.' The Marine punched a four-digit code into the lock and the heavy door swung open.

The three men walked inside. The room's walls were bare cement and without decoration. A glass partition in the center of the room encircled a small round table with six chairs. Corporal Kincaid entered with an electrical wand and scanned the walls, chairs, and table. Then he ran it over the three men. He frowned when the wand activated on Duncan. 'Pacemaker,' Duncan said. The Marine thoroughly frisked him and then checked the security dossier at his desk, confirming that Duncan did wear a pacemaker.

A nondescript man wearing a dark suit entered the room. He was the face in the crowd that no one ever noticed. Officially, Evan Riley was carried on the embassy rolls as an administrative officer. Unofficially, he was the CIA chief of station and a power unto himself. Again, the Marine ran the wand over him. 'Thank you, Mr Riley.' He left and closed the door behind him before activating the jamming circuits. A low hum, almost indiscernible, emanated from the walls, and the four men sat down inside the glass enclosure. They were 'in the bubble', and no known device could monitor their conversation.

'You wished to speak to me,' Riley said.

'First,' Bender said, 'let me thank you for helping Winslow compile a daily intelligence summary on the local situation. It is most helpful.' A little nod from Riley. 'However, I would like for key members of my staff to also see it.'

'That'll take a special clearance from Langley,' Riley said. 'They'll want to clear it before circulation.'

'And we lose immediacy.'

'It can't be helped.'

'Second, I want to open an intelligence channel to the Polish SPS through Mr Duncan in order to—'

Riley shook his head and interrupted him. 'Impossible.'

Bender drilled him with a hard look, '—in order to give the SPS the intelligence they need to effectively target the Russian Mafiya.'

Like most government bureaucracies, the CIA was very protective of its turf. While its main objective was intelligence-gathering, it demanded control over who had access to its information to prevent compromise of the system. In general, it was a good policy. Evan Riley's face was impassive. Above all else, he had to protect his sources, and he knew the danger of working with outsiders. Personally, he trusted no one, especially ambassadors. 'I'll forward your request to my superiors.'

'And I expect an answer tomorrow.'

'Then, sir, your answer will be negative.'

Bender took a deep breath. He had dealt with the CIA before. 'I understand your need to protect sources. By the time we pass the information to the SPS, they'll have no idea where it came from.'

'But you can't guarantee that.'

Bender drummed the table with his fingers. He had to get Riley's attention. 'You probably know that I am in direct communication with Mazana Hazelton.' Again, a little nod from Riley. But James was incredulous and gaped at him. If Bender was reporting to the National Security Advisor, then he had access to the President and was bypassing the Secretary of State. Bender smiled at James. 'That's close-hold information and not to go beyond this room.' He turned his full attention on Riley. 'Have you ever seen the President angry? Let me assure you, you never want to be the object of that anger.'

Riley's face paled. 'I'm quite sure something can be worked out.'

Bender stood and left. He had the CIA's attention.

Air Force One, over Texas

Shaw sat beside Turner as she thumbed through the folder containing the biographies and photos of the Texas oil and cattle barons she would be meeting in less than an hour. 'Don't let the good-old-boy routine fool you, Mizz President. You can cut their Texas accents like butter on a hot griddle and they'll be all Southern charm and smiles, but they didn't get where they are by being fools. All but two are self-made billionaires. Don't be afraid to speak to them in terms they understand.'

Turner raised an eyebrow. 'I'm not about to play the Southern belle.'

Shaw shook his big head. 'Think more like the widow who has to run the ranch to keep the family together. They care about two things: price supports for beef and depletion allowances for oil. And they'll want to hear from you on both of 'em.'

'I'm not in favor of either.'

'Then let Congress take the heat, not you. Sidestep the issue. Tell them money is like manure – you got to spread it around to do any good.'

'What exactly does that mean?'

'A lot to them. I'll back-door a few comments like "The President is more concerned with maintaining low prices than supports or allowances". They'll put the two together and think you can live with the current system as long as they don't get greedy. They'll be reaching for the checkbooks before we're back on Air Force One.'

'It's so manipulative.'

'They know what we're doing, Mizz President. Never forget these gentlemen are gamblers and they hedge their bets. They'll contribute more to whoever Leland backs for president. But they're willing to invest a couple of million to keep the door open just in case we win.'

'Speaking of Leland, what is he up to these days?'

'Like everyone else, lying low until he's sure you've got the wherewithal to run.'

Turner handed him the folder and buzzed for her traveling staff. 'How far is it to Roswell from Dallas?' she asked.

'Approximately an hour's flying time,' came the answer.

'I'd like to stop there for a few hours tomorrow and visit Brian. I've never been to NMMI.'

Worried glances all around. 'That's pretty short notice, Madame President,' Parrish murmured.

'I'm quite sure you can arrange it,' she said.

Warsaw

The call from the third floor of the embassy came at exactly 4 p.m., the last Friday of November. It was Evan Riley. 'Mr Ambassador, I was wondering if we might meet in the bubble room. Could Mr Duncan also be present?' Bender said they would be there in fifteen minutes. Riley was waiting for them when they arrived and actually offered a smile. 'Mr Ambassador, I must apologize for taking so long to get back to you, but the wheels grind slowly sometimes.' They sat down and Riley handed Bender a thin folder.

'Let's see,' Duncan said, enjoying the chance to heckle the CIA head of station. 'On Wednesday morning, General Bender asked for a response in twenty-four hours.' He did the math in his head. 'That was fifty-six hours ago. For the CIA, that's moving at warp speed.'

'Well, we did sidestep some mountains on this one.'

Duncan chuckled, enjoying the exchange. 'You mean you monitored an interesting phone call between the general and the National Security Advisor.'

'For the record, no,' Riley said. 'The ambassador has been the soul of patience on this one. We checked you out. Most impressive, Mr Duncan. I had no idea. How many mobsters have you put in jail?'

'Important ones? Six.'

'Is that why there's a contract on your head?'

'Only one? I'm disappointed.' The two men laughed.

Bender opened the folder and read. 'How good is this information?' He passed the folder to Duncan to read.

'Please, sir,' Riley replied, 'don't ask that question. Let's just say it's worth acting on.'

Duncan shook his head. 'It's too good to be true. A major shipment of money all on one airplane whose last stop is at Modlin Air Base here in Poland. Mikhail Vashin can't be that stupid.'

'That,' Riley said, 'was the initial reaction of our analysts. But we've put together a profile on him that makes for very interesting reading. Vashin is acting within the Russian tradition of grand gestures, big buildings, fancy cars, and beautiful women. It appeals to the Russian character, and success breeds authority and power. There is one story about a bizarre funeral last April that is very illuminating.' He gave a little shudder. 'Anyway, on analysis, this becomes more believable.'

'So who are we dealing with here?' Bender asked.

'An egomaniac,' Riley answered. He paused for a moment. 'I'll get a copy of the profile to you.' Another pause. 'Vashin is emerging as the new Russian strongman.'

'A new Stalin?' Duncan asked.

'Different, but just as ruthless.'

Duncan rubbed his jaw, calculating the probability of

success. 'Sunday night is awfully short notice and I don't think SPS can be ready in time. This'll be their first operation. They need a success the first time out. It's too risky.'

Now it was Riley's turn to press for action. But he had to convince them without revealing, or even alluding to, the source of the CIA's information. The Agency had a spy so highly placed that Vashin was wired for sound. 'Our analysts have correlated this with other intelligence and believe this money shipment is a one-time event. It's a chance to send Vashin a message he understands.'

'How much money are we talking about?' Bender asked.

Again, Riley briefly considered what he could tell them. 'We estimate approximately fifteen to twenty billion dollars in securities, gold, and actual money.'

The buccaneer in Duncan came to the fore and he licked his lips in anticipation. 'This is better than a Spanish treasure galleon loaded with gold.' Another thought occurred to him. 'How much space does that much money take up?'

Riley shrugged. 'At least a plane-load.'

Bender made the decision. 'Pass this on to the SPS.'

'Can you keep Jerzy Fedor at the Council of Ministers out of the loop?' Riley asked.

'Why?' Bender replied.

'That's another question we'd rather not answer.'

Duncan exhaled loudly. 'It's still pretty short notice.'

'You can make it happen,' Bender reassured him.

'What exactly,' Duncan wondered, 'is Vashin going to do with twenty billion dollars?'

CHAPTER SIXTEEN

Moscow

Vashin threw down the latest edition of the *Megapolis Express*. He was furious at the lead article detailing the current successes of Vitaly Rodonov, the Minister of Defense. 'Why isn't Rodonov dead?' he shouted.

'I'll find out,' Geraldine answered, watching carefully for the signs of a fit. She retreated to her office and placed a call to Tom Johnson, the head of security. Then, to be on the safe side, she called Le Coq d'Or and ordered the two girls, Naina and Liya, to come to the penthouse suite. She sat at her desk and scrolled through Vashin's calendar while she weighed her options. Vashin was changing, and that offered new possibilities as well as dangers. Johnson arrived and they went into the penthouse, where Vashin was still standing in front of the big picture window overlooking Moscow.

'Mikhail,' Geraldine said, bringing him back to the moment.

'Why isn't Rodonov in the ground?'

'He didn't take the honey trap,' Johnson said. 'Apparently he's a happily married family man.' Vashin shot him a deadly look. 'We can't blame the girls,' Johnson hastily added.

'Then use more direct means.'

'That's an easy solution with potentially bad consequences. No one must be able to trace it to you or your organization. We made one failed attempt.'

Vashin's head jerked up. 'I didn't know there had been an attempt on his life.'

Johnson gave a little nod. 'Perhaps you remember the car the Belorussian separatists blew over the Moscow Business Bank in Minsk?'

Vashin looked puzzled. 'But that had nothing to do with Rodonov.'

Johnson said glumly, 'Rodonov was in Minsk for a secret meeting. We discovered he would be driving down Serafimovicha Street. So we planted a bomb like those the Belorussians use in the sewer and waited for him to drive over it. We got the wrong car.'

'Why wasn't I told about it?'

Johnson was brutally frank. 'For two reasons. First, because we failed. Second—'

Vashin interrupted him. 'So it could never be traced back to me.'

'Exactly.'

Vashin looked out the window. 'Very good.' Johnson took that as a dismissal and left.

Geraldine sensed the timing was right. 'Why should you be concerned with Vitaly Rodonov? He's beneath you, not worthy of your concern. Besides, he did go to NATO and saved our European landing rights. The gateway is still wide open.'

'But not as open as it was before,' Vashin muttered.

'Progress is not a straight road. You taught me that.' She sensed he was in a receptive mood. 'Vashin Towers is a major junction on that road and a symbol of what you can do. But it is a building. Now the people need to see the man behind the great accomplishments. Perhaps it is time for grand gestures and maybe even forgiveness. Show the people, your followers, that great power also means mercy.'

Vashin liked what he was hearing. 'Perhaps you're right.'

She reached out and touched his arm. 'Are you still having the same dream?' He nodded, not looking at her. 'Only the gods live in clouds, Mikhail. I'm certain it's a message. What else can it mean? Everything you do, all that you touch, should be big and godlike.'

The Hill

The Box echoed with commands and, at exactly eleven o'clock Saturday morning, the Corps marched out of Hagerman Barracks. The ranks were a little straighter, the turns sharper, and their step more purposeful as they came on to the parade field. The Tactical Leadership Advisors watched nervously as their charges passed by and, occasionally, cast furtive glances at the waiting crowd. The grandstands were overflowing and the field lined with spectators. What had promised to be a normal Saturday morning parade attended by a few townspeople had turned into a major event.

The reason for the sudden interest was sitting on the reviewing stand with General McMasters, his wife, and the commandant, Colonel Nelson Day. 'Madame President,' Lenora McMasters asked, 'have you ever seen a military parade before?'

'This is my first time,' Maddy replied. 'Does the town always turn out like this?'

'Sometimes,' Lenora answered. 'It's probably because you are the first sitting president to ever visit Roswell.' The Corps moved on to the field.

'I think Brian has mentioned you three or four times. He calls you the Cookie Lady. How many have you baked?'

Lenora laughed. 'I quit counting after the first year. It's such a little thing, even silly, but for some reason—'

Maddy reached out and touched her hand. 'Thank you.' They fell silent as the superintendent stepped up to the microphone. He began by calling for the chaplain to give the invocation. The appropriate honors were played for the President, and Adjutant's Call was sounded. 'Colonel Day,' Maddy asked, 'what's happening?'

The commandant beamed with pride as he explained a standard military parade. Then it was time for the Corps to pass in review. McMasters and Day escorted her to the front of the stand to review the cadets as they passed by. The commands were sharp as Alpha Troop approached, its guidon lowered. 'Eyes right' echoed over the field. As one, the cadets' heads snapped to the right.

'They're wonderful,' Maddy said. 'You must be very proud of them.'

'We are, Madame President,' McMasters said. He gave a low laugh. 'And sometimes they're show dogs.' Maddy looked at him, not sure how to interpret his remark. 'They're still kids, Madame President. But they know when to shine.'

'Indeed they do.' She watched as Brian's troop marched by. She barely recognized her son and her eyes misted over.

It had been a long day and finally Maddy was alone with Brian in his room. 'I can't believe how neat and clean it is.'

'We had a big room inspection this morning.'

'Before the parade?'

'And we had an open-ranks inspection before that.'

The mother in Maddy came out. 'That's asking too much.'

'Ah, Mom. I got it all locked up. Thanks to Maggot and the Trog.'

Maddy looked at her son, hearing something new. He was not the same willful, very spoiled boy she had sent to New Mexico. 'Are you happy here?'

Brian shrugged. 'I got some good friends.' He fell silent. Then added, 'I want to come back next year.'

Near Modlin Air Base, Poland

A steady stream of small vans and cars started arriving at the old redbrick warehouse shortly after dark on Sunday evening. The routine was the same for each vehicle: the driver stopped and gave the recognition signal to the guard, then the two or three passengers would get out and clear their weapons as other guards escorted them to the side of the warehouse, then another team would search the vehicle to ensure it was not booby-trapped or carrying weapons. Finally, the vehicle was waved into the warehouse, where it was quickly unloaded. The driver would proceed through and load his passengers on the back before rapidly driving away.

Inside the warehouse, the canvas money bags or suitcases that had been delivered were loaded into three Brinks-style armored trucks. It was hard to tell who was more nervous, the Polish Mafia delivering the money or the Russian Mafiya receiving it. But the collection point worked well, and soon the last vehicle arrived – a dark gray Mercedes-Benz sedan. It went through the same routine and was waved inside.

The moment the car stopped, a cloud of gas erupted from the trunk, out of the grill, and from underneath. The last thing the driver did was to throw open his door to escape. That only triggered another burst of gas. Within six seconds, everyone in the warehouse was unconscious.

Outside, the guards heard a brief commotion as warnings were shouted. Then all was quiet. Two guards ran for the door to check. But when they opened it, escaping gas knocked them out. Bright lights clicked on and froze the remaining guards in an illuminated tableau as a bullhorn ordered them to drop their weapons and freeze. One guard fired his AK-47 blindly into the night. A single shot dropped him before he got off four rounds.

Black-uniformed men stepped out of the shadows and secured the area before going inside, where the occupants were starting to regain consciousness. All but one would suffer from a splitting headache and have a bitter taste in his mouth. The exception was dead from an asthmatic reaction to the gas. The commander of SPS drove up in his command Humvee and got out. He spoke briefly to his men before going inside. The prisoners were all gagged, blindfolded, and bound with plastic flex cuffs. He allowed himself a tight smile as the Mercedes was recharged with gas and the small convoy reformed, ready to move.

Near Pozan, Poland

The bunker at Crown Central was unusually busy for a Sunday night. Normally, only the radar operator was awake at eleven o'clock, and his main problem was to find something to read. But tonight the entire crew was awake and still in a state of euphoric shock mixed with childlike delight over the new radar system the Americans had finished installing the day before. They had never suspected that a system like the AN/TPS-59 even existed. The contrast between the US-built radar with its phased-array antenna, built-in anti-jam circuits, and sophisticated computer system and the old Soviet Barlock radar was extreme. A vague image of the Wright brothers' Flyer and a modern jet fighter flitted through the back of the young radar operator's mind.

The American technician stood over the radar operator's shoulder as the target they had been waiting for appeared on the scope, 165 miles to the west and still over Germany. 'Roll the control ball and place the cursor over the target,' he explained. 'Now press down on the ball until you feel the first detent.' The computer analyzed the target and spat out a wealth of digital information, displaying the key numbers on the screen next to the target, an Ilyushin 76. 'Good,' the American said. 'If you want the system to track the target, press the ball to the second detent.' The Pole did as he said and the system flashed. The target became a green inverted V. 'Now you can leave it or tag it up as a bandit – a hostile aircraft.'

'It's a Vnukova aircraft,' the radar operator explained. 'That's a Russian diplomatic flight. We get two or three a week. They often land at Modlin Air Base near Warsaw when they are going to Europe, but never on the return flight.'

'It's hostile,' a man standing behind the American said. He was dressed in black combat fatigues and armed with an automatic strapped on his hip. Only the small patch on his right shoulder announced he was with Special Public Services.

The American reached over the radar operator and punched at the keyboard. The inverted green V turned red. A warning light flashed and the display went to a backup mode. 'I'll be damned,' the American said, 'he's jamming us. I didn't know the Ilyushin had a jamming capability.' His hand reached for the anti-jam circuits on the overhead panel.

The SPS officer grabbed his wrist, stopping him. 'This is a special flight. We don't want to scare them off. I want him to land.'

'But eastbound flights never land,' the radar operator said.

'This one will,' the SPS officer predicted.

Now they had to wait. With each passing minute, the SPS officer looked more worried. Finally, the altitude readout on the target started to decrease. 'The Ilyushin is descending,' the radar operator said. 'He's on track for Modlin Air Base.'

A look of triumph flashed on the SPS officer's face as he reached for the telephone. 'Put me through to Jerzy Fedor at the Council of Ministers,' he told the operator. As expected, Fedor could not be reached, and the SPS officer left a message. 'Please tell Mr Fedor that we have a Russian aircraft landing at Modlin Air Base without diplomatic clearance.'

Modlin Air Base, Poland

The Ilyushin coming from Europe touched down just before midnight and squealed to a halt, its brakes howling from the heat generated by landing on the short runway. Its rear cargo doors opened and armed men wearing camouflaged uniforms streamed out to secure the area before the plane taxied in. They were not regular military but a special unit recruited from disaffected former members of Speznatz, Russian special forces. They ran into the surrounding trees and set up a perimeter. Satisfied, they radioed that the area was secure.

But they should have gone fifty feet deeper into the trees.

The Ilyushin lumbered clear of the runway and moved slowly to the parking ramp, where a bank of portable floodlights was switched on, creating an island of light around the Il-76. The aircrew shut down engines as a fuel truck drove up under the plane's wing. The pumper got out of the cab and connected the hose to the single-point refueling valve. Following procedures, the aircrew shut off all power and then got off the aircraft with the remaining guards. The older Ilyushins had a bad habit of not grounding correctly and generating unwanted sparks, which could be very unhealthy during refueling.

The men guarding the perimeter were tired and bored. They had gone through a similar drill at six pickup points in the last fifteen hours without incident. Soon they removed their night vision goggles and cigarettes were passed around. They came alert when the convoy approached. Eager to finish, they pulled back to the edge of the trees as a dark gray Mercedes led the three armored trucks up to the Ilyushin. One heard some movement in the trees behind him. He listened for a few moments and then wrongly decided it was an animal disturbed by their presence.

It all happened at once. The pumper disconnected the fuel hose from the aircraft, the men standing around the Mercedes-Benz collapsed to the ground, and the portable floodlights went out. The rear doors of the armored trucks burst open and men wearing gas masks poured out, surrounding the aircraft. A hail of gunfire rained from the trees and cut down the perimeter guards. It was over as quickly as it had begun.

Men dressed in black fatigues emerged from the trees and quickly examined the guards. No mercy was given, and twice a single shot rang out as they finished their work. Without a sound, the men dragged the dead guards into the trees. Except for the pools of blood, no trace was left. Four men emerged from the undergrowth and sprinkled an absorbent material that resembled kitty litter on the blood. They swept it into a box and then disappeared into the shadows.

Two trucks drove up as the team who had assaulted the aircraft gave the aircrew and remaining guards an injection. They would be unconscious for another two or three hours. More men joined the assault team as they rapidly unloaded the aircraft, passing bag after bag of money down the ramp and throwing them into the trucks. Then came the suitcases and boxes filled with negotiable securities. The two trucks drove away and a cargo loader approached. Offloading the gold was another matter. Two pallets of bullion rolled out the back of the Ilyushin and the cargo loader groaned under the weight. The aircraft seemed to ride higher on its landing gear.

The cargo loader drove slowly away as two more trucks approached. But this time they carried a grisly cargo for loading. The bodies of the perimeter guards were carried one by one on to the cargo deck and carefully arranged with their weapons and equipment. Then the aircrew and guards who were still unconscious were loaded into the trucks and driven to safety.

The commander of SPS drove up in his Humvee. He got out and inspected the area, obviously very pleased with the operation. He checked his watch. They were ahead of schedule. He gave an order and thermite charges were placed in the Ilyushin. The last went into the single-point refueling valve. Radio-controlled igniters were inserted and the men moved away. The commander gave the order and the thermite charges were sequentially detonated. A small explosion flashed and the right wing of the aircraft crumpled to the ground, severed at the root. A series of explosions tore at the aircraft as flames engulfed the fuselage. Soon it was a roaring inferno sending a beacon of flame and smoke high into the night sky.

'Sparks during refueling,' the commander said. 'The politicians in Warsaw will understand.'

The blue-and-white helicopter circled the still-smoldering wreckage before landing. Little was recognizable other than the black scorch marks that roughly outlined the airframe of the Ilyushin. Jerzy Fedor got out of the helicopter. His normally lean and ravaged face was even more cadaverous as he spoke to the cluster of officers and firemen waiting for his arrival.

'The survivors are all requesting political asylum,' the base commander told him.

'Why?' one of Fedor's assistants asked.

Fedor snorted. 'Consider who we're dealing with. If you were a Russian who survived this, would you want to go home?'

'But it was a refueling accident.'

'A very convenient accident, yes?' Fedor climbed back into his helicopter and took off. But instead of returning to Warsaw, it headed for an old country manor house that had served as a resort for the communist élite and their families during the heyday of Soviet rule. Now it was a dilapidated eyesore. The helicopter landed in the paddock beside the stables and Fedor climbed out and walked quickly inside, where the commander of SPS greeted him.

'Why wasn't I told of this?' Fedor demanded.

'I thought you were,' the commander replied. 'Perhaps you should speak to President Lezno.'

'I will.'

The commander led Fedor into the stables. Fedor froze, struck dumb by the sight. 'How much is here?' he asked.

'We haven't even tried to count it.'

Fedor's face became animated. 'My God! What do we do with this much money?'

Moscow

A very worried group of men clustered around Geraldine Blake on the main floor of the action room in Vashin Towers. 'I think you should wake him and tell him now,' one of the men counseled. She hesitated, not sure what to do.

'Treat it as a state crisis,' another offered.

'Do you know what was on that airplane?' she asked. No answer. 'Thank God it was an accident.'

'Mikhail Vashin does not believe in accidents,' a third voice said. From his tone, he was dismally contemplating his longevity.

'Who planned the shipment?' the first voice asked. They needed a scapegoat. Head shakes all around.

'Did the American have anything to do with it?' This from the third speaker.

'Not that I know of,' Geraldine answered. 'But one hand never knows what the other is doing here.' She thought for a few moments. 'I'll wake him.' She walked quickly off the floor and returned to her office, where she placed a call to Le Coq d'Or and ordered Naina and Liya to come immediately to the penthouse suite. The manager said they were with clients and it would take an hour. 'I want them here in thirty minutes,' she said, banging down the phone. Then she called Vashin's doctor and told him to come over. Finally, she called Tom Johnson, just in case.

The girls arrived last and Geraldine gave them all final instructions. Then she went to the restroom off her office and undressed. She combed out her hair, slipped on a silk dressing gown, and stepped into high-heeled slippers. She took one last look in the mirror and walked to Vashin's bedroom. Tom Johnson was with the guard on duty and gave Geraldine a nod as she went in. A blue light glowed from one corner, casting a soft light over the room as she approached the huge bed. She nudged the girl sleeping beside Vashin and motioned her to leave. Then she dropped her robe and sat on the side of the bed. She reached over and stroked Vashin's penis until it was hard. He groaned in his sleep. Slowly, he came awake.

'Mikhail,' she whispered.

'Yes.' He was now fully awake. She continued to stroke him. 'There's bad news.' She felt him grow even more rigid. 'There's been an aircraft accident.'

'Is it the money?'

'I'm afraid so.' She bent over and took him in her mouth.

'What happened?' His voice was amazingly calm and she wished she could see his face.

She raised her head. 'There was a fire on the ground.' His hand grabbed her hair and jammed her back on to him. She used her teeth and tongue until he came.

'Are you sure it was an accident?'

'We're not positive. The details are still coming in.'

He pushed her away. 'Get Yaponets.'

Vashin was dressed and drinking tea when the senior godfather of the *vor* arrived. 'Did they tell you?' Vashin asked. Yaponets nodded. He was still groggy from lack of sleep. 'What do you think?' Vashin demanded.

'There are no accidents.'

'Who is responsible?'

'My guess? Since it happened in Poland, the SPS. My sources say they are led by the Devil himself.'

Vashin grunted. 'They are only an arm. Who made the decision?'

'There's only one head.'

'I want it *cut off*.'

Yaponets considered his answer. 'I made many contacts in prison.'

'Do it quickly.'

'It will be difficult. I'll do what I can.' Yaponets stood and paced the room. 'You have a leak.'

'That's why we are speaking alone.' He waited. 'Now we need a diversion.'

'One of your spells?'

'Give me a few minutes then call them in. This will be a bad one. Make sure there are no sedatives.'

The White House

'Seventeen days and counting,' Patrick Shaw said, claiming the undivided attention of the six people who made up Maddy Turner's reelection committee. They were gathered in her private study off the Oval Office. 'After the President declares, the bastards will be in high gear and going for the jugular. Count on 'em hitting us with legal action to tie us up in knots in the courts and waste money hiring lawyers.'

The hungry look on his face reminded them of a Great White shark contemplating its next meal. 'Lawyers and the courts are the weapons of choice these days, the new checks and balances for the politically incontinent. Well,' he drawled, 'I don't mind playing that game one little bit. So we're gonna set them up.'

Turner shook her head, stopping him in full flow. 'We're not going to run that type of campaign,' she said, her tone quiet but firm.

Shaw dropped his Southern accent. 'Madame President, think of a vaccination against a disease. If the disease stays away, no harm is done. But if the disease hits, our defenses are ready. The ball's in their court and they can do whatever they want with it. But if they take the bait, we'll play them like hooked flounders. They'll come down with the worst case of political herpes on record.'

'Political herpes?'

Shaw gave a wicked laugh. 'Yep. You get it from screwing around where you shouldn't and then when you think you're over it, it comes back.'

Turner laughed. 'You're mixing your metaphors.' Her voice turned hard as granite. 'I repeat, we will not play those kinds of games.'

The meeting was over, and the committee left murmuring about their latest instructions. Shaw held back for a moment. 'Madame President, are we locked in concrete on this one?'

'We are, Patrick.' He shook his head as he left. Mazie came in. Since no sitting president is ever alone with one staff member, Richard Parrish sat in a far corner. 'I wanted to speak to you in private,' Turner said. Mazie arched an eyebrow but said nothing. 'What's the story behind the item in the PDB about the Poles capturing a major shipment of drug money last night?'

'It's a success story, Madame President. We provided the Poles the intelligence they needed and they acted on it.'

'Who acted on it?'

'An internal security organization called Special Public Services. You might call it the focus group for our security aide package.'

Turner drummed her fingers on her desk. 'Richard.'

Parrish cleared his throat. 'Senator Leland called about it this morning.' Because Leland was the chairman of the select committee on intelligence, he was the only senator who saw the President's Daily Brief. 'He's concerned that we're supporting a fascist organization in Poland.'

'The SPS a fascist organization?' Mazie said. 'He needs another visit to the Betty Ford Clinic.'

'We are going to have to respond,' Parrish said.

Mazie thought for a moment. 'I'll brief him this afternoon.

The National Security Advisor going to his office should stroke his ego.'

'One thing puzzles me,' Parrish said. 'Why is he involved?'

'I'm more worried about Vashin,' Mazie said. 'We hurt him and he'll react.'

'What will he do?' Turner asked.

'I don't honestly know, Madame President.'

'At least we've got honesty on our side.'

CHAPTER SEVENTEEN

Vandenberg AFB, California

Noreen Coker's dark brown eyes followed Air Force One as the beautiful blue-and-white Boeing 747 taxied in. 'What does it cost to fly that thing?' she asked the Air Force colonel standing next to her.

'The last I heard, ma'am, it was over fifty thousand dollars an hour.' The colonel escorted her to the waiting helicopter that would fly the President to the outdoor rally in San Luis Obispo. A Marine escorted her up the air stairs and into the passenger compartment.

'Those seats are for the President,' the Marine said, pointing to two airline-type seats facing each other and flanking the window on the left side of the aircraft.

Noreen laughed at the thought of Maddy Turner needing two seats. 'But she's such a little thing.'

The Marine didn't see the humor. 'The rear-facing seat is for whoever the President wishes to talk to.'

'I see,' Noreen said. She settled into the seat on the opposite side of the aisle and waited for Turner to arrive. She pulled out her speech introducing the President. Key phrases leaped off the page and she committed them to memory: . . . *my best friend . . . the little girl from San Luis Obispo who had a dream . . . a woman whose vision reaches across generations and into the future . . . possesses a rare courage and integrity.* Noreen leaned back and smiled at what was coming. Madeline O'Keith Turner would end her speech by announcing her candidacy for the presidency of the United States. Maddy was going to run in her own right.

Dennis was the first of the presidential party to climb on board. 'The weather is perfect,' he said. 'It's hard to believe Christmas is only five days away.'

'Is Maura here?' Noreen asked.

'She's already at the rally,' Dennis replied. 'Along with Sarah, Richard, and most of the press corps.'

The pilots started the engines, a sign that the President was only minutes away. Dennis stood by the door and waited for her arrival. Moments later, Madeline Turner stepped through the entry way and made her way to her seat. 'Dennis,' she called, pointing to the seat facing hers, 'please join us.' Dennis beamed as he sat down in the rear-facing seat. 'We need to talk,' she said as the steward buttoned up the cabin. It was amazingly quiet for a helicopter. 'Noreen, you're looking quite glamorous today. Have you lost weight?'

Noreen's laugh was silky smooth. 'I got rid of that no-good man.' She strapped in and the helicopter lifted off, heading for the park in San Luis Obispo, forty miles due north. 'Don't say it, you warned me.' Their laughter mingled as the helicopter turned out of the pattern. As always, it received priority clearance and Air Traffic Control diverted all traffic.

Pismo Beach, California

On a side street just off Highway 101, a white panel van pulled out of a ramshackle garage. The woman sitting in the passenger seat listened to a VHF radio scanner. She turned to the man in the back. 'Leon, the helicopter is airborne.' Leon zipped up his fire-retardant Nomex suit and pulled the hood over his head. He bent over the aluminum case that resembled a small coffin and unsnapped the cover. The driver wheeled on to the on-ramp and headed north toward San Luis Obispo. The woman checked her stopwatch. 'Eleven minutes.'

'We'll be there,' the driver promised.

Leon checked the battery pack.

Near San Luis Obispo, California

Dennis leaned forward in his seat and handed Turner the final draft of her speech. 'It's the same except for the introduction. We punched up the hometown angle.'

Turner read the speech. It was short, perhaps twenty minutes, not counting applause. She read it again, this time half aloud. She made one correction to the opening statement; it sounded too much like Shaw. 'Schedule,' she said. Dennis handed her and Noreen a detailed listing of the day's events following the rally. Turner leaned back in her seat and closed her eyes. Her hand reached out for Noreen's. 'Thank you for coming.'

'Girl, I wouldn't miss this for the world.'

The white van approached the last bridge on Highway 101. The front-seat passenger duly noted the two Secret Service agents standing at the rail checking traffic. 'Not enough,' she muttered to herself. 'Leon,' she said to the man in the back, 'check the backside of the bridge for scanners.'

Leon moved against the windows in the rear door as they passed underneath. 'Yeah. Two shits on this side. One's got a camera. The other a radio, I think.'

'It doesn't matter,' the woman said.

'I can see it,' Leon said, the calm in his voice not matching what he felt.

The woman checked her watch. 'Right on time. Go.' They started the routine they had practiced over fifty times. Leon moved into the center of the cargo compartment and dropped the panel that had been cut into the roof. He looked up, checking his field of view. He could see the helicopter off to their rear left. 'It's at our seven o'clock coming to four o'clock.' The woman picked up her laser rangefinder and held it in her lap as she rolled down her window and focused intently on the van's wing mirror. 'Four o'clock,' Leon said. He adjusted his oxygen mask and blast goggles. He bent over the aluminum case and extracted the deadly shoulder-held surface-to-air missile.

'I've got it,' she replied, her words coming more quickly. She raised the laser rangefinder and aimed it at the mirror. She didn't want to be seen aiming anything directly at the President's aircraft. The moment the helicopter was in the crosshairs, she pulled the trigger. The LED window flashed and she immediately lowered the rangefinder out of sight. 'Two point four miles,' she read. The helicopter was in the heart of the envelope. The woman drew the blast curtains, sealing Leon in the rear, and placed her hand on the release lever to the back doors.

Leon dialed 2.4 into the Strela and raised the missile to his shoulder, aiming it out the open roof. He placed the crosshairs on the helicopter and pulled the trigger to the first detent. The cryogenically cooled infrared seeker head locked on. The tracking light flashed and he pulled the trigger to the second detent. 'FIRE!' he shouted. The solid propellant booster filled the cargo compartment with smoke and flame as the four-and-a-half-foot missile leaped skyward. At the same time the woman pulled the release lever and the rear doors snapped open. The powerful fan they had installed in the van switched on and vented the cargo compartment, laying a smokescreen behind them. The doors slammed shut and the van raced for the next exit.

The sustainer rocket ignited as the missile reached its maximum speed of 1.76 Mach. The Secret Service agent on the bridge a mile back saw the rocket plume and yelled into his radio. 'MISSILE! ON YOUR LEFT, NINE O'CLOCK!'

The cameraman focused his Betacam on Liz Gordon. They did a sound check and she started to talk. 'It's a gorgeous December day here in San Luis Obispo and I can see the President's helicopter as it approaches to land. There is an unconfirmed rumor that Madeline Turner will announce— OH MY GOD THERE'S A MISSILE HOMING IN ON THE PRESIDENT'S HELICOPTER!' She pointed to the sky and the cameraman swung his camera around.

*　　*　　*

It was a contest between the Russian-built Strela-3 and the Sikorsky S-61V helicopter. On one side was a missile with advanced guidance and the capability to defeat flares and infrared jammers. The 4.4-pound high-explosive warhead had both contact and graze fusing. On the other side was a special-built helicopter equipped with flare dispensers and a new reticulated light infrared jammer. But the critical factor was the skill of the Marine pilot.

Without acknowledging the radio call, the pilot turned into the missile and saw it. He pulled on the collective lever and the helicopter shot skyward, forcing the missile into an upward trajectory. Then he slammed the collective to the floor and the big helicopter dropped like a rock as he turned through the missile. Flares streamed into the helicopter's wake.

The missile's warhead briefly acquired the flares and then rejected their heat signature. It reacquired the heat from the helicopter's intake and arched downward just as the pilot called for autorotation. The copilot reached up and retarded the throttles to flight idle, reducing the heat signature coming from the engines. Now a little ruby-red cupola mounted on the side of the helicopter flashed and a stream of conflicting heat signatures burned into the missile's guidance head.

The missile went ballistic in the last two hundred feet and passed over the helicopter. But the fuse sensed a shift in mass and exploded, the graze function working as designed.

A hail of expanding core shrapnel cut into the rear of the helicopter, slicing into the top-mounted engines, chipping at the rotor blades, and rupturing hydraulic lines. But the lightweight ceramic armor plate surrounding the passenger compartment held. The engines burst into flame as a savage vibration shook the helicopter. The copilot's hands were a blur of action as he reached up, pulled the throttles to the off position, and pulled the T-handles that shot the fire bottles, extinguishing the fire. With the power off, the vibration stopped. The helicopter plummeted earthward as the pilot set up for an autorotational landing.

The copilot hit the crash alarm and Dennis desperately held on. He glanced out the window and then at his President. He hit his seat belt release and came out of his seat. Before the Secret Service agent sitting on the jumpseat at the rear could move, Dennis spun Turner's seat around so she was facing rearward, a much safer position. The agent was out of his seat and coming forward as Dennis shoved pillows into Turner's lap. The agent threw a silver fire blanket over her and reached for more pillows.

Liz Gordon never stopped talking as her cameraman tracked the helicopter. 'The missile exploded above the helicopter . . . I saw a brief flash of fire and now can only see smoke . . . It is coming into land on the park near us and I can see something dark streaming out behind the helicopter . . . It's falling fast, way too fast. Oh my God, the President's mother and daughter are in the crowd. They have to be seeing this.

'Oh! Oh! The nose of the helicopter is coming up. I think they're going to make it. No. They're going way too fast! Oh, no!' She gasped for breath.

'Fuel off!' the pilot yelled. The copilot hit the two main fuel switches on the center console. The pilot pulled on the collective to flare and stop the rate of descent. But without power to feed in, they weren't going to make it. As they passed through forty feet, the pilot knew they were going to crash and pulled back on the cyclic control stick to raise the nose. The helicopter banged down tail first. The rotors flexed downward from the impact and cut into the tail rotor drive shaft. The aircraft bounced into the air as it yawed to the right and rolled to the left.

Dennis and the Secret Service agent were not strapped in and they shot forward, crashing into the forward bulkhead. The rotor blades dug into the ground and broke off, cartwheeling across the ground and tearing into the scattering crowd. The last thing the pilot did before dying was to hit the battery switch, cutting off all electrical power. Noreen Coker's seat broke free of its mounts and tumbled forward, smashing into Dennis and the Secret Service agent as the helicopter skidded over the ground on its side. A piece of the transmission shaft pierced the ceramic armor and speared the back of her seat, passing through her body and pinning her to Dennis. A flash of flame engulfed the cabin as the helicopter came to rest.

Liz Gordon was screaming but coherent. 'I can see flames. I can see flames. But the main part of the helicopter is intact. A man is running for the helicopter.'

A Secret Service agent standing by for the landing had grabbed a fire extinguisher and was running toward the helicopter. He threw himself into the flames and stuck the horn of the fire extinguisher into the engine compartment. A fog of retardant billowed up and the fire went out. The agent rolled away on the grass, his face horribly burned.

Liz Gordon and her cameraman ran for the crash. A policeman rushed up and held his hands up. 'It's going to explode!' They skidded to a halt. A crash wagon slammed to a stop beside the helicopter and two medtechs piled out, carrying a crash ax and a fire extinguisher. They were joined by a fireman and four Secret Service agents. Together they shoved the fireman up and on to the side of the helicopter. He swung the crash ax at the window and disappeared into the fuselage. A medtech followed him inside. Two Secret Service agents climbed up and within moments the inert body of the President of the United States was passed into their waiting arms. They passed her down to the other medtech and the two Secret Service agents.

The three men carried her into the crash wagon and it backed away as the helicopter burst into flames. The agents still on the fuselage jumped clear as the medtech and the fireman climbed out of the fuselage and ran for cover, their clothes smoking.

The crash wagon slammed to a halt and its rear doors opened. Two more Secret Service agents jumped in and it started to move, heading for safety and the nearest emergency room. Before the doors slammed closed, they heard someone shout, 'She's okay!'

A Secret Service agent ripped off his sunglasses and rubbed the tears in his eyes. 'Thank you, Lord,' he whispered.

Before the crash wagon had gone fifty feet, it stopped. The rear doors opened and Liz Gordon heard the President of the United States shouting.

'Get out of my way!' Madeline Turner climbed out of the crash truck as a flock of Secret Service agents surrounded her. 'Back off! Give me room!'

'Madame President,' one of them shouted, 'we've got to get you to—'

'I don't give a damn what *you* have to do! There's injured people out there.' She pushed clear of the cordon and started pointing. 'You, establish a perimeter. You! Get Dr Smithson and find out who needs medical attention.' She pointed to the crash truck. 'That's for the injured, not me. Get me a telephone.' For a moment, no one moved. 'Dammit, move! Get the police to clear a lane for emergency vehicles. Are you listening?'

For a moment it was chaos around her. Then there was order. A Secret Service agent handed her a cellphone. 'You're talking to our command post, ma'am.'

She took it. 'Connect me to the National Military Command Center and contact the Vice-President.' She waited. 'Please find my mother and daughter and tell them I'm okay,' she said to the nearest Secret Service agent. A voice came on the line. 'This is President Turner. I'm alive and well, there is no change of command.' She waited for a moment and then authenticated.

The Vice-President came on the line. 'Sam, I'm okay. Take care of things at your end.' Dr Smithson, her personal physician, scurried up. 'Hold on, Sam.' She turned to the doctor. 'Check me out. Here. Be quick.'

The doctor placed both hands on her temples and studied her eyes. 'Take three deep breaths.' He listened and smelled her breath as she breathed deeply. Her eyes and lungs were clear. 'Follow my finger.' He waved a finger in front of her eyes and measured her response. He pressed her ribs. 'Any pain?' She shook her head. 'I don't see any bleeding. Do you feel wet or warm under your clothes?' She shook her head. He ran his hands over her arms and shoulders, feeling for broken bones. Then he felt her pulse. 'You're in a mild state of shock, but other than that, you seem okay. We need to get you to a hospital for a complete physical.'

'Take care of the injured first,' she ordered. 'Sam, you still there? Listen, get on to Patrick and tell him everything is on hold.'

In the background, Liz Gordon faced the camera. 'We have witnessed a miracle here. President Turner is totally unscathed.' Her cameraman panned to the burning pillar of flame reaching into the sky. 'All others on board perished in the crash.'

The White House

Patrick Flannery Shaw was staring at the TV set and listening to Liz Gordon when the phone rang. He picked it up and listened as the Vice-President relayed Turner's message. 'Thanks, Sam,' he said, hanging up. He stared at the image of the burning helicopter on his TV. His knees gave out. He sat down and held his head in his big hands, shaking in relief.

The Western White House, California

Maura closed her eyes and listened to her daughter. Maddy's voice was calm and measured as she talked to Brian on the telephone. 'It happened so fast,' she told him. 'It's really hard to remember. One moment we were all over the sky and the next they're dragging me out of the helicopter.' She listened for a moment. 'No, I'm fine, I really am.'

Sarah never took her eyes off her mother. At first, the eleven-year-old girl had simply clung to her like a baby. Now she was safe and secure, her world back in place, and content to cuddle up to her grandmother. But she could hear something different in her mother's voice. 'Grams, is Mom going to be okay?' she whispered.

'She's still a little shaken,' Maura said. 'But, yes, she's fine.' She got up and walked down the hall, finding Richard Parrish.

'Richard, call the Air Force and get Matt Pontowski here as quickly as possible. He's at Luke Air Force Base in Phoenix.'

Luke AFB, Arizona

Like most everyone in the squadron, Pontowski was glued to the TV set in the pilots' lounge as the story of the failed assassination of the President unfolded. All the pilots in the 309th Fighter Squadron, better known as the Wild Ducks, had heard the rumors about his friendship, or affair, depending on who was spreading the rumor, and accorded him a respectful distance. The fact that he was a brigadier general also added to his isolation.

Behind him, a group of young lieutenants learning to fly the F-16 clustered around the bar and tried on different attitudes to cover up the horror of what they were seeing. They all knew it could happen to them.

'Crispy critters,' one lieutenant said.

'Looks like they had a bad day,' another offered.

One kept score. 'Bad guys one, Marines zero.'

A sergeant skidded through the door. 'General Pontowski, the colonel needs to see you ASAP.'

Pontowski came to his feet and they fell silent. 'The bad guys killed a lot of good people today,' he told the lieutenants. 'Remember that, if you ever have a chance to nail one of the bastards for real.' He walked out of the room.

The lieutenant-colonel commanding the Wild Ducks was waiting for him at the scheduling desk. 'Sir, we just got a call from the head shed. They want you at the Western White House pronto, like an hour ago. We got a D model laid on and an instructor pilot preflighting it right now.' The D model of the F-16 was a two-place fighter. 'The flight plan's filed direct Vandenberg.'

Another sergeant ran up to them carrying Pontowski's personal equipment. 'A van's waiting outside,' she panted. Pontowski grabbed his helmet, parachute harness, and G-suit, and ran for the van that would take him to the F-16. The instructor pilot was in the back seat of the F-16 ready for engine start when he arrived at the jet.

Vandenberg AFB, California

The straight-line distance from Luke Air Force Base to Vandenberg is 417 nautical miles and, at .96 Mach, Pontowski was calling for landing clearance forty minutes after taking off. Five minutes later, he touched down and rolled clear of the runway. An H-60 Blackhawk helicopter emblazoned with 'United States of America' on the fuselage had its engines running when he taxied in.

The Western White House, California

Maura was standing on the veranda when the Blackhawk touched down at the Western White House sixteen minutes later. 'We need you,' was all she said, leading him inside the house. He walked into the family room where Maddy was talking to Parrish. The chief of staff excused himself and left with Maura. They were alone.

'Matt,' she said, smiling at him, speaking in a rush. 'What brings you here? I've never seen you in a flight suit before. No wonder you turned Maura's head when she first met you.' She paused, a haunted look in her eyes. 'I guess I should have zigged when we zagged.' It was an echo of the lieutenants' banter at the bar. Another pause. 'I'm talking too much, aren't I?'

'It's a natural reaction. You should've heard me the first time.'

She was in his arms, shaking, finally letting go. They stood there in the fading twilight, his arms around her as tears streaked her face. Gradually she regained control and her breathing slowed. 'Why me?'

'I've often asked the same question. That's the way it is

in combat. There's no rhyme or reason to it. Only survivors.'

For a moment, he felt her body stiffen. Then she relaxed, still safe in his embrace. 'Is that what combat's like?' She felt him nod as he caressed her hair. 'How can anyone do that to another human?'

'I don't know. But it's our job to stop them.'

'Mom,' Sarah said from the doorway, 'are you okay?'

Maddy turned away from Pontowski and held out her arms. 'I'm fine, now.'

Sarah ran into her mother's embrace. 'I saw it, Mom. I saw it all.'

'I know, darlin', I know. It's okay to talk about it, if you want.'

Washington, D.C.

The Old Executive Office Building next to the White House was lit up like a wedding cake in the night as more and more of its denizens rushed to their offices. Lacking any real reason for being at work on a Friday night, many of them milled around the black-and-white-tiled corridors, anxious to glean any information they could about the attempted assassination. But most of all, they were worried, not only for the President, but for a woman they simply called Maddy.

However, there was no lack of purpose on the third-floor offices of the National Security Council. Only the rap of hard heels echoed down the hall as the chiefs of America's national security and intelligence agencies gathered in Mazana Kamigami Hazelton's conference room. Two of the men were so deeply buried in Washington's infrastructure that only the Director of Central Intelligence knew who they were and what they did.

The last to arrive, in a wheelchair, was Nelson Durant, the head of Century Communications. They all knew why he was there: Century Communications had built the world's most advanced information-gathering computer system for the United State's intelligence community. But only Mazie and the DCI knew that its successor was on-line and undergoing testing.

Mazie walked in and stood at the head of the table. 'I just got off the phone to the President. She's fine.' The room broke into spontaneous applause. 'She's directed that we form a special committee to investigate and gather evidence. I've asked Mr Durant to head the committee and he has accepted. We, and I mean all of us, are here to help him.' She gave them a meaningful look. Everyone in the room was a power and controlled a bureaucratic empire with congressional or presidential support. But not one of them was a match for Nelson Durant. Mazie concluded by saying, 'We're going to catch the bastards. Mr Durant, it's all yours.'

Durant leaned forward in his wheelchair. 'You may be wondering why a few key players are not here. That's because we checked out every one of you first. You're here because you're clean.'

'Mr Durant,' the director of the FBI protested, 'you may have overstepped your bounds.'

'Really?' Durant replied. 'Are you aware that your assistant director has a mistress and a call-girl, both on the FBI's payroll?' Durant's assistant gave each of them a bound document. 'This is a list of everyone in your organization who came up dirty. What you do with the information is up to you. But do not use them in this investigation.'

There was silence as the men and women stared at the lists. 'I thought,' the representative from the Department of Justice said, 'that Beatrice was specifically programmed *not* to do this type of investigation on US citizens.' Beatrice was the code name for the information-gathering computer system Durant had created.

'She can't,' Durant said. 'This was done by the system replacing Beatrice. I call her Cassandra.'

The DCI was impressed. In the CIA alone, the new computer system had rooted out three sleepers left over from the Cold War, six spies who had penetrated CIA headquarters at Langley, and thirty-eight double agents out in the system. 'What else has Cassandra uncovered?'

'She's discovered that the missile used in the attack was a Russian-built Strela-3. It came through Poland.'

The DCI was incredulous. 'The Poles are involved in this?'

Durant shook his head. 'Apparently not. But we're still looking at them.'

'Vashin,' Mazie half whispered.

'Perhaps,' Durant replied. 'Turn to the back pages of your handout. Each of you has an action list to start working on.' He looked around the room, his eyes deadly calm. 'We're going to shake the tree until someone falls out.'

CHAPTER EIGHTEEN

Moscow

Vashin stared out the big picture window of his new penthouse, deliberately ratcheting up the tension as a fresh storm moved in. 'That was not what I wanted. *You* stirred a hornet's nest.' At the emphatic *you*, Yaponets felt a warmth in his crotch. Vashin spun around and Yaponets almost lost it. 'I wanted Lezno sewn up, not the bitch!'

Yaponets rubbed his close-cropped gray hair and willed his bowels to be still. Sweat streaked the forehead of the burly sixty-four-year-old. His carefully crafted image as a Russian samurai was dissolving in front of the Council of Brothers. 'A misunderstanding,' he pleaded. 'We had talked about the Turner woman. I thought you meant her.' His eyes darted back and forth, first to Vashin, and then to Oleg Gora, the torpedo who had earned his place on the Circle of Brothers at Boris Bakatina's funeral. 'There is no one who can stop you. So after the money was stolen—'

Vashin snorted, interrupting him. 'It was stolen in Poland. There is only one head in Poland who matters – Adam Lezno.' He spun around and glared at Yaponets. 'The Americans will not rest until they find out who was behind this.'

Yaponets tried to look confident. It didn't work. 'They will never trace it to us.'

Vashin didn't answer. He turned slightly and nodded at

Gora. Yaponets lost control of his bowels. Vashin snorted as he rushed from the room. Gora started to follow him. 'Let him be,' Vashin ordered. He turned back to the window and Gora sat down, disappointed that he would not be able to demonstrate his skill. Outside, Geraldine Blake guided Yaponets to the room set aside for people to clean up after soiling themselves in a meeting with Vashin.

In the penthouse, it was time to cast judgment on Yaponets. 'If you're going to kill the emperor,' a godfather said, 'you must not fail.'

'Americans hate emperors and love martyrs,' the senior godfather said.

'The Americans are fools,' another godfather said, citing mitigating circumstances in evidence. 'They will only find who we want them to find.'

Vashin agreed. 'Perhaps you're right.'

'Yaponets has served you well,' the same godfather continued, making a plea for Yaponets's life.

Geraldine's advice about mercy and making grand gestures was still fresh in Vashin's thinking. 'Indeed he has.' The trial was over, and the men talked quietly about the state of the *vor* and routine matters until Yaponets returned. He smelled strongly of cologne. Vashin waved him to a seat. 'No more misunderstandings, my old friend,' he said, pacing in front of the window, his hands clasped behind his back. 'The Poles are garbage and garbage does not steal my money and live to talk about it. We are going to teach them an object lesson. Sew up Lezno. But I want the arms and legs as well.'

'The SPS carried it out,' a godfather said.

'Eliminate them.'

'The Americans are supplying the Poles with intelligence,' another godfather said. 'The new ambassador is behind it.'

'That is not good for his health,' Vashin said. The men laughed, appreciating his humor.

Yaponets wanted to be sure there was no misunderstanding this time. 'Is he one of the arms to be amputated?'

Vashin mulled it over. Did he want an American ambassador killed so soon after a failed attempt on Madeline Turner? Would that focus the CIA on the *vor*? He didn't know. What if that assassination failed? 'No. We can neutralize the Americans in other ways. If this ambassador becomes a problem we will reconsider our options. For now, I want Lezno to experience an unfortunate coincidence. The Poles will get the message.'

'There are no coincidences,' another godfather intoned. The men all nodded in agreement, their paranoia in harmony. Vashin turned to the window and stared into the falling snow. The meeting was over and the men left silently. Outside, Geraldine called for their limousines and bodyguards. Yaponets was the last to depart and she helped him with his coat. 'I do hope everything is going well with Mr Vashin.'

Normally a woman was beneath Yaponets, and he would have ignored her. But his instincts warned him she enjoyed a special status with Vashin. The cunning savagery that had served him so well as he rose through the ranks of the *vor* gave way to a new urge: survival. The words his father had taught him to say as a child when referring to Stalin came back. 'I'm a mere mortal in the presence of greatness,' he repeated automatically. She walked him to the elevator and waited for the car to arrive. The image of his headless body falling down the dark shaft flashed in his mind. 'Is it still the same?'

She didn't answer but smiled a goodbye when he stepped into the elevator. She returned to her desk and waited for the inevitable call. It came six minutes later. 'I want to see Gabrowski,' Vashin ordered.

'The Pole with the amber cufflinks,' she said, confirming the identity of the man. Automatically, she considered the problem. What had the Council of Brothers been discussing that provoked such fear in Yaponets? Gabrowski must know something about the money shipment or might even be involved. But to what depth she didn't know. If he was, he would be a fool to come to Russia. And he struck her as anything but a fool. Then she considered the other side of it. Would he need to sleep with her again so they could be alone? 'How soon do you want to see him?'

'Tomorrow. Monday at the latest.'

'You know the Poles. He might not want to come, considering Christmas is Wednesday.'

'Tell him he'll be home the same day.'

'Yes, sir. I'll get right on it.'

The plane from Warsaw landed before noon on Sunday. Geraldine and one of Vashin's silver Bentleys was waiting for the lone passenger. He walked down the stairs bundled against the frigid wind and stepped into the car. 'Welcome to Moscow, Mr Gabrowski.'

Jerzy Fedor took off his hat and gloves and looked at her, his lean and ravaged face red from the cold. 'Why the urgent summons?'

'Mr Vashin wants to know where his money is,' Geraldine told him.

Fedor sighed. It was against all his principles to give anything back once he had it. 'I wish I knew.'

She knew the conversation was being recorded. 'That's most unfortunate.'

The White House

The residence was alive with laughter as Maddy Turner's family and friends gathered around her for a Christmas Eve celebration. Downstairs, the chief usher hovered at the entrance of the South Portico, waiting for one particular car to arrive. When it rolled up, he rushed forward, anxious to greet Pontowski and his son. 'Good evening, General Pontowski. It is good to see you again. May I wish you an early merry Christmas?'

'You always were the smooth-talking devil, James. I don't believe you've met my son, Matt.' Matt stepped forward and shook the older man's hand. 'James was an usher during your great-grandfather's administration,' Pontowski explained.

James grew very serious and looked at Matt. 'President Pontowski was the finest man I have known. It was an honor to have served him and his wife. Your great-grandmother was an elegant lady.' He motioned Pontowski to enter. 'I believe you know the way.' He watched the father and son walk down the hall to the staircase leading to the second floor.

'Making points?' a voice asked.

The chief usher shook his head. 'Touching the future.'

'What does James do?' Matt asked as they climbed the stairs.

'The chief usher is like a hotel manager,' Pontowski answered. 'He supervises everything from social events to repainting. It's his job to know all that goes on behind the scenes. What maid or butler is having personal problems, who's sick, what needs fixing. The guests may come and go, but the staff stays.'

An intern met them on the second floor and led them to the Yellow Oval Room. Sarah rushed up and took Pontowski's hand, demanding a kiss on the cheek. 'I like your dress,' Pontowski said. She pirouetted away as her full, floor-length skirt billowed around her. Her blonde hair flowed and twisted with her, creating the charming illusion of a dancer on center stage.

Then she was back. 'Is this the first time you've been to the White House?' she asked Matt. The teenager nodded dumbly, not sure what to say. Then she danced away to greet other guests.

'I think she likes you,' Pontowski said.

'Gimme a break, Dad. She's only eleven.'

Pontowski laughed. 'Going on sixteen.'

'Maggot!' Brian called from across the room. He rushed up. 'Has Chubs been buggin' you?'

'She's not fat,' Matt replied, defending Sarah.

'Yeah. I know. But it bugs the—' He cut off the word he was thinking of, '—out of her. Come on, I'll show you my room.' Matt looked at his father, who nodded. The two boys disappeared.

Matt wandered through the residence and, as before, the memories rushed back. For a brief moment in time, he was a lieutenant again and his grandfather was the President of the United States. As always, Tosh was there, his anchor and real mother.

'A penny for your thoughts,' Maura asked, breaking into his reverie. One of the White House photographers capturing the party snapped a candid photo of them together.

'Thinking about times past.'

'Let's find Maddy. I know she's looking for you.' She took his hand. 'I think she's going to introduce you to the family. I hope you're ready for it.'

'Have we reached that stage?'

'Dammit,' Maura said, surprising him, 'you better have.' Then she added, 'Take care of her, Matt Pontowski. She's still not over the crash.'

'It takes a while.'

She squeezed his hand and led him into the family quarters.

Maddy was wearing a floor-length red skirt and white blouse. A gold chain matching her earrings snared her narrow waist, and for a moment Pontowski could not take his eyes off her. She laughed, not seeing him, and the empty void in his life was gone. She turned and noticed him. 'Matt, I'm so glad you could make it.' Her words were still coming a little too fast. She took his hand and reached up, kissing him on the cheek. He was aware that every eye in the room was on them, and that the photographer had taken at least three shots recording the scene. She was announcing a change in their relationship.

Most of the guests had left and only a few of the family were still hanging on. Two of the older aunts, Vera and Kathy, had taken an intense interest in Pontowski and were hovering around him. 'Well, ladies,' Maura announced in a loud voice, 'your pumpkin has arrived. It's time to get you two old biddies to bed.'

'Careful who you're calling an old biddy,' Vera countered. But she conceded the point and gave Pontowski a hug. 'You'll do – for now,' she said. Maura walked them out.

'They like you,' Maddy said. She was smiling at him. 'Where are the boys?'

'I haven't seen them all evening.' He followed her into the family lounge. They were alone. She sat on the couch by the fire. 'Sarah was acting very grown-up tonight,' he said.

'Too grown-up.' She shook her head. 'You should've seen the first dress she wanted to wear. Right out of the Mata Hari collection. Fortunately, Maura talked her out of it.' She tilted her head. The enchanting smile was back and she gave him a questioning look. He sat down next to her and she scooted closer. Her hand reached out and held his. For a moment they were silent as she slowly relaxed. He felt her hand tremble. 'The nightmares keep coming,' she said finally.

'It helps to talk about it. Maybe a minister or counselor.'

'I've talked to Reverend Ford. But can you imagine what Senator Leland would do if he learned I was talking to a counselor? He'd claim I had lost my marbles.'

'Surely he can tell the difference between a counselor and a shrink?'

'In politics they're one and the same.' Again, silence. She moved a little closer. Instinctively, he put his arm around her and she cuddled against him. He was surprised at how small and fragile she felt. 'Two of my best friends died. I loved Noreen and if Dennis hadn't turned my seat around or if Rick Bower – he was the Secret Service agent – hadn't covered me with a fire blanket—'

He stroked her cheek and felt the tears. He gently brushed them away. 'Greater love hath no man than this, that a man lay down his life for his friends.'

'Is that how you handle it, by reading the Bible?'

'No. I do it by remembering.' Slowly, he recited a list of names, each one vivid and alive. 'Jack Locke, Mike Martin, Frank Hester, Skeeter Ashton—' The list grew longer. Then he said, 'Shoshana.' His voice was calm. The pain was gone and only memory lingered on.

'Your wife.'

A simple 'Yes.' He went on, 'Because of them, I know what I have to do. And I will never forget.' He felt her relax.

'Neither will I,' she promised. They were silent as they looked into the fire.

A discreet knock at the door caught her attention. Pontowski moved over to the far side of the couch. 'Come,' she said.

The door opened and James, the chief usher, entered. 'Madame President, all the other guests have left. Um, here are the proofs the photographers took tonight. I thought you might like to see them.' He handed her a cardboard tray half full of photographs. He stood as they sat together on the couch and thumbed through the photos, waiting for them to see it.

Pontowski saw it first. 'Oh-oh.' He pulled the photo out of the tray.

Maddy stared at it for a moment and then sighed. Sarah was in an awkward embrace with Matt; they were kissing. Her eyes were closed and his were wide open. 'She'll be twelve in June and I was hoping I wouldn't have to deal with this for another year or so. How old is Matt?'

'Fourteen. He knows better.'

She laughed. 'This is harmless, almost cute.'

'Maddy, this is the White House and you are the President.'

'I know. In the wrong hands—' She rolled her eyes to the ceiling in amused frustration. Then she faked a big sigh. 'Perhaps a little lesson?'

Pontowski caught it immediately. 'Just enough to get their attention?'

'Right. James, please send the miscreants in.'

'Immediately, Madame President.' The usher quickly left.

Maddy relaxed into the couch and stretched, enjoying the moment. 'This will take some faking.'

Brian arrived first. Sarah and Matt trailed in behind. Maura came in and sat down. Maddy handed them the photo. 'What were you doing?' she asked, trying to act stern.

'Yuk!' Brian said. 'I can't believe Maggot kissed Chubs.'

Sarah glared at her brother. 'I was giving Matt a tour. He's never been to the White House before.'

Pontowski looked at his son. 'That is you in the photo?'

'Yes, sir,' Matt answered. He looked embarrassed.

Maddy said, 'Sarah, I'll talk to you later.' She fixed Matt with a serious look, and for the rest of his life he would remember it. 'We live in a goldfish bowl here. We have to be very careful what we do.'

'Yes, ma'am,' Matt replied.

'We'll talk later,' Pontowski said to him.

'Folks,' Maura said from her corner seat, 'this was just two kids kissing under the mistletoe. Let's not make something out of this when it's not. Okay?'

'Kissing Chubs,' Brian added. 'What a downer.'

Sarah glared at him. She whirled around and ran from the room, tears streaking her face. 'Sarah!' Maddy called, concern on her face.

Maura stood slowly, tired from the long day. 'That's the trouble with this place. Everything turns into a federal case. We just need to let kids be kids. I'll take care of it.' With a very audible sigh, she left the room.

'We best go,' Pontowski said. 'Thanks again for the invitation.' He took her hand in his. As before, her touch was warm and soft. They said goodbye and he led Matt into the hall. 'What were you thinking of?'

'She kissed me, Dad.'

'Did you kiss her back?'

'Naw. I was too surprised.'

Pontowski laughed. 'Welcome to the wonderful world of women, son.' He gave Matt a light slap on the back. 'If you like her, wait a while.'

'President Turner isn't mad at me?'

'Not a bit.'

'Are you sure?'

'Trust me on this one.'

Warsaw

Bender carried the tray with the silver tea service into the bedroom. He set it down beside the bed. 'How are you feeling?'

Nancy struggled into an upright position. 'It's just morning sickness. It should pass in another week or two.' She groaned. 'This is all your fault, you know.'

His laugh was low. 'I take full responsibility.' He poured a cup of tea and handed it to her. He watched her as she sipped the tea and slowly woke up. It was one of the things he loved about her, the way she woke to the day, always eager for what was coming. She placed the half-empty cup on the tray.

'Oh,' she said, seeing the small package. She picked it up.

'Merry Christmas, love.'

She slowly unwrapped it, touching the paper and savoring its texture. 'What lovely wrapping.' She opened the box. Inside was a small brooch in the shape of a floral spray. Gold and silver strands twisted together to hold droplets of amber. She looked at him, her eyes moist with tears. 'It's beautiful. Wherever did you find it?'

'Ewa Pawlik knew a jeweler.'

Nancy reached out and took his hand. 'I didn't get you anything half as nice.'

He sat on the edge of the bed and rested his hand on her stomach. 'I think you did.' They talked for a few moments and she started to feel better. Finally she rose to get dressed and he walked into the morning room and sat down. The phone rang and he picked it up. Even though it was Christmas, he was still the ambassador. 'Bender here.' It was the embassy duty officer telling him that he had a phone call from Jerzy Fedor requesting an emergency meeting. 'Get Peter Duncan to cover it,' he said.

Evan Riley sat in Bender's office while they waited for Duncan to return from the meeting. 'Poland shuts down over Christmas,' Riley said. 'It must be important if Fedor is jumping through hoops.' He snorted. 'Hell, we've all been jumping through hoops since the assassination attempt.'

'Anything new on it?' Bender asked.

'Not that I know of. Apparently the missile came through Poland. But this place is a wide-open pipeline for the Russian Mafiya. Personally, I think the Poles were innocent bystanders on this one.' He grew expansive. 'They're a victim of their geography, caught in the middle.' They fell silent when a steward brought in a fresh pot of coffee. Riley helped himself to a cup. 'That was a smart move sending Duncan to meet Fedor. We don't trust him. Too much travel to Russia and the Ukraine.'

Peter Duncan returned an hour later. He was unusually animated and paced the carpet. 'The fuckin' Russian Mafiya's doing it again. They found out where the gold is stored and are going after it Monday morning. We're talking major assault on a bank right after it opens. The audacity of the bastards!'

Riley's eyes darted back and forth. 'How did Fedor find out?'

Duncan shook his head. 'He wouldn't say. Obviously, he knows someone or has his own sources. At least the Poles had enough sense to separate the gold from the money. The cash is easily dispersed. The only bank with a vault large enough to hold so much bullion is CreditPolska on Zlota Street.'

'So what does Fedor want us to do about it?' Bender asked.

'He wants us to tell the SPS so they can save the bacon.'

'Or in this case,' Riley added, 'the gold. But if the SPS acts and anything goes wrong, we get blamed because our intelligence was wrong. Why do I smell a set-up?'

'My thoughts exactly,' Bender added.

Duncan flopped into a chair. 'So how do we make it go right?'

'We need to exploit the Mafiya's weaknesses,' Riley said, 'not play to their strengths. They're smart and vicious street thugs who are dangerous on their own turf. We need to make 'em play our game where training, fast reaction, good command and control, and movement are the deciding factors.'

'How do we do that?' Bender asked.

Riley asked, 'Fedor said it's planned for Monday morning?'

'Correct,' Duncan answered. 'That gives us four days to put a response together.'

Riley shook his head. 'It also gives them four days. I want

to take that away from them. We force them to act prematurely by moving the gold bullion tonight.'

Duncan tried not to grin. 'Not quite.'

A very discreet gold-lettered sign on the double glass doors announced that Exclusive Studios occupied the top floor of the building on Zlota Street. It was a good location for business and close to the central train station and the Palace of Culture and Science, the tallest building in Warsaw. Normally, Exclusive Studios was open twenty-four hours a day, seven days a week, for any lonely businessman, preferably an elderly Asian, willing to pay the going rate of five hundred to a thousand dollars for an intimate encounter with one of the most beautiful prostitutes in Warsaw. But on Christmas even businesses owned by the Russian Mafiya were closed.

But that was not to say Exclusive Studios was unoccupied. It also had an unobstructed view of Bank CreditPolska on the opposite side of the street and line-of-sight communications with an office high in the tower of the Palace of Culture and Science. The office in question was the hub of Vashin's legitimate business interests in Warsaw. But its real function was to serve as a communications and coordination center for Vashin's more normal enterprises.

The girls at Exclusive Studios, who were kept under lock and key when not dispensing their charms, were celebrating Christmas and a party of sorts was going on. Consequently, their guards, who should also have been watching the bank, found themselves distracted when the convoy of three trucks, four armored personnel carriers and one command car lumbered down the street and turned into the alley that led to the rear of the bank.

And that was the problem.

Peter Duncan sat in a truck parked across the street. On the outside, the truck looked like a large delivery van. But inside was some of the world's most sophisticated communications monitoring equipment. 'Jesus H. Christ,'

Duncan said to the SPS communications specialist. 'Did anyone see the convoy?'

They wanted the Mafiya to think they were moving the gold. Actually, the trucks were the cover to insert a team of SPS commandos into the bank. The gold bullion would stay in the vault. Duncan and the SPS were betting the Mafiya would focus on the convoy and go after it. Or better yet, split their forces to hit both targets in a knee-jerk reaction. No matter what, they were walking into the waiting arms of the SPS. But the Mafiya needed time to react.

The young Pole looked perplexed. 'There's been no communications with the Palace of Culture.' He rotated the sound boom on top of the van toward Exclusive Studios and listened. 'I can still hear music and laughter.'

'Damn,' Duncan muttered under his breath. 'It must be one hell of a party.'

He called the SPS commander on the secure radio. 'They didn't see you arrive at the bank. Drive around the block and make a little noise when you pull up.'

'We'll unload first,' the commander replied. Duncan waited and, in his mind's eye, he could see the black-suited SPS spilling out of the trucks and moving silently into covering positions and into the bank. Within minutes, the commander radioed, 'Moving. Any reaction?' The communications specialist in the van shook his head. The Mafiya lookouts were still partying. When the convoy reappeared six minutes later and turned on to Zlota Street, there was still no reaction from Exclusive Studios.

'Slow down,' Duncan ordered. The trucks did as ordered and chugged slowly down the street, gearboxes whining and engines revving. Still no reaction. 'They must be screwin' themselves deaf in there,' he muttered to himself. 'How in the hell can they miss this?' Desperate, he radioed, 'We need an accident. Have one of the APCs side-swipe a parked car.'

On cue, the last armored personnel carrier brushed against a car. It was meant to be little more than a kiss, but the mass of the six-wheeled APC crushed it. The convoy pulled around the wreck and slowly turned into the alley leading to the back of the bank, again disappearing from view. The communications specialist scanned his instruments and shook his head. 'I can't believe this,' Duncan grumbled. He pointed to one of the men dressed in civilian clothes. 'Go ring their doorbell and ask if that's their car that was hit. Tell them who did it.'

The man jumped out of the van and ran to the double glass doors to Exclusive Studios. On the third ring, a voice on the intercom said they were closed. The man shouted back, describing the accident. From the van, Duncan pointed to the bank and signalled him to say more. The man added that the APC that had done it was still parked behind the bank with a convoy of trucks. Duncan motioned him to leave when a shadow appeared at one of the studio windows. In the van, the communications specialist gave Duncan a thumbs-up. Someone had finally made a telephone call. Now they had to wait.

Forty minutes later, the SPS commander called on the secure radio. 'Are they coming?'

'The road watch teams report negative activity,' Duncan said.

'It's too obvious if we stay here any longer,' the commander said. 'Moving now.' The convoy started engines and reappeared from behind the bank. It drove slowly past the studio and turned south on Chalubinskiego Street.

The communications specialist listened to the telephone traffic and gave Duncan a thumbs-up. 'They saw you leave,' Duncan radioed. 'Drive slowly and go straight ahead. Maybe someone will follow you. Make it easy for them to find you.'

Two minutes later, the road watch teams reported a string of cars approaching Zlota Street from the north. Duncan radioed the convoy. 'They've taken the bait. They wanted you to move. Expect guests in a few minutes. They're coming up behind you.' But much to his surprise, all the cars turned into Zlota Street and stopped well short of the bank. Duncan swore under his breath, certain the Mafiya was playing a game. He keyed his radio and called the convoy. 'Is anyone following you?'

'Negative.'

'Slow down and stand by,' Duncan transmitted.

Men jumped out of the cars and gathered in a large group in the center of Zlota Street. They wore on hip-length black leather jackets and a few carried AK-47s. The communications specialist swung the van's sound boom around to pick up what they were saying. 'They're drunk!'

'Damn,' Duncan groused. 'They like to party at Christmas. That's why it was planned for Monday. They needed time to sober up.' Another car skidded around the corner and slammed to a stop, scattering men in front of it. A tall man wearing a full-length leather trench coat got out and shouted orders. 'Get this on video,' Duncan ordered. One of the specialists trained the infrared camera on top of the van on the man and punched at the video controls. Another specialist readied a hand-held camera.

The newcomer had created some semblance of order and four men carrying AK-47s ran down the alley to the rear of the bank. Two trucks drove up and more men jumped out of the back, adding to the confusion. The trucks started to back up, but three more cars arrived and blocked their exit. A loud argument broke out and peaceful Zlota Street turned into a mob scene. Duncan was incredulous and keyed his radio, relaying the scene to the SPS commander. 'These guys are clowns and can't make up their minds what to do.'

A single shot rang out. 'What was that?' Duncan asked. The communications specialist roared with laughter as he replayed the videotape. A thug was waving his AK-47 around and had accidentally fired a single shot. He fell to the ground, holding his foot.

'One just shot himself in the foot,' Duncan radioed.

'We better put them in the bag before they hurt someone else,' the commander replied.

Duncan shrugged. 'Why not.'

It was easily coordinated, and the APCs from the convoy raced back. They roared into position and blocked off both ends of Zlota Street as the commandos inside the bank surged out the back. The four Mafiosi covering the rear raised their hands without transmitting a warning and the commandos moved up the alley. A bullhorn on one of the APCs ordered the men in the street to surrender and it was over.

Four SPS commandos kicked in the door to Exclusive Studios and charged inside, closely followed by one of the communications specialists with a video camera. They pounded up the stairs, where they received a warm welcome from the girls and hard looks from the Mafiya guards. Then the girls turned their wrath on the guards, all of which was duly captured on tape.

The SPS commander arrived in his Humvee in time for the first head count. He spoke into the radio. 'All secure. Sixty-seven in the bag.'

'What do we do with them?' Duncan asked.

'Call the police.'

'What's the charge?'

The commander was perplexed. He had assumed the clean-up would be a problem for the morgue and street sweepers. 'They're Russians,' he said finally.

CHAPTER NINETEEN

Camp David, Maryland

Shaw guffawed loudly, making Maura uncomfortable. She moved away from the TV set and the small group watching the videotape with her daughter. *Noreen could deflate you with two words*, Maura told herself. She missed Noreen Coker. The tall black congresswoman from Los Angeles had been a caustic but vital member of Maddy's kitchen cabinet, and her unfailing good humor and common sense had helped avoid many partisan potholes on the political road to success. And in Maura's eyes, Patrick Flannery Shaw was the biggest pit in the pavement.

Can anyone replace Noreen? she thought. She knew how her daughter needed people as a sounding board and how vital a close circle of friends was to her. *At least it won't be Shaw.* An image of Matt Pontowski flashed in the back of her mind. But he was leaving for Poland. She smothered her distaste for Shaw by falling back on the social amenities and freshening their coffee.

'Mizz President,' Shaw managed to say between bouts of laughter, 'this may be Warsaw's funniest home video.' He especially enjoyed the last scenes. But Maura failed to see the humor of a man writhing on the ground in pain and holding on to his foot. Then the scene shifted to the inside of Exclusive Studios where four partially nude women were kicking a man rolling around on the floor. He couldn't decide what needed the most protection, his head or his crotch. The women had no trouble making a decision and worked on both ends. 'Smack-dab between the old uprights,' Shaw observed in response to one well-aimed kick.

Maura deliberately spilled some hot coffee in his lap. 'Oh, I *am* sorry. I hope it didn't hurt.' She dropped a large napkin on his huge stomach.

'What would Noreen say?' Vice-President Sam Kennett asked, ignoring Shaw's discomfort.

Gwen Anderson laughed. 'It's all in the follow-through, girl!' The Secretary of Health and Human Services was enjoying herself. 'Why don't we release this to the media?'

Shaw finished dabbing at his pants and fixed Anderson with his I-can't-believe-you-said-that look. But he sugar-coated his words. 'We might want to hold off on that one for a while, Mizz Anderson.' His Southern accent was thick and honey-sweet. 'We need a bogeyman to scare Mr and Mrs Joe Voter, not make 'em laugh.'

'One of your famous aphorisms?' Anderson scoffed. She doubted that he knew what an aphorism was.

Shaw did. His answer was instinctive, honed by years of dealing with politicians. He became very serious. 'Never diminish your enemy because it diminishes you.'

'Why not release the part showing the prisoners being rounded up and loaded on trucks?' Kennett said. 'It's a graphic statement that our foreign aid program is working.'

Shaw shook his head. 'Better to show peace and prosperity in our time. We might want to do some "before and after" sound bites for TV later on. But for now, stick to domestic issues.'

Turner held out her cup for a refill. Shaw moved back when Maura passed too close with a full carafe. 'It might help with the speech,' Turner said, referring to her State of the Union address that was less than three weeks away.

Gwen Anderson agreed, anxious to recover what she might have lost in the exchange with Shaw. 'It's a good chance to sample voter response on that issue.'

'We know how the voters feel on foreign aid,' Shaw

muttered. 'They don't like it. At best, it's a non-issue. Let it lie.'

Turner made her decision. 'We'll release a clip like Sam said and see how it flies.' Gwen Anderson swelled with satisfaction and Shaw knew better than to press his case after the President had made up her mind.

'That's not what I wanted to talk about,' Turner said. 'When should I announce my candidacy?'

'You have two choices,' Shaw said. 'Announce before the State of the Union and go in as the grand hero. Or save it until afterwards and keep them on pins and needles. Believe me, they won't miss a word you say.' He chuckled. 'Guaranteed to keep them awake.'

'By announcing later,' Kennett said, 'it will keep them focused on your speech. They all know you're running. The question is, on what issues? They'll be looking for every clue they can find.'

The discussion went around the room and Turner decided to announce after the speech. 'I'm going ahead with an independent commission to investigate combat readiness.'

Anderson's head came up, instantly alert. 'Why? We've never been more prepared militarily.'

'Then why are people getting out of the services in record numbers?' Kennett asked.

Anderson leaned forward, her hands clasped together. 'Maddy, don't do it. The Neanderthals in the Pentagon will use it to reopen the issue of women in combat. We've come too far to lose what we've attained. Our military has never been more combat ready because we're using the best of our people.'

At first, Shaw only listened, trying to think of a way to dissuade Turner. Combat readiness was not a bone he wanted to gnaw on during an election campaign. But more worrisome was the tone in Anderson's voice and what she was saying. He was in the presence of a true believer – Gwen Anderson had an agenda beyond her allegiance to Maddy Turner. But how far beyond? 'Madame President,' he said finally, 'I think Mizz Anderson is right. This would be counterproductive until after the election.'

'And even then,' Anderson snapped.

'Gwen,' Maddy said, soothing her friend, 'I know how you feel about women in the military. But what I want is an honest appraisal of our state of combat readiness. That's why I want you to head the commission. I know you'll be fair.'

'I appreciate your confidence,' Anderson replied. 'I'll be glad to do it.'

Shaw's chin dropped to his chest. Maddy Turner had made two mistakes in less than ten minutes.

Warsaw

The young man at the immigration counter barely glanced at Pontowski's official passport before stamping it. Then he did a classic double-take and rechecked the identification page. His eyes opened wide and he stood to hand the passport back. 'Welcome to Poland, General Pontowski.' Pontowski gave a little nod and headed for the baggage carousels. The young man watched him leave and picked up his phone.

The carousel cranked to life and baggage appeared on the moving ramp. His two suitcases and old parachute bag came through the opening, but before they reached him, two brown-uniformed guards snatched them up and walked toward him. They sat the bags down and came to attention, their eyes fixed on his face. 'Welcome to Poland, General Pontowski.' He heard his name murmured in whispers behind him as passengers waiting for their bags flowed toward his carousel, anxious to get a look. 'Customs is this way,' one of the guards said, picking up the parachute bag. The crowd parted, opening a corridor to customs.

Every customs agent on duty was lined up behind one counter while more security guards cleared a path. The agent-in-charge glanced at the name tags on the bags and checked them through. 'Welcome to Poland, General Pontowski.' The five words of greeting were becoming a chant. Scattered applause followed him as he went through the double exit doors into the main terminal, his two baggage carriers in tow.

The big surprise was holding a neatly lettered sign with

his name. Ewa Pawlik smiled at him. 'Welcome to Poland, General Pontowski.' She stepped forward and extended her hand as she introduced herself. Pontowski's first impression was of a young woman in her mid-twenties, on the heavy side, with soft brown hair that cascaded to her shoulders in gentle waves. Her doe-shaped hazel eyes held him for a moment and he was certain, without doubt, that she was the most beautiful woman he had ever met.

Smile, he told himself. He muttered some words, hoping he didn't sound like a complete idiot, as they shook hands.

'Mr James asked me to meet you,' she said. 'He's the Deputy Charge of Mission. An embassy car is outside.' The crowd parted like the Red Sea as he followed her out. Again, scattered applause echoed over him.

'I don't understand,' he said. She held the car's rear door open as the driver opened the trunk for his bags. 'You'd think I was a celebrity.' She walked around and got in the front passenger seat. The two guards who had carried his bags stood at attention and saluted as she drove away.

She turned in the seat and faced him, her look matter-of-fact. 'Your grandfather was extremely popular and is revered by many of our people.'

Pontowski gave her his lopsided grin. 'Local boy makes good.'

Ewa was not amused. 'He was the first President of the United States of Polish descent. My mother still has a picture of him in her surgery. It is next to Karol Wojtyla.'

'Hanging next to the Pope. Gramps would be impressed.'

'My mother always hoped he would visit Poland,' she said.

'He wanted to.'

'That is the story of Poland. So many want to, but when history is written, they did nothing.'

There was no admonishment in her voice, only the dull recitation of fact. Pontowski would have liked to have been able to explain why his grandfather never visited the land of his ancestors, but he didn't know the reason. He changed the subject. 'Your English is perfect.'

Again, the serious look. 'I learned from my grandmother. She was born and raised in Chicago.' She spoke to the driver in Polish and he turned down a side street, taking a back way to the embassy. 'Traffic is very heavy,' she explained.

'Warsaw reminds me of New York,' Pontowski said. 'Without the skyscrapers.' She didn't answer and they rode in silence to the embassy. The gate guard waved them to a stop and a security team checked the car for a bomb. The driver pulled ahead and stopped at the side entrance.

A Marine guard opened Pontowski's door and came to attention, snapping a perfect salute. 'Good morning, General Pontowski. Welcome to Poland.'

Pontowski returned the salute and followed Ewa inside. 'Does everyone know who I am?'

'You look very much like your grandfather.'

Bender was waiting for Pontowski in his office with Peter Duncan, Evan Riley, and Winslow James. 'Welcome to Poland,' Bender said.

Pontowski laughed. 'I can't tell you how many times I've heard that today.'

Bender sat down and steepled his fingers. 'I'm not surprised. The Pontowski name carries weight over here.'

'Is that why you asked me to head the ODC?' ODC was the legation's Office of Defense Cooperation.

'Partly. Peter, why don't you fill Matt in?'

Duncan cleared his throat and explained what they had accomplished with SPS. 'It turns out the Poles are capable of taking care of themselves. But they do need help in certain areas.'

'Like current intelligence,' Riley added.

'In the case of the Polish Air Force,' Bender said, 'we want to enable them to control their own airspace, which the Russians apparently consider their private preserve. But we are not sure exactly what they need or how receptive they will be to our suggestions.'

'Your name,' Winslow James added, 'will overcome a great deal of resistance.'

'We have discovered,' Riley said, 'that Russian organized

crime is somewhat arthritic and doesn't respond quickly. We're on a roll right now and want to keep up the momentum.'

'I'll see what I can do,' Pontowski said. 'If I read you right, the SPS was a force in being and only needed good intelligence. It won't be so simple with their air force.'

'For now,' Bender said, 'get settled in. We'll talk more on Thursday when you're over jet-lag and have been briefed on the situation.'

Winslow James checked his notes. 'I have a series of briefings arranged for Wednesday morning. I've also detailed Miss Pawlik as your translator and assistant. She'll help you as needed.'

'A lovely girl,' Duncan added wistfully.

'Matt, we need to speak privately,' Bender said, dismissing the other three men. He waited until they had left and the door was closed. 'You should fit in well here. Duncan has done wonders and will help you in any way he can.'

'What about the CIA?'

Bender grew thoughtful. 'Riley has been very cooperative, but I sense that could change in a heartbeat. Be careful how you handle the staff. The foreign service is very touchy about the way they do business and anything moving faster than a snail upsets them. James is coming around but he can still get fussy.' He thought for a moment. 'Matt, there is something we must get straight.' He paused, searching for the right words.

'What's that, sir?'

Bender came right to the point. 'Your relationship with President Turner.'

'I've heard the rumors.'

'The papers and the wires are full of it. Please remember, you're still in the Air Force. I will not have an officer working for me sleeping with a superior officer who, in this case, is his commander-in-chief.'

'Sir, I am a subordinate officer and respect your position. But I don't think this is any of your business.'

The two men looked at one another. Both wanted to avoid a confrontation but they had to clear the air. 'Matt, it's called fraternization.' Bender stood and paced the carpet.

'We have to set the example or the troops won't follow. I've seen the havoc a pretty private or cute second lieutenant can play with good order and discipline.' He shook his head. 'But sex seems to overpower everything and it always gets us in the end.'

Pontowski laughed. 'That's where it's supposed to get us. Don't worry, sir. Maddy Turner understands the game better than any of us. Nothing untoward has happened, or will, as long as she's President.'

Bender relaxed. 'I hope I can count on that.'

'You can, sir.'

The rest of the week rushed by, filled with briefings and the normal routine of settling in. Thanks to Ewa, he found an apartment in Wilanów, not too far from the ambassador's compound and the American School. He was shocked at the rent, but Ewa assured him his station allowance would cover it. He ordered a car through foreign and military sales and settled into his office. The two lieutenant-colonels who worked for him, one Air Force and one Army, were eager over-achievers anxious to prove themselves. Consequently, there was little for him to do other than signing the voluminous amounts of paperwork that appeared, as if by magic, on his desk every day.

Problems started when he asked to visit a Polish fighter squadron. The air attaché, an Air Force colonel, disapproved his request, saying such a visit was outside the Office of Defense Cooperation's area of responsibility. Pontowski was about to march into the colonel's office for a quick head-knocking session when Ewa stopped him. 'Let me speak to his secretary first,' she said. She bought some flowers on her lunch break and, later that afternoon, the request was approved.

'What would I do without you?' Pontowski asked.

'You wouldn't see the Polish Air Force,' she replied.

The traffic on the road leading to Okecie airport slowed and came to a halt. Pontowski shifted his weight and looked out the car window. Three tour buses were unloading what looked like Russian soldiers in front of a huge monument on the other side of the street. Ewa followed his gaze. 'That's a monument to the Russian soldiers who were killed liberating Poland from the Germans in World War Two. They remember.'

'Is that all the Russians did for Poland?'

She shrugged. 'They built the Palace of Culture and Science as a gift to the Polish people.'

Pontowski twisted around in his seat. The ugly brown building dominated Warsaw's skyline. 'It's a monstrosity.'

'It's useful,' she replied, 'and it serves as a reminder.' The traffic started to move, and a few minutes later the staff car pulled into the barracks next to the airport. Pontowski buttoned his uniform coat, adjusted his scarf, and belted his topcoat. First impressions were everything.

A Polish brigadier general and two other officers saluted when he entered the building. 'Welcome to the First Air Regiment,' the brigadier said. They shook hands. 'We were the first to fly the F-16 and like to think we are the premier air defense unit in our air force. We are at your service.' They talked while a staff sergeant got Pontowski's parachute bag out of the car's trunk. 'I see you brought your flying gear,' the brigadier said nervously. 'Perhaps we can accommodate you with a flight in our D model if the weather cooperates.' He sounded hopeful that it would not. As expected, the Polish Air Force had put its best foot forward for Pontowski's visit, wanting to impress him. But he knew what to look for. The office equipment was old, the building needed repair, and no flights were posted on the scheduling boards.

'How much flying time do your pilots get?'

The brigadier hesitated. 'Fifty-five to sixty hours a year.'

Pontowski was shocked. A fighter pilot had to fly five times that much to maintain minimum combat proficiency. He wasn't so sure he wanted to fly in the back seat with a pilot who was, at best, marginally proficient in basic flying skills. 'I would consider it an honor to fly in the front seat. Of course, with an instructor pilot in the back.'

'Of course,' the brigadier replied. He was not a happy man and spoke to his aide in Polish. 'Arrange for General Pontowski to fly as pilot. I want our best instructor to go with him.'

It was a long drive from the barracks to the far side of the airport where flight operations were hangared. Pontowski felt better when they drove up. He knew a fighter squadron when he saw one. 'Matt!' a voice boomed when he got out of the car. It was Emil, the Polish officer with the unpronounceable last name who had flown with him at the air show when Sammy Beason had crashed. 'No crashes today!'

'Not if I can help it.'

'Good. I'm flying on your wing as number two.' He escorted Pontowski into the locker room, where they changed into their flight suits.

The IP, instructor pilot, flying with Pontowski briefed the mission while the two pilots jotted down notes on their knee-boards. The flight was little more than a familiarization ride in the jet and would be totally undemanding. Afterwards, the IP asked Pontowski about the squadron patch above his right chest pocket. 'The 303rd is an A-10 squadron?' he asked.

'It's a reserve outfit at Whiteman Air Force Base. I was the squadron commander for a while.'

The IP studied the patch. 'A most unusual coincidence. In the Battle of Britain, the 303rd was a Royal Air Force squadron made up of Polish pilots. They flew Hurricanes.'

'My grandfather flew with the RAF in the big one.'

The IP nodded. 'Yes, I know. He flew Mosquitoes.'

The patch was on Velcro and Pontowski pulled it off. He handed it to the IP. 'As a souvenir of this flight.'

Pontowski preflighted the F-16 with the ground crew chief. The jet was in pristine condition and glowed with tender loving care. But he sensed something was wrong. 'Don't your pilots preflight their own aircraft?' The crew chief shook his head. 'Ah, I see. It's the way we do things. Flights can be very demanding.' The ground crew chief was not convinced. 'Have you ever been up for a ride?'

'It is not allowed.'

'Maybe I can change that. Then you'd know why it's best to double- and triple-check everything.' The resistance he felt coming from the sergeant melted away.

Within moments, he was sitting in the front seat of the cockpit, his hands running through the familiar checklist. The ground crew chief helped him strap in and pulled the boarding ladder away. Engine start and taxi went smoothly, and within minutes they were at the end of the runway waiting for clearance to take off. Pontowski was surprised there was no quick-check crew waiting for them to do a final inspection for leaks, loose panels, or cut tires before they took the runway. At the last minute, the IP changed the takeoff and called for instrument departures. Pontowski shook his head in disapproval. The weather was improving and more than adequate for a formation or twenty-second in-trail takeoffs. Weather was always a problem in Europe and a fighter jock had to learn how to handle it or he would spend most of his days on the ground. Also, an instrument departure would burn a lot of fuel before they joined up. He made another note.

The takeoff and climb out were routine as the two fighters followed radar vectors and were passed over to Crown East, the GCI site near Bialystok. The GCI controller split them and set them up sixty miles apart. When they were headed directly at each other, the controller identified Emil as the target and Pontowski as the interceptor. Pontowski cringed when he realized it was going to be a simple stern conversion where the controller gave him vectors that hooked him around into Emil's six o'clock. It was enough to bore a man silly, and even the controller did not sound enthused. On the fourth set-up, when Pontowski was the target for the second time, he realized they were accomplishing nothing. 'We're boring holes in the sky and my attitude,' he told the instructor pilot in the back seat. 'Emil needs practice playing with an aware bandit.'

'What's an aware bandit?' the pilot asked.

'It means the guy you're trying to hose out of the sky knows you're on him and has a clue. Let me put my nose on Emil and see what he does.'

'What should he do?' the pilot asked. The fact that they were having such a leisurely conversation revealed how relaxed the mission was.

'Take over the intercept and use the vertical to maneuver into weapons-firing parameters.'

The pilot was shocked. 'It's not allowed.'

Pontowski gritted his teeth as Emil swung around in a level turn to his six o'clock position, still following the vectors from the GCI site. He was frustrated, because a pilot with the F-16's radar and black boxes could run a better intercept than any ground controller. This was not his idea of how to fly and fight.

He felt a sense of relief when the IP called Crown East for vectors back to Okecie for landing. They had been airborne forty minutes and accomplished nothing in the way of training. 'Fuel is a consideration,' the IP explained. Pontowski made another note.

Approach control split them up for radar vectors to an ILS final, an approach the airlines preferred. Since Pontowski had more fuel remaining than Emil, he landed last. The weather was still improving and the field was bathed in sunlight with fifteen miles' visibility. 'Okecie Tower,' Pontowski radioed, 'request an overhead recovery.' An overhead recovery was the standard circling approach fighters flew when returning from combat.

Before the IP could object, the tower called, 'That approach is not allowed.' Pontowski made another note and effected a straight-in landing. The ground crew chief marshaled them into parking and chocked the wheels. Pontowski climbed out and collected his thoughts as they walked in for the debrief. Tact and diplomacy were high on his agenda. But there was no debrief. He made another note.

In the locker room, Emil motioned for Pontowski to wait until the IP had changed and left. 'Polish pilots don't like to hear criticism,' he said.

'Is that the reason you don't debrief?' A nod from Emil confirmed his suspicions.

'I would never criticize you,' Emil confessed.

'Then you're not doing your job.'

'It was not a very demanding mission,' Emil said.

Pontowski thought for a moment. *How do I tell them the truth and still keep the doors open?* 'At least I learned something.' The eager look on Emil's face demanded he say more. 'You're a good pilot and can fly the jet. Now we have to get you enough fuel and flying time to learn how to fight the F-16.'

'To fly and fight,' Emil repeated. 'I remember you saying that before we took off at the air show.'

Pontowski's face was deadly serious. 'That's what this business is all about.'

The White House

Maddy Turner's maid hovered in the background as she undressed for bed. Of all the rooms in the residence, she loved her bedroom best. It was personal and feminine, and free of the showroom look demanded by Washington's political establishment. *What would Matt think?* she asked herself, trying to envision his reaction to her room. To her bed. 'Laura,' she called from the dressing room next to the bath, 'you can go. Have a nice weekend.'

'Thank you, Mrs President,' came the reply.

She was alone as she slipped a simple white silk nightdress over her head. It fell to mid-thigh and was low-cut. *It's almost nothing,* she decided, studying herself in a mirror. She sat at her makeup table and brushed her hair. She laid the brush down and pushed the narrow straps of her nightdress away. *What would Matt see?* She looked at her breasts. She stood and pulled on a full-length terry-cloth robe. But rather than go into her bedroom, she sat back down.

She tried to let her mind wander down some pleasant lane of remembrance. But the present was too strong and demanding, the future too near, and her State of the Union address only five days away. *How are people seeing me? How am I coming over?* She chastised herself for constantly linking her self-image to her political image. 'Is that all that's left of me?' she said aloud.

When should I announce? And where? Do I do it at a press conference? Maybe at the conclusion of a speech? For a moment, her mind's eye saw a children's hospital in the background. She discarded that image. The press would say she was using children as props for her political ambitions. *Maybe it should be an intimate setting with my family?* She made a mental note to speak to Shaw about the how and where.

She sat still for a moment, trying to understand the reflection in the mirror. *Am I letting too much show or not enough? Noreen would know.* Her friend's laughter echoed in her memory. Now the images were back, sharp and clear. For a moment, she was still in the helicopter and Dennis was spinning her seat around as they plummeted to the earth. She forced the memory away.

The image in the mirror seemed to blur and fade, a gossamer mirage in the wind. *So fragile. So fragile.* She reached for the phone. 'Please call Reverend Ford.' She waited. Within moments, the minister was on the line. 'I'm sorry to disturb you,' she began, 'but it's the crash. It keeps coming back.'

'That's the way a sane mind deals with an insane act. For now, don't be afraid of facing it and talking about it. It will become less urgent with time and should fade.'

'I keep asking myself, why me? Why did I survive and no one else?'

'No human knows the answer to that question and no one can speak for God. But there must be a reason.'

'Why do I find that so hard to believe?'

'To believe otherwise invites chaos. Perhaps we won't ever know the why of our existence. But we must keep faith, not only in ourselves but in each other. Your friends will not have died in vain if you keep their memory and honor them by doing what is right. But no matter what happens, remember them.'

Ford's words washed over her like a soothing breeze, carrying a comforting echo of what Pontowski had so gently revealed to her. 'I will,' she promised.

CHAPTER TWENTY

Moscow

Tom Johnson dropped the videocassette on Geraldine's desk. 'That's the unedited version,' he told her. 'I got it through one of my contacts in Washington. You need to see it first.' Geraldine glanced at the camera that was part of the elaborate security system in the Towers. Vashin had been fixated on the short news clip run by CNC-TV news and any delay was out of the question. Besides, she already knew what was on it, which would have been an even bigger surprise for Johnson.

She picked the cassette up and marched into his office. 'Mikhail, we have the unedited videotape from Warsaw.' She readied the TV as he settled on a couch. He nodded and she hit the play button. The tape started with the image of a tall man issuing orders in the middle of Zlota Street. 'He appears to be the only one not drunk,' Geraldine said.

Vashin watched impassively as four men ran to the back of the bank. Then the camera zoomed in on a man rolling on the ground in pain, holding his foot. 'He accidentally shot himself,' Geraldine explained. Vashin gave her a quick, questioning look. She bit her lip at the inadvertent slip. She was getting careless. The scene abruptly cut to four men running up the stairs to Exclusive Studios and kicking in the door. Released from their captors, the girls descended on their former guards like vengeful banshees. Even Vashin flinched when one drove the point of her shoe into a prostrate man's groin. He watched in silence as sixty-seven men were rounded up and loaded into their own trucks.

'What happened to them?' he asked.

'The police held them for a week and then kicked them out of the country. Unfortunately, they were all photographed, fingerprinted, and typed for DNA before being released. Their records were turned over to Interpol, the British, and the Americans.'

Vashin grunted and replayed the tape. Geraldine watched him for signs of a fit, but nothing happened as he replayed the tape again and again. 'We look like clowns,' he said finally. 'Get Yaponets.' Geraldine hurried out of the room to summon the godfather.

Vashin walked across the room to the big picture window overlooking Moscow. *The archangel Michael must love heights,* he told himself. He stared out into a dark gray nothing. A winter storm was battering Moscow with a fierce intensity and the window shook. He mentally reran the tape. *They made us look like idiots.* In the back of his mind, he could hear people laughing at the sight of his men, at the mention of the Russian Mafiya. AT HIM! The laughter grew louder and seared his soul. The storm beating against the Towers was a perfect reflection of his anger and frustration. *I will not have it!* Vashin felt the power in the storm as the building swayed.

Who is stronger, the gods or me? His peasant's soul trembled in fear at the challenge as the huge window rattled in its frame. Suddenly, the wind died and the clouds parted over the center of Moscow. The domes of the Kremlin were bathed in a golden light. He stared in amazement. It was the same as his dream! Or was he still dreaming? For a moment he wasn't sure. His eyes opened wide. *This is real!* Then the break in the storm moved away from the Kremlin, trailing the golden light like a spotlight sweeping the ground. It came to rest over Vashin Towers as the storm stalled over Moscow.

In his mind's eye, he saw the Towers from the Kremlin, glowing in the sunlight that had once been on it. With a certainty he had never felt before, he knew it was a message. *It is me! This is my destiny!*

Yaponets found him still standing in front of the window, staring into the gray snowstorm that lashed Moscow. He was a patient man and sat down. He studied the set of Vashin's shoulders, the way he held his head, and the rigidity of his stance. An inner sense warned him that Vashin had changed. 'Mikhail,' he said in a low voice. Vashin turned and Yaponets felt an overpowering urge to escape. The look on Vashin's face reminded him of an evil priest in an old Eisenstein movie he had seen as a child. He fought the impulse to run.

'You need to see this,' Vashin said. He played the videotape and they watched in silence, the two men alone as the windows rattled in the storm. The tape played out. 'People are laughing at me.'

'Not in public,' Yaponets replied.

'Adam Lezno is laughing. First, he steals my money and now this. A Pole laughing at me! I won't have it.'

Yaponets tried to soothe him. 'He's a dead man the moment he flies in his—'

'He didn't do this alone. Who helped him?'

'The Americans, of course. The new ambassador is in league with the Devil.'

'I want him sewn up. Dead. With Lezno.'

Yaponets nodded. 'We can do that.'

Warsaw

Bender and Jerzy Fedor stood together as Adam Lezno's limousine arrived at the aircraft. 'I appreciate the chance to go with the President,' Bender said. 'I've never seen a ship launched.'

'I suggested it when they were arranging the christening. It's the first of our new Gdansk-class frigates. Very modern and powerful. Besides, you'll have a chance to meet Lech Walesa. A most unusual individual.'

'I'm looking forward to it.'

Lezno got out of the limousine and sat in a wheelchair designed for boarding aircraft. 'Good morning, Mr President,' Bender said. 'A nice day to fly.'

'I prefer the train,' Lezno replied. 'But I've got to be back this afternoon.' An aide tugged the wheelchair up the stairs. 'Jerzy, I want everyone in place when I return.'

'We will be ready,' Fedor assured him.

'You're not going?' Bender asked.

'A last-minute change of plans. A bureaucratic – what do you Americans say? – snafu.'

Bender laughed. 'Situation normal, all fouled up.'

'I thought the *f* stood for a much better word than "fouled".'

They shook hands and Bender climbed the steps and entered the two-engine business jet that served as the President's official aircraft for travel in Poland and Europe. Because it was crowded, Bender had to sit at the rear for the short twenty-five-minute flight to Rebiechowo, the airfield on the western side of Gdansk where they would land. Lezno turned around and asked, 'Is it true pilots hate it when they are not at the controls?'

'Absolutely,' Bender replied.

'Once a pilot,' Lezno said, 'always a pilot.'

Bender gave him his best fighter-pilot grin and strapped himself in. The takeoff was as expected and the weather cooperated for the short hop. Bender tried to relax and gazed out the window, taking in the landscape. As he was near the engines, he heard the change of pitch as the aircraft started to descend. When they were established on an arc around the southern side of Gdansk and passing through 4,000 feet, he leaned back and tightened his seat belt.

A loud explosion rocked the aircraft and the window he had been gazing out of moments before shattered in a shower of acrylic, peppering the woman across the aisle from him. At the same moment, he saw a bright flash off the left wing and again the aircraft rocked from the blast. A man tumbled into the aisle, screaming in pain. Lezno turned to Bender and shouted, 'What's happening?' Fear was writ large on his face as the aircraft nosed over and banked to the left.

Bender was out of his seat. 'Two fucking missiles,' he shouted, pulling himself forward.

A woman grabbed at him. 'We're going to die!'

'Not if I can help it,' he growled. He pulled free of her grasp and fought his way forward. A blast of air beat at him and he could see the copilot slumped over the center console on the flight deck.

The man rolling in pain in the aisle clutched at Bender's legs and wouldn't let go. It was a death grip Bender couldn't break. 'Let him go!' Lezno roared, his voice carrying over the chaos. The man eased his grip and Bender kicked free, stepping over him. The aircraft's bank tightened into a spiral as Bender pulled himself into the narrow space between the pilots. The copilot was dead and the pilot slumped forward over the controls.

The ground was rushing at them and they had only seconds to live.

Bender's reaction was automatic, honed by years of experience and flying combat. He grabbed the pilot's shirt and pulled him off the controls, back into his seat. He reached for the control column. 'Come on!' he shouted, bringing the nose of the aircraft to the horizon. With agonizing slowness, the nose came up and the sink rate slowed. 'You can do it,' Bender cajoled. Finally, they were level at less than 300 feet above the ground.

Twenty-six miles away, in a wooded clearing, two men were loading an aluminum case that resembled a small coffin into a van. Their radio squawked, telling them the aircraft was still airborne. Without a word, they opened the cover and pulled out the deadly Strela-3, the shoulder-held surface-to-air missile that NATO called 'Gremlin'.

A fire warning light flashed at Bender. 'Left engine,' he said, more to himself than anyone as he pulled the left engine control lever to the off position. He didn't realize he was shouting. The pilot's hand moved toward a T-handle on the top of the instrument panel. Then it fell away as he passed out. But it was enough.

Bender pulled the handle and felt it go into a detent. He twisted and pulled again, firing the halon fire extinguisher. The fire light went out. 'I need help,' he shouted. A man appeared behind him. 'Help me with the pilot.' He released the pilot's safety harness with his left hand while he flew the aircraft with his right. Together they managed to drag the unconscious pilot out of his seat. Bender slid into the pilot's seat, aware that his left hand and arm were covered with blood. He pulled the pilot's headset on and hit the radio transmit button on the yoke. 'Mayday, Mayday.'

A cool voice answered him. 'Aircraft calling Gdansk, please identify yourself.'

'This is Falcon One with an emergency. We have been hit by two missiles. Left engine out, pilots incapacitated. President Lezno is on board, condition unknown.'

'Identify yourself and say the condition of the President,' Gdansk answered.

Bender silently cursed the controller. He was concentrating on the wrong things and would have to be told what to do, the one thing Bender did not have time for. 'I'm declaring an emergency and want a discrete frequency for vectors to the nearest airport. Scramble the crash crews and clear all airspace.' He ignored the controller's repeated request for identification and concentrated on flying the aircraft. He scanned the flight and engine instruments to see if everything tallied. It did. He checked the hydraulic pressure. It was slowly bleeding down. 'How long?' he wondered aloud. And what systems would he lose? He slowed the aircraft and ran a controllability check. The jet responded as it should.

To be on the safe side, he reduced airspeed even more and lowered the gear. Three lights flashed green on the instrument panel as the gear clunked down. He turned in his seat and yelled. 'Everyone strap in!' The controls started to feel heavy and he knew he didn't have much more time. 'Gdansk Approach, I have a field in sight. It is to the west of town with a long west-to-east runway. I am losing my hydraulic pressure and am landing. Clear all traffic and request tower frequency.'

'Falcon One,' the Gdansk controller answered. 'Do not land without proper identification. I repeat, do not land.'

Bender shouted, 'Fuck you in the heart, buddy!' He punched at the radio, finding the frequency for Guard, the universal emergency channel. 'Airport west of Gdansk, this is Falcon One with an emergency, left engine out and losing hydraulic pressure. I am five miles for a straight-in landing' – he checked his compass – 'on Runway One-One. President Lezno is on board. Scramble emergency vehicles.'

A different voice answered. 'Rebiechowo Tower has you in sight. Wind is easterly at seven kilometers. You are cleared to land. Emergency vehicles are scrambled.'

Bender worked to control his voice. 'Rog, Rebiechowo.' *Fly the airplane!* he yelled to himself. He checked his airspeed. 'Too slow.' He pushed the right throttle full forward. But the controls were growing more stiff. 'Rebiechowo, I'm experiencing control problems.' He looked out the left-side windscreen. *Too many trees.* If it had been open farmland, he would have sucked up the landing gear and made a controlled crash landing. But the trees were growing denser as he approached the field.

'There,' the man said, swinging the Gremlin on to the approaching airplane. He sighted the missile, laying the crosshairs on the nose.

'Wait,' his partner said. 'He's low and slow. Take an aft shot.'

'He'll be over the approach lights,' the shooter replied.

'He may crash,' his partner said. 'Better for us.'

The flight controls were heavy as Bender crossed the approach lights, still thirty feet in the air. He fought for directional control but the stricken airplane yawed into the dead left engine. He stomped the right rudder, hard. Slowly, the aircraft responded and straightened out as he lined up for touchdown.

He never saw the missile streaking after the aircraft, homing in on its one good engine.

The White House

'Madame President.' The woman's voice was not loud but urgent. Maddy Turner fought against it, not wanting to wake up. 'Madame President, we have a situation that needs your attention.'

She came awake. It was Laura, her maid. 'What time is it?'

'Just after four in the morning.'

Turner sat on the edge of the bed and pulled on a robe. 'Why are you here so early?'

'I have the morning shift this week,' Laura said. 'A message came in. The night duty officer is outside and Mr Parrish is on his way. He should be here in ten or twelve minutes.'

Still groggy, Turner stepped into her slippers. Laura handed her a hairbrush and she smoothed her hair back with a few quick strokes. She stood and walked into her private office in the residence. The duty officer was standing there, a worried look on his face as he nervously fingered a message. 'The President of Poland was killed early this morning,' he said.

'Adam Lezno is dead?' Turner said, coming fully awake.

'Yes, ma'am. His plane crashed while attempting an emergency landing at Gdansk.' Turner took a deep breath and gave a little nod. The duty officer plunged ahead. 'Madame President, apparently Ambassador Bender was at the controls.' Turner stared at him. 'Everyone perished in the crash.'

Madeline O'Keith Turner folded her arms around herself and hung her head as she rocked back and forth. For a moment, the duty officer was afraid she would collapse. But her head came up and her voice was icy calm as tears streaked her face. 'What happened?'

'The details are still coming in, but apparently President

Lezno's aircraft was hit by two missiles. The pilots were killed and General Bender tried to save the aircraft. They crashed on landing.'

'Has Mrs Bender been told?'

'I don't know, ma'am. I'll have an answer in a few minutes.'

The President's words were cold steel and the orders came fast. 'Tell Richard to meet me in my study. Activate the situation room, and call Mrs Hazelton. I want to meet with the National Security Advisory Group and anyone else she deems necessary.' She walked to her bedroom door and stopped. Without looking at him, she asked, 'Do they know what kind of missiles?'

'No, ma'am. Not yet.'

'Thank you, Den—' She almost said Dennis.

'It's William, ma'am.'

'Thank you, William.' She walked through the door, her eyes dry, the tears gone.

The President of the United States walked into her private study next to the Oval Office twenty-five minutes later. She was dressed in a charcoal-gray business suit, her hair pulled back. Richard Parrish was waiting for her as Felipe, her favorite steward, hovered in the background. 'Coffee and toast will be fine, Felipe.' She sat down behind her desk. 'Any more news?'

'Yes, ma'am. CNN, Fox, and CNC-TV have video coverage.' He turned on the TV and selected CNC-TV news.

They watched in silence as Liz Gordon's face appeared on the screen. Her voice was solemn as she related what was known about the crash. She turned to the screen behind her. 'This footage was shot from the control tower as President Lezno's plane attempted to land.' Turner's face was frozen as the scene unfolded. The jet was touching down as it fireballed, cartwheeling down the runway, strewing wreckage in its path. Finally, it came to rest upside down as crash trucks converged on it. Men reached the fuselage but flames drove them back.

The scene ended as the plane exploded, sending a pillar of smoke and fire into the clear morning air. 'No one,' Gordon concluded, 'survived the holocaust.'

'My God,' Parrish whispered. 'He almost made it.'

Felipe entered with a tray and served coffee. 'Mrs President,' Parrish said, 'I know General Bender was a good friend. Maybe you should—'

She interrupted him. 'He was more than a friend, Richard.' Her mind cast a long look into the recent past. 'During the Okinawan crisis, he stood by me. When we were on the brink, he was a rock. I sent him into China and would have sacrificed him—' Her voice cracked. Then she was back in control.

'Mrs President, I was going to suggest that you mention him in the State of the Union tonight.'

Turner looked at her best advisor. 'Were you afraid I would postpone it?'

'The thought had crossed my mind.' The phone rang and he answered. 'It's Mrs Bender.'

Madeline Turner picked up the phone. 'Nancy, I'm so sorry, so sorry.'

Parrish heard the anguish in her voice and left, closing the door behind him. Mazie Hazelton was waiting for him in his office. 'How's she doing?' the National Security Advisor asked.

'I don't know. I've never seen her like this.'

Madeline Turner hated the situation room with its austere walls and military atmosphere. She preferred the light and openness of the West Wing with its bustling activity, and often joked that she was going to turn the situation room into an arboretum. But on this day, Wednesday, 22 January, less than twelve hours before her State of the Union address, the situation room was a perfect reflection of her will and determination.

Mazie Hazelton entered the room ahead of the President. 'Gentlemen, the President.' The seven men were already standing and came to attention as Turner took her seat.

'Please be seated,' Turner said. All but one sat down. She

leaned back in her chair and nodded at the Director of Central Intelligence, who was still standing. He pressed a button and the large video screen opposite Turner came to life as he recounted in measured tones the assassination of the President of Poland and all on board his aircraft.

'We now have a copy of the audio tape recorded by Gdansk Approach and the control tower,' the DCI said. He jabbed at a button and they heard Bender's voice declare a Mayday and describe the emergency.

'He's a cool one,' General Wayne Charles, the chairman of the Joint Chiefs of Staff, murmured. He gave a slight grimace when Bender shouted the grandfather of obscenities at the controller when he was told not to land.

The door opened and a man in a wheelchair was wheeled in. The DCI stopped the audio playback and said, 'Mrs President, I don't believe you've ever met Nelson Durant. Mr Durant is leading the investigation into the attempted assassination on your life.'

'Please forgive me for being late,' Durant said. 'But sometimes this gets in the way.' His reference to the wheelchair was a cover for his poor state of health.

'I'm glad you could make it,' Turner replied.

The DCI restarted the audio tape and they heard Bender tell the tower he was experiencing control problems and might have to land short of the field. His words were still measured but the strain was obvious. 'That was the last transmission,' the DCI said. 'However, we have recovered the crash recorder and it is being flown to the States for analysis.'

A frame froze on the screen, showing the aircraft just as it touched down. The DCI used his laser pointer to highlight a small streak of flame a few yards behind the plane. 'This,' he said, 'is a surface-to-air missile homing in on the functioning engine. That is what destroyed the aircraft.'

'Who did this?' Turner demanded.

'I can address that issue,' Nelson Durant said. 'On the face of it, a dissident group of Polish right-wing radicals. They hated Lezno and considered him a traitor. They're so far to the right that they consider the Ku Klux Klan a leftist organization.'

'Then Robert was killed,' Turner said, 'because he just happened to be traveling with President Lezno at the wrong time.'

'Apparently so,' Durant replied. 'We do have communications intercepts that indicate the missiles were supplied by the Polish Mafia.'

'Which is logical,' the DCI said. 'The Polish Mafia will sell anything to anyone.'

'But what is interesting,' Durant added, 'is who is financing this group of Polish right-wing nuts. It's a long trail that goes through Germany, to the United States—'

'To who?' Turner snapped, interrupting him.

'A militia group in Arizona,' Durant said. 'We were looking at them because we thought they might have something to do with the attempt on your life. Three days ago, we monitored a telephone conversation between the militia's commander and an old prison buddy. But the phone call didn't make much sense until the next day, when the militia transferred a large amount of money from its account in an offshore bank in the Bahamas to another account in the same bank, which happens to belong to the Polish Mafia. Two hours later, the missiles were delivered to the nutcases in Poland. We believe it was the payment for the missiles.'

'Where did the militia get the money in the first place?' Mazie asked.

'We don't know. But the old prison buddy who made the phone call was the cellmate of one of Yaponets's stooges when he was in prison.'

Turner stood and paced back and forth, her face a grim mask. 'So I can assume that Russian organized crime is behind this. Can you prove it?'

Durant shrugged. 'Enough to convict anyone in a court of law? Probably not.'

'How deep does this go?'

'We're still digging.'

Turner stopped pacing and faced her advisors. There would be no diplomatic or legal solution. 'I need your honest opinion. Is there any doubt who's responsible for General Bender's murder?'

$\star$ $\star$ $\star$

The doors to the chamber of the House of Representatives swung wide and the Door Keeper of the House stepped through. 'Mr Speaker,' he intoned, his voice carrying over the large assembly, 'the President of the United States.' The Supreme Court justices, senators, representatives, all the collected heads of the United States government, came to their feet as Madeline Turner entered. She walked down the aisle with measured solemnity, carrying a thin leather folder in the crook of her left arm. The applause that greeted her was not of the country fair or conquering hero variety but rather subdued and respectful. Every man and woman knew of the tragedy in Poland and the bond between this president and her general.

Senator John Leland was mindful to join the applause when the TV cameras were trained on him. But even so, it was a hollow gesture. The phone call from Dan Beason that morning had reminded him all too clearly that there was an outstanding debt and that payment was due. Leland fancied himself a philosopher and believed that vengeance was a dish best served cold. But it was all too apparent that Dan Beason still burned with a desire for revenge for the death of his son.

Leland watched the President's progress, gauging the temper of his colleagues. It was time to set matters straight.

People extended their hands as she made her way to the rostrum, wanting to touch hands and share the moment. General Wayne Charles, the chairman of the Joint Chiefs of Staff, took her hand in his. 'He was the best we had,' he said. Turner moved on. She opened the folder, handed the Speaker a copy of the speech, and stepped to the podium. Her voice was calm and measured as she read the opening words. Then she paused and looked up.

'Early this morning, I was awakened with the news that the President of Poland had been killed in a plane crash. With him was my good friend and United States ambassador to Poland, General Robert Bender. You have all heard the details and know the tragedy that has been inflicted upon one of our best allies. In so many ways, it was a blow against all that is good and decent in our world. We will consult with our friends and allies to discover who is responsible. But let me assure you, the American people, and yes, the world, that I will do whatever is necessary to bring these criminals to account.'

Only Leland and the small group around him remained seated as the chamber came to its feet and applause echoed over her. She waited patiently for it to subside before continuing. Leland followed her speech on the printed copy Turner's staff had given him as a courtesy moments before he entered the chamber. He circled those proposals that were dead in the water before they ever reached the Senate. Finally, he turned to the last page. His head jerked up when the words on the sheet in front of him did not match what he was hearing.

'My fellow citizens, the Constitution requires that from time to time I report to Congress on the State of the Union. I can say without hesitation that we are secure and confident, ready to meet the challenges facing us in this new century. We are a united people and, if I may borrow from Abraham Lincoln's second inaugural address, the mystic cords binding the union together are strong because of Americans like Robert Bender.'

She bowed her head as if in prayer and waited, taking the beat from those in front of her. And only when the chamber arose as one and thundered their approval with applause did she look up. Leland joined in the tribute, assuming he was in the presence of an astute politician milking the moment for all it was worth, letting words substitute for action.

Part Three

CHAPTER TWENTY-ONE

Warsaw

The Marine corporal standing guard at the front entrance to the embassy opened the door for Pontowski and came to attention. Pontowski was certain the young Marine was more rigid than normal, if such a condition were possible. 'Good morning, Corporal Kincaid,' Pontowski said.

'Good morning, sir,' Kincaid replied. There was a slight crack in his voice. Then he did the unthinkable. 'Sir, a moment?'

'Certainly,' Pontowski replied, puzzled by the breach in protocol.

Kincaid stared over Pontowski's right shoulder. He gulped. 'I, er, we shall miss the general. Please extend our condolences to Mrs Bender.' The young corporal looked Pontowski directly in the face, tears in his eyes.

'Thank you. I will.'

Pontowski took the stairs to the second floor, thankful for the exercise. It helped relieve the grief boiling inside him. At the head of the stairs, he almost collided with the middle-aged woman from the communications section in the basement. She was hurrying down the hall like an officious mouse, anxious to deliver the morning's cables. For a moment she stood there, not moving. Then the folders slipped slowly from her arms and scattered on the floor. 'Are you okay, Miss Clement?' he asked.

She bent over and scooped up the folders. Pontowski stooped to help her. 'No, I am not okay,' she announced, her voice firm. They stood together. She looked at him, her chin shaking. 'He knew my name.'

'That was the general,' Pontowski murmured.

They stood there for a moment, silent. 'They only kill the good ones,' she said. Then she was gone, scurrying down the hall.

The protocol officer was waiting for him outside his office. 'I'm so sorry,' she whispered. Then she too rushed away. Pontowski stood there, deeply moved by the emotional reaction of the staff to Bender's death.

Winslow James beckoned to him from across the room. 'What was that all about?' James asked.

'She's upset.'

'Of course she is,' James replied, giving Pontowski a patronizing look. 'But we all have a great deal of work to do, especially now. We must not be distracted from our duties.' He spun around and walked into his office as Pontowski fought the urge to strangle him.

Behind him a voice said, 'James is a raving asshole.' Pontowski turned, surprised to see it was Peter Duncan. 'Yes,' Duncan said, 'I've been drinking. It's the time-honored way the Irish mourn a friend's death.' Automatically, their right hands clasped in friendship. 'He was a fine man, none better.'

'Most assuredly,' Pontowski replied, sounding exactly like Robert Bender. *I will remember*, he promised himself.

The White House

Joe Litton, Turner's press secretary, grinned like the Cheshire cat and almost purred in satisfaction. 'The reviews are in, Madame President. Your State of the Union address was a hit. All told, a most positive reaction. But a few of the reporters are asking for clarification on one minor point.' He managed to look apologetic. 'When you said, "I will do whatever is necessary to bring these criminals to account", did you mean "to justice"?'

'That's our goal,' Turner replied. 'But we have to work with other countries and their idea of justice may not be the same as ours.' The answer satisfied Litton, and he hurried back to his office to feed the hungry lions waiting for him.

'A thankless job,' Parrish muttered under his breath. He checked the day's schedule and wished she would replace Dennis or detail someone else to manage the daily schedule. 'A full day, Madame President.' He handed her the list and unconsciously stepped back. He felt he had to give her room.

She scanned the agenda, automatically balancing each item against the long list of issues, concerns, and problems she carried around in her mind. It was a list she constantly shifted and ranked, working on whatever needed the most attention but never forgetting what was in the background. She hesitated when she saw Senator John Leland's name on the afternoon schedule. 'What does *he* want?'

'I only talked to his staff. He'd like to discuss General Bender's replacement.'

Turner stood up, anger flaring. It was such a rare display that Parrish took another step backward. 'My God! The man's not even buried yet.'

'Leland's concerned about Poland, Madame President.'

Turner paced in front of her desk as she cycled through her mental action list. Poland was definitely in the top ten and moving up. Soon it would challenge the problem of when to announce she was running for a second term. As always, she mentally circled the problem, looking at it from different angles. Slowly, she drew Poland into sharper focus. She shifted the counters on her mental abacus and came up with a new priority. But an image of Nancy Bender hovered in the background, demanding a claim. 'Have Mazie and Stephan at the meeting,' Turner said.

Parrish made a note to have the National Security Advisor and the Secretary of State in attendance.

'Richard, as long as Mazie and Stephan will be here, make some time after Leland leaves for us to meet with Mr Durant.' She thought for a moment. 'Have Sam and the DCI join us.' Parrish added the other two members of the National Security Advisory Group to his list. He knew what the topic was.

Senator John Leland was all white hair, jowly cheeks, and old-fashioned charm when he entered the Oval Office. 'Madame President, thank you for seeing me on such short notice.' Turner extended her hand and they sat on one of the couches in front of her desk. Leland nodded at Mazie and the Secretary of State. 'Mrs Hazelton, Stephan, good to see you again.' Besides being charming, the senator was an accomplished liar. He barely tolerated Stephan Serick and hated Mazie with every ounce of passion in his political soul.

They exchanged the usual pleasantries and Leland complimented Turner on her State of the Union address. 'Most moving, Madame President. I agree with your concern over the growing instability in eastern Europe. We must not desert our friends in that part of the world, especially Poland.' The discussion was low-key as Leland made a case for appointing a new ambassador. 'We need to reaffirm our commitment to the Polish people during this difficult time.'

'It's a question of finding the right person,' Serick said.

'I'm quite sure there are many names we would find mutually agreeable,' Leland replied. 'I'll have my staff send over a short list of possible nominees my committee would consider favorably.' He paused. 'Mrs President, may we speak in private?'

Turner hesitated. Without a witness, Leland would interpret whatever was said to his advantage. 'It would clear up many misunderstandings,' he urged.

Against her better judgment, she agreed. When they were alone, Leland said coldly, 'Madame President, I am told that our government exchanged a Russian criminal in one of our prisons for a nuclear weapon.'

'We did,' Turner said, her voice flat and noncommittal.

'Then I assume the other part is true.' No answer from Turner. 'The weapon we received in return for setting this criminal free was a fake.'

'Actually,' Turner said evenly, 'it was a training device. Perfect in all respects but one.'

'Regardless, Madame President, we were snookered. That misguided venture embarrassed our country and weakened our position in eastern Europe. You should have consulted me first. I would have cautioned you against such a rash move. However, I'm confident this can remain between just you and me.'

'I see,' Turner said. It was a simple enough deal: in exchange for his silence, she must nominate the ambassador he wanted.

Nelson Durant felt the tension the moment he was wheeled into the President's private study off the Oval Office. He immediately made the connection to Senator Leland, who he had seen leaving as he entered the White House. Maddy Turner stood to greet him warmly and motioned him to a place next to her chair. The four members of her National Security Advisory Group looked at him hopefully. 'I wish my investigation had something positive to report,' he began. 'Unfortunately, we are running into too many stonewalls. But we are finding some cracks.'

'You have no idea who was behind the attempt on the President's life?' Mazie said.

'I didn't say that. We know who did it: three crazies from the California Militia. It's just a matter of time until we find them. We also know the missile and payoff money came from the Russian Mafiya. Our problem is that we don't have hard evidence.'

'Is there any connection to the Lezno and Bender assassinations?' Vice-President Kennett asked.

'It all goes to the same source,' Durant replied. 'Again, proving it is another matter.'

The DCI coughed for attention. 'We know who's behind this – Mikhail Vashin. He's nothing but a vicious street thug gone national. Expect more of the same.'

Turner folded her hands on her desk, her face a mask. 'I'm willing to consider other options.'

Mazie chose her words carefully. 'Sanctioned covert operations are out of the question.' Everyone in the room knew she meant assassinations.

'Why?'

'It's a moral question. We simply don't do it.'

Again, the DCI coughed for attention. 'There's a very practical reason. They tried it on you and look at the reaction. Do we want to risk getting into the same pickle? I think not.'

Turner leaned back in her chair and closed her eyes. 'I agree with everything you've said. So continue with the investigation for now.' She looked around the room. 'Anything else?' The meeting was over.

Outside in the main hallway, Mazie asked the DCI to come to her corner office. Once the door was closed, she said, 'I'm worried.'

'That she'll authorize me to go after Vashin?'

'That she's even considering it.'

'No one kills an American ambassador and gets away with it,' the DCI replied.

'So what are our options?'

'We don't have many. Congress has seen to that.'

'So you're telling me there is nothing more we can do.'

'I didn't say that. Through its oversight function, Congress sets the bounds for intelligence, especially covert operations. However, they haven't drawn a hard line in concrete but rather laid down a broad chalk line. My shoes are white with dust from standing on that line. There are things I can get away with, but the President cannot.'

Mazie drew into herself. *Am I reading the signs right? Maddy wants us to do something, but what? No matter what we do, plausible denial must be the rule.*

'This is a tough one,' the DCI said, thinking the same thing.

'If she brings it up again,' Mazie said, 'we'll have to do something.'

For the first time since Mazie had known him, the DCI smiled. 'I'll work on it.'

The Hill

It was Monday afternoon between the end of classes and supper roll-call, when a cadet had some time of his own. The time was even more sweet because they did not have to form up to march to supper. Brian almost ran back to their room to change into his gym clothes, looking forward to some time on the basketball court in the Godfrey Athletic Center. Lately, the coach had been talking to him about trying out for the team, and some of the older cadets were actually treating him as a species of subhuman, a big improvement over his Rat status.

But before he climbed the stairs to the second stoop, Matt corralled him. 'We gotta talk to the Trog.'

'Gimme me a break. What's she want now?'

'She maxed a chemistry test.'

'This is a problem?'

'The teacher says she cheated. No one's ever maxed it before.'

Brian was dumbfounded. 'The Trog, cheatin'? You gotta be kidding.' Matt only shook his head. 'Come on, we gotta find her,' Brian said, the basketball game totally forgotten.

They finally found her on the parade field. She was running lap after lap, pushing herself to exhaustion. The Regimental Executive Officer, Rick Pelton, was running with her, and on the next lap he shot them a worried look. 'Zeth,' he called, pulling up beside the boys, 'I need a break.' Zeth ignored them and continued to run. Pelton bent over, his hands on his knees, gasping for breath. 'Wow, is she mad.'

'Is she okay?' Matt asked.

Pelton shook his head. 'She's talking about resigning.'

'That's dumb,' Brian said. 'She loves this place.' He pulled into himself and, for the first time in his life, thought hard about helping another person. 'We need to talk to the Dean and tell him that Maggot tutored her.'

'Who's gonna believe a Rat can do that for third-class chemistry?'

Matt squared his shoulders. 'Gimme a chance and I'll convince 'em.'

'He'll need proof he did it,' Pelton said.

'Ah, shit,' Matt said, sounding like Brian. 'How we gonna get proof?'

Brian almost shouted. 'I got it. I was with you most of the time and the Secret Service saw us. I bet they even got a log.' Brian and Matt followed Pelton into the TLA's office where Chuck Sanford, the lead Secret Service agent, worked.

'Pelton's okay,' Brian acknowledged.

'Yeah,' Matt muttered, not so sure he shared Brian's opinion. But he couldn't say why.

Warsaw

The telephone call from the brigadier general commanding the First Air Regiment came on the last Wednesday in January, exactly two weeks after Pontowski's flight with Emil. The brigadier was ecstatic: his regiment had received a train-load of JP-8 jet fuel from NATO and for the first time his fuel dump was full. 'And there's more on the way,' he said. 'Thank you.'

'My pleasure,' Pontowski replied.

'Now I have two problems,' the brigadier said. 'How to use it effectively and how to keep it from being stolen.'

'I've got the man you need to speak to. His name is Peter Duncan and he's a security expert.' A meeting was quickly arranged, and Pontowski thought that was the end of it.

Then, very hesitantly, the brigadier said, 'My pilots have much to learn. Perhaps you would like to fly with them again?'

'I'd love to. Any time. All we need is good flying weather.'

'If you are available today, we currently have ten miles' visibility, broken overcast, clear on top.'

Pontowski felt the old itch and suddenly the day got much better.

★   ★   ★

Pontowski stood in front of the scheduling board in the squadron and tried to pronounce the names of the three pilots who would be flying on his wing. He had serious misgivings about leading a four-ship training mission so early on. But he liked the aggressive spirit behind the idea. 'I won't be flying with you today,' Emil said, obviously disappointed. 'My brigadier wants to expose as many pilots as possible to your style of flying.'

'How about scheduling me in a D model and you fly in the pit? That way I've got an interpreter and some-one who knows the local area.' Emil readily agreed and it was easily arranged. They walked into a small briefing room where the three nervous pilots were standing behind their chairs.

'Sit down and relax,' Pontowski said. He started a standard briefing by listing the sequence of events on the chalk board. 'Since the weather is cooperating, we'll do a formation takeoff in pairs with twenty-second spacing between elements.' From the worried looks on their faces, he sensed it was wrong, too aggressive. Or perhaps they didn't trust him. He changed his mind. 'Make that single-ship takeoffs with twenty-second spacing. I'll turn out to the left and hold three-fifty knots. Join up in fingertip formation, with number two on my right wing.'

'That means I'll have to cut you off on the inside of your turn and then cross underneath,' his wingman said.

'That's correct,' Pontowski replied. 'Take your time. I'll give you plenty of throttle. When three and four have joined on my left, I'll use our radar to clear the airspace and find a break in the clouds to punch through on top.'

The three pilots scribbled furiously as he covered the details of each event. When he was finished he quickly recapped what they would be doing. Finally, they stepped to the waiting aircraft. Emil was quiet as they walked up to the two-place F-16. 'Perhaps,' he hedged, 'we're doing too much for the first mission?'

'Then we'll play it by ear,' Pontowski said.

He found out exactly what Emil meant on takeoff. As

briefed, he turned out to the left, carving a graceful arc around the southern part of Warsaw. It took his wingman almost three minutes to cut him off, cross under, and move into place on his right wing. By then, he couldn't find his second element of two aircraft and wondered where they had gone. He called approach control on the radio and asked for radar vectors for a rejoin. But the ground controller was confused. Finally, Emil had to tell approach control exactly what they wanted him to do. From the tone of Emil's voice and the brisk flurry of Polish, Pontowski was sure most of the adjectives Emil was using would never be found in a Polish/English dictionary. He made a mental note for the debrief.

Twenty minutes after takeoff, he found the missing two F-16s circling at 24,000 feet. He called for a fuel check and groaned inwardly. The back seat in his D model F-16 replaced the forward fuselage fuel tank and he took off with 1,400 pounds less fuel than the other three jets. Yet his number two and three wingmen had less fuel than he did! For a fighter jock, running out of fuel was one of the cardinal sins. He made another note to talk about fuel management and throttle technique in the debrief.

Emil's warning about doing too much on the first mission echoed in his mind. He had to slow down. Once he had them flying straight and level in a reasonable wingtip formation, he practiced formation turns. The first one was a fiasco, the second one better, the third perfect. He made a further note for the debrief.

Then he moved them out into a line-abreast formation with the second element 4,000 feet to his left and his wingman 500 feet off his right wing. He worked them through a classic fluid-four turn where they turned ninety degrees and still came out in the same formation. It would have been perfect except they lost number four. Again, Emil got on the radio and had approach control vector them for a rejoin. By now they were getting good at rejoining and Pontowski had their measure. They were fast learners and good pilots, who suffered from lack of flying time and aggressive training. He would talk about it in the debrief. He went into an extended-trail formation with the second element three miles behind him. He turned to the right, pleased that his wingman was now welded in position on his right wing. The second element closed for a turning rejoin and moved smoothly into formation.

Pontowski called for a fuel check; it was time to head for the barn. He called approach control and broke the flight up, sending three and four home first. He called his wingman. 'Okay, partner, how are you on overhead recoveries?'

'It's not allowed,' Emil said from the back seat.

'It is now,' Pontowski replied. He briefed his wingman on exactly how to fly the traditional recovery flown by fighters returning from combat.

Most of the squadron's pilots were standing outside the operations building and saw the two F-16s as they approached from the southwest. Pontowski locked their airspeed at 300 knots and their altitude at 1,500 feet above the ground. When they were over the approach end of the runway, he keyed his radio. 'In the break.' He racked the jet into a turn and peeled off to the left, aligning the missile rail on his left wingtip with the runway for offset. Five seconds later, his wingman did the same. 'Watch your spacing,' he radioed, cautioning his wingman as he bled off airspeed. Then added, 'Gear down.' His left hand flicked out and hit the gear lever, dropping the gear and the flaperons.

When he was abeam the touchdown point, he circled to land. The airspeed bled off nicely as he came down final. He kissed the concrete at exactly 140 knots. Good landings in the F-16 were easy, but great landings were a gift from God. 'How's he doing?' Pontowski asked Emil.

Emil twisted around in his seat to watch the other F-16 land. 'Perfect.'

'Well, at least one thing went right today.' He turned off the runway and waited for his wingman. They taxied to the squadron area as a team and parked. On cue, their canopies came up together and he cut the engine. 'Cheated death again,' he told Emil.

Twenty minutes later, the two pilots walked into the briefing room expecting to see the other three pilots. The room was deserted. 'Where did they go?'

Emil looked embarrassed. 'We never debrief.' He started to explain, but his voice trailed off.

'They're not used to criticism,' Pontowski said. 'Emil, the debrief is the most important part of the mission. That's where we all learn from our mistakes and how not to make them again.'

It was after six in the evening when Pontowski returned to the embassy. He walked down the deserted hall to his offices and, as expected, found the two officers who worked for him still there. They briefed him on the message traffic that had to go out, he signed the releases, and sent them home to their families. Then he took off his coat and worked through the folder on his desk detailing a training package for the Polish Air Force. It was a good proposal but it didn't feel right, not after that afternoon's flight.

'Damn,' he muttered under his breath. He fished the videocassette from the mission out of his briefcase and popped it into his VCR. The familiar picture recorded through the F-16's head-up display appeared on the TV screen and his voice was loud and clear over the radio. Again, his frustration built as the mission unfolded. *They're decent enough pilots*, he reasoned. He glanced at the training proposal and knew it was all wrong, then threw the folder against the wall in frustration. Its pages fluttered across the floor. He leaned back in his chair and closed his eyes, the strain from the mission demanding its price. He dozed.

'General,' Ewa said, 'would you like some coffee or tea?' His eyes snapped open. She was standing in front of his desk holding the offending folder, all neatly arranged and in order. She tilted her head, waiting for an answer.

'Please sit down,' he said, motioning to a chair. 'I've got a problem. The folder you're holding is a training proposal for your air force. It's a good plan, but for some reason I know it won't work.'

She scanned the folder and then read a few pages. 'Whoever wrote this doesn't understand Poles.'

He sensed she was right. 'So what do I do?'

'You need to talk to my mother.' Without waiting for a reply, she picked up his phone and dialed a number. She spoke briefly in Polish and turned to him. 'Have you ever had pierogi with a good Polish beer?' He shook his head.

Dr Elzbieta Pawlik pushed through the door of the crowded pub and spoke to a heavy-set man behind the counter. He looked around and led them to a table with three empty seats. The young couple scooted to one end and went on talking and smoking as if they weren't there. 'So, what don't you understand about us?' the doctor asked, coming directly to the point. The couple next to them fell silent, obviously listening for Pontowski's answer.

'I guess the Polish character is totally beyond me.'

'That's because we're a mixed people, speaking a Slavic language, with a European culture. Look at the people around you. Most of them are very young. But never forget they were all born in the Soviet dark ages.' A waitress brought a platter of pierogi and a pitcher of beer. Elzbieta pointed to a pastry. 'Try that one.'

Pontowski bit into it and found it delicious. 'It reminds me of a Cornish pasty.'

'It should remind you of Poland,' the doctor said. 'That is why you don't understand us. We are a hard-headed people, Matt Pontowski, and learn by example. Your name – what do you Americans say? – has weight here. We want to trust you because of who you are. Try not to disappoint us.' She took a healthy swig of beer. 'We have been occupied so often and for so long that we distrust words. Authority. Foreigners.'

The young man sitting next to Pontowski snorted. 'Especially Russians.'

'My father,' his girlfriend said, 'hates all Germans and Russians.'

'So given a chance,' Elzbieta asked, 'which would he kill first?'

'Germans,' a man at the next table called.

'Why?' Elzbieta asked.

'Duty before pleasure,' another man shouted.

Elzbieta fixed Pontowski with a hard stare. 'Now you are talking to Poles. Are you listening?' She turned and left.

The girl leaned across the table. 'Are you the grandson of President Pontowski?'

Pontowski gave her his best grin. 'Guilty as charged.'

For a moment, he was surrounded by silence. Then the talking, laughter, and drinking really began.

The price of the evening was a hangover the next morning. It pounded at Pontowski with an intensity he hadn't felt since he was a young lieutenant at Luke Air Force Base in Arizona. Ewa took one look at him when he entered his office and handed him a cup of coffee. He sipped at it. 'I should know better at my age,' he said.

'Yes, you should,' she chided. But there was amusement in her hazel eyes. 'Did you learn anything else last night?'

'Most assuredly,' he answered.

She looked at him, tears in her eyes. 'Ambassador Bender said that many times.'

Pontowski felt a tug of emotion but quickly buried it. He checked his address book and jotted down a number. 'I'm gonna hire some American fighter jocks to train your pilots. Please call this number in Tucson, Arizona, for me.'

'It's one in the morning there. You'll wake them.'

'He won't mind.'

She went to her office and quickly made the connection. Pontowski picked the phone up and listened for the familiar voice. 'Walderman.'

'Waldo, you current with the Viper?'

George Walderman recognized Pontowski's voice immediately. 'I'm still a weekend warrior. Flying with the 162nd Tac Fighter Group here at Tucson.'

'How would you like to get a life?'

'You want me to play hero again, don't you?'

'Nope. Just train a few.'

'Where?'

'Poland.'

'No one goes to Poland in January.' A long pause. 'When do you want me there?'

'Yesterday.'

'Can do. By the way, who's picking up the paycheck?'

'You'll be a civilian working for the Polish government.'

'That's a different show,' he said.

The White House

Patrick Flannery Shaw sat in the staffroom down the hall from the kitchen and poured a shot of Jack Daniel's. He swirled the whiskey and savored its aroma. But he didn't drink; not when he needed to be at the top of his game. He had spent too many sleepless nights playing out scenarios and had come to the same conclusion every time.

The upcoming election was going to be a squeaker, but Maddy Turner was going down to defeat. And he knew why. The thought of Leland and his buddies running the nation sent a chill down his back. Could he prevent it? Unfortunately, he didn't have much to work with, not given Maddy's scruples. But he had to try. He also knew exactly what she would do to him if she found out. His advice to her about sacrificing subordinates who overstepped the bounds had struck home.

'Patrick,' Turner said, bringing him back to the moment. He stood up. 'Madame President.'

She sat down and poured herself a root beer. 'No *Mizz* President? You must be worried.'

'Yes, ma'am, I am. I know you're under pressure to announce for reelection to avoid being labeled a lame duck. But I think it'd be better if you held off announcing as long as possible.'

'Why?'

'Too many balls in the air. And we need to force Leland's hand.'

'Is he going to run?'

Shaw shook his head. 'The Senate hasn't seen the likes of him since Lyndon Baines Johnson. Leland knows the presidency destroyed LBJ, so why risk what he has in the Senate when he can be a kingmaker?'

She gave a little nod of agreement. 'He is a problem.' In a few short sentences she told him about the private meeting with the senator: the deal exchanging Yaponets for a nuclear weapon that went sour, and what Leland wanted for his silence.

'How in hell did he find out?' Shaw muttered. He looked at the woman who had become the focal point of his life. She was all that he could never be, the sum of all he valued. She walked center stage and commanded the spotlight while he was consigned to the wings. But he didn't care. In his heart, he loved her like the daughter he had never had. His resolve stiffened and he knew what he had to do.

Regretfully, he poured the whiskey back into the bottle and corked it. 'Make the deal.'

CHAPTER TWENTY-TWO

Moscow

It was a business meeting easily arranged. Tom Johnson simply called the headquarters of Transport Aviation, identified who he worked for, and asked to speak to the commander, General Colonel Peter Prudnokov. Two hours later, he walked into the gray and decaying building that was less than a mile from the Kremlin. A severe woman wearing the rank of lieutenant-colonel was waiting for him. She led the way to the only working elevator and they rode in silence up to the third floor.

Prudnokov's office was as austere as the man himself. 'What is the purpose of this meeting?' the general demanded.

'I'm responsible for Mr Vashin's security,' Johnson said.

'I know what you do,' Prudnokov replied.

'It is becoming increasingly difficult to provide the security Mr Vashin requires, especially when he flies. Perhaps your Tupolev can be made available for his use?' The aircraft in question was a VIP version of the Tupolev 204.

'That requires the approval of the Security Council and President Kraiko.'

'Easily arranged.'

'Then I will make the Tupolev available,' Prudnokov replied. 'Is that all?'

'No.' Johnson came to the reason why he was there

personally. 'Last September, Mr Vashin told me to find your daughter.' He handed Prudnokov a photograph. 'Is this her?' The general's face was impassive as he studied the picture. He nodded once. 'I'm sorry to tell you that I have bad news,' Johnson said. 'I'm afraid she's dead.'

'How did she die?'

The image of the naked girl walking to the elevator in Vashin's old penthouse and being shoved down the dark shaft burned in Johnson's memory. 'I'm not sure, but she may have been murdered.' He reached into the bag he carried and handed Prudnokov a small, ornate silver urn. 'Her ashes.'

Prudnokov stared at the American. 'Who did it? I must know.'

'If Mr Vashin approves, I'll find out.'

'I would be most grateful if this was only between you and me.'

'I'll do everything I can,' Johnson said. The hook was set. But first, he had to notify his control that the operation was in motion.

Vashin leafed through the thick notebooks like a child with a new toy. He was fascinated by the wealth of information, photos, and endless trivia about the President of the United States. 'Has Geraldine seen these?' he asked.

'Of course not,' Yaponets answered. 'She knows nothing of your interest.'

Vashin turned the pages of the third notebook. 'Who's this with her son?'

Yaponets studied the photos taken at NMMI. 'The smaller boy is Matt Pontowski. He is Brian Turner's roommate and they're good friends. Brian calls him Maggot.'

'Pontowski. I know that name.'

'The boy's great-grandfather was the President of the United States,' Yaponets explained. 'His father, Brigadier General Matthew Pontowski III, is currently in Poland training the Polish Air Force. In the last folder, there is mention of a romantic connection between Turner and the father.'

'So, the wolves breed more cubs to trouble us.'

Yaponets studied the photos, his eyes hard and unblinking. 'We know where they live.'

Vashin nodded in agreement.

'There is another problem,' Yaponets said. 'My contacts in the States tell me the CIA knows about your dreams.'

Vashin turned to the big window. 'The source of this information?'

'An aide who works for Senator John Leland. He likes high-priced call-girls and talks to impress them. He blabbers about his work on Leland's intelligence committee and what the CIA tells them.'

'Does he know who the CIA spy is?'

'No.'

'So we must find the leak ourselves,' Vashin said.

Yaponets listed the most likely suspects. 'There is me and the Council of Brothers. No one else that I know of.'

'And Geraldine,' Vashin added.

'Kill her,' Yaponets muttered. It was an easy decision. Yaponets and the Council of Brothers were *vory*, the old-guard criminals, and while they might conspire and plot to overthrow Vashin, they would never betray him to an outsider.

At first, Vashin said nothing. His survival depended on a precarious system of checks and balances where he compart-mentalized potential threats to his life. Geraldine and Johnson served a vital purpose and protected him from his fellow *vory*. But when a decision had to be made, there was no choice. 'Have the American bring her in,' he said finally.

Tom Johnson stood at the door of Geraldine's office. 'Mikhail wants to see you.'

This is different, she thought. *Why didn't he just buzz?* She arched an expressive eyebrow as her inner alarm bells went off. Any break in the routines surrounding Vashin signified trouble and, for a brief moment, panic nibbled at the edges of her self-control. She stood and followed the big American into the penthouse. He held the door for her and then left her alone with Vashin and Yaponets. The panic was back when Yaponets smiled at her. She used the only weapon at hand and lifted her chin to give him a condescending nod. But Vashin was looking out the window and didn't see it.

Panic ripped at her when the doors to the private elevator whispered open and two bodyguards stepped out. The doors closed and the guards stood there, blocking that exit. Vashin turned from the window and looked at her. She knew what was coming.

An icy contempt for these men swept over her. 'Really, is this necessary?'

'Undress,' Vashin ordered.

Don't panic! she raged to herself. Slowly, she picked at the buttons on her blouse as her mind raced, looking for a way out. She dropped the blouse casually to the floor. *What will he believe?* With deliberate nonchalance, she unzipped her skirt and let it fall. She pushed the straps to her slip off her shoulders and felt its silky smoothness slip away. An answer came to her. *Can I do it?* She willed her hands not to shake as she unhooked her bra and dropped her panties. Finally she stepped out of her shoes.

Vashin pointed at the elevator and she walked to the closed doors. One of the guards inserted a key into the control box and twisted it counter-clockwise. He stepped aside as the doors opened. Geraldine turned away from the dark chasm in front of her. She raised her head and looked at Vashin. She was regal, the queen going to her execution. 'Why?' Her tone of voice, her bearing, demanded an answer.

'You told the CIA about my dreams,' Vashin said tonelessly.

The irony of it was overwhelming. *How utterly stupid*, she thought. It was enough to steel her nerve. She lifted her chin and stared him down. 'CIA? Please, Mikhail, I *am* British.' She turned to the open door. 'I told Johnson, no one else.' *Ask why?* she prayed.

Vashin held up his hand, stopping the thug from pushing her into the darkness. The pause lasted an eternity. 'Why?'

She didn't turn around as the cold updraft from the elevator well washed over her. *Don't shake! No signs of weakness.* 'He's your chief of security. He had to know.' *ASK WHY!* she raged to herself.

He did and she closed her eyes in relief. 'Who knows how the gods work. What if someone else had the same dream?'

The thug looked at Vashin, waiting for his signal. Vashin hesitated. She hadn't begged for mercy or gone into a long, hysterical explanation. She had simply been Geraldine. His jaw worked and his facial muscles twitched. Was she telling him the truth? The thug moved toward her and raised his hand. Vashin shook his head and motioned him back. 'Give her a lie detector test,' he ordered.

Geraldine turned and walked slowly away. She stepped over her clothes and disappeared into her office, still the queen.

The technician administering the polygraph had worked for the KGB for over twenty years before he found himself unemployed. During that time, he had given thousands of tests to all types of prisoners before, during, and after interrogations. More often than not, the subject was stripped naked as part of the degradation the KGB favored. But he had never given a polygraph to a woman like this one. They could strip her clothes away but never her dignity. His fingers dabbed the gel lightly on her skin and his hands trembled when he applied the sensor pads. He wanted this one to live. He looked at Vashin and began with the standard control questions. Finally, he started the real questioning.

'Is your name Geraldine Blake?'

'No.'

'What is your true name?'

'It's none of your business.'

'Do you work for the CIA?'

'Of course not.'

The technician made a mark on the read-out. 'She's telling the truth.'

Vashin leaned forward, unable to remain silent. 'Who told the CIA?'

'I don't know. Maybe Johnson.'

Vashin picked up a phone. 'Arrest the American.' He listened for a moment and hung up, his face frozen. 'Johnson has disappeared.'

The Hill

The bleachers were packed with teenage girls for the Saturday morning parade, and they all stood when the regiment passed in review. The girls conducted their own inspection of the cadets, using a far different system of gigs and demerits than found in NMMI's Blue Book. The commander of D Troop called 'Eyes right' before reaching the reviewing stand so his two platoons could inspect back. But a little cry of 'Aren't they cute!' from the stands caused a ripple of laughter among the boys in the crowd who were there on their own reconnaissance mission.

It was the old love-hate relationship between the townies and the cadets. But if the truth were known, it was based more on gender than anything else.

'Did you see the buns on that tall guy?' the cadet marching next to Zeth said. 'He was really checking us out.'

'Don't get your panties in a bunch,' Zeth replied.

The Corps marched off the field and into the Box. The squadrons took their respective places and waited for the results of the morning's inspections and parade. The winners were announced over the loudspeaker and the honors were split among three troops, all from different squadrons. The cadets from each squadron roared their approval until the windows shook. They were 'Rocking the Box'. Then the names of cadets newly promoted in rank were read off as the cheering died away. That was the good part. At NMMI, cadets learn early that life is tough. The formation ended as the names of cadets demoted in rank were announced.

The last name was Zeth Trogger.

'This place sucks,' Brian muttered when he and Matt were back in their room. He quickly stripped of his white web belt and hung up his coat, careful to brush it down first and button it up. 'They busted her because they thought she was cheating.'

'I don't know,' Matt said. 'I talked to Zeth's chem teacher and told him I was tutoring her. I answered all his questions.'

'Yeah,' Brian muttered. 'But what about the Dean? Did he believe you?'

'I never talked to the Dean. He used to teach chemistry and I heard he called her in and gave her an oral quiz.'

'Which means,' Brian said, 'he flunked her. She studied hard. Talk about unfair. Let's go talk to her.'

'Too late,' Matt told him. 'Her parents are here and I heard she got a furlough for the weekend.'

'I don't know about you, but I'm pissed. Let's go talk to Pelton and see if he wants to help.'

'Help with what?'

'Nailing the Dean.'

Early Sunday morning, the two Secret Service agents followed the pickup truck out of Roswell. 'Shit,' the driver muttered. 'The little bastards almost got away from us. Who's truck is it anyway?'

Chuck Sanford made a call on his cellphone and within moments had the answer. 'It belongs to a cadet, Rick Pelton. He's the Regimental Executive Officer.'

'Should I let them know we're here?' the driver asked.

Sanford thought for a moment. The boys had gotten a last-minute permit to leave the post for Sunday and had taken off with Pelton. For Sanford, there was only one question. Was Brian safe? The circumstances, the evidence, and current intelligence said yes. But more importantly, Sanford's situational awareness confirmed it. But did he want to intervene? Brian was showing signs of growing up and boys did need some wiggle room. 'Observation only,' Sanford said.

But to be on the safe side, he called for a backup unit.

'I'll be,' the driver said. 'I think they're going to Donaldson's sheep ranch.' The dean of the Washington press corps had attended NMMI and had never lost his ties with New Mexico.

'What the hell are they doing?' Sanford wondered.

Georgetown, Washington, D.C.

Richard Parrish had been a sound sleeper until he became Maddy Turner's chief of staff. After that, his subconscious kicked in and the faintest telephone ring, even in his neighbor's townhouse, snapped him fully awake. It was a rare week when the night duty officer didn't call him at least twice. Usually, he took care of the matter over the phone and seldom went to the White House, where some sharp-eyed reporter would inevitably see him drive in. That report would be good for at least one interruption on the cable news channels and endless enquiries for Joe Litton, the press secretary, to handle.

The phone call that woke him early Sunday morning on Groundhog Day had nothing to do with the rodent seeing his shadow, and Parrish was in his office in less than twenty minutes. The duty officer and Joe Litton were waiting for him. '*Et tu*, Joseph?' Parrish muttered, not trying to be funny in the least.

Litton handed Parrish the news story and the photo taken off the Internet. 'This one has potential.'

Parrish gritted his teeth as he read the news article from the British tabloid. 'Where did they get the photo?'

'It had to come from the US,' Litton answered. 'It crosses the line and there is no way any of our rags would break the story, not even NT.' NT was the *National Tattler*, the most salacious of the rumor-mongering tabloids in the United States. 'So the back-door British gambit.'

Parrish had seen it before. If an unsubstantiated story was too libelous to publish, but too delicious to ignore, a newspaper in the US would leak it to a British tabloid. Then the same newspaper reported what the British were reporting, making it a legitimate story. 'Is it her?' Parrish asked.

Litton shrugged. 'We better ask before we wake the

President.' He thought for a moment. 'We're running out of time. The talking heads will be all over this one.' The talking heads were the political commentators on the Sunday morning TV talk shows.

'Any chance we can kill it?' Parrish asked.

Litton shook his head. 'Like pouring kerosene on a fire.'

'Appeal to their sense of decency?'

'Is this a sanity check?'

Parrish shifted his weight from foot to foot as he stood in the family room waiting for Maura O'Keith. He loved her for what she was: short, plump, gray-headed, and earthly. She was the perfect grandmother and the press adored her. But nothing could protect her from what was coming, if the story were true. He felt like crying when she came through the door. 'Sorry to wake you,' he said. 'But we have a problem.'

Maura adjusted her robe and sat on a couch. She patted the spot next to her for him to join her. He sat and handed her the news article and photo. She glanced at it, put it aside, looked at it again, and sighed. 'That's me.'

'Who's the man?'

'I've never seen him in my life.'

Parrish felt like shouting. 'Then it's a fake.'

'Of course.' Maura studied the picture. 'I *was* a looker.'

'No doubt about it. You still are.'

'I had great boobs in those days,' she said with a nostalgic smile.

'Mother!' Maddy said. She bit her lip, not trusting herself to say any more. Her hands trembled slightly as she looked at the picture. A young and very shapely nude woman sat on a chair. She was gazing down, the look on her face worthy of the Madonna. An equally nude man stood beside her, his hand on her shoulder. The man's penis was crudely blurred out in a way that suggested he had an erection.

'Your father had taken off with some floozie,' Maura

explained. 'One of my customers at the hair salon was a photographer and said she'd pay me to model. The only photo I posed for was of me nursing you. It won third place in a contest.'

'Was I in it? Nude?'

'Maddy, you were two months old. I needed the money.'

The phone rang and Parrish answered. He handed it to Litton. 'The barracudas in the press room are in a feeding frenzy.'

Litton listened for a few moments and said, 'Tell them I'll have a statement as soon as possible.' He broke the connection.

'Get Patrick,' Maddy said.

Parrish made the call summoning Shaw. 'We don't have a lot of time, Madame President.' He studied the picture. 'If we can get the photo from the British, we can prove it's a fake and turn the FBI loose.'

'It would help if we had the original photo Maura posed for,' Maddy said.

'All of which takes time,' Litton muttered. 'Which we haven't got.'

The phone rang and Parrish answered. He listened for a moment and said, 'They can't find Shaw.'

Maddy rested her head against the back of her chair, her eyes closed. For a few moments, silence ruled. Then she said, 'Joe, go down there and be *angry*.'

'Is that all, Madame President?'

'That's all.'

Litton took his place behind the lectern in the press briefing room and fixed the reporters with a stony look. He waited for the room to quieten. 'The President has seen the news article and has no comment at this time.' His words were calm and measured. 'Needless to say, she is concerned and we need time to check it out.' He stopped for a deep breath, leaned forward, and folded his hands in front of him. 'Since you're here at this ungodly hour, I'm assuming you've done your homework and this item is reliably sourced.' He showed his anger. 'Now, I'm going to get personal. I'm *not* speaking for the President. This is just me. I know Maura O'Keith. She's a wonderful, kind, decent woman who's worked hard all her life. Since when have our families become fair game? This stinks. It's a fake, pure and simple.' He straightened up and set the challenge. 'You people know fakes are done all the time with modern technology. It's *your* job to find out where it came from and who's behind it. Do your homework. Then come in here and ask us to respond.'

He spun around and marched out of the room, leaving a wake of silence. Parrish was waiting for him in the hall. 'Perfect. You sounded like you were furious.'

'My response was no fake.' They walked into Litton's office and closed the door. 'How's the President taking it?'

'She doesn't appear too upset,' Parrish replied.

'So what's she going to do?'

Parrish considered his answer. 'I'm not sure. I think she's going to let the press run with it.'

'Why?'

'So someone can step all over his schwanz.'

'I hope it hurts,' Litton muttered.

'When Shaw gets done with them, it will.'

Warsaw

Pontowski was alone in his apartment late Sunday night, coming to grips with the intricacies of the Polish language. 'There's got to be some way to pronounce the unpronounceable,' he grumbled to himself. The horrible consonant sequences were driving him crazy. He tried again, 'Okay, *cz* is like *ch* in China and *ch* like *h*. That's better. *W* is like *v* and the funny *e* is like the French *un*.' He tried a few words. It was starting to come together. Then he listened to the language tape and tried thank you. 'Dziękuje.' He laughed and made a mental promise to hire a tutor.

The phone rang, a welcome relief. 'May I speak to General Pontowski?' a gruff voice said.

'Speaking.'

'My name is Patrick Shaw and I work for Madeline Turner.'

'I know who you are, Mr Shaw.'

'We need to speak soonest. In private.'

'Mr Shaw, all things considered—'

'Like my reputation?'

'Exactly. I would prefer to meet in my office in the embassy. Tomorrow morning. Eight o'clock.' He dropped the receiver into its cradle. 'What the hell?' he muttered.

Ewa Pawlik handed Pontowski a note the moment he arrived in his office the next morning. 'Mr James wants to see you immediately. He's most upset and is with the strangest man.'

'A big guy, curly hair, needs a haircut, flushed face, red nose. Rumpled suit, shoes need polish.'

She nodded at his accurate description. 'Mr James is afraid of him.'

'He's an eight-hundred-pound gorilla from the White House. Not exactly the kind of visitor a DCM wants dropping in unannounced.' He handed her his briefcase and walked directly into the Deputy Charge of Mission's office.

James motioned him to a seat. 'General Pontowski, I've been talking to Mr Shaw and must say I'm disappointed in how you've responded to his requests. I take pride in my legation being most prompt, courteous, and responsive.'

'Then it's all right,' Pontowski said, 'for me to meet with someone from the White House without your knowledge?'

James huffed. 'I wouldn't phrase it that way.'

'This is unofficial,' Shaw said, helping James off the hook.

'So, in unofficial matters, I'm free to act in any way I want?'

Shaw enjoyed watching the two men spar. But that wasn't why he was there. He looked contrite and gave them his most hangdog look. 'I didn't mean to stir the waters.' He deployed his heaviest Southern accent. 'I'm just a good old boy way in over his head here. I'd like to have a few words with the general and get the heck outta Dodge.'

James jumped on the offer. 'Thank you for being so understanding. Please use my office.' He left with as much dignity as he could muster.

Shaw chuckled. 'That boy is about to wet his pants. He needs to learn how to take a precautionary piss now and then. Someday, he's gonna embarrass himself.'

Pontowski ignored Shaw's rough-cut humor. 'How may I help you, Mr Shaw?'

'It's Patrick, son. I'm here to help a friend, Maddy Turner.'

'Does the President need your help?'

Shaw nodded slowly. 'She's running for reelection, General.'

'I wasn't aware she had made that decision yet.'

Shaw's accent faded. His voice took on a friendly tone with a definite edge. 'If your intentions are honorable and you really care for her, you need to put your relationship on a back burner until after the election.' Shaw shifted into his paternal mode. 'You've got a history and must've been pretty wild in your younger days.'

Pontowski accepted the truth of it. He had been wild and irresponsible as a lieutenant and only the prestige of his famous grandfather had saved him from being kicked out of the Air Force. 'People change,' he said with quiet assurance.

Shaw agreed, but it wasn't in his plan to admit it. 'I'll never understand why women are attracted to your type. Nothing but trouble and it's kidney-stone-sized distraction she doesn't need – the voters don't need.'

'Let her tell me that.'

'You don't think I'm here on my own, do you?' Shaw let his words sink in, hoping the lie would take. 'General, I've been with Maddy since the day she got bitten by the political bug. I know how she works. She doesn't want to end whatever there is between you two, but this is not the right time for it to become a public issue. So keep talking on the phone and sending letters, but it's a matter of doing what's right for Maddy.'

'Are you saying I'm a political liability?'

Shaw heaved himself to his feet, his message delivered. 'That's why I like dealin' with you jet jocks.' Pontowski ushered him out and waited while a secretary helped him with his overcoat. 'We have an understanding?' Shaw asked. Pontowski said nothing but put out his hand. Shaw shook it and left.

James rushed up. 'Is there something I need to know?'

'Only that I've been dumped, I think.' He walked back to his office.

'Is the eight-hundred-pound gorilla gone?' Ewa asked.

Pontowski didn't answer. Then he said, 'Ewa I need someone to teach me conversational Polish and help me learn a little about my heritage, where I come from.'

'I would be glad to help,' she replied. 'Do you know where your family lived?'

He was caught off guard. He had meant his cultural heritage and not his genealogy. But the more he thought about it, the more appealing it became. 'My grandfather said something about a village near Crakow.'

'It's pronounced Kra'kov,' she replied.

Shaw hummed a tuneless melody on his way out of the embassy, his mission accomplished. He was slightly puzzled by the sight of a tall and cadaverous man standing beside his car. The man also looked surprised. 'What a fortunate coincidence. Mr Shaw, I presume?'

Yeah, right, Shaw thought. 'You must be Dr Livingstone, I presume?'

The man held the rear passenger door of Shaw's car open. 'May I join you?'

'Depends on who you are.'

'My name is Jerzy Fedor and I would like to officially welcome you to Poland.'

Shaw sized the man up. 'Get in.'

Fedor said with a smile, 'Certainly.'

The limousine drove out the gates and turned left onto Aleje Ujazadowskie. 'What can I do for you, Mr Fedor?'

'Perhaps it's what we can do for you.'

An image of two used-car salesmen standing hip deep in chicken manure while they stabbed each other in the back flashed in Shaw's mind. 'My business in Poland was strictly personal. Nothing official at all.' He wasn't about to tell Fedor why he was there.

'Please, Mr Shaw. It's not every day that the *personal* representative of the President of the United States comes to Poland.'

Shaw was impressed. He had been in Poland less than twelve hours and the government was checking him out. *Time to change the subject.* 'I take it you're from Security?'

'Of course not,' Fedor lied. 'I'm only concerned with economic affairs.' He pointed to a big gray building ahead of them on their right. 'That's the stock exchange, where I work.'

You're a lying sack of shit. You've got access and a clue. Shaw decided it was time to show a little edge. 'Did you work there when it was still Communist Party headquarters?'

'Very good, Mr Shaw. Do you still work in the basement?'

Shaw enjoyed sparring with Fedor. 'I'm moving up in the world.'

Fedor sighed. 'I wish I could say the same thing.'

Shaw sensed he was dealing with a kindred spirit, a man after his own heart. He decided to crack the door open and peek at the other side. 'I've got a plane to catch, but I do have a few minutes.'

'We have a mutual problem, Mr Shaw.'

'We do?' They were still sparring.

'The drug trade. With your help, we were making progress stopping it, but with the death of General Bender—'

Shaw finished the thought for him. 'You're worried we'll cancel.'

'Exactly.' They were on the same wavelength. 'With your help, we can handle the Russians. It's the Germans we're worried about.'

'You want us to pull them up short?'

'It would be appreciated.'

Shaw understood perfectly. Fedor wanted him to back-door a message to the President.

'Why?' He was really asking, *What's in it for me?*

Now it was Fedor's turn to proffer a deal. 'Maybe I can help distract your problem.'

You're good, Shaw thought. They shook hands.

CHAPTER TWENTY-THREE

The Hill

The Dean of the faculty at NMMI was eating breakfast Monday morning when he heard the noise in the back yard. He looked out the window and froze. Two sheep were munching contentedly on his wife's prize azalea bushes. The third animal, a large ram in a much more agitated state, was mounting one of the ewes. The Dean's shock gave way to laughter, and he walked over to Quarters One to tell the superintendent. He didn't see the black Secret Service sport utility truck parked across the street in the parking lot.

McMasters and the Dean walked quickly back to the Dean's house to survey the damage. McMasters's first impulse was to laugh. 'Ranchers take rustling very seriously,' the Dean said, killing any humor and bringing them back to reality.

'I better call the sheriff,' McMasters said.

Chuck Sanford got out of the truck and joined them. 'General McMasters, would it help if we returned the sheep?' He paused. 'Before you call the sheriff. There may not be a problem.'

The superintendent and the Dean exchanged glances. The Secret Service meant Brian Turner was involved and silence was the better part of discretion. 'I'd appreciate that,' McMasters said.

★ ★ ★

Brian stood at attention in front of the commandant, Colonel Nelson Day. 'Mr Turner, are you aware that stealing livestock in the state of New Mexico is a felony offense? It's called rustling. At least they don't hang you for it these days. To the best of my knowledge, the rancher is not going to press charges since the sheep were returned unharmed. So, what are we dealing with here?'

'Sir, I borrowed the sheep and intended to return them. I never lied about it and I was on a permit to be off-post.'

'Barracks lawyers,' the commandant moaned. 'But you are responsible.'

'Yes, sir.'

'I see. And who helped you?'

Brian braced himself even harder and did the most difficult thing he had ever done in his life. 'Sir, since it was my idea and I organized it, I'd rather not say.'

'I understand two others were involved. Are you telling me you're willing to serve their punishments?'

Brian's face turned white. Then he said, 'Yes, sir.'

'Why did you do it?'

'Because the Dean busted my squad leader for cheating on a test when she didn't.'

The commandant shook his head. 'Mr Turner, the Dean didn't bust Miss Trogger. I did. I busted her for a public display of affection. She was caught putting a lip lock on her zoomie boyfriend. About the charge of cheating, after looking into the matter, both the Dean and her teacher agreed that she didn't cheat. In fact, they commended her for her work and her teacher apologized.'

'I didn't know,' Brian muttered.

The commandant kicked back in his chair and studied the cadet. There was still the problem of the sheep. It was a prank that, in his day, would have gotten a cadet twenty tours at worse. Now it was a penitentiary offense. But the young man was standing in front of him and taking full responsibility, which he liked. He made his decision.

'As long as the rancher is not going to file charges and

the Dean is more amused than upset, this is still in my jurisdiction. Sixty tours or suspension for the rest of the year. Your choice.'

Brian never hesitated. 'I'll take the tours, sir.'

The commandant relaxed. 'Very well. A word of advice, Mr Turner. It's always okay to talk about problems with your friends. But next time, either trust the system *or* learn all the facts before you take action. And I'd suggest you make amends with the Dean's wife. Dismissed.'

Brian saluted and beat a hasty retreat. The commandant picked up the phone and called McMasters. He smiled at the thought of the superintendent explaining it all to the President of the United States. Then he laughed out loud. 'That's what he gets paid for,' he said to no one.

Outside, Matt was waiting for Brian. 'How did it go?'

'No sweat. I gotta walk some tours.'

'I'm gonna tell him I helped.'

'Don't even think about it,' Brian said. He told Matt what the commandant had told him. 'Pelton had to know why she was busted.'

'Why didn't he tell us?'

'He's thinking with his prick because he can't get it on with her. So he's causin' some grief.'

The White House

The door to the Oval Office started swinging early Tuesday morning, the first week in February, as a string of people marched in, and then quickly out. Turner worked methodically to clear her agenda of last-minute items before concentrating on her upcoming trip to Europe. Finally, the procession stopped and she was able to relax in her rocking chair. 'I need more exercise,' she told Parrish.

'You haven't swum since—' He stopped before mentioning Noreen Coker.

'I miss her,' Turner said. A little smile of remembrance played on her lips. 'She had a way of keeping things in perspective.' The hurt was easing.

Parrish sensed the moment was right. 'Madame President, perhaps it's time to find a replacement for Dennis, or at least someone else to handle your schedule.'

She reached out and touched Parrish's hand. 'You're right. I have abused you lately.' She considered likely candidates. She didn't want a servant or a yes-man, but someone who was well organized, willing to work long hours and be totally loyal. 'Ask Nancy Bender if she'd like to try it.'

'But she's pregnant and in mourning.'

'So? She still needs a life.' Turner laughed at the look on Parrish's face. 'Who's next?'

'National Security Advisory Group,' Parrish said, finding it hard to switch gears. He opened the door for the four people who were waiting outside.

Turner returned to her desk and opened a folder. 'Any progress on finding General Bender's killers?'

The DCI answered. 'Cassandra, that's Mr Durant's new computer system, has traced the missiles back to their source. There's strong circumstantial evidence the Russian Mafiya was behind it.'

'But we have no hard evidence.' This from Secretary of State Serick.

'And probably never will,' the DCI added. 'A van and three badly burned American bodies turned up in Mexico. They were all shot in the back of the head, doused with gas. Torched. We know it was the same van used in the attempt on your life and we're sure they were the key players. It got interesting when Cassandra traced their movements in Mexico. Our old friend Yaponets fell out of the tree.'

'I'm a patient woman,' Turner replied. 'Keep digging. Any progress on the photo?' They all knew she meant the photograph of Maura that had been published in the British tabloid.

Now it was Mazie Hazelton's turn. 'The FBI has it and is working on it. It's one of the best fakes they've seen. It would help if they had the original to compare the two. They have found the photographer. Unfortunately, she's suffering from Alzheimer's and is seldom lucid.'

'Show her the photo,' Turner said. 'That might jolt her back to reality.' She pointed at Parrish. 'Get with Joe and see how much longer he can hold the media at bay. You can tell him I'm very pleased with the way they have shown some responsibility on this.'

'I'm not so sure how much longer they'll sit on it,' Parrish replied.

Turner mentally checked off that block and went on to the next item, her European trip. 'I read the briefing books last night. I don't see any problems in Spain. I'd like to get out and visit more troops in Bosnia. I need something to announce in Poland. And finally, I'd like to get the Germans' attention. It looks like they're buying western Poland an acre at a time.'

Serick cleared his throat for attention. 'As to the Germans, we don't have much in the way of counters. But it never hurts to voice your concern. At least you might slow them down. For Poland, I'd suggest you announce your choice for the new ambassador. But we need to clear the name through Leland first. We don't need him shooting down our nominee after we've gone public.'

Turner tapped the folder she had been looking at. 'He's acceptable to Leland?'

'Leland recommended him,' Serick said.

'And he has contributed to the party,' Parrish added.

Turner signed the transmittal letter and handed the folder to Serick. 'Send it over.' The discussion went on for another six minutes before they were finished.

'Well, Madame President,' Parrish said, 'it looks like you have some time for that swim.'

The office rapidly emptied. The DCI walked out with Mazie. 'I'm worried,' he said. 'The way she's still in overdrive tells me she isn't over it yet.'

'She's healing,' Mazie replied.

Warsaw

The embassy was controlled chaos as James bounced off the walls getting ready for the President's arrival. As the Deputy

Charge of Mission, he would be in the official party greeting her, and it was his chance to shine. The mandarins in the State Department would have to notice him now. In an effort to cover all contingencies, he had the embassy staff working around the clock and in overdrive.

Ewa Pawlik hurried into her office with a fresh stack of Polish newspaper articles to translate. The Polish press was in a frenzy over Turner's visit. She went to work, frowning at the repeated linking of Matt Pontowski's name with the President's.

'Ma'am?' a soft voice said, drawing her away from the article she was translating. The voice belonged to a short man, barely five feet six inches tall. He was overweight with a large stomach that strained at his suit coat. He had a round face and friendly brown eyes, all topped with a heavy mass of prematurely gray hair that defied his military-style haircut. She felt like smiling at the teddy-bear image until she noticed his corded neck muscles. He was not what he seemed. 'I'm Lieutenant-Colonel George Walderman and I'm looking for General Pontowski.'

Ewa buzzed Pontowski and repeated the name. The door burst open and Pontowski came out. 'Waldo, what took you so long?'

'Ten days and you're complaining?'

Pontowski smiled. 'Ewa, meet Waldo. Don't let the image fool you. He's one of the best fighter jocks who ever strapped on an F-16.' He punched Waldo's big stomach. 'It amazes me how you can still get into the cockpit.'

'Greased shoehorns are a wonderful thing,' Waldo said.

The phone buzzed and Ewa answered. She listened for a moment. 'Do you own a yellow Ferrari with French license plates?' Waldo nodded and explained he had bought it in France while on his way to Poland. 'You need to move it,' Ewa said.

'Will do.' He turned to leave.

'Waldo,' Pontowski called, 'why don't you go with us to meet Air Force One when it lands this afternoon?'

'You got a special invitation?' Pontowski shook his head and Waldo grinned. 'You're slipping, boss.'

Suddenly, Ewa felt much better.

*　　*　　*

Pontowski led Ewa and Waldo through the dense crowd that was packing the airport for Turner's arrival. They reached the entrance to the VIP area and he gave the guards their names. Waldo wasn't on the list and the guard shook his head. Ewa pushed forward and showed the guard her identification. She spoke in a low voice. 'Ewa can work wonders,' Pontowski said.

'She's working wonders with me,' Waldo muttered.

'Sounds like a sexist remark, if ever I heard one.'

'Things are changing in the States, boss. It's okay to admit we're attracted to members of the opposite sex now. Sex doesn't equal harassment.'

'So we're getting back to basics.'

'One hopes.'

Ewa's back was to them but she had overheard every word. *Americans are so naïve,* she thought. But the guard wouldn't let Waldo into the VIP area. She played her trump card. 'Call Jerzy Fedor,' she murmured, handing him her cellphone and a card with a telephone number. The guard punched in the number and paled when the Ministry of Justice answered. He cut the connection and let Waldo enter.

The VIP area was less than twenty feet from the temporary stage where Turner would speak, and they had a clear view of Air Force One as it coasted to a stop. The new President of Poland greeted Madeline Turner as she descended the stairs, and walked with her as she reviewed the honor guard. Then they were on the stage and she was behind the podium.

'She's very attractive in person,' Ewa said. She studied Pontowski's face but couldn't read his reaction. She split her attention between Pontowski and Waldo as she listened to Turner's speech. At first, it was what she expected. But with surprising speed, it changed. 'I can only extend my heartfelt sympathies to the Polish people for the death of your President. I share your grief in a very personal way, for my good friend and ambassador, Robert Bender, died with him. But we must not be so overwhelmed with grief that we lose our way. We must continue what we have started, and I have nominated a new ambassador and sent his name to the US Senate for confirmation. The Senate shares my concern and has assured me he will be quickly approved. Our commitment to Poland remains unchanged as my new ambassador, Daniel Beason, will prove.' Applause swept over the stage.

'I've got to speak to her,' Pontowski muttered. He disappeared into the crowd.

'Fuck me in the heart,' Waldo muttered.

Ewa's head jerked around at the obscenity. 'Is there a problem?'

'You betcha there's a problem. Daniel Beason thinks Pontowski killed his son.'

Ewa was shocked, as much by the change in Waldo as by his news. 'Did he?'

'No. Beason's son couldn't fly worth shit and buffooned his plane into the ground.' Waldo stood close to her and told her about the air show and the accident in which Sammy Beason had been killed.

'You seem to know a great deal about it,' Ewa said.

'We're a close-knit group.'

Pontowski's name was enough to get him through the first security ring surrounding the presidential party. Then he ran out of luck. In desperation, he called James on his cellphone. But James cut him off with an abrupt 'If this is a personal matter, speak to her aide, not me'. The connection went dead. Not about to give up, he followed the flow of people to the press room, where a familiar voice caught his attention.

'Matt Pontowski,' Liz Gordon said. 'I heard you were over here.'

He turned to face CNC-TV News' star reporter. He and Liz went back to the peacekeeping mission in South Africa and, at best, an uneasy truce existed between them. He gave her his lopsided grin. 'I'm with Foreign Military Sales in the embassy,' he told her.

'One of Bender's boys,' she replied. 'I hear you have a history with the new ambassador.'

Pontowski was noncommittal. 'We've met. Any buzz on why Maddy selected him?'

'Conventional wisdom's that she's about to announce her bid for reelection and needs to mend fences with Senator Leland. Daniel Beason is one of Leland's major campaign backers, a real rainmaker. *Voilà* – instant ambassadorship and obligation paid.' Liz paused for a moment, hoping there was an exchange of information in the works.

Pontowski considered his answer. 'The situation over here requires—'

Liz's director rushed up, breaking into the conversation. 'We've got a one-on-one with Richard Parrish. But it's got to go *now*.' An exclusive interview with the President's chief of staff pushed Pontowski off Liz's radar scope and she turned to go.

'Can I tag along?' Pontowski asked. Liz shrugged in response. He took it for a yes and followed them into a temporary studio where Parrish was waiting. A White House staff member stopped him.

'I'm sorry, General Pontowski, but you're not on my list.'

Pontowski arched an eyebrow as if to say 'Do you know who I really am?' But it didn't work. He was up against the hard reality of politics. Power was measured by money, access, and information. At best, he only had the last, and long experience had taught him he was up against a stonewall. Unless Maddy asked to see him, he wasn't going anywhere. He called his office to see if there were any messages. There weren't. He gave up and wandered back to the VIP area to find Waldo and Ewa.

They were waiting by the refreshment stand. 'Well, any luck?' Waldo asked.

'I'm not on her list.'

Ewa felt like singing.

'So what now?' Waldo asked.

'As long as we're out here, it's time you met some jet

343

jocks. You'll like Emil.'

'A chance to fly, I hope.'

Waldo's chance to fly came ten days later when the weather
finally decided to cooperate. Emil joined Pontowski in the
briefing room and waited as the rest of the squadron filed
in to listen to Waldo's first mission brief. Emil kept looking
at the pudgy Waldo, not really believing what he was seeing.
'He's a strange one,' he finally commented.

Pontowski chuckled to himself. Too many others had made
the mistake of misreading George Walderman. 'He's not what
he seems,' Pontowski explained. 'He's prematurely gray and
that pudgy body of his can take some Gs.'

When the room was packed and the video camera on,
Waldo started his briefing. 'There's two types of aircraft in
this world, fighters and targets. Today, I'm going to show
you how to avoid being a target. Every mission starts here in
the briefing room and ends in the briefing room. So today
I'll go through the whole process with General Pontowski
and Emil. Everything will be on videotape. Come back here
after we've landed and watch how we all get better. Okay,
today I'll be leading a two-ship with Emil on my wing as the
student. General Pontowski will be in Emil's back seat as an
instructor pilot.' Waldo turned to the chalk board behind him
and outlined the mission step by step.

Crown Central, the Ground Controlled Intercept radar site forty
miles east of Poznan, cleared the two fighters into the training
area. 'We'll warm up with some G-awareness exercises,' Waldo
radioed, following the exact order of events he had briefed on the
ground. 'In-place ninety-degree turn to the right, NOW.'

Emil racked his aircraft into a tight turn. 'Hold a constant
five Gs,' Pontowski said from the back seat. They rolled out and
did it again. 'This time,' Pontowski said, 'try to hold it without
looking at the G meter.' Emil strained against the Gs and managed a decent constant G turn. 'Not bad,' Pontowski said.

'In-place one-eighty to the left,' Waldo ordered. Again, the two aircraft turned in place.

'Hold a constant seven Gs in a one-eighty turn,' Pontowski told Emil. 'Keep your airspeed near the top of your corner velocity, four-forty knots top.'

The GCI controller at Crown Central came on the radio. 'Waldo flight, can you accept tasking?'

Waldo didn't hesitate. 'That's affirmative.'

'We have an inbound target from the east without a clearance.'

Pontowski keyed his radio. 'Crown Central, this is Waldo Two. Is it a Vnukova flight?'

'It is possible,' the GCI controller answered. 'But we are painting multiple targets.'

'We'll take a look,' Waldo replied. 'We're LOX sweet, twenty minutes' play time, guns only.' He had just told the controller they had plenty of oxygen, twenty minutes' worth of fuel to use, and were armed only with the M61 twenty-millimeter cannon. In combat, the twenty-millimeter Gatling gun was a fearsome weapon. Now it was the controller's job to make the best use of it. He gave them an easterly heading and handed them off to Crown East, who would run the actual intercept.

'Waldo's fangs are out,' Pontowski told Emil. 'Are you up to it? I can take it from back here.'

Emil gave the right answer. 'No problem. I've got it.'

'Go tactical,' Waldo ordered.

'Fly line abreast, five thousand feet apart,' Pontowski said. 'You should be able to make out if he's a fighter, maybe pick up his planform in a turn.' Emil did as directed.

An American voice came on the radio. 'Waldo Flight, you're paired against one, maybe three targets. Visually identify and report only. Snap vector zero-eight-zero for ninety-five nautical miles.' As one, the two F-16s turned to 080 degrees. The target was ninety-five miles on their nose.

Waldo played with his APG-68 radar, trying for an early detection. His radar scope strobed. 'Waldo is being jammed,' he radioed, his voice amazingly cool. 'Crown East, vectors and range only.' Waldo was taking over the intercept and wanted only the bearing and range to the target. 'Bossman, radar standby, weapons cold.'

'Emil's got it,' Pontowski replied.

'Weapons cold, radar standby,' Emil radioed. His voice was high-pitched and nervous. Not a good start.

'Hook-ID,' Waldo said, calling for the tactic they would use. 'Emil is the hook, Waldo the ID.' On cue, Waldo nosed over and dove for the deck, racing ahead of them. He disappeared through the cloud below them.

'I'll talk you through it,' Pontowski said. 'Hold your altitude and airspeed. Waldo's going for the deck. If this were the real thing, you'd arm your missiles now.' At fifteen miles, Pontowski told Emil to turn right for displacement. 'You need room to turn into the target. It's a standard stern conversion where you hook around behind the target.' Again, Emil did as he was told. But now his breath came in short, deep, rapid bursts. 'Control your breathing,' Pontowski said, 'or you'll hyperventilate.'

Emil answered with short, very deep breaths. 'I'm trying.'

'Wait for the radio call from Waldo. It's his job to identify them as friendly or hostile. If this were the real thing, you'd be in position to fire. Today, you're only going to get the target's tail number. Do not get within one mile of the target unless you have Waldo in sight.'

While Emil and Pontowski hooked around behind the target, Waldo was down on the deck, his airspeed meter bouncing off Mach 1.6. When Crown East called the range at four miles, Waldo pulled his nose up and firewalled the throttle. 'Waldo's shooting the moon,' Pontowski told Emil. 'Keep your turn coming. Do you see the targets?' But Emil didn't respond. 'Emil!' The pilot's head slumped sideways; he was unconscious from hyperventilation.

Waldo was going straight up and the target was on his nose. He punched through a cloud deck and saw the Ilyushin 76. 'Target is friendly,' he radioed. 'Repeat, friendly.' Then he added, 'Two chicks in trail! Flankers, Flankers. I have Emil in sight.' He passed behind the Flankers escorting the Ilyushin, still going straight up.

At the same time, the two Su-35 Flankers saw Pontowski's aircraft and turned toward it. 'I've got it!' Pontowski shouted, taking control of the aircraft from the rear seat. He jerked the F-16's nose around, loading the jet with nine Gs. He grunted hard, fighting the G forces. A loud chirping buzz in his headset warned him that one of the Flankers had locked him up on radar for a missile shot. What unfolded next occurred at a speed that defied normal senses. When Pontowski judged they were in range of an infrared missile, he pulled the throttle full aft to reduce the heat signature an infrared-guided missile needed to lock on to. At the same time he hit the flare button on the throttle. A burst of four flares popped out behind the F-16 to capture any heat-seeking missle's guidance head.

Waldo ruddered his jet over on top in time to see one of the Flankers and Pontowski's F-16 come together in the merge in what looked like a head-on collision. Automatically, he keyed his radio and yelled, 'Break left! Take it down!' He snorted in satisfaction as Pontowski's F-16 did exactly that. The other Flanker rolled as its nose sliced toward the ground to follow Pontowski into the dive. 'Shit hot!' Waldo roared over the radio. They had set up a perfect sandwich to have the Flanker for lunch. 'Pitch back now!' Waldo ordered.

'Pitching back,' Pontowski shouted, pulling on his control stick, bringing his F-16's nose up and on to the Flanker that was now heading down but still above him. Then Waldo blasted through, splitting the air between the two Flankers. Immediately, Waldo pitched back into the lead Flanker, the one not engaging Pontowski.

Nothing in the experience of the two Flanker pilots had prepared them for such a close engagement so aggressively executed. A flurry of Russian was exchanged over the radio and, as one, they turned to the east and headed back for the border, trying to act as friendly as possible.

Emil was conscious, his breathing normal. 'What happened?' Pontowski peeled his face mask back and wiped the sweat away with the back of his glove. 'Just doing a Hook-ID,' he replied, trying to sound bored and nonchalant.

'Fuel check,' Waldo radioed. His fuel was low and he suspected Pontowski's was probably lower. He was right. It was time to head home.

By the time they landed, every pilot in the air regiment had heard about the engagement. It was standing room only when Waldo led Pontowski and Emil into the briefing room. Waldo's face was etched with the imprint of his oxygen mask and his flight suit was white with dried sweat. 'This is not going to be a pretty debrief,' he began 'In a Hook-ID, you have a contract with me to not engage unless we have each other in sight. Otherwise, it's turn and run away. Did you see me before engaging?' Pontowski shook his head. 'Then we fucked up, big time.' The room was shocked into silence. Pontowski nodded in acknowledgment and made a note on his knee-board.

The Poles listened in amazement as the two Americans dissected the mission, telling each other what they had done wrong and how to avoid making the same mistake again. The debrief lasted longer than the flight, and afterwards Emil waited to speak to Pontowski in private. 'Thank you for not mentioning that I passed out from hyperventilation.'

Pontowski slapped him on the shoulder. 'You're a good pilot. We'll work on it.' Emil nodded, ready to follow Pontowski anywhere and determined to prove himself.

CHAPTER TWENTY-FOUR

Outside Moscow

Vashin was fascinated the moment he entered the command post. He had never suspected such a structure existed. The long underground corridors showed none of the decay afflicting the rest of the Russian military infrastructure. He told the driver of the electrified golf cart whisking him to the operations center to slow down so he could take it all in. The respect paid by the officers who recognized him was exactly right: an unsmiling face, an inquisitive look, followed by a little nod. The cart stopped in front of a heavy blast door that led to the ops center.

'So, this is where we conduct a war,' Vashin said, still not truly believing he had reached the heart of the Russian military.

The general major escorting Vashin, a one-star, turned him over to the general colonel, a three-star, who would take him inside. Vashin almost laughed when he saw the old-fashioned Plexiglas wall-boards where sergeants still posted information in grease pencil. His own action room buried in the basement of Vashin Towers made this look like a throwback to the Cold War. The three-star led him to a traditional map table that was surrounded by more generals.

A trim colonel stood on the opposite side of the map table with a big screen behind him. 'Good morning, Mr Vashin.

I will be briefing the raid on the headquarters of the Polish SPS. Please interrupt if you have any questions.' The distinctive emblem of the SPS flashed on the screen. 'The double fishhook on the tail of the P has a special significance,' the briefer said. 'It was the symbol of Fighting Poland, the Polish resistance in the Great War.'

Vashin snorted. 'A foolishness we'll soon end.' The generals surrounding him all nodded in agreement.

A map of Poland flashed on the screen and highlighted the location of the target near Kutno, seventy miles west of Warsaw. 'We are employing unconventional forces which will be parachuted in,' the briefer said. 'If you will direct your attention to the large-scale chart in front of you, I will point out the objectives and outline the plan of attack.'

Vashin leaned over the map table and felt himself come alive. This was his destiny, the master planner controlling events, deciding who would live and die. A feeling of absolute power surged through him. Now he appreciated why the ops center continued to use old-fashioned ways of command. The map table, the chart, the pieces moving on the board were tangible, not images on a computer screen. He moved around the table as the briefing unfolded and looked at the map from every angle. Yes! This was the only way to run a military operation. He made a suggestion about the placement of a blocking force.

The generals discussed it briefly and their doubts turned to acceptance. The change was made and Vashin shifted his position, still listening to the colonel giving the briefing.

He had never felt more alive.

The battered Lada crunched down the narrow lane, its half-bald tires slipping on the ice and snow. Large, well-kept dachas, country residences of the rich and powerful, were hidden in the trees. Since there were no addresses or signs, the driver carefully counted the houses, finally arriving at the desired number. He turned off the lane and parked. General Colonel Peter Prudnokov was waiting for him. 'You're a wanted man,'

Prudnokov said. The driver got out of the car and removed the wiper blades. Even in dacha country, theft was a major problem. He put the blades in the pocket of his overcoat.

'Please,' Prudnokov said, motioning toward his dacha set back in the trees. 'I hardly recognized you.'

Tom Johnson bore little resemblance to the man he had been three weeks ago. He had lost weight and the buffalo-like bulge on the back of his neck had almost disappeared. His hair was much longer and dyed a dingy brown. Even his walk was different. Yet his clothes fitted him perfectly and he could blend in with any crowd on a Moscow street.

The two men stomped into the dacha and removed their heavy boots and coats. The slight bulge under Johnson's arm was ample warning that he was armed. 'I'm not going to give you up to Vashin,' Prudnokov said. He had read all the signs correctly and there was little doubt that Johnson was a foreign agent. But while he suspected that Johnson worked for the CIA, he couldn't be sure. Unfortunately, common wisdom in Moscow held that it wasn't good for one's health to cross the CIA.

'I appreciate that,' Johnson said. 'You wanted me to find out who was responsible for your daughter's death.'

Prudnokov only stared at the American. There would be a price to pay for the information. He nodded. 'It was Vashin,' Johnson said. 'He pushed her down an elevator shaft.'

'Personally?' Prudnokov asked.

Johnson shook his head. 'A torpedo. But Vashin ordered it and watched.'

'What is the price?' Prudnokov asked.

'Vashin's flight schedule, drugs, whores. The whole nine yards.'

Warsaw

Pontowski and Peter Duncan drew their fair share of telling looks and hushed words when they entered the VIP lounge at Okecie airport for the ceremonies welcoming the arrival of the new ambassador. More than a few people turned away

351

and engaged in private conversations, not wanting to be seen talking to them, at least not in public. 'I think,' Pontowski said, 'that we're in the leper colony.'

'Not *we*,' Duncan replied. 'The rumor mill around the embassy has it you're *persona non grata*.'

'Shows I'm doing my job right.'

Duncan saw the sumptuous buffet and laid on his thickest Irish accent. 'The lads have done themselves proud. Only the best for the new ambassador.' They moved off to one corner and talked quietly while Winslow James and his wife scurried around, tending to last-minute preparations.

'How are things with the SPS?' Pontowski asked.

'Going very well. They're expanding their training and rolled up two drug rings last week.'

'I didn't hear about that.'

'Few have,' Duncan said. 'The Ministry of Justice wants to keep it quiet for now. Speaking of the Devil himself, here comes Jerzy.' Jerzy Fedor was walking toward them, a glass of champagne in his hand.

'What exactly does Fedor do?' Pontowski asked.

'I'm not sure. He seems to know everyone.'

'A most excellent champagne,' Fedor said. He lowered his voice. 'I've heard a terrible rumor that you were involved in the death of the new ambassador's son.'

'We were flying an aerial demonstration when he crashed,' Pontowski said.

'You make it sound so routine.'

'I'm sorry it happened, but he knew the risks.'

Fedor nodded and sipped his champagne. 'We're going to miss the general.' He turned and wandered away.

'Our boy knows more than he's letting on,' Duncan muttered.

The protocol officer beckoned them. 'The aircraft has arrived. Please join the welcoming party to receive the ambassador and Mrs Beason.' No formal introductions were planned and Pontowski and Duncan joined the two lines of people forming a corridor for the Beasons to pass through. After a few minutes' delay, the door leading from the jetway swung open and the new ambassador stepped into the lounge. On cue, Winslow James and his wife moved forward, welcoming them to Poland. Mrs James handed Mrs Beason a bouquet of flowers and a few words were exchanged. James made a gracious gesture at the welcoming party and escorted Beason toward the door and the waiting limousine.

Applause broke out as the Beasons made their way out. Beason's eyes narrowed into slits when he saw Pontowski. His body tensed and then he moved on. 'Have Pontowski in my office first thing tomorrow morning,' he told James.

'Protocol can be a bitch,' Duncan murmured. They waited until the crowd thinned before leaving. 'I take it your bags are packed?' he said wryly to Pontowski.

The 'tomorrow morning' turned into five days, and it was Tuesday before Pontowski was finally summoned to Beason's office. Winslow James closed the door behind them and moved off to one side, looking very uncomfortable. 'Pontowski,' Beason began, 'you're trouble. Before I left the States, I read a report about you flying a combat mission for the Poles. We do not provide mercenaries for foreign countries.'

'I was flying a training mission negotiated under our Defense Security Assistance program.'

'Whatever. You embarrassed the United States.'

'We were cleared to intercept and identify an aircraft entering Polish airspace without proper clearance.'

'That aircraft,' Beason snapped, 'was a Russian diplomatic flight.'

'Most likely hauling drugs,' Pontowski added. 'It was escorted by two fighters that committed a hostile act in Polish airspace.'

Beason glared at James. 'What's this? I hadn't heard about any escorts or hostile acts.'

James gave Pontowski a cold look. 'That was forwarded through the air attaché's report, not my cable.'

Beason drummed his fingers on his desk. 'Until I can get to the bottom of this, you're relieved of all duties.'

'I can appoint an investigation officer,' James said. 'Of course, General Pontowski will be placed on an administrative hold until it's completed.'

Beason snorted. 'Do it.'

'Sir,' Pontowski said, 'what about the training package we just negotiated? One pilot is already here and more are on the way.'

'Until I'm told otherwise, it will continue. But you will not be a part of it. Is that clear?'

James coughed for attention. 'Mr Ambassador, there is a related issue with the security aid package. We are also supporting the Polish security services. Mr Peter Duncan is in charge of that particular program.'

'I'll talk to him later,' Beason said. He waved a hand, dismissing Pontowski.

Pontowski returned to his office where Peter Duncan was waiting for him. 'Well?' he asked.

'I'm relieved of all duties and on administrative hold while James conducts a formal investigation.'

'What about Waldo?'

'He can continue training the Poles until our new ambassador hears otherwise.'

'Without Bender,' Duncan said, 'that won't be long. So, what are you going to do?'

'Beats me. Maybe it's a chance to go dig up my ancestors.'

'Talk to Ewa. She might have some ideas about sightseeing.'

The White House

The Sit Room, the informal name given to the White House Situation Room, is located in the West Basement across the hall from the White House mess. Behind the guarded and locked door is a relatively small conference room, no more than twenty by thirty feet. It is soundproofed and the walls are surrounded by computer and communications workstations and two small offices. It is always manned by a watch team of approximately five people, but that varies from day to day depending on the crisis at hand.

And Maddy Turner hated it.

She preferred open, airy rooms with windows to the world outside. The Sit Room staff tried to correct this deficiency and fresh flowers were always on the conference table, unless the cranky Secretary of State, Stephan Serick, was present. Then the flowers were removed in deference to Serick's well-known explosive allergic sneezing fits which would have been funny in a lesser man. On the morning of the third Thursday in February, the flowers were gone.

Nelson Durant leaned forward in his wheelchair and studied the communications equipment in the room. He decided it was adequate but not leading-edge. He glanced through the folder in his lap one last time. His investigation into the attempted assassination on the President was complete. Maybe the FBI or CIA could find something else, but he personally doubted they would, since all the key witnesses were dead. But that was the way the Russian Mafiya worked.

'You're first on the agenda,' the NSC's Executive Secretary said. He was Mazie's most valuable assistant, in charge of the Sit Room, and responsible for moving security information and intelligence to and from the Oval Office. 'But you might want to stay for more of the meeting. I think you'll find it interesting.' He was really asking for Durant's seal of approval on what would be a very technical subject.

'I won't take long,' Durant assured the Executive Secretary. The four members of the National Security Advisory Group arrived and took their seats. The guard held the door for Turner to enter. Everyone but Durant stood. 'Please forgive me for not rising,' Durant said.

Turner gave him a warm smile. Durant was growing weaker by the day and was not expected to live much longer. 'Nelson, there's nothing to forgive. Thank you for coming. I know you didn't have to.' They shook hands.

Durant gave her one of his rare smiles. She was the first president in the last thirty years he respected and liked. He handed her his report and waited. It took less than two minutes for her to read the thirty pages. She carefully closed the document and looked up.

'So, the three terrorists who fired the missile, the other material witnesses, are all dead.'

'That's correct, Madame President. When confronted with a problem, murder is the Russian Mafiya's preferred solution.'

'And eleven people were killed because they got their wires crossed.'

'That is based on numerous intercepted telephone calls. Vashin wanted the President of Poland assassinated. You were *not* the target. When Vashin confronted Yaponets about the mistake, Yaponets embarrassed himself badly. The *vory* laughed about it for a week. We also know the Russian Mafiya was behind the assassination of President Lezno and Ambassador Bender.'

'Can we turn anyone in the *vor*?' Vice-President Kennett asked.

Durant shook his head. 'Very doubtful.'

Turner's anger broke through. 'The man's a psychopath. Is there anything we can do?'

The DCI shot Mazie a quick look. She nodded slightly in return. This was the second time Turner had asked the question. Now it was time to act. 'Madame President,' the DCI replied, taking the first step of plausible denial, 'I'll talk to my operations people and review our options. In the meantime, you might want to see this.' He handed her another folder as a large computer screen next to her came to life. Turner opened the folder and blinked twice. It was the glossy black-and-white photo of Maura the British tabloid had published. But this time there was no artful blurring of the man's huge, and very erect, penis.

'This is the actual photo of Maura that the British press published. It isn't a first-generation photo taken from the original negative. Consequently, we cannot undertake our normal checks, like microscopic frame-mark analysis. However, we have undertaken others, such as vanishing-point analysis and stereoscopic viewing. I can tell you, this is one of the best fakes we've ever seen. But it is a fake. We checked the grain pattern using a digital enhancement program. Three separate images were used in this photo. On the screen next to you, look at the disruption of the grain pattern where the man's hand is touching your mother's shoulder.'

Turner studied the screen. 'You said there were three images used. What's the third?'

The DCI blushed. 'Actually, that's what gave it away. Like I said, this is one of the best—'

'Gary,' Turner interrupted.

The DCI's blush grew brighter. 'It's the man's penis. It's not his.'

'Talk about penile implants,' the Vice-President quipped.

Durant asked to see the photo. 'How many people are capable of doing this quality of work?' he asked.

'We're not sure,' the DCI answered. 'I suspect the number isn't large.'

Durant studied the photo for a moment before he committed. This was a perfect test for Cassandra. 'Madame President, I'd like to turn this over to my people and see what they can discover.'

'Thank you, Nelson, I'd appreciate that.'

On her thirtieth lap of the pool, Maddy turned and swam for the far side. Her breath came in an easy rhythm. *I'm not pushing myself*, she thought.

A pretty and athletic Secret Service agent walked along the side of the pool beside her. 'You need to pick up the pace, Mrs President.'

An image of Noreen Coker flashed in front of Maddy. Then it was gone. She stroked harder. Suddenly, she felt better. She increased the pace and flip-turned, determined to do one more lap. The agent was calling the count. 'Stroke, stroke, stroke.'

Maddy touched the edge of the pool and looked up. 'Thank you.'

The agent smiled. 'Almost like old times, Mrs President.' Maddy pulled herself out of the pool and the agent handed her a towel. She wrapped a terry-cloth robe around herself and headed for the dressing room, the agent still behind her. 'Mr Parrish and Mr Litton are waiting for you. But they said they'd sit tight until you were finished.'

Strange, Maddy thought, *important enough to come down here but not important enough to interrupt my swim*. She steeled herself for what was coming.

Both men stood when she entered the dressing room. Litton spoke first. 'Sorry to intrude, Madame President. Liz Gordon back-doored this to us.' He handed her a tear sheet from one of the national scandal newspapers. 'It's hitting the streets this afternoon. It's a screamer.'

PRESIDENT'S MOTHER POSES NUDE

The headline couldn't have been more explicit. Directly underneath was a photo of Maddy and Maura during one of the former's campaigns. 'At least they didn't print *that* picture.'

'According to Liz,' Litton replied, 'they did. It's on page three. But she couldn't get a copy of that. She did say they blurred out your mother's breasts.'

'Does my mother know?'

Parrish shook his head. 'The crisis team is waiting in the Oval Office.'

She stared at them, rigidly holding the offending article. 'What is the matter with these people?'

Litton was embarrassed. 'They're reporters, ma'am.'

Warsaw

The chief of the American embassy's Administrative Section thumbed through his notebook, making sure all relevant questions were answered. Of all his duties, he disliked formal investigations the most. Most of the time, he knew the person being investigated and that put him on the spot. But more importantly, he was at risk if the person was well connected and could boomerang the investigation back on to the investigating officer. And the subject of this investigation could certainly do that. Like so many things, survival depended on who you knew. He glanced at his watch. It was just after eight in the evening.

'It is late, General Pontowski. Thank you for being so patient.' He reviewed Pontowski's answers, looking for a way to exonerate him and, at the same time, please the new ambassador. 'You mentioned the fighters, Flankers, which, I believe, are Su-27s.'

'Actually, they were Su-35s, a much-improved variant of the Su-27.'

'I see. Does that make a difference?'

'It does if you're up there hassling with them.'

'I see.' Of course, he didn't, but maybe someone important would. Back to the original question. 'You mentioned that the fighters committed a hostile act. What exactly was that?'

'They were actively jamming us in Polish airspace. That's a hostile act. We always have the right of self-defense. That's what all the maneuvering was about.'

The Admin Officer allowed himself an inner sigh of relief. He had found what he was looking for and survived another investigation. Now he had to delay submitting the report until some crisis or intervening event would bury it. He calculated five to six weeks would do the trick. Pontowski would be bored, but he too would survive. 'Sir, thank you again for your cooperation. Until the ambassador resolves the disposition of your case, you are on administrative leave and relieved of all duties. Your office and most of the embassy are off limits. I'll need your keys and electronic swipe card.'

Pontowski dropped his keys and swipe card on the desk. Once he left, he would effectively be locked out of the embassy. 'Can I clear my desk?'

'Of course.' The Admin Officer closed his notebook and waited. Pontowski gathered up the photograph of his son, his address book, and a few mementos from previous assignments. It wasn't much. Then he walked out and the Admin Officer locked the door behind him, pocketing the key.

Pontowski sat at Ewa's desk and stared at his hands. Then he left her a note to please call him at his home. *Damn!* he raged to himself. *How humiliating.* He forced himself to calm down, feeling the need to talk. *It's after two in the afternoon in Washington. What the hell. Why not?* He picked up the phone and asked the operator to dial the White House.

The White House

'Take a seat,' Turner said when Shaw entered the Oval Office. The heads of the six people who made up Turner's crisis staff turned as one as he found a chair. Shaw's presence could only mean one thing: she was taking off the gloves and going bare-knuckle. She paced the carpet, her arms folded. 'I have done some distasteful things in my life,' she said, 'but telling my mother about this tops the list. So how do we stop it?'

'I'm not sure we can,' Press Secretary Litton said. 'As far as the media are concerned, it's now a legitimate story. That means we have to start responding to their questions.'

'Treat it as brush-fire and stomp it out. I don't care how, just do it.'

Shaw waited, focusing on her every move and gesture as the crisis team discussed their options. *Fuckin' fools*, he decided. The moment was right when Turner sat down and leaned back in her chair. Now she would listen. 'Mizz President, have Joe here call some of his publisher friends and tell 'em this is all a crock. He's got it from the *highest source*. Maybe a little warning about getting too close to this dog because it's full of fleas.'

Parrish shook his head. 'I can hear the *New York Times* or *Washington Post* hitting the roof. Don't do it.'

Shaw shrugged, not pushing. But he knew Turner was considering it. She stroked her cheek before nodding. The press secretary picked up a phone and asked the operator to connect him to the publisher of the *Times*.

'Joe Litton here. We've seen the headlines and are very concerned.' He listened for a moment, hand over the mouthpiece. 'They're going to run it as a straight story.' Then he was back on the phone. 'Right. I'm not telling you to kill the story. But let me tell you, this is a crock. And I've got that from the highest source. If you're going to use it, keep going with your own investigation. It'll prove what I'm saying. If you go with the story as is, there will be a price, a very steep price.' He banged the phone down. 'She got the message.'

'Perhaps,' the domestic affairs policy advisor ventured, 'it would be best to let Maura respond as a private citizen who has been libeled.'

Before Shaw could step on that, the door burst open and Turner's secretary rushed into the room. 'Madame President, it's your mother. She's had a heart attack—'

'Damn those bastards to hell!' Turner blasted. She ran out of the office.

The secretary returned to her desk, deeply worried. The phone rang and she picked it up. 'I'm sorry, General Pontowski, but, but—' She broke down in tears, unable to talk.

Shaw took the phone. 'Patrick Shaw.'

'I want to speak to Maddy,' Pontowski said.

'Maybe I'm having a touch of Alzheimer's here, but didn't we discuss this? The President can't take your call.' He dropped the phone into its cradle with finality.

CHAPTER TWENTY-FIVE

Warsaw

Evan Riley sat at his desk and read through the stack of cables, faxes, telephone-call transcripts, and e-mail the CIA had monitored coming into the embassy. It amazed him that the foreign service assumed he didn't do this type of thing. What he learned from this surreptitious activity reinforced his cynical nature while providing many humorous stories for the CIA agents working on the third floor.

As a result, he saw the cable from the State Department ordering the CIA to stop providing intelligence to the SPS before anyone else. But he had also monitored the back-door messages between Bender and the National Security Advisor. He knew what the President wanted. And this wasn't it. The conflict was not new and, in the give-and-take of foreign policy, it meant only that the mandarins in the State Department were in the ascendancy. Because he considered himself a professional spook, loyal to his masters, he could live with that.

His computer buzzed at him. He spun around in his chair and read the flash message. The CIA had posted a Category 2 warning that the Russian Mafiya was going to attack the SPS in less than eighteen hours. And it didn't get much better than a Cat 2.

Now he had a problem. 'This sucks,' he muttered to no one. He checked his watch. Knowing how the embassy worked, it would take at least two hours before the first message was formally processed and worked its way to him. Then he would have to act on it and stop providing intelligence to the SPS. He made a decision and phoned Duncan's office, but there was no answer. He was hesitant about calling Duncan on a cellphone as the call could be easily monitored and, coming from Riley, would set off alarms.

Frustrated, he phoned Ewa Pawlik, trusting her discretion. 'Ewa, would you and Peter Duncan care to join me at Blikle's for coffee? Say, in about two hours, around four o'clock?' She said she'd be delighted and would pass the invitation on to Mr Duncan. Riley rapidly cleared his desk and left, telling his secretary he would be out for most of the afternoon. How could he act on a message he hadn't seen?

As usual, the cake shop on Nowy Swiat Street was crowded. Ewa spoke to a waiter and he pointed to the back room where there was an empty table. Duncan followed her, fully aware she was drawing more than a few appreciative glances from the men and hostile stares from the women. They sat down and, before they could order, Evan Riley joined them. He handed Duncan a note with a simple 'This is the telephone number you wanted'. They exchanged a few pleasantries and Riley left, finally able to return to the embassy, where his desk was piled with paperwork and the message he knew was waiting for him. Once he had read it, he would make sure that no more intelligence was passed to the SPS.

Duncan waited until after they had finished their coffee before whipping out his cellphone and dialing the number. A pleasant woman's voice answered and told him about an apartment that was available in Konstancin. But he had to act immediately. She gave him an address.

Duncan cursed the heavy traffic as he drove south out of Warsaw. It took him an hour to reach Konstancin. After flailing around in the dark trying to find the address, he asked a teenage boy for directions. Much to his surprise, the address was across the street from a dingy yellow army barracks located in the heart of the suburb. He turned into a gated drive and was greeted by a Caucasian Shepherd, a huge, shaggy gray watchdog. A middle-aged woman came out, tethered the dog, and opened the gate.

Inside, another woman was waiting for him. 'I'm sorry, but the apartment has been rented,' she said. 'I'm not sure you would want it.' She gestured across the street at the barracks. 'In the old days girls worked here servicing them.' Duncan almost laughed. The house was a CIA listening post that had been a brothel. She held out her hand and he gave her the slip of paper with the phone number. The way the number was written was his entrée. 'Forget this number and address.' He nodded and she spoke in a low voice. 'The SPS compound at Kutno will be attacked tonight by the Russians. We're not sure of the exact time or how.'

Again, Duncan nodded. He glanced at his watch. Where could he find Jerzy Fedor at this hour to pass on the warning?

'Do not contact Fedor,' she said, anticipating his next move. 'He may be compromised.' Duncan reached for his phone to call the SPS. She reached out and stopped him. 'Don't. They're monitoring the phones at the SPS.'

'Oh, shit.' Duncan ran for his car.

Ewa was still at work at 6.30 that same evening, wading through the paperwork that had piled up on her desk while she was out with Duncan. The last item was a big envelope from the Ministry of Culture and Tourism. She carefully opened it and read the cover letter. Suddenly, the long, frustrating day turned wonderful, full of promise. She reached for the phone and hit the speed-dial button.

'Pontowski,' the familiar voice answered.

'This is Ewa. I have a most interesting letter from the Polish government. They're offering you a chance to visit your family cottage which has been restored as a tourist attraction. Of course, there will be some photographers at the cottage for publicity, but other than that, you'll be free to explore your heritage.'

'I didn't know there was a Pontowski cottage. Grandpop only said we were descended from good, lusty peasant stock.'

'Then it must be a farmhouse,' Ewa told him.

'Where is it?'

She checked the letter. 'It's near Jankowice on the Vistula river. I don't know where that is. But you' – she almost said *we* – 'will be staying in Krakow. So it must be near there. You'll love Krakow. It's a very pretty city, even in winter.'

'Sounds good. Do I get an interpreter or guide?'

'I'll check into it,' Ewa promised.

Bethesda, Maryland

The doors leading into the Bethesda Naval Medical Center swung open and the waiting reporters and cameramen automatically stepped forward. Just as quickly, they stepped back when Maddy Turner came out. The respectful hush lasted three steps. 'Madame President,' a reporter asked, breaking the silence, 'how's your mother?' Turner stopped as more questions were shouted at her.

'She's stable. The doctors are very optimistic.'

Another question from the back carried over the crowd. The speaker had a deep baritone voice that carried weight and could not be ignored. 'Was it because of the photograph?'

Turner didn't answer at first, and fixed the reporter with a hard look. Maura was a tough, savvy woman who knew how the system worked, and it had been only a matter of time before the doctored photos were published in the US. More importantly, Maura had a history of minor heart problems. But for Turner, it was a moment a politician lives for. It was an opportunity to beat up the media. 'I can tell you she was very upset.' Her words came faster, building in momentum. 'My God, the woman's sixty-nine years old. She didn't deserve this.' Just as quickly, the storm passed and she was in control. 'But did that cause her heart attack? I don't know.'

366

The deep baritone questioner was back. 'Then you don't hold the press responsible?'

The sharp look on her face said more than any words. But her answer was calm. 'I like to think that the media and I have the same moral values. Joe Litton will have a statement in your hands within the hour.' She walked toward the waiting cars.

'Madame President,' a woman said, her voice cracking, 'please give our best to your mother. Our prayers are with her.'

Patrick Shaw was waiting for her in the presidential limousine. Her departure from the hospital had been as carefully staged as a Broadway production and he was pleased. The reporter with the deep voice he had planted had triggered the answers he wanted. But Shaw was still a very worried man.

Maddy climbed in and sat down. She leaned back in the seat and closed her eyes. 'She's fine. It was a minor attack.'

The iron bands around Shaw's heart eased. 'That was a perfect exit, Madame President. You held them by the neck and kicked them where it did the most good.'

'I'm not finished yet. Those bastards are going to learn to play by the rules.'

The bands were back, clamping Shaw's heart.

Near Bialystok, Poland

The operator on duty in the bunker at Crown East radar site was like a child with a new toy: he couldn't keep his hands off the controls of the new TPS-59 radar. Unbidden, his right hand rolled the control ball until the cursor was over the only target on the screen. He pressed the ball to the first detent and the computer displayed a wealth of information. The aircraft was a Russian Antonov 124 transport. The huge cargo plane was the Russian answer to the American C-5 Galaxy and was rarely seen outside Russia, much less at night. The operator checked the flight plan. The Antonov was on a routine mission and not one of the troublesome diplomatic flights.

He tracked the westbound aircraft as it flew past Warsaw. He almost called the tactical threat officer when the aircraft slowed to 140 knots ground speed. But when it remained at 32,000 feet and on the same heading, he changed his mind. The crazy Russkies were probably having mechanical problems.

Near Kutno, Poland

The six-man crew on the Antonov 124 were warm and comfortable on the fully pressurized upper deck. On command, the flight engineer depressurized the cargo deck and closely monitored the cabin's pressure as the rear cargo doors opened. The pilot felt the big aircraft pitch up slightly as the ninety-four men in the rear bailed out. He readjusted the trim while the cargo doors closed and the copilot pushed the throttles back up to cruise speed.

Outside, the jumpers deployed their highly modified parachutes, checked their oxygen for the long descent, and clapped their hands to stay warm in the freezing night air. Thanks to the small GPS receiver each man carried, they had no trouble steering for the target fifteen miles away. The lead man checked the big watch strapped to the emergency chute on his chest. They would be on the ground in twenty-one minutes.

The commander of the SPS was caged fury when Duncan told him about the impending attack. But he was far too professional to act rashly. He glanced at his watch: almost midnight. 'They'll be monitoring us, if they're any good.'

'Assume they're good,' Duncan replied. 'If the attackers are in place, activity in the compound will key the attack. If the attackers are still moving into position, activity will probably force an abort.'

The commander uttered a fine Polish profanity. 'They'll go for the communications center first. Unfortunately, most of my people here are cadets. My instructors have taught them "silent alert" procedures but we've never practiced them.' He studied the clock on the wall for a moment and made his decision. 'We still have some time.' He picked up the phone and set the alert in motion.

The communications center responded first. The duty officer prepared an attack message and opened a line to the army's central command post. The two sergeants on duty secured the bunker doors and opened the weapons safe. Inside the barracks, two instructors moved silently from bed to bed, waking cadets. The commands were simple. No lights and no noise. Wear battle fatigues, vests, and helmets. Stay low and gather by the door. On command, run for the armory and draw your weapon. Go to a defensive position as instructed. *This is not a drill.*

Duncan followed the commander to the armory, where they had to wait for a weapons custodian. It seemed an eternity before the sergeant arrived. The commander told Duncan to stay and help pass out weapons until more custodians arrived, then join him in the command post. The commander was issued a sidearm and a Heckler and Koch MP-5 submachine-gun. A smooth bolt action and long silencer made it the perfect weapon for close-in fighting. Then he disappeared into the night. Duncan felt the tension slowly coil like a spring being wound up.

The first batch of cadets piled through the door and were rapidly issued weapons. An instructor sent them to guard the command post and the communications center. 'Try not to do yourselves an injury,' he said, motioning them into the night. He swore when they collided with the next group of arriving cadets. Two more weapons custodians arrived and Duncan was issued a sidearm, vest, and helmet before he too left for the command post.

Outside, he paused for a moment to let his eyes adapt to the night. He wished he had night vision goggles, but the limited number available were going to squad leaders. The third group of cadets ran past him, heading for the armory. Duncan took a deep breath as primeval instinct emerged from its hidden niche. Adrenalin surged through him and he was more alert and alive than he had been in years. He looked around, now fully accustomed to the night. Instinctively, he glanced up. Four dark shadows drifted across the darkened sky.

Parachutists! Duncan raged to himself. His heart raced as

the shadows passed overhead and drifted over the trees south of the compound. For a moment, he couldn't move, frozen with fear. He had never been trained for this type of combat and it was totally beyond him. *Run!* he told himself. Another thought came to him. *These are my friends. I've got to warn them.* He ran for the command post.

A cadet stopped him with a challenge. 'I don't know the fuckin' password,' he growled. 'Look up.' The cadet did so as two more shadows passed overhead. 'Those are parachutes. Pass the warning.' The cadet ran into the command post and the heavy steel door banged shut, stranding Duncan outside. 'Ah shit,' he moaned, his fear back. Another dark shadow drifted over, this time much closer to the ground, obviously about to land. Duncan crouched in the shadows as the parachutist touched down. The man gave a little grunt on impact, his feet protesting in pain after the long exposure to the cold. He expertly collapsed his parachute, his back to Duncan.

Duncan never hesitated. He glided across the thirty feet separating them as he drew his weapon. He held the automatic low on his waist as he poked the rigid forefinger of his left hand against the man's neck, just below his left ear. 'Freeze, asshole.'

The man's reactions were quick and sure, the result of years of training and conditioning. He whirled on Duncan and his left arm came around in a sweeping motion. His right foot was a blur as he aimed a kick. Normally, it would have been all over. But adrenalin was still pumping through the American and he stepped back, rattlesnake quick, avoiding the kick. The man was almost as fast and his knife was out, a blur coming at Duncan.

Duncan shot him in the stomach.

The single shot echoed over the compound and into the trees. The loud shriek of a mortar round echoed back. Duncan grabbed the man by the collar and dragged him toward the command post. The mortar round tore into the first barracks and exploded, sending a bright pulse of light over the compound. In that split second over forty cadets were framed, some running for the armory, others away. Round after round pounded the compound, killing and wounding cadets caught in the open. Duncan was also exposed, and he rolled under the body he was dragging, the only protection available. Shrapnel tore into the corpse, but he was safe.

As quickly as it started, the barrage stopped. Shrieks of pain and cries for help shattered the sudden silence. Duncan knew what was coming next and scrambled to his feet. He was a mess, caked with blood-soaked dirt, but unhurt. He dragged the body the last few feet to the command post and banged on the steel door. 'I've got one of the bastards!' he yelled in English.

Duncan's adrenalin rush crashed just as men hurried from the nearby trees, firing on the run. The distinctive rattle of AK-47s permeated the air, filling him with terror. Duncan fell to the ground and fumbled with the AK-47 still strapped to the dead parachutist's side. The buckles were unfamiliar and it took a moment to free the weapon. He worked furiously as a sapper reached the door of the command post, unaware that Duncan was only a few feet away. The sapper planted an explosive charge against the door as Duncan came to his feet and charged the AK-47. He squeezed off a short burst and cut the sapper down before he could set the detonator.

Duncan fell to the ground and rolled into deep shadow as more men charged into the compound. But it was only a matter of moments before one of the attackers spotted him through night vision goggles. He was as good as dead and knew it. An uncontrollable rage claimed him. He came to his feet and emptied the AK-47. He slapped another clip into the weapon and kept firing. He never saw the grenade rolling across the ground toward him.

Duncan's fire had delayed the attackers long enough for six cadets to move into position and block the attackers from moving past the command post. For a few moments, the firefight hinged on the low concrete structure, and the attackers were unable to move past it. Finally, another sapper reached the door and set the detonator. A cadet poked his submachine-gun around the corner and cut him down before he could retreat to safety. A blast knocked the heavy door off its hinges and an assault team of four men rushed inside the darkened bunker.

But the command post was empty. The commander of the SPS had ordered its evacuation through an escape hatch in the rear wall. Contrary to popular belief, night vision goggles do not work in total darkness, and the four men were essentially blind. One of them lifted his goggles and flicked on a flashlight. He saw the escape hatch in time to see four grenades tumble out. The last thing he heard before the explosion was the hatch clanging shut.

Flames from the burning barracks cast an eerie light over the compound as the firefight dissolved into chaos. There was no coordination, just pockets of resistance fighting for their lives. Suddenly, a helicopter flew across the compound at full speed. It made no attempt to slow or turn. But it was enough.

A series of frantic radio calls demanded to know if there were more helicopters inbound. Lacking an answer, an assault team trying to flank the command post withdrew to the trees. In itself, it was a trickle. But the team next in line stopped advancing, made a radio call and, finding they were on the flank, decided to withdraw. That was when the SPS commander ordered a counterattack by the twelve cadets on the opposite side of the compound. The trickle turned into a stream and the attackers were in full retreat, rushing for the trees.

Part of the genius of military leadership is knowing when to exploit an advantage, a willingness to sacrifice lives, and having the force of personality to make it happen. The commander of the SPS keyed his radio and calmly ordered his cadets to counterattack, driving the last of the invaders into the trees. The fighting was hand to hand and vicious as the cadets avenged their fallen comrades. Finally, they broke through to the fields on the other side of the trees.

Another part of the genius is knowing when to stop. The commander listened as the gunfire withered away. Satisfied that he had a defensible perimeter, he ordered the cadets to stand and hold. The battle was over.

★　　★　　★

'Sir,' a cadet said, 'we found Mr Duncan.' The young man led the commander to the side of the command post. The fragmentation grenade had turned the body into a bloody pulp, almost unrecognizable. The cadet threw up. The commander waited patiently, remembering his first firefight. 'The American did well. Look.' He counted the bodies. 'He gave us warning and killed seven of our enemies. The man was a friend.'

The commander looked at the burning barracks and the carnage around him. Half of his cadets had been killed or wounded. The body count for the attackers stood at twenty-six and was going higher. 'This is not a victory, only a warning.' He pulled out his cellphone and called Jerzy Fedor. They had to talk immediately.

CHAPTER TWENTY-SIX

Outside Moscow

The commander's balcony overlooking the operations center appealed to Vashin's enjoyment of heights and gave him the overview he craved. Yet it was not so far removed to put him out of touch. The trim army colonel took the main stage, holding a long, old-fashioned wooden pointer. He jabbed at the large-scale chart of the SPS compound on the sliding wall-board directly behind him.

'Our forces have successfully withdrawn as planned. The trucks are now *en route* to Belarus and should cross the border at first light. The border guards have been bribed and there will be no trouble.'

Vashin liked the colonel's optimism. He reached for the microphone clipped to the side of his seat. 'Casualties?' he asked. His voice echoed over the operations center with a tinny, harsh sound.

The colonel shrugged. 'Does it matter? We achieved our objective. The SPS no longer exists as a functional unit.'

Vashin accepted the colonel's logic and stood to leave. The generals rose as one, a fraction of a second behind him. The constant deference they paid Vashin, their total subservience, were survival techniques born of desperation when Stalin ruled, refined under Khrushchev, institutionalized during Brezhnev's regime, and almost forgotten when Gorbachev tried to reform the system. Instinctively, the generals saw in Vashin a new Stalin, and reverted to the submissiveness that had worked so well in the past. 'Your positioning of the blocking force was masterful,' one of them said. 'They were able to stop a counterattack which saved the operation. You are to be commended, sir.' The other generals nodded in unison.

Vashin acknowledged their praise and left. The generals were silent until the door closed behind him. As one, they sat down and the real briefing began. The generals would willingly lie and deceive their political masters, but not themselves. The colonel dropped his long wooden pointer and slid the wall-board back. A large computer-driven display appeared with video images. The colonel now flashed a laser pointer at the screen. 'We lost the element of surprise when one of our men landed inside the compound. Since most of the force was in position, the commander opted to initiate the attack. In retrospect, that was a mistake and the commander will be disciplined. The SPS had been warned and were waiting. The Poles were so confident that they used cadets. For them, it was a training exercise. Nevertheless, our men were still able to inflict considerable damage before withdrawing.'

'Casualties?' a gruff voice asked.

This time the colonel answered. 'We inserted ninety-four and left forty-one behind on withdrawal. Most of those are presumed dead.'

The image on the screen changed and a late-breaking CNN story appeared. A news team was at a border crossing between Poland and Belarus, where a large group of men were being offloaded from trucks. Many were wounded and bandaged. The on-scene reporter sorted through a large stack of weapons, describing their make, origin, and use. Most of the generals spoke English and did not need an interpreter. 'An unmitigated disaster,' one of them muttered.

'Without doubt,' a two-star replied. 'But is it for us to tell him?'

'Not me,' a three-star said. 'He sent my wife a new car. A Mercedes-Benz. My daughter loves it.'

'He knows where we live,' the two-star said.

★   ★   ★

Geraldine Blake arrived at her office next to Vashin's penthouse at the usual time. Normally, she had one or two hours in which to finalize the day's schedule and only saw Vashin after the girl left. But this morning she was surprised to hear the television tuned to an English-language station. *Most unusual*, she thought, since Vashin's English was very limited. She listened. It was an English-language edition of CNN, and the late-breaking story of the capture of a large force of escaping Russian terrorists on the Polish border was getting full coverage. *This will be a problem*, she thought.

She checked her appearance in the mirror, picked up her slim leather notebook and walked through the door. The TV was still on but Vashin was not paying attention. He was sitting on a couch, thumbing through the big picture albums that detailed the life of his nemesis, the woman he called the bitch. Lately, he had become obsessed, and the albums were updated daily. He closed the books and walked to the big window overlooking Moscow.

'It was a fiasco,' he muttered.

'I'm sorry,' she replied, 'but I don't know what happened.' It was a gentle rebuke to the effect that she could not help him if she was kept in the dark.

Vashin stared into the mist swirling around the Towers, his hands clasped behind his back. 'We are losing Poland.' He spun around and glared at her.

'Why? I thought the Polish Mafia was under your thumb and you were in control there.'

'I was until the Americans started helping them. This Special Public Services of the Poles, it's a front for the CIA. I can sense it in my bones. That's why I had to eliminate them. The generals told me the operation was a success. Why did they lie to me?'

He's obsessing, Geraldine thought. *He knows the CIA has nothing to do with the SPS.* She fought for time. 'Maybe the generals thought the operation was a success. CNN reported that one of the Americans helping the Poles, a Peter Duncan, was killed in the attack. According to our sources, Duncan was in Poland with the US Defense Security Assistance Agency administering the security package negotiated by the last ambassador. With Bender dead, the new ambassador might scale back their aid. That only leaves one person in Poland still working with the Poles.'

'Yes, I know. Pontowski. *Her* boyfriend, the grandson of a president. I can't touch him.'

'Under the circumstances, a very wise decision.' She gracefully rose and walked to the window. She touched his shoulder. 'Mikhail, what would Peter the Great do?' As she said it, the mist parted and the sun broke the eastern horizon far to the south.

He turned to her, his face glowing as if he had seen a vision. 'You're right. I must look to Russia.' He pointed to the sun. 'The sun is breaking over the south.'

'The south?' she asked, not understanding.

'The Ukraine is Russia's granary. It's vital to the Russian empire, our survival. The German minister I met in Bonn, von Lubeck, used a word, a very good word. *Anschluss*.' He paused, striking a pose. 'I want to see the Pole. Get him here and tell him to bring the money that was stolen from me.'

'Certainly, Mikhail.' She turned to leave.

'And,' he said, halting her, 'call a full council of the *vor* for next week.'

Geraldine panicked. To gather the heads of all the families that made up the *vor* took several weeks, maybe months, to arrange. Egos had to be stroked, ceasefires between feuding families negotiated, security arranged. An arbitrary summons on such short notice was impracticable, even for Vashin. 'That will be difficult.'

Vashin glared at her, knowing she was right. 'As soon as possible, then.'

She gave him a radiant smile as a reward for his understanding, turned and left. Vashin watched her go, his eyes narrowing. 'Can I really trust you?' he muttered. Since Johnson's disappearance, he had become obsessed with his security. Twice he had almost purged the ranks of the *vor* in a bloodbath that would have rivaled Stalin's purges. But common sense had prevailed before he gave the order. He forced himself to be rational and returned to the couch to watch TV. His English was much better than Geraldine suspected and it was clear that the attack on the SPS had been a disaster. 'There is always a price to pay,' he said to no one. He flipped open one of the albums, fully aware that Maddy Turner was beyond his reach. His eyes narrowed when he saw a photo of Brian, Zeth, and Matt in their uniforms. He closed the book and walked back to the window to bathe in the new sunrise.

Warsaw

The wind lashed at Pontowski when he got out of his car. He glanced at the sky as traces of sleet stung his face. For once, the weather matched his mood, solemn and gray. He looked around to see if anyone else from the embassy had come to the airport for the ceremony. He was alone. He jerked at the belt of his uniform overcoat and jammed his hat down more tightly against the wind.

Across the parking ramp, he could see the gray outline of the Air Force C-17 that would carry the mortal remains of Peter Duncan home.

An officer and a cadet from the SPS met him at the gate. They were wearing black combat fatigues with their winter field jackets. The cadet held the gate open and the officer saluted. Without a word, the three men walked across the tarmac toward the small group of people huddled under the tail of the waiting aircraft. Pontowski was surprised to see Evan Riley, the CIA's chief of station, standing beside Jerzy Fedor.

They exchanged greetings and waited as the SPS marched on to the ramp. The commander of the SPS led them, his measured pace matching the somber occasion. The SPS was not an organization given to drill and ceremonies, and their ranks and cadence were far from perfect. But the numerous head bandages and arm slings were ample tribute to who and what they were. The commander brought them to a halt behind the C-17 and ordered them to split into two ranks, forming a corridor to the aircraft. An honor guard bearing the Polish flag flanked by the Stars and Stripes and the SPS standard led a black hearse across the ramp.

Six pallbearers from the SPS were waiting for the flag-draped casket. They raised it to their shoulders and, in perfect step, moved slowly toward the aircraft. The standard of the SPS was lowered in tribute as they passed. The SPS came to attention and the commander shouted an order. They saluted together. Pontowski came to attention and held his salute as the pallbearers carried the casket into the aircraft.

'He was a friend,' Fedor murmured. 'Like the general.'

The commander barked another order and the SPS marched off the field. Pontowski turned to leave. 'We need to talk,' Fedor said. 'The three of us.'

The three men sat in Fedor's limousine and sipped hot coffee, glad to be out of the biting wind. 'The wind always blows coldest from Russia,' Fedor said.

'Are we talking about the weather?' Riley asked.

Fedor's smile reminded Pontowski of a grinning skull. 'Of course,' he replied.

'Are we going to spend all day talking around it?' Pontowski asked.

A heavy silence ruled the car for a few moments. 'We are receiving mixed signals from your government,' Fedor said.

'That's the nature of the beast,' Riley replied.

'We want to resolve the Vashin problem,' Fedor said. 'Can you help us?'

'No help here,' Pontowski said. 'I'm cooling my heels pending a formal investigation. I can't even go into my office.'

Fedor nodded. 'So I've heard.'

'Now who told you that?' Riley asked, hoping as always for a lucky hit. Fedor looked surprised, as if they were discussing common knowledge. The CIA agent conceded the point. 'You can't blame me for trying.' He thought for a moment. 'Let me run your request by my people. I'll get back to you.'

The meeting was over and Pontowski reached for the door handle. 'General Pontowski,' Fedor said, 'my government would be most appreciative if you would visit your ancestor's cottage. Tourism, you know.'

'Was this your idea?' Pontowski asked.

'Of course not. Perhaps in two weeks?'

'Sure. Why not.'

'We'll be in touch,' Fedor said.

Pontowski watched as the limousine sped off, Riley still inside. He walked back to his car and drove to his apartment in Wilanow where, much to his surprise, Riley was waiting for him. 'What the hell is going down?' he asked.

'I'm not sure,' Riley answered.

'Do you trust that sonofabitch?'

'*Of course not*,' Riley said.

'So why are you here?'

'Instincts. This is one ride we don't want to miss. Until I find out exactly what we're looking at, I'd like for you to hang around for as long as possible.'

'Why?'

'The Poles don't trust anyone, with good reason. But your name carries weight and if they think you're involved – well, let's just say that gives me leverage.'

'So I'm a pawn.'

Riley scowled. 'More like a poker chip.' His face turned to granite and his voice grew hard. 'First the general and now Duncan. I don't know about you, but I'd like to even the score.'

'Count me in.'

Washington, D.C.

For the first time since his prostate operation, Shaw was turgid and erect. He closed his eyes and stroked the girl's blonde hair as she worked her Saturday night miracle. Or was it the penile implant? 'You can't keep a good man down,' he muttered.

She felt his scrotum, her fingers gently prodding. 'Is this how it works?' She gave the pump embedded next to his testicles a little squeeze. The cylinder in his penis grew harder.

'Whoa, easy,' he said, not sure how much it could be pumped. She licked at him and gave another squeeze. Now he was fully erect and hurting.

'What would happen if I kept pumping?' She was a professional who enjoyed her work – when it put her in control.

He felt her fingers start to contract and his pulse raced. 'I don't even want to think about it.' She gave a playful squeeze and he sucked in his breath. 'For God's sake, if it pops—' The phone rang, claiming his attention. He picked it up. 'Shaw.' He listened for a moment while the girl played with him. 'Certainly, Mizz President.' The girl looked up at him and found the release cap on top of the pump. 'I'll be right there.'

The girl squeezed the release cap and the pressure bled off. Suddenly, Shaw was very limp and totally uninterested. 'What's the matter, hon? You look worried.'

The uniformed Secret Service guard on duty at the entrance to the West Basement checked Shaw's identification and noted the time in his visitor's log. Shaw took the first right, walked down a few steps and passed the White House mess. Farther down the hall, he turned into the small break room where Maddy Turner was waiting. He had never seen her so tired and haggard. Judging by the way her clothes were hanging, she had lost weight. She smiled at him when he sat down. 'Just like old times.' She pushed a bowl of popcorn across the table.

He grabbed a handful and stuffed some in his mouth, mumbling, 'Sure is, Mizz President. How's your mother doin'?'

'Much better, thank you. It was a minor attack and she's very strong.'

Shaw gulped and took the plunge. 'If you want, I can call in a few markers, find out where that photo came from, and crunch some skulls.'

382

She shook her head. 'Only as a last resort.' He poured himself a glass of Jack Daniel's, and for a few moments they were in a time warp, back in Sacramento when she was a confused, lonely, and very junior state senator struggling to find her way. But an alarm kept buzzing in his head, warning him that things had changed. 'Patrick, what went wrong with Matt?'

The alarm turned into a blaring Klaxon. Matt Pontowski was the one subject he did not want to discuss. 'Geography, most likely. You know these flyboys. Out of sight, out of mind.'

The old intimacy was back as they mulled over the day's events and gossiped about the personalities who bracketed their lives. 'Speaking of Poland,' Maddy said, 'did you hear the latest?'

'About the attack? Sure did. Looks like the Poles can take care of themselves.'

'Thanks to Bob Bender. His security aid program gave the Poles the edge they needed dealing with the Russians. But that's only half the matter.'

Shaw sensed they had come to the reason for the meeting. 'You got me there. What's the other half?'

'The Germans. They're systematically buying up the western half of Poland and the Poles are going to end up as tenant workers in their own land. The Germans have got to stop.'

'That's going to make for some sour Krauts.'

Turner ignored the pun. 'Please, this is serious.'

'Sounds to me like a poker game between Germany and Russia with Poland as the pot. Is it winner take all?'

'I don't think so. Mazie is predicting a fifth partition.' She fixed him with a look he hadn't seen before. 'I won't have it. Not on my watch. The problem is that I don't have any counters to put on the table.'

Shaw took a long pull at his drink. 'It's a shame you don't play poker, Mizz President.'

'I played strip poker with my husband. I won. Stripped him bare every time.'

'Why am I not surprised? In poker you learn to bluff. Maybe it's time to find out how good the Germans are at poker.'

'You mean bluffing.'

'Actually, I'm wondering how willing they are to call a bluff. There's a big difference.'

'Patrick! Pay attention. What do I put on the table?'

'Something that will cause their sphincter muscles to slam shut.'

'Such as?' She listened to his answer, surprised at its blatant transparency. 'That will never work.'

'Won't it? Pick the right players and it will.' He gave her a wicked grin. 'Talk to Herbert von Lubeck. He fancies himself a poker player.'

'You've played with him?'

'Yes, ma'am. Stripped *him* clean.'

'Why am I not surprised?' She paused, sipping at her root beer. 'Patrick, there's something else.' He tensed, waiting for the ax to fall. 'When do I announce for reelection?'

His heart slowed and he smiled broadly. 'Good question, Mizz President.'

CHAPTER TWENTY-SEVEN

The White House

Maddy Turner paused and gazed out the window of her bedroom. April was still a week away but the morning carried a hint of an early spring and, for a brief moment, she wanted to escape the White House, the cares and pressures and, most of all, the Imperial City itself. As quickly, the feeling was gone. This was her time and place. This was what she wanted.

Out of long habit, she glanced in a mirror. But it was only a cursory inspection to check her hair and makeup. She didn't really see the person looking back at her. She walked into the dining room for breakfast, where Maura joined her, wearing a brightly colored robe. 'That's new,' Maddy said.

'We were out shopping yesterday and Sarah picked it out.'

Maddy looked worried. 'You've got to be careful and not strain—'

Maura interrupted her. 'The exercise is good for me.'

The door opened and Sarah came through, wearing a tight little miniskirt and a revealing top. The two women looked at her without a word as she sat down. 'Well?' Sarah challenged.

Maddy sighed. 'Well what?'

Sarah didn't answer and ate in silence while Maddy and Maura discussed the day's schedule. When they were done,

Maura touched Sarah's arm. 'Maybe it's time to think about makeup and accessories. We've got time before school.' Sarah beamed at her. 'I'll get my bag. No, meet me in my bedroom.' The girl bolted for the door. Maura heaved herself to her feet. 'I'll talk her into changing.'

'Thanks, Mother.'

'She's definitely discovered boys.'

'So soon?'

Maura gave a little snort. 'As I recall, you were the same age.'

Madeline Turner was a well-studied subject in the White House and, like most of her staff, Mazie took her cue from the office the President was using. If she was in the Oval Office, any meeting would be short, formal, and very businesslike. If Turner was in her private study off the Oval Office, the atmosphere would be relaxed and chatty. 'The President is in her private study this morning,' Turner's private secretary announced when Mazie appeared for her scheduled 8.30 meeting. Mazie thanked her and walked in.

'Please, sit down,' Turner said.

Long experience had taught the National Security Advisor that the chair closest to the President was the most comfortable. 'I received a phone call a few moments ago,' Mazie said. 'Nelson Durant passed away. Congestive heart failure.' Turner gave a little nod. She hadn't heard but her staff would automatically issue the proper condolences and statements to the press. Mazie handed her a folder. 'He sent this yesterday afternoon with his apologies for not delivering it in person. I believe it was one of the last things he did.'

Turner opened the folder and read Durant's summary of his investigation into the photograph. Mazie caught the slight working of her jaw but said nothing. Turner's eyes turned glassy hard. 'That bastard. So it was Leland.'

'Actually, it was Senator Leland's chief of staff. It's safe to assume Leland knew about it.'

'That's not even an assumption. No staff member would do this on his own.'

'Not unless he was suicidal,' Mazie added.

'So where did Leland get the photo?'

'That, Mr Durant did not discover. Unless the right someone starts talking, we'll never know.'

Turner was out of her seat, pacing back and forth, clearly very angry. 'Damn him! Damn him to hell! I've tried to be accommodating and this is what I get in return. Dealing with that man is like falling in a snake-pit. No matter what you do, you're going to get bitten.'

'Keep him busy protecting his backside and he won't be a problem.' Mazie's words were an echo of Noreen Coker's. Turner sat down and leaned back in her chair. Now she was ready to listen. 'Shaw has it right,' Mazie continued. 'When you're losing, leak. Point the media at Leland.'

'Who and how much?'

'That's the tricky part,' Mazie conceded.

'I need to think about it.' Turner leaned forward, indicating a change in subject. 'I want you to tell the Germans to cease and desist in Poland.'

'I doubt if they're in a mood to listen since we have almost nothing to put on the table.'

'I realize that. Can you use your connections to arrange a meeting with Herbert von Lubeck?'

'My mother-in-law knows him.'

'Ah, yes. Elizabeth Martha, the Bitch Queen of Capitol Hill. Will she help?'

'She likes to be involved. Once you let her in, she'll want access.'

Turner thought for a moment. Politics was like a bazaar where you had to give something to get anything. And access to the President was a very big something. Was it worth what she would get in return? 'Do it,' she said simply.

Mazie was in the Executive Office Building across the street from the White House late that same afternoon. She kept mulling over her conversation with the President. Frustrated, she telephoned the Director of Central Intelligence. 'Gary, we need to go secure.' They both turned the keys in their STU-IV telephones and their voices became tinny as they were filtered through the encryption circuits. She told him about the meeting Turner wanted with the Germans.

There was a long pause. 'All very interesting,' he said finally. 'It might help turn down the heat over there.' Another pause. 'The Poles are going after Vashin in retaliation for Lezno.'

'Can they get away with it?'

'Probably. Most of the players think he's out of control.'

'He is,' Mazie replied. It was time to talk nuts and bolts. 'Does that meld with what we're planning?' The DCI didn't answer and she snapped at him. 'Am I talking to myself?'

Much to her surprise, he laughed. 'You sound like Noreen Coker.'

'Not even a hint,' she retorted.

'We can support them.'

'How?'

'We'll ask.'

Mazie sensed that was all he was going to say. 'If you're going to kill the king, don't fail.'

'I hear you,' the DCI said. He broke the connection.

For God's sake, do this one right, Mazie thought. She pulled into herself, scrutinizing the German side of the problem. 'It's all in the timing,' she murmured to no one.

She picked up the phone and called her mother-in-law, the redoubtable Elizabeth Martha.

Turner leaned back in her chair and closed her eyes, her fingers interlaced. For the first time since breakfast, she was alone. She breathed deeply, forcing herself to relax. But it didn't happen. She sat upright and glanced at the carriage clock on the mantel. It was after six o'clock and time to send her staff home. She pressed the intercom to her secretary. 'Let's call it a day,' she said.

Again, she leaned back in her chair. But this time, she let

her mind roam. Sooner or later, whatever was bothering her would bubble to the surface. Leland's face came into sharp focus. She mulled the problem over, looking at it from different angles. Suddenly, it all clicked into full view, crystal clear, no longer hiding. 'So obvious,' she murmured. She picked up the phone. 'I need to speak to Patrick Shaw.' She dangled the phone from her fingertips, and within seconds Shaw's familiar, deep-rumbling voice was there.

'I hope I'm not calling at a bad time.' *I hope there's a bimbo there to see your reaction*, she thought.

'Not at all, Mizz President.'

'Patrick, we know the source of the photo.' She paused for effect. 'It was Leland.'

'Sonofa*bitch*.'

'Exactly. He overstepped the bounds on this one. What do you suggest we do?' She listened, fixed on the sound of his voice more that the actual words.

'For right now, nothing. Keep it in reserve. Timing is everything.'

'Thank you, Patrick.' She hung up. *That got your attention.* She settled back in her chair again, more alone than ever.

The Hill

Matt slammed into the room, threw his backpack down, and climbed into his bunk. 'This place sucks!' he announced to the ceiling.

Without looking up from his computer, Brian said, 'This from Mr NMMI?'

Matt rolled over on his side and glared down at his friend. 'They give out rank to the shitheads like candy here.'

'And when did you learn that? The bit about the shitheads getting promoted.'

Matt's basic honesty kicked in. 'Ah, most of 'em are okay. It's fuckin' Pelton.'

Brian laughed. He had never seen Matt so upset. 'So what's cadet superfucker up to now?'

'He's saying he got it on with the Trog.'

'Only in a wet dream,' Brian replied.

'Yeah, well, he says she's got a buff bod but small tits.'

Brian frowned. 'He's got to learn to keep his mouth shut.' He pushed back in his chair. 'Chow time.' The one constant in their life was the amount of food they consumed each day. Since there was no formation for supper roll-call on Wednesdays, they Rat Walked to Bates Dining Hall and joined the serving line. Rick Pelton was behind them with two of his buddies. 'Hey, Turner,' he said, 'you still walking tours for bonking ugly sheep?'

Brian bit off a reply and shoved his tray down the line, waiting to be served.

But Matt wouldn't let it go. 'I didn't know you were an expert on screwin' ugly sheep.' He added a respectful 'sir'.

'Careful, boy, or you'll be walking tours until you grow up.'

Matt whirled on Pelton. The older cadet was five years his senior, six inches taller, and outweighed him by forty pounds. But at that exact moment, Matt wanted to fight. 'I'll be walking tours for beating the living shit out of a lying—'

Brian was there, pulling Matt back. 'Let's eat.' He pushed his friend down the line.

Pelton laughed, playing it up for the cadets in line, who were taking in every word. 'Hey, did someone build Pontowski a backbone and jam it up his ass?'

'Someone needs to jam the truth up yours,' Matt muttered.

'The truth shall make you free,' Pelton said, misquoting the famous line.

Brian grabbed Matt's arm and pulled him down the line. 'Over there,' he said, pointing to a table well away from everyone else. They sat alone and attacked their meal. Zeth walked over and stared at Matt's back for a moment before she bent over and whispered in his ear, 'I fight my own battles, meathead.'

'He's spreading a bunch of lies,' Matt protested.

'It was none of your business,' Zeth said. 'Everybody knows Pelton's full of bullshit. Nobody was paying any attention and it would've gone away. Now you shot off your mouth and made it a federal case.'

Matt twisted in his seat and watched her walk away. He felt miserable. 'Eyes front and center, Rat!' an upper classman called.

Warsaw

Ewa slid back the door to the first-class compartment and lifted her small suitcase on to the overhead rack. Pontowski was right behind her and did the same. 'It's been over twenty-five years since I've been on a train,' he told her.

She gave him a sideways look and took off her hat, shaking her long hair free. 'How unusual. I suppose you Americans either fly or drive your own car.' She threw her heavy coat on to the rack and sat down. 'We have the compartment to ourselves.' She shed her heavy boots and curled up on the seat, hiding her feet under her long skirt.

Pontowski sat opposite her by the window and watched as the train pulled out of Warsaw's central station. The door slid open and the conductor asked for their tickets. Ewa rummaged through her bag and handed him two travel folders. The conductor glanced at the names, came to attention, and gave a half-bow. 'I hope you enjoy your journey, General Pontowski. If you need anything, I'll be outside.' He closed the door and sealed off the corridor for the journey to Krakow.

'It looks like we're getting the first-class smooze,' Pontowski said.

'The government wants this to be a big success,' she told him. 'Personally, I don't like the constant attention. It makes me feel so . . . so watched.'

Pontowski smiled to himself. Ewa was going to be watched no matter where she went.

An extremely attractive middle-aged woman, a photographer, and a driver were waiting for them on the platform when the train arrived at Krakow. The photographer started shooting picture after picture. 'I'm Renata Brandys,' she said, leading them to a waiting Mercedes-Benz. 'I'll be your guide. You're scheduled to tour Krakow this afternoon and visit your family cottage tomorrow morning. But after that, we are at your disposal for whatever you care to see.'

'Thank you,' Pontowski said. 'Your English is excellent.'

Renata smiled. 'I earned my doctorate at the University of Missouri.'

'I live not too far away,' Pontowski said. 'Warrensburg.'

'What a coincidence,' Renata replied.

'I doubt it,' Ewa murmured under her breath in Polish. The two women smiled at each other.

An early morning mist was rising off the Vistula river when Pontowski and Ewa met in the lobby of the luxury hotel for the drive to the cottage. Renata bustled up, all crisp efficiency. Her hair was carefully arranged and she wore a very stylish coat. 'Good morning,' she sang. 'The car is waiting.'

It was disturbingly quiet when they stepped outside. Pontowski paused and looked across the river at the royal castle in the center of Krakow. It faded in and out of the mist, briefly overshadowing the town before disappearing. 'Beautiful,' he murmured.

'It's so much a part of us that we don't notice it,' Renata said.

'But it's always there.' He crawled into the back seat next to Ewa, very much aware of her soft fragrance. 'New perfume?' he asked.

She gave him a little smile and shook her head. Her hair flowed around her face, enchanting him. 'It must be the shampoo. I washed my hair this morning.'

'You were up early,' Renata said in Polish, her voice silky sweet.

The traffic going in their direction was very light. Renata spoke with an insider's knowledge, describing what they were passing and where they were going. Ewa listened carefully and recorded most of what she said in a little notebook. Just before they arrived at the cottage, she scribbled a note for Pontowski. *She knows too much. Look at that beautiful coat. She's not a guide. Be careful.*

Pontowski nodded but said nothing.

Two more photographers, a videographer, and the curator of the cottage were waiting for them. Renata got out and held the door for Pontowski. 'Ewa is such a lovely child,' she said. 'And her English is perfect.'

The curator led them to a small wood-framed house painted a bright blue while the photographers snapped away rapidly. The videographer moved with them, constantly zooming in on Pontowski's face. 'This is a typical peasant farmhouse for the area,' the curator explained. 'Only two rooms, a large kitchen where the family lived and one large bedroom where they all slept.'

'Their families were very large,' Renata added.

Pontowski sat on the large bed and looked around. Two trundle beds and two cribs filled the room. 'They didn't have much privacy,' he said.

Renata gave a little smile, knowing what he was thinking. 'Farm children learn the facts of life at a very early age.'

Ewa blushed brightly and asked questions about how they cooked and what they ate. 'Mostly vegetables and bread,' the curator said. 'Meat was a rarity.'

'I'd like to look around outside,' Pontowski said.

'Ah . . . ah,' the curator stammered, 'it's very muddy.'

'That's okay,' Pontowski replied. 'I've stepped in worse.' He walked out with the curator in close tow. 'Where's the barn?'

'They were too poor. They did have little sheds or manmade caves.'

Pontowski looked around and it hit him. This was his heritage! It had always been there, hiding in the mists and taken for granted. An overpowering urge to explore and learn all he could swept over him. 'Were the fields this way?' The curator tried to stop him but Pontowski ignored him and walked into the trees.

Renata rushed up. 'General, we have a meeting planned with the local priest to show you the parish records—'

'In a few minutes.'

'We're short of time.'

He came out of the trees and stopped. At first, the rusted, twisted barbed wire and stone foundations made no sense. Then he saw the guard tower. 'What was this?' he demanded.

Renata's voice was matter-of-fact. 'This was a concentration camp.'

Pontowski stared at her. 'I didn't know about it.'

'Of course, your family was not responsible for this. They had the misfortune to live where the Germans decided to build a camp. The inmates worked in the fields.'

Pontowski relaxed. 'Oh, I thought—'

'You thought right,' Ewa said. She was standing behind them. 'This is part of Auschwitz.'

'Are we that close?'

'We're less than ten kilometers away,' Renata said. 'We thought you knew. Surely, your grandfather told you.'

'No, he didn't.'

Renata was the cool professional, dispassionate and objective. 'There were fourteen separate camps that made up the Auschwitz-Birkenau complex. Most were for manufacturing things like uniforms.'

'You said my family was not involved. Are you sure?'

'You have relatives who still live in the area. One of your grandfather's third cousins is still alive. You can speak to her if you wish to discover the truth for yourself.'

Pontowski stared at the ground as conflicting emotions tore at him. 'Damn! God damn it to hell! I don't want to know.'

Renata said evenly, 'Would you like to see the parish records? They go back to the 1600s.'

'No. I want to see Auschwitz.'

Renata's voice was an echo in his mind while they drove over the bridge and followed the road as it curved through the barren field. A light drizzle fell, and he could make out the camp's rail entrance piercing the tower in the center of the long dark façade. Then he saw train tracks that led through the arch under the tower. 'Birkenau, not Auschwitz, was the main death camp,' Renata said.

He got out of the car, forgetting his hat. Renata waved Ewa to remain behind with the driver. Long experience had taught her how to handle what was coming. She led him through the arch. 'It's so quiet,' Pontowski said. They stopped for a moment as he stared. A few wooden barracks were still standing, as well as most of the permanent brick buildings. Concrete fence posts with barbed wire outlined the perimeter and divided the camp into compounds. 'I didn't realize it was so big.'

She walked straight ahead, leading him into the heart of darkness. 'In front of us are the unloading platforms.' The gravel walkway turned into mud as they made the long walk. 'The selection was done there.' She pointed to a small concrete platform next to a low building. 'If they pointed you to the right, you were immediately put to death.' They continued to walk, her words reverberating in his mind. 'On your left are the remains of the gas chamber, which was underground.'

The depthless evil of the gas chamber and all it represented flailed at his soul. This was not a carefully composed photograph, nor an eloquently written essay. It was reality, and he was part of it. The drizzle turned to rain and streaked his face. 'How did they live with themselves?' he whispered.

It was a question Renata couldn't answer. Instead she said, 'The monument in front of you was built on the rubble of—' Her voice trailed off. He was motionless, staring at the dark monstrosity in front of him. She waited. Physically, he was with her. But he was lost in the pandemonium of his emotions. Again, experience had taught her how long to wait. She touched his elbow and gently propelled him forward. 'The monument in front of you is built on the rubble of crematorium number two.' They halted in front of the black structure. It was twisted, low to the ground, with a line of plaques in front, each mounted on a low pedestal.

Renata stood in front of one and looked at him. 'They all say the same thing in different languages. *Forever let this place be a cry of despair, a warning to humanity.*' She waited. Then, when she judged the time to be right, she prompted, 'Come, let's get out of the rain and find some coffee.'

Pontowski nodded dumbly and turned to follow her. He took a few steps and stopped, looking down at his feet. His shoes and pant cuffs were caked and splattered with mud. He raised his eyes, his anguish overflowing. 'It's the same mud.' His words at the cottage about stepping in worse things came crashing down on him. 'There isn't anything worse.'

Pontowski came out of the shower, finally feeling clean. He pulled on the hotel's heavy white terry-cloth robe and toweled his hair dry. He padded across the room to the minibar and poured himself a cognac. Certain one miniature would not be enough, he called room service and ordered a full bottle. 'When all else fails, drink,' he told himself. He stood in front of the window, looking across the Vistula as he sipped. Krakow and the castle were obscured by the night mist.

A knock at the door claimed his attention. Without checking, he opened it. Ewa stood there. 'I thought you were room service,' he said. He held the door open for her. 'What brings you here?'

She sat down. 'Renata told me to come.'

'Renata?'

She gave a little nod. 'We talked. I was right. She's not a guide.'

'What is she?'

'Remember when she said she had earned a doctorate? She's a psychiatrist.'

Pontowski snorted. 'She's also a liar. How could my family live with what I saw today and not be involved?' Another knock at the door stopped him. This time it was room service with the bottle of cognac. He tipped the waiter, then sat down beside her and poured a healthy shot into his snifter. 'Care for one?'

'That won't help,' Ewa said. 'Renata said your family was not responsible. She never said they were not involved.'

He drained the glass. 'So they were part of it.'

She took the glass away from him and touched his cheek. 'They did what all our families did. They did what was necessary to survive. They had no choice.'

He closed his eyes and took a deep breath. The truth was so simple, yet so hard to accept. What would he have done? Or his grandfather? Then he knew. They would have resisted and probably been killed. But hopefully, whoever they left behind would have lived and rebuilt the future. Could he fault them for that? Could he accept that for the truth? He didn't know and he was lost. He sensed her hand draw away. Suddenly, he felt cold and lost again. He opened his eyes. Her face was close to his, her eyes filled with tears. She took his hand and held it to her breast. He felt her heartbeat, sure and strong. 'Our hearts tell us to live, Matt Pontowski.' She leaned forward and kissed him lightly on the lips.

Then she was in his arms.

Later, she cuddled against him, her hair soft against his face. 'I thought there was friction between you and Renata.'

'There was.' She kissed him on the neck. 'We settled our differences.' She opened up to him. 'Renata was worried you had assumed too much of the guilt. She's seen it before and thought you needed someone to talk to.'

'Why didn't you tell me?'

'Tell you what?' she murmured.

'That I was the first.'

'Does it matter?'

'You're damn right it matters.'

'You Americans can be so sentimental. We'll talk about it in the morning.' She drew him to her, kissing his face again and again.

Ewa was gone when he woke. Certain that she had returned to her room, he showered and shaved, savoring the hot water. He slowly dressed, enjoying the sunshine streaming in the window.

He found his cleaned and polished shoes outside the door and slipped them on. Then he went down to the breakfast buffet, hoping to find her there. When he didn't see her, he called her room, a little concerned.

'I'm sorry, General Pontowski,' the operator said. 'Miss Pawlik checked out early this morning.'

CHAPTER TWENTY-EIGHT

Moscow

Jerzy Fedor rubbed an amber cufflink with his right hand and tried to remain calm. His eyes darted to the open doors of the elevator that had carried him to Vashin's penthouse. But there was no car waiting to take him to safety, only a black pit, a yawning chasm. An image of a beautiful girl flashed in front of him. With a jolt, he remembered her name. Little Dove. Was he next?

'I want the money the SPS stole from me,' Vashin growled. 'All of it.'

Fedor gestured helplessly at the four large aluminum suitcases. 'This was all I could find – over a billion dollars in negotiable securities.' The look on Vashin's face was ample warning that it was not enough. 'There may be more,' Fedor conceded.

'Find it,' Vashin ordered. He turned his back on the flustered Pole.

Geraldine motioned Fedor to the elevator. He was surprised to see that the car was now waiting. *When did that happen?* He took a few tentative steps, still not believing he was going to get out of the meeting alive. Geraldine touched his elbow and stepped with him into the elevator. The doors closed. Geraldine's presence and the soft hum of the machinery reassured him that he was going to make it.

Geraldine scribbled a note on her pad for him to read. *Do not leave Moscow until we talk.*

Geraldine was practiced economy as she went down her checklist. Everything was ready for Vashin's meeting with the Circle of Brothers. She hurried to change into something more appropriate for a meeting with the seven men who made up the inner sanctum of Russian organized crime. Satisfied they would be adequately impressed by the black evening gown she had chosen, she returned to Vashin's penthouse in time to greet Yaponets. He was always the first to arrive and the last to leave. 'Oleg Gora will not be here,' Yaponets told her.

Geraldine gave an inward sigh of relief. It had been exactly one year since Gora had strangled, then quickly decapitated, Yegor Gromov in the snow at Boris Bakatina's funeral. 'He's never missed a meeting,' she said.

'He's doing a little job for Mikhail,' Yaponets said. Geraldine glanced at him with feigned lack of interest. 'Oleg enjoys his work,' Yaponets explained. 'Besides, he's never been to the States before.'

Geraldine filed the information away for follow-up. Few things were more important than a meeting of the Council of Brothers, and it had to be a very sensitive contract for Vashin to send Gora. At that moment, the elevator arrived and three more members of the Circle arrived. Their arrival and departure followed a strict protocol. The last two men arrived together and the Circle was complete. She knocked on the bedroom door.

Vashin came out, freshly showered and shaved. A young girl followed him and quickly left. Geraldine handed him a folder for the meeting and took her usual seat by the wall to be of instant service. He thanked the men for coming and opened the folder, ready to turn to business.

'Mikhail,' Yaponets said, 'as our brothers in the States are fond of saying, we have a cash-flow problem.' A low, hungry growl worked its way around the room. The drug money from Europe had been shut off, which was having the same effect on the *vor* as the loss of the Spanish treasure galleons did on the Spanish Empire in the eighteenth century.

Vashin stared them into silence. 'A temporary setback. Nothing more.' He waved his hand at the four aluminum suitcases still stacked in a corner. 'There should be over a billion dollars there. Take it. More is coming.'

The oldest godfather cleared his throat to speak and they fell silent, more in deference to his age and experience than the power he wielded as the head of the fifth-largest family in Russia. 'A year ago there were three hundred and twenty-one active godfathers in Russia. Today, the number is over four hundred. Many are acting on their own. Our unity is our strength. They must be brought under control or we will be destroyed.'

Vashin nodded slowly, as if he were giving great weight to the godfather's words. 'That is why I'm calling a meeting in Yalta. Everyone will be invited – the *vor*, the Mafiya, everyone.'

'Why should they come?' a godfather asked. 'Why Yalta?' He answered the last question himself. 'Brilliant. Yalta is in the Ukraine, neutral territory. Everyone will be safe.' His eyes opened in admiration as more pieces fell into place. 'You're inviting our Ukrainian brothers.'

'And the Belorussian families,' Vashin added. 'Geraldine will explain.'

'Mr Vashin selected Yalta because it is a resort where security is already in place. Many vacation dachas are available and all the amenities will be provided. Also, it will be spring and a welcome break from winter.'

The old godfather wouldn't let it go. 'But why will they come?'

'Because Stalin settled the fate of the world after World War Two at Yalta,' Vashin answered. 'They can either join me as I build the new Russia and reap the benefits, or they can die on the trash heap of history.'

Fedor was wide awake at the sound of the door lock clicking

open. He reached for the small automatic under his pillow and thumbed the safety off. The door to his hotel room swung open as he raised the pistol. A woman was silhouetted in the light. 'Jerzy?' Geraldine called in a soft voice. He lowered his weapon and turned on the light. She closed the door, dropped her topcoat on a chair, and stepped out of her shoes. She sat on the bed beside him and stroked his chest.

'We need to talk about Yalta,' she whispered.

The Hill

Brian buffed his boots, applying the finishing touches for Saturday morning's inspection and parade. He chanted, keeping cadence with the strokes. 'One more month of shining brass,/ then this place can kiss my ass.'

'What you doing over vacation?' Matt asked, arranging the shelves in his locker.

'I'm thinkin' of going to summer school and then trying out for football.'

'I thought you hated this place.'

'I do.'

'Yeah, right.'

A pretty Rat who had her eye on Brian poked her head round the door. That was as close as she could get without getting stuck and placed on report. 'You heard the latest?' she asked. 'Pelton and the Trog are getting it on. He says she's pregnant.'

'No way,' Brian said. 'Pelton's living in a wet dream because he can't score.'

'Yeah,' Matt muttered, feeling responsible, 'the guy's pure hogbreath. Full of—' He didn't finish the sentence.

'Well,' the girl said, having the last word, 'everyone in Saunders Barracks is talking about it.'

'That's gonna piss her off,' Brian said. The girl flounced away, teasing him with her walk. They went back to work, bringing the room up to inspection standard, and finished thirty minutes before Call to Quarters.

Zeth knocked at the open door. From the look on her

face, they knew she had heard the latest rumor, and Matt felt like crawling headfirst into the nearest trash can. 'Zeth, I'm sorry. I should have kept my mouth shut.'

'Pelton's mouth is the problem,' she said, 'not yours. Don't worry about it.' She paused, looking at them. 'You two are all right.' Then she was gone.

'What was that all about?' Brian wondered.

'It was almost like she was saying goodbye,' Matt replied.

The Box echoed with commands as the cadets marched off Stapp Parade Field. The Saturday morning parade had been a little ragged, not up to the Corps' usual standard, and the cadet regimental commander was not happy. He huddled with his staff as the troops marched on to their assigned walks. Rick Pelton looked over the CO's shoulder and froze. Zeth was standing in front of her troop and going through the standard manual of arms, her rifle flashing in the sunlight. 'What the hell?' Pelton said. Every cadet was watching her, and a hush fell over the Box, the only sound the slap of her hands on the rifle.

When she had finished, she held the rifle by the upper stock and lowered the butt to the ground. Twice, she rapped out two sharp clicks, the metal butt plate striking the pavement, demanding everyone's attention. Then she right-shouldered the rifle and marched up the center walk, straight for Rick Pelton. As she neared, her hands flashed and she lowered the rifle, as in bayonet practice. She held the trigger guard by her right hip and the muzzle pointed forward, slightly lowered.

'Cadet Trogger,' the CO barked, 'return to ranks.'

Zeth ignored him and halted directly in front of Pelton. She jammed the muzzle between his knees and jerked upward, hard, catching the front sight under his crotch. He groaned in pain. Then she ripped the muzzle back, holding it inches from his crotch. Her right forefinger squeezed the trigger and the click echoed over the Box.

'You're lucky the bore's blocked, trashmouth,' she said, her voice amazingly calm and matter-of-fact. She executed a perfect about-face, right-shouldered the rifle, and marched smartly back to her troop.

Warsaw

The short drive across the Vistula river into Praga was like stepping through a time warp for Pontowski. The five- or six-story ramshackle brick buildings, clanging trams, and sidewalks full of people hurrying to work reminded him of the time he had accompanied his grandfather on a tour of eastern Europe as a child. The cab driver easily found the address on a side street and deposited him at the corner, saying it was perfectly safe to walk in the morning since the muggers were still asleep.

Pontowski walked down the street until he located a painted wooden door with a brass plaque announcing the surgery of Dr Elzbieta Pawlik. Inside, he found a waiting room full of people. Since there was no receptionist or nurse on duty, he stood, waiting until someone came in for the next patient. One of the men recognized him and stood up, offering Pontowski his seat. Pontowski smiled, shook his head, and thanked him. An old woman studied his face. 'Is he the Pontowskis' son?' she asked in Polish.

'General Pontowski,' the man said, 'is indeed President Pontowski's grandson.'

The side door opened and Elzbieta Pawlik looked in to call her next patient. She glanced at Pontowski and motioned him inside. 'I've been expecting you.'

'I can wait,' he said. 'They were here first.'

'They know who you are,' she said, pointing to a seat.

He sat down, surprised to see a photograph of Maddy Turner on the wall next to one of his grandfather. 'I'm looking for Ewa.' The doctor didn't answer. 'Can you help me find her?'

'No.'

'Why not? It's important.'

'Because you slept with her?'

'It's much more than that,' he replied.

Elzbieta gave a little snort. 'She's confused and needs time to think.'

'Maybe I can help.'

'You would only confuse her more.' She pointed to the wall with the photographs. 'Ewa is no match for her.'

'There's nothing between us. Not now.'

'It's not that easy, Matthew Pontowski. We're an emotional race, tied to our history. Why are those photographs on my wall?'

Pontowski thought for a moment. 'Because my grandfather was the first Polish-American president. Maddy, I don't know.'

'Because she is the forty-fourth President of the United States.' She snorted at the confusion on Pontowski's face. 'One of our most famous poets was Adam Mickiewicz. He lived in the nineteenth century when Poland was partitioned between Russia, Prussia, and Austria. He wrote a play, really an epic poem, called *Dziady*, "Forefather's Eve". You've heard of it?' He shook his head. 'I'm not surprised,' she said. 'But that's why you don't understand us. In the play, Mickiewicz prophesied the coming of Forty-four, the mysterious savior of Poland.'

'Coincidence,' Pontowski muttered.

'Perhaps,' she replied. 'In the play, Forty-four is a man. But how much coincidence do you believe in? You commanded the 303rd Fighter Squadron, yes?' He nodded. 'The 303rd was a famous fighter squadron in the Royal Air Force in World War Two. The pilots were all Polish and they fought in the Battle of Britain.'

'Still coincidence.'

'Then why did the forty-fourth President of the United States send you here?'

'It had nothing to do with a prophecy.'

'Tell a Pole that and he won't believe you.'

'But you said Forty-four was a man.'

'That is why my daughter is confused. Maybe Mickiewicz had that part wrong or had left something out. Leave her alone for now.' She pointed at the door. 'I have sick people to see.'

Pontowski stumbled outside, a very confused man. The cab driver was waiting for him. 'The American embassy,' he said. At least he could still use the small library in the basement.

'General Pontowski,' the Marine guard on duty at the embassy entrance said, 'Mr Riley would like to speak to you. He's in his office on the third floor.'

'At least it's not on the forty-fourth,' Pontowski muttered, heading for the elevator. He stepped inside and hit the button, not certain the elevator would stop at the third floor. It did. A trim young woman he had never seen before was waiting for him. She led him into a windowless inner office where Evan Riley was hunched over a large desk, reading a pile of messages. He waved Pontowski to a seat. 'James forwarded the final report of your investigation to Ambassador Beason this morning. It clears you and Waldo.'

'I hadn't heard.'

'Beason still has to sign off.'

'He won't. He hates my guts.'

'He doesn't have a choice.' Riley handed him a message stamped TOP SECRET and for the ambassador's eyes only. The State Department directed Beason to fully support the Office of Defense Cooperation. Effective immediately, Brigadier General Matthew Pontowski was placed on inactive status from the US Air Force and released to the Polish Air Force as a civilian training officer.

'What the hell?' Pontowski muttered. 'You're not authorized to see this.' Another thought came to him. 'Why are you showing it to me?'

'I need someone to take Duncan's place.'

'Doing what?'

'I may need you to pass key intelligence to the right people at the right time.'

'You've got formal channels for that,' Pontowski said.

'Don't be cute,' Riley muttered. 'We can't trust half the players the way things are.'

'So why me?'

'Because the Poles trust you. It sends the message that we're behind them.'

'Behind them on what?'

There was no answer from Riley.

Over Ohio

Maddy Turner studied the first photos of the damage caused by the spring storm that was lashing at the Pacific Northwest. She had never seen such devastation, and was flying out to view the damage and marshal the government's relief efforts. Nothing in her experience galvanized the bureaucracy more than a few well-placed presidential questions after a personal visit. Richard Parrish handed her the latest weather report. 'The meteorologists are talking about the storm door being wide open. Another big cell should hit early next week and there's more behind it.'

She studied the satellite printout. Another major storm was forming over the central Pacific and a bigger one was building farther to the west. She leaned back and gazed out the window of Air Force One. They were headed west and chasing the setting sun. Golden hues laced the evening sky, turning into shades of red. Streaks of blue split the clouds like a master artist's brush strokes. 'It's so beautiful and peaceful here,' she murmured.

The phone beside her seat buzzed and she picked it up. It was Brian. 'Mom, I got troubles.' She tensed, expecting the worst. She relaxed as Brian told her the story of Zeth's revenge on Pelton and how Matt was involved.

'Did you or Matt know what she was going to do?'

'Naw. But we saw it. Mom, they're gonna kick her out.'

'There's not much I can do.'

'Can you talk to General McMasters?'

The Pacific Northwest is drowning and he's worried about this? she fumed to herself. *Well, at least he's thinking about someone else for a change.* 'I'll have my staff check into it.'

'Thanks, Mom.' He broke the connection.

Maddy stared out the window. *He's turning into a young man and I'm missing it.* She felt the tears start to form, but just as quickly they were gone. She had important work to do. 'Please have Mazie and Gary come in,' she told Parrish. Within moments, the National Security Advisor and the DCI were sitting down next to her. 'Richard,' Turner said, 'we need some privacy.' Her chief of staff quickly left, closing the door behind him.

'This storm,' Turner said, 'is going to occupy a great deal of time in the coming weeks. However, I want to stay on track with the Germans.'

'I'm meeting with Herbert von Lubeck in Bonn this coming Tuesday, April fifteenth,' Mazie told her. 'All off the record and very unofficial.'

The DCI frowned. 'I'm not very hopeful. I don't see us bluffing the Germans on this one. We've got to bring something to the table.'

Turner stared at him. 'It's not too late to cancel. I'm willing to consider other suggestions.' She drummed her fingers on the arm of her chair, a sure sign it was time to move on to the next subject.

'Sorry, Madame President,' the DCI said. 'We just don't have a lot of options on this one.' He shuffled through his notes. 'I have one more item, a request from the Poles. Most unusual. They're asking for some very specific help in dealing with the Russian problem.'

'Do what you can, but I don't want an Iran-Contra affair haunting us like it did poor President Reagan.'

'I see no problems at this point,' Mazie assured her. 'There are a few other items that you should be aware of.' She quickly ran down her list, bringing Turner up to date. Then they were finished and gone. The meeting had taken less than ten minutes.

Joe Litton stuck his head round the door. 'More photos from Oregon,' he said. 'It's getting worse.'

Turner bent over the coffee table in front of her and thumbed through the photos. She shook her head. 'And the worst is still to come.'

Outside, Mazie huddled with the DCI in a corner. 'How close are the Poles to acting?' she asked.

The DCI shook his head. 'I don't know. They seem serious enough. I wish I knew what they were up to.'

'The right something might get the Germans' attention. You must have a source inside the Polish government?'

'I'll try to find out what's brewing,' the DCI promised.

Mazie's head jerked up when she saw Patrick Shaw walk past. 'I didn't know he was on board.' They watched suspiciously as he entered the President's stateroom.

'Mizz President,' Shaw said, waiting for her to acknowledge his presence. She looked up at him and he slouched into a chair. 'I've been working with Stammerville and Holt about announcing your reelection. They've come up with a new strategy.' He paused, carefully selecting the right words.

'What is it?' Turner asked impatiently.

Shaw took a deep breath. 'You don't. Instead, you go silent and get drafted. Popular demand for you to run again.'

'Is that a chance we want to take?'

'No chance about it. We'll organize it at the grass-roots level and when the news is breaking our way, a huge clamor and gnashing of teeth will arise from the multitudes demanding you lead them out of the wilderness. The bandwagon will roll right out of the heart of America and over anyone who gets in the way.'

'You make it sound so cynical.'

'It solves a lot of problems.'

'Like the fact I'm a woman.'

'And a widow,' he added. He took a deep breath. 'And Pontowski.'

She was irritated. 'I wasn't aware he was a problem.'

Shaw hung his head and tried to act contrite. 'He's not right for you, Mrs President. He's got a history.'

'That was a long time ago, Patrick.'

He dropped the folder he was carrying on to the coffee table. 'These were taken in Poland ten days ago. He was out discovering his roots.'

Maddy looked through the photos, seeing the one Shaw

had carefully buried, enough to be hidden but where she would definitely find it. Pontowski was standing in the door of his family's cottage, gazing out. Ewa was looking up at him, her eyes glowing, her face bright. 'A beautiful girl. Who is she?'

'His interpreter, Ewa Pawlik. She works at the embassy.'

'Are they close?' Maddy asked.

'Look at her face. That tells me everything I need to know.'

'Fire her.'

'We can't do that.' The President's frown demanded an explanation. 'Hell, Mizz President, everyone screws the Polish.'

CHAPTER TWENTY-NINE

Warsaw

'Please review this,' Winslow James said. 'Check the concur box and sign at the bottom.' He handed Pontowski the completed report of investigation with Ambassador Beason's letter of transmittal on top.

Pontowski gritted his teeth as he read. 'You want me to agree to this?' James nodded. 'That means I accept Beason's so-called corrective actions?' Again the diplomatic nod. 'Did you bother to read the report?'

'Of course I read it.'

'Then how do you get from a report which clears Waldo and me of doing anything wrong to Beason's cover letter?' Pontowski flipped to the letter and read aloud. '"You are hereby reprimanded for acting in a manner that brought great discredit to the United States, this legation, and yourself."' He threw the report at James. 'Shove this next to your favorite hemorrhoid. The one you think with.'

Nothing in James's career had prepared him for this. Years of experience in the foreign service had conditioned him not to make waves, to speak in a low voice, and to pass the buck. Becoming aggressive when faced with a problem simply was not done. And no one spoke to a Deputy Charge of Mission like that. 'Please remember I represent the President of the United States.'

'I'm sure you do.'

James grimaced, trying to regain his composure. 'Your attitude is totally uncalled for. However, you must respond, in writing, to close this investigation.' Pontowski grabbed the report and lined out the concur block. At the bottom he scribbled NOTED and placed his initials next to it. James shook his head in nervous disbelief. No one ever mutilated an official document like that. He stood up. 'Please wait here.' He almost ran out of his office, reminding Pontowski of an officious mouse as he scurried across the Red Room to Beason's office. He was back in a few moments, his face two shades of pale lighter. 'The ambassador will see you immediately.' Pontowski followed him on the return journey. The two secretaries watched them in silence.

'Don't sit down,' Daniel Beason muttered. He looked up and tapped the report on his desk. 'I'm sick and tired of you flyboys who think the rules don't apply to them.'

'What exactly are the rules when somebody wants to shoot you down?'

'That is not my concern here,' Beason snapped. 'Because of political influence, you are beyond my control.' He handed Pontowski the official cable from the State Department detaching him to the Polish Air Force as a civilian training officer. 'Let me make this perfectly clear. You get into trouble and this embassy will take no action to save your worthless skin. You are on your own and will receive no help from this government. Further, I am holding conversations with the Polish government to have you declared *persona non grata*.'

'Is that all, sir?' Pontowski asked. Without waiting for an answer, he executed a perfect about-face and walked out. Gathering up his raincoat and briefcase, he headed for the elevator. He punched the button to descend to the lobby and was surprised when the car rose to the third floor. Evan Riley was waiting for him when the doors opened.

'I heard,' was all Riley said, leading the way to his office.

'You don't miss much.'

'When are you moving over to the Polish Air Force?'

'Soon as I can get out of here.'

'Good. We'll be in contact as soon as we have any significant intelligence that needs to be passed on.'

'You called me here to tell me that?'

Riley shook his head. 'To warn you about Jerzy Fedor. Don't trust him. Also, you need to spend a few minutes with my operations officer.'

The 'few minutes' Riley mentioned turned into three hours as the station's ops officer provided Pontowski with dead drops, passwords, and telephone numbers linking him with cutouts. The exposure to basic tradecraft gave meaning to what it meant to be out in 'the cold'. Finally, he was finished and able to drive to the squadron at Okecie.

It was now a different organization, full of hustle and purpose. The walls were freshly painted and the floors were clean. But more importantly, the pilots were in offices and briefing rooms hitting the books and 'hangar-flying' missions. Pontowski walked past an exercise room where two pilots were working on weight machines, strengthening their neck muscles. He found Waldo in a briefing room, finishing a training report from a mission. A very unhappy young pilot sat at the table with him. 'Don't get discouraged,' Waldo told him. 'You're doing much better than I did at this stage.' He handed the pilot his training folder and the young man beat a hasty retreat.

'Welcome to the real world,' Waldo deadpanned.

'It looks like they're getting serious about flying the Viper.'

'Believe it,' Waldo said. 'You prepared for a shocker?' He led Pontowski through a guarded door and into the mission planning section. Emil and the squadron commander were huddled with a civilian over the chart table.

'I believe you know Jerzy Fedor,' Emil said.

Pontowski and Fedor shook hands. 'What brings you here?' Pontowski asked.

'Yalta,' Fedor replied. He pointed at the chart, showing Pontowski a target complex on the Black Sea. A black line connected it to Rzeszow, an airbase in southern Poland. 'We

413

have some accounts to settle with the man who killed President Lezno and General Bender.'

Automatically, Pontowski measured the distance: 640 nautical miles. 'That's a bit far to haul bombs without refueling,' he said.

'Can it be done?' Emil asked.

'With the right profile and some careful planning.'

'Will you help us with tactics?' Emil asked.

'Tell me the threat,' Pontowski replied, 'and I'll tell you the tactics.'

The Hill

McMasters stood and walked to the center window of his office. For a moment, he fixed his gaze on the bronze statue of the rearing bronco, NMMI's symbol and mascot. Behind the statue, cadets hurried through the sally port into Hagerman Barracks, anxious to get out of the rain. For the superintendent, the Sally Port was the true symbol of the Institute, not the bucking bronco. 'What a stupid teenage thing,' he said to the commandant, who was standing beside his desk. Colonel Day didn't answer. He knew how McMasters worked and his need to verbalize his decisions. 'I suppose there is a rough justice here,' McMasters continued. 'I wish we could ignore it.'

'But we can't,' Colonel Day said. 'I had to suspend her. It's a pretty clear-cut case of assault.'

McMasters nodded in agreement. 'And in front of the entire Corps. Miss Trogger does pick her moments.'

'She's never been a retiring wallflower,' Day added.

'Is Pelton going to prefer charges?'

'So far, he hasn't,' Day replied. 'I think he's waiting to see what you do with her appeal.'

McMasters stifled a sigh. He knew what he had to do. 'I could overlook a fight, even one between a boy and a girl. But I cannot tolerate an assault.' He returned to his desk and buzzed his secretary. 'Please send Miss Trogger in.'

Zeth marched through the door and reported in. She stood at attention in front of the superintendent's desk, her eyes focused on the wall behind him. She was very aware of the commandant standing to her right as he shifted his weight from one foot to the other. She chanced a sideways glance. Day was a very unhappy man. His decision to suspend her had not been easy.

'I don't have many options here,' McMasters said.

'Miss Trogger's past record has been exemplary,' Colonel Day said. 'And she has taken full responsibility for her actions.'

'That's commendable,' McMasters said. 'Unfortunately, my hands are tied in cases of assault.' He tried one last gambit, searching for any excuse. 'Did you know you were committing an act of assault on Mr Pelton's person before you did it?'

'Yes, sir, I did.'

'But you went ahead anyway.'

'Yes, sir,' Zeth said. She almost added that Pelton had assaulted her reputation. But she knew that wasn't an excuse.

'I have no choice,' McMasters said. 'I must deny your appeal. You are to clear your room and be off campus as soon as possible, no later than by Call to Quarters tonight. If your parents can't pick you up, we will provide a hotel room and meals until you can arrange transportation home.'

'I can hook a ride to my folks' ranch in the Hondo Valley,' she said. 'It's not far.'

He looked at her sadly. 'I can't tell you how much I hate doing this.'

Zeth came to attention. 'I understand perfectly, sir.'

McMasters thought for a moment. 'I know you want to attend the Air Force Academy. It will be my privilege to write a letter of recommendation should you decide to apply.' *And speak to a few old friends*, he mentally added.

'Thank you, sir.' She threw him a perfect salute. He returned it. The two men watched her leave.

Colonel Day said, 'She's too good for you Zoomies. West Point needs cadets like her.'

'Hands off,' McMasters ordered.

'May the best service win.'

*   *   *

The two boys stood in the doorway, watching her pack. Their hats and ponchos were still dripping from the rain. 'Come on in,' she said.

'It's my fault,' Matt said. 'If I hadn't've shot off my big mouth—'

Zeth interrupted him. 'It's not your fault.'

'I can get my mom to help,' Brian offered.

'No, you won't,' she replied. She zipped up her last bag. 'Look, I knew it was wrong and I went and did it anyway. Get this through your thick heads. I'm responsible. Now I've got to live with the consequences. That's what leadership is all about. Even Colonel Day agrees with me on that one.'

'But Pelton deserved it,' Matt said. 'Everyone in the Corps says so.'

'Since when has a vote determined what is right or wrong?' She picked up her bags. 'Time to go.'

The Western White House, California

Maddy stood at the deck rail taking in the sunset. She was alone and savored the moment. It was her favorite time of year in San Luis Obispo, when the hills were green with spring. For a moment, she was free of the Imperial City on the Potomac, with all its posturing and deception, greed and unfettered ambition. A breeze washed over her, carrying a hint of rain, bringing her back to the moment and why she was on the West Coast. *Is it really going to get worse?* she asked herself. *I hope the meteorologists are wrong.* The irony of it struck her. The major test of her administration could be the storm building in the Pacific.

A slight shudder made her clasp her arms to her body. 'Are you cold, Madame President?' It was one of the ever-present Secret Service guards. She shook her head. Ever since the helicopter incident, they had been more protective and more attentive, if that were possible. It was as if they had to atone for the crash.

She wanted to do something, to meet the storm head-on. But it wasn't going to happen. All she could do was wait and trust others to carry out her wishes. *Like tax reform*, she thought. How hard had they worked on that? Yet in the end, the bureaucrats had gone their own way and done exactly what they wanted. Her lips compressed into a narrow line. She could correct that. Or could she? Who could she trust? Images floated through her mind. It was not a big gallery and was even smaller with the deletion of Dennis and Noreen Coker. How she missed those two.

Another image drifted out of her subconscious. 'Ah, Mazie,' she said to herself. *How I use you. But why do I sense you know it and don't mind?* Yet the facts were clear. Mazie was up to something because of what she had said.

And there was Bender. 'My brave general,' she whispered. The breeze increased, turning into a cold wind.

'Madame President. You might want to come inside. It's starting to rain.' Maddy turned to her new personal assistant. It was Nancy Bender, five months pregnant and beautiful. Maddy walked slowly inside to wait for the storm to arrive.

Bonn, Germany

Herbert von Lubeck carefully stoked the burning logs in the huge fireplace. He was a tall man and had to bend over to reach the hearth. Although it was mid-April, a winter's cold held the continent in its grip. He wanted his guest to be comfortable. It was one of the amenities of which he was proud. He glanced at the doll-like woman cuddled up in the high wingback chair. *So different from her mother-in-law*, he thought. *Turner should have sent E. M. Hazelton if she wanted results.* He shuddered at the thought of doing business with the Bitch Queen of Capitol Hill.

'May I get you something to drink?' he asked.

'Brandy, please,' Mazie answered.

He poured her a snifter from his private reserve. It carried no label, but it was the finest brandy in the world. He handed it to her, remembering the last time he had been in this same room with Mikhail Vashin. *So different. And so much easier.*

Mazie held the snifter up and examined the golden liquid. She took a delicate sip. 'Magnificent,' she murmured. She drew her legs up, settling into the chair. For a brief moment, von Lubeck pictured her nude. *Concentrate!* he warned himself. *Save the distractions for later.* He fought the urge to light up a cigar. *Let the brandy do its magic.*

'E.M. tells me you like cigars,' Mazie said. 'I love the smell of a good Havana.'

Von Lubeck bestowed his most charming smile on her and reached for the humidor. 'I understand the storm is causing widespread damage on your West Coast.'

'It's the worst recorded storm in history,' Mazie said, again taking a sip. 'It looks like it's spreading inland.'

'Global warming, no doubt.'

'So the scientists claim. Which is one of the reasons I'm here.' She raised the glass and drank. 'This is excellent.'

The conversation had taken an unexpected turn. Von Lubeck puffed at his cigar, wanting time to think and for the brandy to give him the edge he needed. But Mazie pressed ahead, taking it away from him. 'Our scientists are mostly agreed that it's due to the greenhouse effect. Automobiles are the major source.'

Von Lubeck sighed. 'Ah, the automobile. I do not see you Americans giving up your beloved cars.'

'We won't have to,' Mazie said. 'Perhaps you've heard of our research in fuel cells? Our scientists may have made a breakthrough.'

'A development to be desired,' von Lubeck murmured, calculating what Germany could do if it controlled that invention. Dealing with the Arabs then would be an absolute delight. 'Our scientists tell me a usable, cheap, mass-produced fuel cell is a ghost on the wind, a fairytale like cold fusion.'

Mazie smiled. 'I understand you have spent billions chasing that particular ghost.'

It was a body blow and von Lubeck almost flinched. 'So close,' he murmured.

'Fuel cells are not imaginary,' Mazie said, taking a longer sip of the brandy and cradling the glass in her hands. It was time to offer the carrot. 'We have so much in common – a desire for a stable Europe, strong economies, advanced technologies.'

The pieces fell into place for von Lubeck. 'We hold some patents you need,' he said, cutting to the heart.

She smiled at him. 'Perhaps.'

'Germany would be most interested in participating in the development of your fuel cells.'

'Nothing is free,' Mazie said.

Von Lubeck nodded. 'You mentioned a stable Europe earlier.'

'Exactly. President Turner is very worried about Poland and certain disturbing trends.' She took the gloves off and picked up the stick. 'If Germany continues its massive purchases of land and businesses, western Poland will become your vassal state like the West Bank of the Jordan river. That is unacceptable to President Turner.'

The brandy had done its work and she had laid out the quid pro quo too soon. Fuel cells in exchange for an independent Poland. It was easy to counter the offer. 'Ah, but it creates a barrier between my country and what the Russians are doing in eastern Poland.'

Mazie ignored his excuse. 'If you persist, we will stand aside and let events in Poland play out. Maybe the Russians will prevail and extend their influence right up to the German border. Regardless, we will deal with whomever is in charge after the dust settles.'

Von Lubeck almost laughed. She was saying too much. 'You're bluffing. You have nothing to offer us.'

'I am sorry you believe that,' Mazie said. She stood up.

Von Lubeck said, 'I pity Poland. Your country likes to make promises and encourage others to do the heavy lifting. Then you abandon them at the first sign of trouble. Show us you can contain the Russians and stop the drugs. Then we might be interested.'

'We do need a strong partner in Europe,' Mazie agreed curtly. 'There are others who are interested.' They exchanged the usual words of departure. Then she was gone.

Von Lubeck stared into the slowly dying fire. He snorted. 'Fuel cells.' He had used the carrot-and-stick approach too many times to fall victim. Still, there were reports that had come across his desk. He dismissed them. His world was geopolitics and he called up his mental map of Poland. 'Stupid woman,' he muttered, thinking not of Mazie but of the President of the United States. He threw his cigar into the fire and turned to leave. He glanced at Mazie's snifter of brandy. It was full. His eyes opened wide.

CHAPTER THIRTY

Moscow

It was a ritual the old man adhered to with the rigor worthy of a true believer. Every Wednesday afternoon at exactly three o'clock, his old Russian-made Fiat wheezed up to the newly renovated Sandunovsky Bath and the old man would get out. An attendant would wait for him at the door and escort him inside, where the restored statues and tiles of the bathhouse glittered again with Czarist splendor. The old man would fish a few rubles out of his pocket and pay the cashier. That was as much a part of the ritual as the weighing-in, soaping, steaming, and rinsing.

After the first round, the old man would sit in the changing room with a sheet wrapped around him and gossip with the other regulars, happy to be among friends. Nothing about him, his clothes or actions, suggested he was one of the most powerful godfathers in the Russian Mafiya, a member of the Circle of Brothers, and wealthy beyond a Czar's wildest dreams. In fact, he had saved the baths and paid for their restoration, a minor out-of-pocket expense.

Two other men, lesser lights in the world of Russian crime, joined him. Common knowledge held they were in competition to be the old man's heir. The regulars moved away, creating a circle of privacy. 'Are you going to Yalta?' the younger asked.

'No,' the old man answered.

'Others may follow your example.'

'That is for them to decide.'

'Mikhail will be insulted.' This from the elder of the two.

'He is outside the law.' To accuse Vashin of breaking the codes and rules of the *vor* was the worst accusation the old man could hurl at anyone.

'It will be dangerous not to go,' the younger man said.

'At my age, danger is the only thing that gives me a hard-on.' Their laughter joined and the tension was broken. Two men, fully dressed and wearing black leather topcoats, walked into the changing room and stood in the doorway. For a moment, the old man and his friends gossiped about the infidelity of a young wife and traded obscene comments. The old man shot the newcomers a disdainful look and jerked his head for them to leave. When they didn't move, he knew. 'Vashin?' he muttered.

A slight nod answered him, and he sighed in resignation. He stood and walked into the steam room as if for another round of sweating. One of the men drew a sawed-off shotgun from under his leather coat and motioned for the men in the changing room to lie on the floor while the other man threw a grenade into the steam room. He jammed a wedge into the latch and stepped back, pulling out a submachine-gun. The explosion blew the door of the steam room off its hinges. The two men sprayed the room with gunfire, killing any witnesses before walking nonchalantly to a waiting Mercedes-Benz.

'Who was the wife they were talking about?' one asked.

'A new widow,' the other answered.

Vashin liked the old-fashioned way in which Geraldine had organized the Yalta meeting. Easels were erected around her office holding charts diagramming the accommodations where the godfathers and their large entourages would be quartered. In one corner, a big board held the arrival schedules of the aircraft and the number of limousines, cars, and trucks that would be necessary to transport the arrivals to their dachas. It was a carefully integrated flow plan that kept the vehicles in constant motion.

'By controlling transportation,' she told Vashin, 'we control all movement.'

'And thereby control them,' Vashin said, seeing the marvelous logic of it. One of his aides entered the room and whispered in his ear. It was a long message. Vashin nodded twice and walked over to the easels. He picked up a black marker pen and struck out three names, one of them a member of the Circle of Brothers. 'We suddenly have vacancies,' he told Geraldine.

Vitaly Rodonov, the Minister of Defense, was eager to escape the Kremlin and return home after a long and frustrating day. He glanced at his watch. Almost ten o'clock. A telephone rang and an aide answered. He listened for a moment. 'The woman wants a meeting. Tonight.'

'Tell her the usual place and time.' He hurriedly gathered up his briefcase and coat to make the meeting. By the time he had descended the Red Steps, his car was waiting for him. He gave the driver directions and settled in for the short drive. At the designated corner, the black limousine turned into a side street and slowed. A woman stepped out of the shadows and the limo halted long enough for her to enter.

'He made a mistake,' Geraldine said. She told him of the execution of the godfather and his heirs.

Rodonov leaned back in his seat and closed his eyes. 'Finally,' he murmured.

'It's an opportunity we may not have again,' Geraldine said softly, telling him the obvious.

Tom Johnson drove past the block and checked the balcony of the third-floor apartment. A tattered rug was draped over the railing, the signal for a meeting. As long as the rug was hanging there, the meeting was hot and the street was being watched. He made a U-turn, acknowledging the signal. He had exactly seventeen minutes.

He drove to Gorky Park and left his battered Lada on the street. He scanned the night to ensure he was not being followed before taking a few steps down a path leading into the park. It was too dangerous to go any farther at night. Even the police waited until light to pick up the bodies.

'Here,' Peter Prudnokov, the commander of Transport Aviation, said.

Johnson stepped into the shadows. 'Face to face is dangerous,' he muttered.

'I have information. But my family needs protection.'

'From who?'

'Vashin. Who else?'

Johnson gave a little nod. 'We'll do what we can, but it depends on what you have.'

'My command is providing the airlift for Vashin's conference in Yalta.'

'I'm not impressed.'

'We know when, what airplane, and the route Vashin himself will be flying.'

'That we can use.'

Warsaw

It was after midnight and Pontowski was still awake, hoping for a phone call. The embassy's copy of Adam Mickiewicz's *Dziady* lay in his lap. It had lost much in translation. Yet he could feel the strength and emotion of the poet's words. *It must be my Polish blood*, he told himself. At exactly one o'clock, the phone rang. It was his son, who called at the same time every week. 'How's it going?' he asked.

'Not good, Dad.' He told Pontowski about Zeth and how he felt responsible for her expulsion. The remorse and pain he felt reached across two continents. 'Would it help if I talked to General McMasters?'

'It wouldn't hurt,' Pontowski replied. 'But I doubt if it would change anything.' They spoke for a while until

Pontowski ended the conversation by saying, 'Son, the ball is in your court. You gotta do what you think is right.' They broke the connection and Pontowski leaned back and closed his eyes. *It's tough doing the right thing*, he thought. Unbidden, an image of Maddy Turner danced in his mind's eye, tantalizing him with promises of what might have been. 'What went wrong?' he wondered aloud. He tried to dismiss the image. But it persisted with a life of its own, beckoning him into the future. *I'll make it right*, he promised himself. *If I can*. Then he fell asleep in his chair, the book still on his lap.

A knock at the door woke him. Morning sunlight streamed in the window and he was stiff from sleeping in the chair. He padded to the door but no one was there, only an advertisement for maid service tucked into the jamb. It was a signal that Evan Riley had a message for him. He had the procedure memorized and started on the trail that ultimately led to the dead drop. At the second stop, the trail changed and he was given an address in Konstancin, an upscale community south of Warsaw. It took him thirty minutes to find the house across from the drab yellow army barracks in the heart of the suburb. Riley was waiting for him inside.

'Was this an old brothel?' Pontowski asked.

'Now it's a safe house.' Riley pointed to the barracks across the street. 'When the Soviet Army was here, that was an intelligence headquarters and this was a whorehouse. They pumped the girls and we pumped them.' He chuckled. 'Those were the good old days.' He sat down. 'What are the Poles going to do about Vashin?'

'Bomb the hell out of him at Yalta.'

'So they are serious. Have they got the right target?'

'According to Jerzy Fedor they do.'

Riley shook his head. 'The only guy more twisted than Fedor is on our side, what's-his-face Shaw.' He handed Pontowski a manila envelope. 'You might find this interesting. It's Vashin's flight plan.'

The Western White House, California

The rain sheeted down, pounding the big picture window.

Inside, the rattling glass forced Maddy to take two steps back. 'I've never seen it rain like this,' she said.

'It's much worse up north,' Parrish replied. 'Portland and Seattle have lost over half their normal phone service. Thank God for cellular phones.' He checked his clipboard. 'But even they're out in some areas where the wind's knocked down towers.'

'How's FEMA doing?' she asked. FEMA was the government's Federal Emergency Response Agency.

'In place and responding.' Parrish looked worried. 'But it's going to take much more.'

'Alert the Pentagon,' she said at once.

'They haven't much to offer.' Parrish gave her a folder. Inside was a list of every operation, peacekeeping mission, and deployment the Department of Defense was supporting around the world.

'I hadn't realized they were stretched so thin,' she said.

'It's a problem.' He thought for a moment. 'Knowing Wild Wayne, he's ahead of us and knocking heads and kicking backsides.' General Wayne Charles was the Chairman of the Joint Chiefs of Staff and had a habit of living up to his nickname. 'They'll come through.'

The computer buzzed and Parrish played with the mouse, clicking on the conference icon. 'We're ready to go with the National Security Advisory Group,' he told the President. She sat down in front of the computer and the video cam. The images of the four members appeared on the screen. 'Good morning,' she said into the microphone. 'Mazie, how did it go with the Germans?'

'Not good, Madame President. They want to see some action on our part reining in Russian organized crime before they back off.'

'Madame President,' Stephan Serick said grumpily, 'you should have consulted with me before sending Mrs Hazelton off on this venture. I've dealt with von Lubeck. He doesn't bluff.'

'The Poles may give us what we need,' the DCI said.

'What exactly are they up to?' Vice-President Kennett asked.

The DCI was uncomfortable. 'Vashin is attending a conference at Yalta and they're planning to attack his villa. It's in retaliation for the assassination of President Lezno.'

'What the Poles do is not our concern,' Turner said. 'Mazie, wait a few days and then follow up with von Lubeck. If the Germans are still dragging their feet, tell them I'm reconsidering our trade policies.'

'Madame President,' Serick said, 'I must protest. The Germans are among our best allies. We can't treat them this way.'

'They're on the edge here,' Turner replied. 'I want them to step back and do the right thing in Poland, take the honorable course.'

'And letting the Poles assassinate Vashin for us is honorable?'

'I believe,' Turner said icily, 'they are doing it for Poland.'

Washington, D.C.

The images had barely faded from Mazie's computer screen when her telephone buzzed. It was the DCI. They made the line secure. 'Serick may have shot off his foot,' the DCI said.

'He was very angry,' Mazie conceded. 'But he made a valid point. The Germans are good allies.'

'But we need to get them back on the reservation in regards to Poland,' the DCI added. 'So what do we do now?'

'Wait,' Mazie answered.

The Hill

Brian stomped up the steps to the second-floor stoop and shook off his poncho before going inside. 'Hey, Maggot,' he called, 'talk about getting pissed on! Have you heard?'

'Heard what?' Matt answered.

'All classes and formations are canceled for the next couple of days. Lots of people got flooded out and General McMasters is gonna let them use NMMI as a relief center. We may have to double up with some kids from town and we're gonna send teams to go get some stranded families. The commandant is asking for volunteers.'

Matt came outside and leaned over the railing. He studied the weather. 'It's letting up.'

'About time. You want to volunteer? I am.'

'I'm worried about the Trog. I called her ranch but can't get through. Not even on a cellphone. I think she's there all alone.'

Brian recalled the time they had ridden there by horseback from the Escalante family compound. It seemed like an eon ago. 'Ah, she'll be all right.'

Matt made up his mind. 'The weather's breaking. I'm gonna go check on her.'

'You still feeling guilty?'

'Yeah, I guess so. Besides, I gotta talk to her.'

'How you gonna get there?'

'Beats me.'

'Chuck Sanford is going off duty,' Brian said. 'Maybe he'll take us.' The two boys hurried down the steps to the TLA's office and corralled the Secret Service agent.

Sanford listened and nodded. 'Yeah, let's do it. We should be able to get there before dark.' He looked at Brian. 'But you gotta stay here.'

'Come on! Gimme a break.'

'Sorry,' Sanford told him, 'but that's the way it is. We don't know what the conditions are and we can't take the chance. Matt, you go sign out while I finish up here.'

Brian stifled an obscenity. If Sanford wouldn't allow him to go after Zeth, there was no way the commandant would allow him to volunteer for relief work. Why couldn't they treat him like everyone else? 'See you when you get back,' he muttered. He wandered through the sally port and gazed at the sky. The rain had stopped and the weather was definitely improving. There were times he hated being the President's son. 'No way,' he said to himself. He ran back to his room and grabbed his poncho, scribbled a note, and left it on his desk. Then he ran for the parking lot, hoping Sanford had left his truck unlocked like everyone else in Roswell.

Sanford drove slowly up the highway toward Ruidoso, slogging through the mud and debris that covered the highway. The drive had taken much longer than expected and the dark evening sky indicated that a new storm was moving in. He mentally cursed weathermen and tried to call his office at NMMI. The cellphone was out of contact with a relay tower. He keyed his radio, with similar results. Finally, he checked the locator beacon the Secret Service had installed in the truck. It was on and transmitting. At least the Service would know where he was. Out of long habit, he glanced in the rearview mirror. A dark gray sedan was following them. 'I can't believe someone else is out here,' he muttered to Matt.

'The turnoff is just ahead,' Matt said.

'Got it,' Sanford answered, turning on to the dirt road that led to the Trogger family ranch. The mud and snow tires of the four-wheel-drive sport utility truck kicked up a shower of mud and gravel. Ahead of them, the Rio Hondo had overflowed its banks and water was splashing through the deck planks of the low wooden bridge. Sanford got out and walked across, testing it. He came back. 'It'll be okay. You get out while I drive across. You can tell them where to look for the body if it gives way,' he said, half joking.

Matt got out and waited while Sanford eased the truck across the bridge. Then he ran to catch up. He jerked open the rear door to throw his poncho in. Brian was lying on the floor, grinning at him. He held a finger to his lips, cautioning Matt to be quiet.

CHAPTER THIRTY-ONE

New Mexico

It was dark when Sanford pulled up in front of the ranch house. A lantern flickered in one room, offering proof that Zeth was there. 'Electricity must be out,' Sanford told Matt. He hit the horn and Zeth opened the front door. Matt was out of the car and up the steps. He skidded to a stop, suddenly embarrassed.

'I was worried,' he said.

'I didn't realize you had grown,' she said, looking at him with fresh eyes.

Brian bounced out of the truck and ran up the steps.

'Oh, no,' Sanford groaned. 'Where did you come from?'

'No way I was gonna miss out on everything,' Brian replied. It was a typical teenage answer, expressing the need to be included and not left out.

Sanford grabbed his radio and cycled through the channels, trying to contact any station to establish a relay. Nothing. He tried his cellphone and again came up dry. Finally, he gave up. 'I need to tell the detachment where you are.'

'No problem,' Brian said. 'I left a note on my desk and told them I was going with you.'

'They still need to know you're okay. I got to tell you, good buddy, it would've been a hell of a lot better if you had stayed at NMMI.'

'I didn't mean to cause trouble,' Brian said, now genuinely contrite.

'I know,' Sanford said, remembering when he was Brian's age and how much he hated being odd man out. He turned to Zeth. 'You heard a weather report lately?' She shook her head. He stared at the night sky. The rain was starting to fall again. 'I need to find out what the weather's doing. We gotta decide if we're gonna stay or go.'

Moscow

Geraldine was ready to leave with Vashin. Her bags were already at Vnukovo, the airport used by the Kremlin's leaders when traveling out of Moscow. She cleared her desk and, with a few minutes to spare, checked her e-mail. There was only one message, from someone who claimed to be an astrologer. That puzzled her. Few people knew her mailing address and none of them were fortune tellers. She called up the message. Nothing in her expression betrayed the shock she felt. It was from her handler. Your horoscope says don't fly today.

Warsaw

Pontowski and Waldo sat at the back of the small room and tried to act as if it were a routine briefing. Emil stood in front and kept looking their way for reassurance. But they were not flying the mission and there was little they could do. The Polish officer fingered his note cards as the seven other pilots took their seats. Then he cleared his throat one last time and started the detailed mission briefing. 'Good morning,' he said. 'Our mission is Target Yalta.' Waldo cycled the graphics for Emil and a small-scale chart of the route flashed on the screen.

Slowly, and with increasing confidence, Emil warmed to the briefing. The Poles had been planning and practicing over a week, so nothing was new and the briefing was essentially a final wrap-up. When Emil got to the ingress phase and reviewed the attack sequence on the compound where Vashin was staying, Pontowski was certain they could bring it off. Emil carefully went over target identification, even though the pilots had spent hours in target study. 'The attack is scheduled for first light tomorrow morning when we can be sure the objective will be sleeping.'

A grainy photo of Vashin flashed on the screen. He was getting out of his limousine at the funeral of Boris Bakatina.

'Look at their faces,' Waldo whispered, gesturing around the room. 'They want his ass.'

'Indeed,' Pontowski murmured, his own face a perfect reflection of the other pilots'.

The door banged open and the brigadier general commanding the First Air Regiment entered. He crisply called everyone to attention, and the three-star general commanding the Polish Air Force stomped into the room. Jerzy Fedor was right behind him. 'The mission is canceled,' the general barked.

'I'm sorry,' Fedor said. 'But I have received information that the objective will be moving constantly while he is in Yalta and we don't know where he will be at any given moment.' Fedor rushed out, not wanting to answer any of the astonished questions.

'I cannot allow the mission to continue,' the general said to the hushed room. 'I will not kill innocent people in a hunt for Vashin.'

Pontowski closed the door. 'I know where he'll be,' he said quietly, just loud enough to be heard. He cycled the mission graphics on the screen to an area chart. He traced Vashin's flight plan on the screen. 'We know when his aircraft will be here, here, and here.' He pointed to the waypoints the aircraft would overfly and circled the town of Kremenchug in the Ukraine. 'His airliner will be here at exactly ten-twelve hours our time today.'

'Holy shit,' Waldo said, 'the Yamamoto option.'

'What my eloquent friend is referring to,' Pontowski said, 'is the operation in World War Two when we intercepted and shot down the aircraft carrying Fleet Admiral Isoroku Yamamoto. He was the genius who planned the attack on Pearl Harbor and the Japanese never recovered from his loss.'

Emil studied the chart and measured the distances. He shook

his head. 'We would have to take off in forty-five minutes to make the interception. We can't possibly mission-plan and brief in that short time. Besides, we have practiced for a bombing mission, not an air-to-air mission. We don't have the experience to do it.'

'Me and Waldo can do it in our sleep,' Pontowski said.

Waldo groaned loudly. 'My momma warned me about doing this.'

'Doing what?' the general asked.

'Volunteering to get my ass shot off.'

New Mexico

Sanford tuned Zeth's radio, trying to work through the static. By changing channels, he was able to piece together a weather report. 'It's improving. But they're predicting local flooding. Let's head back and see if we can get across the bridge. Go get your things,' he told Zeth. She ran upstairs while he again tried to contact somebody to relay a message. He briefly considered pressing the emergency button on the truck's locator beacon. But they weren't in trouble, and with all the real emergencies going on he didn't want to create a false alarm.

Zeth came back with her bag and a large flashlight. 'Ready,' she said. Sanford slipped the truck in gear and headed back down the dirt road, slipping and sliding in the mud. Twice they became bogged down and the boys had to get out and push the truck free. The second time Brian slipped and was covered with mud when he got back in the cab. 'I always knew you were good for something,' Zeth told him. Brian grinned at her.

Warsaw

The brigadier general commanding the First Air Regiment left the briefing room and went to his office. He punched a number into his new telephone and waited. A woman answered on the fourth ring. He hung up, waited exactly two minutes, and dialed another number. This time Evan Riley answered. 'It's a go on the second option. But there is a problem. Pontowski and Walderman are leading the mission. Should I cancel it?'

A long pause. 'When do they have to take off?'

The brigadier checked his watch. 'In thirty-five minutes.'

Another long pause on Riley's part. 'Without Pontowski and Walderman, they can't do it. Let it go.'

The brigadier broke the connection and thought for a moment. Then he called Jerzy Fedor.

The Western White House, California

She was in front of a mirror, her nightgown in disarray. A bare-chested Matt Pontowski was standing behind her, his arms around her, his lips gently nuzzling her hair.

'Madame President.' The woman's voice was soft but demanding. Maddy's dream was shattered. 'Madame President.' Maddy's eyes came open. A low light illuminated the woman's face and, for a moment, she didn't know where she was. Then it all snapped into sharp focus. 'We have a situation that you should be aware of,' the woman said.

Maddy sat up and swung her legs over the edge of the bed as the woman handed her a robe. 'What time is it?'

'Almost midnight.'

Maddy stood and stepped into her slippers, still groggy from less than two hours' sleep. She paused briefly at her dressing table and ran a brush through her hair before walking into the family room. 'Patrick, I didn't know you were here.'

Shaw stood. 'Yes, ma'am. I flew in on the shuttle. The Secret Service is cycling agents back and forth so I bummed a ride with them.'

It was a flimsy excuse and she knew it. 'We can talk later.' The night duty officer waited for her to recognize him. 'What do you have, Bill?'

'General McMasters at NMMI called. Brian has left the campus with Agent Sanford and they're out of contact. There is some concern because of the flooding that has hit the area.'

Fear froze her and, for a moment, she was a mother, worried about her firstborn. 'What happened?'

'We don't have all the details, but Matthew Pontowski, who is his roommate—'

Maddy interrupted him. 'I know who his roommate is.'

'Sorry, Madame President. Agent Sanford and Mr Pontowski drove to a ranch to check on another cadet, Zeth Trogger, who had been expelled. Your son left a note saying he was going to sneak along with them.'

'Sneak along?' Maddy said.

'Yes, ma'am. That's what Brian's note said. Consequently, General McMasters thinks Brian is with them. Because of the storm and flooding, they're out of contact and isolated. However, Agent Sanford's truck is equipped with an emergency locator beacon and since it hasn't been activated, we think they're okay.'

'I want to speak to McMasters,' Maddy ordered, her worry giving way to anger.

The duty officer handed her the phone. 'He's on hold, Madame President.'

She took the phone. 'General, what the hell is going on out there?' She listened and her anger slowly eased. Then she asked, 'Isn't that near the Escalante ranch? Is it a safe area?' Her face paled when McMasters said the Hondo Valley was subject to flash flooding. 'Please let me know as soon as you learn anything.' She broke the connection.

The head of the Secret Service detail entered the room and waited to be recognized. 'We've established an open line to the detachment at NMMI. They're trying to recover contact with Agent Sanford but can't send a vehicle because of the flooding. As soon as the weather breaks, they'll launch a search helicopter.'

The anger was back, driving her. 'What do we pay you people for?' she snapped, immediately regretting it. 'Please forgive me. I'm upset, but that's no excuse.'

'Nothing to forgive, Madame President,' the agent said. 'If it was my son, I'd be breaking down doors.'

'Please keep me informed,' she said, dismissing him. Parrish was beside her, looking half asleep and disheveled. 'Well, since we're all awake,' she said with mock good humor, 'let's go to work.' A secretary went to the kitchen for coffee as more of her staff reported in. The Situation Room duty officer traveling with the mobile command post entered and spoke quietly to Parrish. He handed the chief of staff a folder and left. 'The storm?' Maddy asked.

'No, ma'am. We'll have an update on that in a few minutes. This is a report from the CIA. The Poles are launching eight F-16s to shoot down an airliner carrying Mikhail Vashin.'

'That's their decision,' she replied. 'Contact the good Senator Leland and tell him.' She thought for a moment. 'No. Do it in the morning when it's too late to do anything about it. Our official position is that we learned about it after the fact, gave no orders, and had no hand in it.'

Parrish looked sick. 'The CIA report says two American pilots are leading the mission. General Pontowski and a George Walderman. Technically, they're civilians and they're acting on their own accord. But that does involve us.'

The President steepled her hands and rested her chin on her thumbs, her eyes closed. 'Whatever the legalities, whatever Leland does, and no matter how this turns out, I'm not going to apologize for our allies removing an extremely dangerous enemy.' Her eyes snapped open. 'Vashin refuses to play by the rules and there is no doubt in my mind he'll do everything in his power to destroy this country. Can you imagine what he'll do if he controls a nuclear arsenal?' She challenged them to answer.

'Well, Mizz President,' Shaw drawled, 'if you pull this one off, you'll take first prize at the county fair. If it goes bust, they'll feed us all to the pigs.'

'Thank you, Patrick. I needed to know that.'

Patrick Shaw looked at his president, fake resignation on his face. 'Talk to Maggie Thatcher. She can tell you how it works.' He laughed. 'If you want, I can have Leland so busy jumpin' through hoops he won't give a damn what we do to the Russkies.'

'How are you going to make that happen?' Parrish asked.

'I can see Matt Drudge on TV now. "Highly reliable sources confirm that the revealing photo of the President's mother was a fake and that Senator Leland ordered it passed to the British tabloids."'

'The Drudge Report strikes again,' Parrish muttered.

'Do it,' Maddy said. 'I need to get dressed. Please have an update on the storm ready when I return.' They stood until she left the room.

Her maid was waiting for her. 'I laid out some clothes in case you were going back to work.'

She dropped her robe. 'Thank you, Clara.' She caught her image in the big mirror over the dresser and the dream was back, sharp and clear. An empty feeling swept over her. Then, for a brief moment, she was back in time, young again, her face fresh and unlined. She closed her eyes and savored the memory. When she looked again, a middle-aged woman stared back at her. Her eyes were heavy with worry, her face careworn. 'Is that who I am now?' she asked. She closed her eyes and Matt Pontowski was back with her, his arms around her. 'There will be a time for us,' she promised.

She opened her eyes and picked up the phone. 'Please tell Mr Parrish I want to return to Washington as soon as possible.'

Warsaw

Pontowski was moving fast when he reached his F-16 and clambered up the boarding ladder. The ground crew chief followed him and helped him strap in. Pontowski's hands were a blur as he ran the before-engine-start checklist. Then he looked over at Waldo, who was waiting patiently for him to finish. 'I'm getting slow,' he mumbled to himself. His right forefinger hit the electrical switch and the VHF radio came alive. 'Radio check,' he transmitted. The flight checked in. He waved a forefinger in a tight circle at the ground crew chief for start engines and brought the big Pratt & Whitney F100 kicker to life. With the engine on-line, he cycled his Have Quick radio, thankful they had the jam-proof frequency-hopping radio that an enemy could not monitor. He was going to be doing a lot of talking.

Again, he checked the flight in on the radio then taxied for the runway. The eight aircraft parked in a line, noses pointed into the wind, for their weapons to be armed and a final quick check before takeoff. He waited, the old tension mounting. For a moment, he was back in time on his first combat mission, holding at the end of the runway just like now. He knew what Emil and the other pilots were feeling, and for one split second wasn't sure that he and Waldo could bring it off. A ground crew chief ran out from under Pontowski's wing and held up a handful of red safety pins with red streamers. His weapons were ready for flight.

Can we do it? he wondered. He honestly didn't know the answer. He made the decision and tapped the front of his helmet with his fist, the signal for lowering their canopies in unison. Waldo sent the signal down the line and eight canopies were lowered simultaneously. Only the ground crew chiefs saw it, but it was the first step in the pilots coming together as a team.

Pontowski keyed his radio. 'Takeoff single-ship, twenty-second intervals.' Waldo answered by clicking his transmit button once. Six more clicks echoed in acknowledgment. Pontowski grunted in satisfaction. It was a good beginning. He called for takeoff clearance from the tower and taxied on to the runway. The others followed him, taxiing into a staggered pattern to avoid jet blast.

'Cleared for takeoff,' the tower radioed.

'Rolling,' Pontowski replied, starting the clock.

New Mexico

It was one o'clock in the morning when the headlights of Sanford's truck raked the swollen Rio Hondo. He got out and checked the bridge. It was under three inches of water. He hurried back to the truck. 'Zeth, you've lived here most your life. Do you think it's safe to cross?'

'My dad used to drive across all the time when it was under water. I guess it's okay.'

'Let's try it.' He grabbed a rope out of the truck and tied one end to the front bumper and the other end to himself.

'I'm gonna walk across and check it out. If I fall in or get swept away, I'd appreciate a little help on the rope.' The teenagers played out the rope as he walked across the bridge. He made it across and was coming back when, suddenly, a single shot rang out.

Sanford fell into the raging current as a volley of shots shattered the truck's windshield. The teenagers fell to the ground and rolled under the truck. But Zeth kept crawling and pulled herself on to the floor of the front seat. Two more shots slammed into the truck, spraying glass over her. She reached up and pressed the button on the emergency locator beacon. But the set was dead, shattered by a bullet.

CHAPTER THIRTY-TWO

Moscow

An honor guard at Vnukova airport stood at attention in the morning sun as the motorcade drove up to the boarding steps of the waiting Tupolev Tu-204. The Russian military had converted the twin-engine turbofan airliner for VIP use, and it was the flagship of Transport Aviation, rivaling Air Force One in comfort and luxury. The motorcade coasted to a halt.

General Colonel Peter Prudnokov, the commander of Transport Aviation, saluted Vashin as he emerged from his limousine. 'We are at your service, Mr Vashin.' Vashin nodded, taking the salute as his rightful due. He climbed the steps.

Vashin hesitated at the door and looked over the assembled crowd below him. The sun streamed on to his face, and a sense of euphoria lifted him upward until he was flying on his own, ever closer to the sun. 'This way, please,' a uniformed steward said, bringing him back to earth.

He stepped inside, and the forward entrance door was closed. He heard the whine of an engine as it came to life. The sense of euphoria was back. His time had definitely come.

General Prudnokov stood with the honor guard and saluted the Tu-204 as it taxied out. The salute wasn't for Vashin but for the crew and his beautiful airplane. 'For Mother Russia,' he vowed quietly.

Over Poland

Pontowski was talking to Waldo over the Have Quick radio as they climbed to the east. 'Fuel's going to be a problem. We need to jettison our bombs.' Each of the eight F-16s was carrying two Mark-84 2,000-pound bombs that were intended for the target at Yalta. Now they were excess baggage.

'There's a bomb range to the south,' Waldo said. 'We can jettison them safe over there. But I doubt if the range officer is on duty or if the range is open.'

Fuel is always a problem in a jet fighter, and hesitation meant valuable fuel lost. 'Let's do it,' Pontowski said. 'Enter the range single-ship, one mile in trail. I'll come off the range and turn downwind for the rejoin. Form up in two flights of four, fingertip formation. I'll lead Red Flight with Emil on my wing as Red Two.' He named the other two pilots who would be Red Three and Red Four. 'Waldo, you lead Blue Flight.' Again, he called off who would be Blue Two, Three, and Four. Seven clicks on the mike buttons answered him.

They turned toward the range. 'Select jettison safe,' he radioed. Seven more clicks answered as the pilots hit the selective jettison button on the right multifunctional display. Then they highlighted stations three and seven, the hard points under the wings where the bombs were carried. But Waldo's wingman, Blue Two, accidentally selected station eight, where an AIM-9M air-to-air heat-seeking missile was carried.

'Master arm on,' Pontowski radioed as he approached the range straight and level. When he judged he was clear, he hit the pickle button. He felt the two bombs come off but visually checked to be sure. Since they weren't armed, there was no explosion, only a cloud of dust.

'Six o'clock at three hundred meters,' Emil called, scoring the drop. He pickled off his bombs and one by one the fighters followed. Waldo's wingman, Blue Two, hit his pickle button and the bomb on the left wing separated cleanly. The AIM-9 on his right wing leaped off the rail and headed straight for Waldo.

The number-three pilot in Waldo's formation, Blue Three, saw it and yelled, 'WALDO! BREAK LEFT!' Waldo's reactions were honed by years of experience and he rolled his F-16 to the left and buried his nose, loading the aircraft with eight Gs. The missile flashed by, barely missing him.

'Jesus H. Christ!' Waldo shouted over the radio. 'What asshole—?'

'Blue Two,' Pontowski transmitted, overriding him, 'break right and fall in behind the last man. Select the correct station and pickle the bomb.' It was a bad start to the mission and Pontowski had to get it turned around. If Blue Two could not get his bomb off, Pontowski was going to send him home and would fly the mission with seven aircraft. But everyone's confidence would be shaken. He watched as Blue Two circled. The bomb came off cleanly. Pontowski breathed more easily. 'Join up as briefed,' he radioed. The eight aircraft turned to the east.

A torrent of Polish filled Pontowski's earphones as Emil gave Blue Two a tongue-lashing. While the Americans didn't understand a word said, the meaning was obvious from the tone. It had to be a devastating barrage. Pontowski waited for the first break to set things straight. His top priority was to keep them functioning as a tight team. 'We all make switchology errors,' he radioed. 'Our job is to learn from it. When you make a mistake, correct it and get on with the mission. You can sort it out on the ground, after you land. The key is to always press ahead. Remember that. PRESS!' He hoped they all got the message. 'Blue Two, you and Waldo owe Blue Three a beer. That was a good call and he saved your worthless ass.'

Waldo knew exactly what Pontowski was doing: staying focused on the mission, keeping their confidence up. He keyed his mike and joked, 'Hey, a kill's a kill. But next time, make it a bad guy.'

'Sorry, Waldo,' Blue Two transmitted. 'I fucked up. Bad.'

Pontowski heard the anguish in the young pilot's voice. He had to get them all back on track. 'We've got an old saying: no harm, no foul. Press.' Seven clicks answered him. They were all back as a team. 'Weapons safe,' Pontowski radioed. He didn't need to waste another missile.

New Mexico

Brian and Matt were under the truck and pulling on the rope tied to the bumper. 'We can't budge it,' Brian said. 'It's hung up on something in the river.'

'How long has he been in the water?' Matt asked.

'Fifteen, maybe twenty minutes,' Zeth replied. 'Too long.'

'If I can get into the front seat,' Brian said, 'I can start the engine and back up. We can pull him out.'

'No,' Zeth ordered. 'You'll get shot.' Suddenly, the rope snapped free and snaked across the ground, running downstream. Zeth saw it immediately. 'The current's pushed him against our bank.' She pointed into the dark. 'He's down there, about the length of the rope away.'

'Let's go get him,' Matt said, crawling out from under the truck. Brian was right behind him. Now the numerous times they had run the confidence course at NMMI paid off. They were into the brush in seconds and moving fast.

Zeth waited, the minutes ticking, the tension tingling in her. She almost screamed when Brian rolled back under the truck. 'We found him. He's alive and hung up in driftwood that's piled against a tree. He can see where the shooter is and he said not to come get him or we'll get shot.'

Zeth thought for a moment. 'Where is the bastard?'

Brian pointed to a shadow on the far bank. 'Right about there.'

'How long do you think it will take to get Chuck out of the water?'

'A minute, maybe.'

'The shooter's got to be using a night vision scope,' Zeth said. 'You go back and when you're ready, yell "Go". I'll shine my flashlight at him and wash out his scope. My TAC officer did it once to me during training and I was blinded for about a minute.'

'Got it,' Brian said. He disappeared into the night.

Zeth crawled out from under the truck and reached into the back seat. She groped around until she found the flashlight. Then she stood, using the angle of the truck as a shield, and held the flashlight on the hood. She crouched behind the fender, her hand over her head, and aimed the flashlight at the spot in the darkness.

Over Poland

Now it was up to Emil to get them safely through Belarus and into the Ukraine. He punched a new frequency into his UHF radio. 'Minsk Control,' he radioed in his accentless Russian. 'This is Vnukova One and Two, climbing to thirty-four thousand feet, destination Kiev.'

'Vnukova aircraft,' the ground controller replied, 'our radar paints two aircraft and we do not have a flight plan, or clearance, for your flight to transit Belarus. Remain outside Belorus airspace.'

The first part of the plan had worked and the Belarus radar was painting each formation as a single return. Now Emil had to bluff their way into Belorussian airspace. 'We are a diplomatic flight of two aircraft returning from Poland. We filed a flight plan but the Polish pigs are asleep.'

'As usual,' the controller replied. He had handled many of the diplomatic flights. 'Say type of aircraft,' he radioed, bored with the whole thing.

'Ilyushin 76s.'

'Roger, Vnukova flight. You are cleared to proceed on course. I will obtain clearance for you to enter Ukrainian airspace. Expect further clearance in five minutes.' They were in.

'Radar standby,' Pontowski told them over the Have Quick radio, certain that no one on the ground could monitor the transmission. They had to act like two transports, and he didn't want some air defense early-warning site detecting their radars. He called up his navigation display and punched in new numbers. He was a little rusty and it took longer than normal. Vashin's flight route appeared on the screen.

Pontowski punched in more numbers and let the computer work the problem. If Vashin was on schedule, they would intercept his airliner near Kremenchug in the Ukraine in fifty-two minutes.

It was a long time to fly in tight formation. 'Waldo, we need to talk tactics,' he radioed.

Over Russia

Vashin stood at the window of the Tupolev Tu-204's VIP suite immediately aft of the flight deck as they leveled off at 34,000 feet and headed south toward the Ukraine and Yalta. His hands were clasped behind his back, his feet apart.

Far below, the broken cloud layer tantalized him with hints of the land beneath. In his mind, there was no doubt that he was master of his vast domain. For a few moments, he was at peace with the world. But just as quickly, the feeling was gone, replaced by pure hate. An image of Madeline O'Keith Turner filled his mind's eye. His fury grew as he consigned her to hell. 'I will send you there,' he muttered. *Be patient,* he told himself. *Cut off her arms and legs first.*

An eager steward overheard him mumbling. 'May I be of service?'

Vashin shrugged off the man's offer before reconsidering. 'When will Miss Blake arrive at Yalta?' The steward hurried forward to relay Vashin's question to the communications officer on the flight deck. A warning tickled at the back of Vashin's mind and his eyes narrowed as he stared out the window. Why had Geraldine begged off at the last minute? She had pleaded that final details needed clearing up and had said that she would follow him in a few hours. But it wasn't like her to leave loose ends until the last minute. That bothered him. In his mind's eye, he saw the climax he had so carefully orchestrated for the conference. *Perhaps,* he thought, *Geraldine should be a part of it.*

His eyes opened wide and fear caught in his throat when a jet fighter popped up a hundred meters off the left wing. Then a second and a third appeared, stretched out in line, tapering back to the left. He spun around and looked out the other side of the airliner. Three more fighters were echeloned to the right. He hurried forward to the flight deck and burst through the door. The pilots were gazing out the side windows and seemed totally unconcerned.

'We have an escort,' the first officer told him.

'Is there a problem?' Vashin asked.

'None at all,' the first officer assured him. He keyed his radio and spoke to the lead pilot. The fighter rocked its wings. 'Think of them as an honor guard,' the first officer said.

Vashin's euphoria was back.

New Mexico

The waiting was killing Zeth as the seconds turned into days. Her arm was cramping but she didn't move, afraid to take her hand away from the flashlight.

'GO!' Brian finally yelled.

She flicked on the flashlight. Its beam cut through the night and fired the brush on the other side of the river with light. She saw the man holding a rifle and kept him illuminated. He rolled into the bushes but she kept the light on him. Finally, he disappeared. She swept the bank and focused on his car, which was parked just short of the bridge. 'Hurry!' she shouted.

'We need more time!' Matt answered.

A shot rang out, smashing into the far side of the truck, inches below the level of the flashlight. She saw the muzzle flash and aimed the beam at that spot. Again, she saw the shooter, who was shielding his eyes from the bright light. Then he was gone. She guided the beam in a sweeping motion, still holding the flashlight at arm's length and crouching behind the fender. Her head kept bobbing up for a quick look, first over the hood, then around the grill. She couldn't see him but kept the light moving.

A single shot rang out and the big flashlight exploded in her hand. She almost passed out from the shock and rolled on the ground, her hand a bloody mess. She was vaguely aware that the truck was still shielding her. She reached into the back seat and found a dirty towel Sanford used to clean the windshield. She wrapped it around her hand. Two more shots rang out, this time not aimed at her. 'Watch out!' she yelled. 'The bastard can shoot!'

There was no answer.

Over the Ukraine

'Fuel check,' Pontowski radioed.

In order, the pilots checked in with the fuel they had remaining. Each added, 'Tanks dry, internal only.'

'Jettison tanks now,' he ordered. On cue, the empty fuel tanks tumbled away. This time there were no switchology errors. He checked his navigation display. The waypoint where they would intercept the airliner was 240 nautical miles on the nose. He punched more numbers into the display and selected a descent point. Once they dropped off Ukrainian radar, alarm bells should go off. *Keep it high as long as possible*, he thought. *Conserve fuel.* He selected a descent point 140 nautical miles short of the intercept point when they would be abeam Kiev, their supposed destination. That would look like a normal descent for landing and might delay those alarm bells.

New Mexico

Zeth was passing in and out of consciousness. Then Sanford was over her, water streaming down his face. 'Sorry to take so long.' His skillful fingers unwrapped the bloody towel. 'Matt, there's a first-aid kit in the back of the truck. Get it. Be careful. Don't let him get a shot at you.' He touched her cheek. 'Nice work with the flashlight.' Matt handed him the kit and Sanford bandaged her hand, talking as he worked to reassure her. 'Your hand must hurt like hell, but I don't think it's as bad as it looks. The guy's good, but not that good. He missed me but I slipped and fell into the water. They almost had me out when he got off the two shots at us. I could've sworn he was aiming at Matt.'

'Maybe Matt was the only one he saw,' Brian said.

'Maybe,' Sanford replied.

They heard the shout. 'Hey! We talk, okay?'

'What kind of accent is that?' Brian asked.

'Russian,' Sanford answered. He crawled into the front seat and reached under the dashboard, extracting a nine-millimeter Glock. 'Zeth, how you doing?'

'Better,' she answered, her voice gaining strength.

'Good. I want you to do the talking so he'll think he's dealing with a pushover. I need some time, so count to one hundred before you start. Tell him I'm wounded and need a doctor. Tell him anything, but keep him talking. I'm going upstream. I'll swim across. The current should carry me to the other side. I'm gonna get behind him.' He handed the automatic to Brian. 'Use this if you have to.' He pulled his own weapon out of his shoulder holster and checked it. Then he was gone.

Zeth slowly counted to one hundred. 'What do you want?' she yelled.

'We talk.'

'My father's hurt. I need to get him to a hospital.'

'I let you go after you give me the boy. A deal, yes?'

Zeth looked at the boys and whispered, 'It's a kidnapping. He must think Matt is Brian because we're with Sanford.'

'Tell him Brian fell in the water and disappeared,' Matt said.

'Brian fell in the river,' Zeth yelled. 'He got swept away.'

'Not him. The other one.'

Zeth stared at Matt, her eyes wide. 'I need to think about it,' she shouted.

Near Kiev, over the Ukraine

It was time to descend. 'Emil,' Pontowski said, 'tell Kiev Control we have a problem with our landing gear and want to check it out during descent.' He listened on the UHF radio as Emil made the call. After a brief exchange in Russian, Emil's voice came over the Have Quick radio.

'We're cleared to descend at our discretion and maneuver to check our landing gear.'

Pontowski held them at altitude for a few more minutes to conserve fuel. The lower they went, the greater their fuel consumption. 'Throttles idle, airspeed two-ten,' he ordered. It was a maximum-range descent in which they would trade altitude for miles at the lowest possible fuel consumption.

They leveled off at 300 feet, well below radar coverage. For a moment, Pontowski was tempted to bring his own radar to life for one sweep to find the airliner. But if the Tu-204 was equipped with radar warning gear, that would set off all sorts of alarms. 'Let's do this one visual if we can,' he transmitted. 'Go tactical.' Each formation spread out into a big box, roughly 3,000 to 5,000 feet on a side.

'Okay, troops,' Waldo said, 'heads up. A Tu-204 looks like a Boeing 757. Except it's got winglets.'

The pilots searched the sky.

New Mexico

Zeth checked her watch. 'Chuck should have made it across by now.'

'Hey!' the man yelled. 'Time's up. Give me the boy and you okay.'

Matt stood up. But Brian tackled him just as a shot rang out, splitting the air above their heads. 'No fuckin' way, Maggot. I don't know why he wants you, but he's gonna kill us all.' They rolled back under the truck.

'Give me the boy,' the man yelled.

'How do we know you won't shoot us?' Zeth yelled.

They heard the car start. The headlights came on and the car slowly moved on to the bridge and stopped, blocking it. Oleg Gora got out, standing in an inch of water that was still flowing over the top of the wooden planks.

'The water's going down,' Zeth whispered, shielding her eyes from the lights. They watched as the man walked in front of the car and held the rifle above his head. He threw it into the water.

'He's out of ammo,' Brian said.

'I'll bet he's still got a sidearm,' Zeth commented.

'Now it's okay, yes?' the man shouted.

The teenagers looked at each other, not sure what to do.

Near Kremenchug, over the Ukraine

Blue Two redeemed himself for the switchology error on the range when he called, 'Tallyho! Two o'clock. High. Eight miles.' Seven sets of eyes focused on that part of the sky; first one click echoed in Pontowski's headset, then six more. They had all found the target except him. His vision wasn't what it used to be. Then he saw it. The airliner was a speck in the sky. He was padlocked, afraid to take his eyes off it and lose contact. 'Waldo, take spacing, two miles in trail.' Waldo acknowledged and flew a weave as his flight fell into trail.

The information Riley had given him was accurate. They were at the airliner's four o'clock and closing to its deep six o'clock. He estimated they were 35,000 feet below it with a good look-up angle for AMRAAM missiles. The slammer would do the job nicely. His fangs were out. This was not the glamorous undertaking of chivalrous knights of the air, but the work of assassins. Yet he had no compunctions about shooting down the airliner and killing innocent people to nail Vashin. How many more innocent Poles would he save? Faces flashed in his mind, and he was back in the pub with Ewa and her mother. He forced himself to concentrate. He and Waldo had done what they came for.

'Emil, take the shot. Use the slammer.'

'My pleasure,' the Polish pilot answered.

'I'll talk you through it,' Pontowski replied.

Red Three saw the threat first. 'Bandits! In trail on the Tupolev. I count six.'

Pontowski strained to make them out. Then he saw the six small specks flying a V formation with the airliner. 'Escorts,' he radioed. 'I can't make out what they are.'

'Press,' Waldo said, warning him they were rapidly running out of fuel and time.

Pontowski checked his gauges. They had less than a minute's playtime to engage the fighters and shoot down the Tupolev if they were to make it back. His orders came fast. 'Waldo, lean right. Red Flight, check left thirty degrees.' Waldo's flight turned away to the right while Pontowski's turned to the left. Now they had the fighters bracketed as they closed. 'Select heaters,' Pontowski radioed, telling the pilots to use AIM-9s for the engagement. 'Master arm on.' His voice was calm, but this wouldn't last for long. The fighters were almost directly overhead. 'PULL! he shouted, shoving his throttle into afterburner. The four Vipers headed straight up for the fighters.

Fifteen seconds later, Waldo keyed his radio, his voice much calmer. 'Blue Flight, pull.'

Pontowski sorted the aircraft as they climbed, assigning each member of his flight a target. 'They don't see us,' he radioed. 'Hold your shot until you're in range.' A low growl filled his headset. The seeker head of his missile was locked on and tracking. 'Su-27s, Flankers,' he radioed, finally identifying the bandits escorting the Tupolev. But he was wrong. The six aircraft were Su-35s, the much-improved version of the Su-27.

'Damn!' Pontowski shouted. A missile was streaking toward the Flankers, its smoke trail etching the sky. Emil had buck fever and had fired too soon. The missile went ballistic.

The AIM-9 is unbelievably fast and it shot straight up, passing harmlessly between the Flankers, leaving a smoke trail that led directly to Pontowski's flight of four Vipers. One of the Flankers rolled for a belly check and saw the fighters climbing toward him. The Flanker buried its nose and headed down. Immediately, three others followed, leaving two behind to protect the Tupolev. Two Flankers headed straight for Pontowski's Red Flight while the other two fighters headed for Waldo's Blue Flight, which was lower and farther away.

'He's good,' Waldo said, warning Pontowski. He personally doubted if he could have reacted that fast and sorted out the attack, pairing two against Pontowski's flight while peeling off two to engage Blue Flight. Neither Waldo nor Pontowski feared the Su-35, but they had good reason to fear the man leading them.

'PRESS!' Pontowski shouted. What happened next took less than twenty seconds, and with twelve fighters in less than five miles of airspace, it was a true furball as the two groups of aircraft merged, the Flankers going straight down, the Vipers straight up. The only mutual support that existed was knowing there were friends in the area. But it was every man for himself

The Tu-204 rocked violently, throwing Vashin to the floor. He picked himself up and fell again, rolling forward as the big airliner dove for the ground. He was furious and struggled to his feet, half stumbling, half skidding toward the flight deck. He burst through the door. Warning bells and the shouting pilots deafened him. 'What are you bastards doing?' he shouted, adding to the confusion.

'We're being attacked!' the captain yelled.

'Where are they?' Vashin shouted back.

The captain pulled back on the control column and the big plane leveled off. 'We can't see them,' the first officer answered.

Vashin's mouth contorted in fury, his paranoia in full flow. He fully believed his own pilots were trying to kill him.

Pontowski jerked the nose of his Viper on to the lead Flanker and pointed straight at him. He had every intention of shooting him in the face. The Flanker's nose jerked once as the pilot fought for separation. Instantaneously, Pontowski's nose was back on him. His right forefinger was depressing the trigger as they came together in the merge. The twenty-millimeter cannon fired as Pontowski rolled ninety degrees and brought the Flanker on board canopy to canopy. The Flanker's cannon was also firing but the golden B-B, the lucky round, came from the Viper. The Flanker exploded as Pontowski flashed by with less than fifty feet separation.

★　　★　　★

Vashin found his voice. 'You fools,' he rasped, 'I'll have you—' The words froze in his mouth when he saw the tumbling wreckage of one of his escorts. A fighter he didn't recognize flashed by, going straight up. For the first time in his life, he knew true fear.

Still going straight up at .92 Mach, Pontowski twisted in his seat, searching for the two Flankers he knew had to be there. He saw a bright flash that had to come from Blue Flight. *Theirs or ours?* Then he was back in it, fighting for situational awareness. Much to his surprise, another F-16 was at his seven o'clock and 500 feet away. It was Emil in a fighting wing formation. Where were the other Flankers? The Tupolev? He checked his fuel gauge as he ruddered his aircraft over and headed straight down, Emil still covering his six o'clock. Instinctively, he found another Flanker. But an F-16 cut in front of him and fired an AIM-9. Pontowski crossed less than 100 feet behind the F-16, shaking violently when he hit the other's jet wake. A nearby flash almost blinded him. But this time he was sure it was the Flanker.

He pulled up, yelling over the radio, 'BINGO! BINGO! BINGO!' They had to disengage or they would all flame out for fuel starvation before landing safely.

But Waldo was on top of it. 'Blue Three. Disengage to the west. Now. Blue Two and Four, I have you in sight, your six is clear, head for homeplate.'

Pontowski saw a Viper nose over and streak past a Flanker going in the opposite direction. Then it hit him: the Flanker was also disengaging. The fight was over. 'Red Flight,' he transmitted, 'disengage and RTB.' He listened and his spirits soared as his flight checked in. Everyone was accounted for! 'I repeat,' he radioed, 'return to base.' He scanned the sky. He rolled for a belly check and saw the Tupolev in the distance, 10,000 feet below him and crossing from his right to left.

'Damn!' he raged. The airliner was too far away to chase down with the fuel he had remaining. They had come all this way for nothing and shot down three good pilots who were only doing their job. He hit the auto acquisition switch on his throttle, bringing his radar to life. He had a lock on in less than a second. The airliner was seven miles away, closer than he thought, and on the hot side of the intercept. The decision was there, made for him. He nosed over and shoved the throttle forward into mil power. He hit the option select button on his right multifunctional display and called up an AMRAAM missile.

Emil's voice came over the radio. 'I'm still with you.' Then, 'Bandits at three o'clock.'

Pontowski's head jerked to the right. Two small dots were turning into them, the second a mile behind the first. They were the two Flankers that had remained behind to escort the Tupolev.

'I'm engaged,' Emil transmitted, turning into the new threat, meeting the Flankers head on. Pontowski banked to follow – his turn to offer mutual support. He zoomed for separation, hoping one, or maybe both, of the Flankers would come after him. But the Flankers didn't take the bait and, by climbing, Pontowski had effectively left Emil out in front and all alone. 'God damn it!' he raged. He watched as Emil and the lead Flanker closed and simultaneously launched missiles at each other. Now it was a race to see who had the fastest missile as both fighters jinked wildly, trying to avoid the oncoming missile. Emil's missile flashed by the Flanker, missing completely. At the same instant, the proximity fuse in the Flanker's missile detonated, sending a shower of shrapnel into Emil's aircraft.

Pontowski felt sick as Emil's jet disappeared in the missile's fireball. Then he saw the F-16 again, still flying but trailing a plume of fire. 'Eject!' Pontowski yelled over the radio. He watched in horror as Emil and the Flanker collided head on.

'Oh shit,' Pontowski moaned to himself. A cold anger claimed him as he looked for the second Flanker. But it was far below him, headed straight down in afterburner, running from the fight. He turned on his radar, searching for the Tupolev.

*   *   *

'There!' the Tupolev pilot shouted, pointing at his ten o'clock position. Vashin's eyes followed the pilot's finger and he saw Pontowski's F-16 as it surged into view, dropping on them like a bird of prey. 'Do something!' he yelled. The captain jerked at the controls and turned into the fighter.

It was the only thing he could do.

Pontowski saw the nose of the Tupolev turn into him and he gave the pilot high marks for trying. Without emotion, he hit the pickle button, sending a fire signal to an AMRAAM missile. The slammer came off the rail and picked the first target its radar head detected. The missile headed straight for the Tupolev. Pontowski mashed the pickle button a second time and sent another missile on its way.

Vashin saw the two smoke trails etching the sky as the missiles came directly at him. An image of the archangel Michael launching thunderbolts flashed in his mind's eye. Then he shouted at the pilots, his voice cracking with anger. He wanted to kill them because they were so helpless. It came to him in a flash. 'Geraldine!' he shouted. 'You cunt!'

His fury grew into a satanic rage, consuming him with hate, as the first missile closed. 'It's not my time!'

But it was.

Pontowski climbed at mil power and headed to the west. He was alone in the sky and desperately low on fuel. He hit the navigation button on the multifunctional display and called up the nearest friendly airfield where an F-16 could land. Rzeszow flashed on the screen, 450 nautical miles away. He leveled off at 40,000 feet, read the distance to the airfield, and checked the fuel gauge again: 3,200 pounds of fuel remaining. He wasn't going to make it. Maybe, with a lot of luck, he could make it to Poland.

He unclipped his oxygen mask and wiped the sweat away from his eyes. The aftershock hit him and he ached with weariness, sick of it all. 'You did good,' he murmured, recalling Emil's face.

New Mexico

'He's just standing there,' Brian whispered. 'Like he's got all the time in the world.'

'He's testing us to see if we'll shoot at him,' Zeth said. 'By now, he probably figures we don't have a gun.'

'The fucker's wrong,' Brian growled, raising the Glock Sanford had given him.

Matt saw a shadow move on the opposite bank. 'Look,' he whispered. It was Sanford. They watched as the Secret Service agent raised his automatic in a two-handed stance to shoot the man in the back. But nothing happened. Sanford disappeared into the shadows.

'His gun must've jammed,' Zeth whispered.

'I'm coming across,' Gora shouted. He started to walk over the bridge which was now out of the water.

A shadow materialized on the far side of the bridge, gliding up behind him. 'Chuck,' Zeth whispered.

Sanford was behind him and threw a carotid hold around Gora's neck, cutting off the blood supply to his brain. Normally he would have been unconscious in five to ten seconds. But Sanford slipped on the wet boards and the men crashed to the deck. Brian stood up to get a clear shot but the men were on each other, gouging and tearing at one another's eyes and throat.

Matt jumped into the driver's seat of the truck and switched on the headlights to give Brian more light. He started the engine. Brian tried to get off a clean shot but Sanford was in the way. Gora kicked at Sanford's knee and the agent went down. Brian fired and missed. Gora kicked Sanford in the head and knelt down behind him, pulling him up by his shirt as a shield. A knife flicked open in his hand. He held the blade to Sanford's neck.

'Throw the gun in the river!' he yelled.

Sanford's forefinger moved in a tight circle, the signal to start engines. Then he pointed at the truck and beckoned them forward. Matt understood immediately. 'Brian, do it,' he ordered. Matt slipped the truck into gear.

Brian heaved the gun into the water just as Matt stepped on the accelerator. The truck leaped ahead and on to the bridge. Gora's head jerked in surprise as Sanford kicked free and rolled off the side of the bridge. Matt mashed the accelerator. Gora stood up, his automatic in his hands, and fired three shots into the oncoming truck. Matt slipped as low as he could behind the steering wheel and held it steady.

The front bumper of the truck caught Gora head-on and smashed him against the grill of his car. His scream shattered the dark night.

CHAPTER THIRTY-THREE

Over the Ukraine

The altimeter read 12,000 feet when the F-16's engine flamed out for fuel starvation. Pontowski automatically checked his position: nine miles short of the Polish border. He allowed himself a tight smile. The Viper had a one-to-one glide ratio: for every 1,000 feet of altitude lost in a descent, it traveled one mile forward. With a little luck, he'd cross the border with 3,000 feet to spare. But that was cutting it close.

He wired the airspeed at 210 knots and scanned the cockpit to make sure everything was securely stowed. A loose pen or checklist could play havoc. He locked his shoulder harness and watched the altimeter unwind. He ran the tally. Assuming Waldo got them all back, it was his and Emil's F-16s for the Tupolev and four Flankers. And Emil for Vashin. He had to believe it was a good exchange.

The altimeter passed 3,000 feet and he glanced outside. He was above a low cloud deck and couldn't see the ground. An abandoned airfield or a stretch of road would have been tempting. He waited for a moment, and when the altimeter touched 2,500 feet, approximately 2,000 feet above the ground, he placed his feet against the rudder pedals, pushed into the back of the seat, pulled in his elbows and reached for the ejection handle between his legs.

He pulled the handle straight up.

Chuck Sanford sat alone in the front seat as he drove slowly down the highway toward Roswell. Wind and rain pounded at him through the shattered windshield and he shivered. He glanced in the rearview mirror at his precious cargo. Brian, Matt and Zeth were very quiet. 'How's the hand?' he shouted over the wind noise.

'Hurts like hell,' Zeth answered. 'But I can move my fingers.'

'That's good,' Sanford said, certain she was going to be okay. But Matt was another story. 'Matt, how you doing?' No answer. Sanford wanted to stop the truck and cradle the boy to him, comforting and reassuring him. But that wasn't possible. 'I gotta tell you, that was the bravest thing I've ever seen.'

'No kidding!' Brian said. 'I saw it. I couldn't've done that, not with a guy shooting at me like that.'

Sanford pitched his voice just right. 'You saved my life, Matt. I owe you big time.'

'Come here,' Zeth said, putting her good arm around Matt and gathering him to her.

'Hey,' Brian said, 'no fraternization.'

'Get your body over here,' Zeth said. 'I'm cold. You two Rats gotta be good for something.' Sanford smiled at the commotion going on in the back seat.

'I got an idea,' Brian said. 'My mom's house is close to the beach. Maybe we can do some serious surfing over vacation.'

'I've never surfed,' Matt said, breaking his silence.

'Nothing to it,' Brian assured him. 'Maybe we can get your dad to fly out. That'd be fun. How about it, Trog? You wanna do it?'

'My dad can teach you to fly,' Matt said, increasing the offer.

'I'll think about it,' Zeth replied.

Sanford listened to them chatter away, plotting their vacation. 'Hey, Maggot,' Brian said. 'Do you think my mom and your dad would like to see each other again?'

Zeth laughed. 'You better believe it.'

'That would be okay,' Matt said.

Sanford relaxed. They were going to be fine. All of them.

The Western White House, California

Maddy Turner's simple request to return to Washington, D.C., as soon as possible set an incredible chain of events in motion. The Secret Service was alerted, the Federal Aviation Agency started to reserve airspace for the flight, and maintenance crews at Vandenberg Air Force Base inspected Air Force One with infinite care, preparing it for flight. However, the flight crew remained undisturbed, so they would be fully rested and fresh in the morning. The White House communications section was in overdrive as it prepared to switch its focus from the West Coast to Air Force One and finally to the White House. And the list went on and on.

Joe Litton took a devilish delight in rousing the press corps that traveled with the President with the news. He rationalized that if he was up and working at four in the morning, so should they be.

In the midst of all this activity, the Western White House was an oasis of calm purpose. The President was dressed for travel and sitting in her makeshift office in the family room. She showed no fatigue from being up most of the night and was busily at work. Her staff was fully used to her workaholic ways, certain they could sleep most of the way to Washington.

Nancy Bender, Maddy's new personal assistant, was with her, reconciling her personal schedule. When they had finished, Nancy stood to leave. 'Mrs President, please have the duty officer call me the next time you wake early.'

'Nancy, you're five months pregnant. I'm not a slave-driver.'

Nancy smiled. 'Yes, you are. But I knew that when I took this job. When I can't do it, I'll tell you.'

'I do worry about you.'

'Thank you, Mrs President. But I'm fine.' And she was.

Parrish was next. 'The latest weather report,' he said, handing it to her. 'The storm's finally breaking up. We should have some good weather for the next seven or eight days.'

'It's about time. Have FEMA be ready with a full assessment when we get back to Washington. I want to brief key members of Congress on the situation and our relief efforts. And I'll need to speak to the country.'

Parrish made the appropriate notes. 'Mazie's in the command post reviewing the latest message traffic from the Sit Room.'

'Show her right in when she's ready.' Maddy leaned back on the couch and closed her eyes. 'Any news on Brian?'

'I'll check,' Parrish said.

'Am I becoming obsessive?'

'He is your son. Like I said before, I'd be beating down the doors at NMMI if my kid was missing.'

'He's not exactly missing, just out of contact.'

Parrish hurried out to check the hotline the communications section was keeping open to NMMI.

Maddy let her mind wander for a few moments, to Brian, so much a part of her life. At times, his image and Sarah's joined. Her beautiful children, whom she loved more than life itself. Then another image appeared – Matt Pontowski. She opened her eyes. Mazie was poised in the doorway, immaculately dressed and all business.

'Good morning, Mrs President.' She sat down and handed Maddy the PDB. 'This just came in. Vashin is the lead topic.'

For once, Maddy did not read it. 'Did they get him?'

'The Poles shot down the airliner he was supposed to be on. His death hasn't been confirmed yet. There is bad news. Two of the Polish aircraft are missing.' She paused. 'You did know Matt Pontowski led the mission?' A short nod answered her. 'One of them is his aircraft.'

'Is he dead?'

'I was with him in China. The man's a survivor.'

The images came flooding over her. Maddy was with him

in his room at the Escalante family ranch looking at the portrait. Their lips brushed. She forced the memories back into their carefully guarded niches. She was still the President. 'Tell me as soon as you learn anything.'

'I imagine,' Mazie continued, 'the Germans will reconsider their position in Poland and be very anxious to get on board now.'

'Tell von Lubeck they missed the boat.'

Mazie sketched a little smile. 'That will turn up the heat.'

'Indeed,' Maddy answered, steel in her voice.

'That's all I have, Mrs President. But there's one thing I've always wondered about. What was it that put you on to Vashin so quickly?'

'It was the heads, remember? It was such a bizarre gesture. It told me everything about him. I couldn't ignore it.'

Again, Maddy leaned back into the couch and closed her eyes. The waiting was unbearable. Mazie didn't move. Then she reached out and gently touched the President's hand. 'They'll be okay,' she predicted. Their hands clasped, and for a few moments the two women sat there, alone, as the world swirled around them.

The phone buzzed and Mazie picked it up. She listened and, without a word, handed it to Maddy. Brian's voice came on the line, full of life. 'Mom!' Maddy had to pull the handset away, his voice was so loud. 'You can't believe what happened!' He was bubbling with excitement.

'Are you okay? You're not hurt?'

'Naw. A little scraped up, maybe.' He started to babble again, eager to tell her the whole story.

A duty officer from the mobile command post came to the door and motioned to Mazie. He handed her a message and left. Mazie quickly read it and passed it to Maddy. It was from Poland. Maddy's spirits soared. 'Brian, slow down. I can hardly understand a word you're saying.'

'Mom, are you crying?'

EPILOGUE

Moscow

The door clanged open and light streamed into the small, dank cell. Geraldine shielded her eyes from the blinding glare, barely able to see the two hulking silhouettes standing in the doorway. She fought for control of her bowels. The old Soviet system might have been dead and buried for over a decade, but this was still the dreaded Lubyanka, once the home of the KGB and now the headquarters of the Federal Counter-Intelligence Service. 'Miss Blake,' one of the shadows said, 'please come with us.' She followed them into the corridor, surprised at how clean and bright it was. They led her to a shower room where a woman handed her fresh clothes from her apartment.

'Please hurry,' the woman said, pointing to a shower. 'President Rodonov is waiting.'

'President Rodonov?' Geraldine asked. 'Vitaly Rodonov, the Minister of Defense?' The woman nodded and handed her a bar of soap and a towel. Geraldine dropped the gray prison dress she had worn since being arrested and stepped into the shower. The hot water coursed over her and, slowly, her mind started to function. She wasn't dead yet.

Rodonov placed his teacup down when Geraldine joined him, her hair still wet from the shower. She wasn't wearing makeup, but her clothes were perfectly arranged and she still carried herself like a queen, a far cry from the West Acton railroad estate in London where she grew up. He motioned her to a chair. 'Vashin is dead.'

She nodded at the obvious. Rodonov had used the time since his reprieve wisely. Sooner or later, Vashin would have ordered his execution, and it had been a matter of who could strike first. 'Who killed him?'

'The Poles shot down his aircraft.'

'And you let them?'

'Let's say we encouraged them. Of course, we had to defend his aircraft in case he survived.' He sipped his tea. 'The loss of a Tupolev and four escort fighters was a small price to pay to save Russia.'

'Why are you telling me this?'

'You know more about the *vor* and the Mafiya than any other person, yet you are not one of them. I want you to work as my special assistant.'

The offer was predictable. She was the ultimate insider, and what she knew would be critical in any fight against the *vor* and the Mafiya. And it would keep her alive. 'If I refuse?'

Rodonov shrugged and looked at his feet, toward the cells in the basement. She understood. 'Aren't you worried that I work for the CIA?'

'Don't be stupid,' he scoffed. 'Johnson works for the CIA. Marshal Prudnokov developed that connection for us.'

'Another promotion? I didn't know commanding Transport Aviation could be so rewarding.'

'The rewards of success are great,' Rodonov reminded her.

'Since Mikhail is dead and there is no question as to my loyalty—'

Rodonov interrupted her. 'We know you work for the British.'

'MI6 does pay well,' she murmured.

'We pay better.'

'I do hope so,' she replied, sealing the deal.

Warsaw

The doctor bent Matt Pontowski's right leg and prodded the

muscle. Pontowski groaned loudly, the pain intense. 'Very good,' the doctor said, obviously proud of his handiwork. 'You were lucky we saved your life, never mind the leg.' His fingers felt the kneecap. 'You Americans have done wonders with artificial joints. But I'm afraid you'll never fly again.'

'Maybe not a jet,' Pontowski said, gritting his teeth. What should have been a routine ejection from the F-16 had turned into a disaster. He had punched out under ideal conditions thirty miles short of the airfield. But he had not separated cleanly from the seat and had landed unconscious. The parachute shrouds had twisted around his leg and the inflated canopy had dragged him into a fence, where he had almost bled to death before a farmer rescued him. At some point he had shattered his knee, probably on landing.

'Please see your own physician when you're in America,' the doctor said, dismissing him.

Pontowski thanked him and said goodbye to his nurses, who seemed both sad and happy to see him go. He limped out of the hospital and into a bright spring day. He stood in the sunlight, glorying in the moment. It was good to be alive. *Matt's vacation starts in three weeks*, he thought. *Plenty of time to get home*.

A silver-gray Mercedes-Benz sedan pulled up and Jerzy Fedor stepped out. 'May I offer you a ride?'

'Why?'

'I would like to thank you.'

'For what?'

'For helping us.'

Pontowski felt the anger boil to the surface. This was the man he had been warned repeatedly not to trust. 'What's your game, Mr Fedor?'

Fedor smiled, his cadaverous face for once full of life and warmth. 'The game we Poles have played for centuries: survival. Think of it as all ends against the middle.'

'And I was one of the ends.'

'Actually, a means to achieve an end.' He could tell that Pontowski didn't understand. 'It's difficult to explain. Poles have always needed men we can believe in if we are going to act. Look at our recent history: Kosciuszko, our poets—'

Pontowski interrupted him. 'Like Adam Mickiewicz.'

'And our composers, like Chopin. Men of action like Josef Pilsudski. Men of God like Archbishop Stefan Wyszynski and Karol Wojtyla. They give us focus. Yet, sometimes, we are our own worst enemies when we follow the wrong star.'

'What was my role in all this?'

'As long as you were involved, we were certain the United States would not desert us.' Again, the smile. 'Perhaps it's best that you're leaving.'

'There's someone I want to see first.'

'Ewa Pawlik, no doubt.'

'I could have sworn she came to my room when I was still delirious.'

'Let her go. She served her purpose.'

'To keep me involved.'

'Would you have flown that mission if you had not—?' Fedor let his voice trail off.

'I don't know.'

'That's because you have a Polish heart,' Fedor said. He extended his hand in friendship.

The White House

Patrick Flannery Shaw came through the southwest gate of the White House. An escort hurried him up West Executive Avenue and into the West Basement. The President sat in the small break room next to the mess, stirring a bowl of popcorn and talking to the on-duty chef. 'Patrick,' she said, 'would you like something to eat?' He shook his head and the chef left, closing the door behind them.

Shaw sat down and poured himself a healthy shot of Jack Daniel's. He had been expecting this conversation, but not quite under these circumstances.

'Stephan Serick wants to resign,' Maddy said.

Shaw sipped the whiskey. 'I hadn't heard.' A mental picture of the crusty Secretary of State stomping down the hall with his cane played in the back of his mind. 'He got his feelings hurt over the way you handled the Germans. Tell him you need him, give him a few ego strokes, and he'll roll over like a puppy dog.'

She stirred the popcorn with a forefinger before taking a nibble. 'How much harder should I push Leland over Maura's photo? I think he wants to declare a ceasefire.'

'It kept him preoccupied. Not a single word from the jackass about Poland.'

'Poland was a sideshow,' Maddy said.

'But it could have blown up in your face,' Shaw replied. The President sat in silence, thinking. When she looked at him, Shaw's stomach lurched. He had never seen that look before. 'Mrs President, is this a come-to-Jesus meeting?'

She didn't answer, which only made it worse. 'Patrick, you gave that photo of Maura to Leland's staff.'

Shaw gulped. His worst nightmare had just come true. 'I only dangled the bait. They were so eager, they took it hook, line, and sinker. I was lucky to get my hand back.'

'Why?'

'So you'd have a damn big club to beat Leland with.'

'Have I ever played the game that way?'

Shaw was genuinely apologetic. 'No, ma'am, you haven't.' He had to explain himself, justify his actions. 'I was certain Maura could handle it, might even enjoy it. I never figured her for a heart attack. She's so strong.'

'Indeed she is.' Silence. Then she asked, 'Why Matt? Why did you drive him away?'

Shaw heard the tone in her voice and he sighed loudly. This was his swan-song, probably the last time he would ever speak to her. He lowered his head, waiting for the guillotine blade. 'Look at his track record.' He snorted. 'Women chase him down the street tearing their clothes off. My gawd! He's got more temptation coming his way than half the state of Texas.'

She gave him a sad look. Shaw would never understand that passion was a law unto itself, without rhyme or reason. It was simply there, or it wasn't, and no person could control it. 'He is exciting,' she admitted.

'Mrs President, beneath that crooked grin and those straight teeth is a certified aerial assassin. He may look civilized, but he's got a switch somewhere inside him that turns him into pure aggression. And based on what happened with Brian, his son is a chip off the old block. It's gotta be in the genes.' He took a deep breath. 'He's all wrong for you.'

'Why?'

'Because people love scandal and Leland was going to use him as a club. He was gonna cost you the election.'

'True.'

Shaw's mouth fell open in awe. She had used him! She had held him close enough to do the dirty work and still kept him at arm's length. 'If I'd screwed up, you'd have nailed me to the wall.'

'In a heartbeat,' she replied, mimicking his tone.

'But you'll never forgive me for chasing him away, will you?'

She reached across the table and touched his hand. 'I'll find my way back to him.' She smiled. 'At the right time. But in the future, he's off limits to you.' They sat there, still old friends. 'Patrick, when *do* I announce for reelection?'

RICHARD HERMAN

AGAINST ALL ENEMIES

A B-2 Stealth Bomber is lost on its way to destroy biological weapons in the heart of the Sudan. Captain Bradley Jefferson, from American intelligence, is accused of betraying the mission.

The trial at the Whiteman Air Force Base, Missouri, becomes a political minefield, exploding the millennium madness. Capitalising on the affair, a new leader emerges to consolidate his power base and shake the government apart.

Suddenly Jefferson changes his plea to guilty. Just as the prosecutor discovers he's innocent. And then the Captain turns up. Dead . . .

'Truly Edge of the seat exciting' Dale Brown

'Imaginative action . . . told to perfection' Clive Cussler

HODDER AND STOUGHTON PAPERBACKS

RICHARD HERMAN

MOSQUITO RUN

Three women, two men: captured by pirates off the Malaysian coast. Now held captive by a drug warlord somewhere in the jungle interior.

Rich kids. One of them the daughter of a US Senator. A man with powerful political clout.

The president knows that his only hope is to send in the top guns from Delta Force, the crack counter-terrorist unit, in a high risk rescue mission.

A mission that has unnerving parallels with his own World War II experience, flying an RAF Mosquito on a deep penetration, precision raid into the heart of enemy territory . . .

MOSQUITO RUN

'This is the sharp end, with vivid descriptions of air combat, the smell of hot oil and fear' *The Times*

'Could very well be tomorrow's headlines' Clive Cussler

HODDER AND STOUGHTON PAPERBACKS